A Shaper's Tale

by Jane Prétat

Copyright © 2017 Jane Prétat

All rights reserved.

ISBN-13: 978-1546427728
ISBN-10: 1546427724

ACKNOWLEDGMENTS

My life has been blessed with the friendship of a variety of creative people like the Shapers of my story. Some I have met only briefly. Others I have known well for years. I am filled with gratitude for each encounter, whether brief or prolonged.

A primary recipient of my gratitude is Eclipse Neilson who is the director of Woman Soul where I was first a staff member and then a camper at Rowe Camp and Conference Center. It was Eclipse who encouraged me to become part of this group, then called WomenCircles, back in the 1990's. It was also she who encouraged me to accept the Iris Award and get this fiction book published. She was the book's first editor while feeding both my body and spirit through years of friendship and support.

Two other editors have also come from our circle. Jayleigh Lewis took on the arduous job of editing the book back into shape after both my computer and my iPad crashed. Mosa Baczewska not only designed and completed the extraordinarily beautiful book cover but also did the final edit and formatting. I owe them both an enormous debt of gratitude.

I also want to thank friends at the Jung Institute-Boston where many of my ideas about creativity and dreams began to shape and take on their own form. My life and thought have been richly fed by Jungian literature as well.

I especially want to thank my friend Mary Ann Jones with whom I have traveled and done workshops in places like Jamaica and Ireland. She has fully supported this book and me in our many transformations while doing her own research and writing on the healers of Jamaica.

Last but not least I want to thank my children, grandchildren and extended musical family, both those who still bring song into my life today and those already sung to "the Land Beyond the Stars." My heart is full of love for you all.

PROLOGUE

As sea mist and fog swirl across the surface of night seas, the thoughts and dreams of the sentient Alph move over the intergalactic oceans of sleeping minds. Made only of light, and nearly invisible as they float at the edges of the Great Unknown, the Alph long always for the form only Shapers can give to their dreams. The Shapers among us can often feel their magic flowing in, sometimes soft as sleep, other times hard as the breaking slap of waves, urging us toward the cliffs of creation. Though they have existed since before the beginnings of time, few humans know of them anymore. Shapers often think they themselves are the source of their inspirations.

In ancient Earth days the Alph were often intuited and labeled as giants, fairies, dragons, elves and a variety of other magical creatures. During one Earth era, it was popular to identify them as ghosts and spirits. In Earth's last days, scientists first described them as refractions of light or urges from the depths of black holes, later as nanots, tiny robots in the brains of humankind.

After Earth was destroyed there were no labels until the Alph dreamed a dream of redesigned humans. With the help of two Shaper species of old, the Las from their own dimension and the Nus from another, their dream became a reality. Redesigned humans were brought into being and settled on a tiny green planet called Mem, where tall mountains and wide purple seas bordered fertile fields, and black sand beaches nestled under a warm sun and three small moons.

One of the Las, a female named Astraea, was chosen to become Mem's first goddess-queen-mentor. She was a beautiful woman twelve feet tall who established an agricultural society of calm and peace, leaving as her legacy a hereditary line of queens as well as an established cultural practice of dream shaping through creative arts and rituals.

Pronouncing the experiment a success, the Nus returned to their own dimension and vanished. Eventually the Las also disappeared. From their stasis rest, the Alph continued to send their night visions to the Shapers among the new humans. Memmians kept up the practices they had learned from Astraea, but as time passed they forgot her reality and came to see her as a holy icon who existed only in the heavens, her stories preserved mainly in the tattered fantasies of children's tales.

When Atrid was born that was the state of affairs. Although she was hereditary Queen of Mem, her ability to Shape was sadly compromised by a determination to rid Mem of what she saw as the nonsense of rituals and dreams. Her shaping was born of her own power and a determination to expand her empire to the edges of a multiverse that she would rule forever.

At first the Alph continued to sleep, but when the chaos Atrid created shook them awake, they knew they must respond.
Talin was their response. Half Alph and half human, though he didn't know this for a long time, he was created to be their Shaper: the one who would bring about their dream of a renewed future for Mem, and for all the worlds.

CHAPTER 1

Atrid was born at midnight on the night of the Turning, when the purple sea carried the melting ice of Mem's cruelest winter in memory out to the distant horizon. Though it was the dark of her moons, for the planet's people it was a night of celebration. The tides had turned. The Greening would finally begin. On black sand beaches big bonfires of winter debris burned, as musicians played and Memmians danced. In the deep sky above stars spun circles of bright light, as if eager to share the joy of the happy humans circling below.

As they had done for centuries, mage-priests and priestesses rode their shaggy ponies down from the distant mountains to float offerings of tiny folded paper boats filled with sweets out onto the violet waters; they then hobbled their mounts and joined the dance while children splashed into the shallows to snatch the prizes before they sank to the spirits below.

Neither mage nor citizen gave much thought to their aging Queen as she labored in the birthing room of her mountain aerie. Queen Arian was far too busy giving birth to care that both her people and the stars were dancing. When the skies cleared at midnight, and the dance of the stars became visible, she was already exhausted, hardly able to whisper a word of gratitude as her babe took its first breath.

Mira, her mage-midwife, was so concerned for the Queen's condition that she hardly had a moment to spare for the child. At her nod one of her six handmaidens took the baby.

"Look, look!" the young women cried, trying to encourage the Queen to awaken. "See your beautiful daughter!"

"Arian is exhausted," Mira scolded them in a whisper, bending over her patient, desperate to save her friend. "Take the baby away and leave the Queen to me."

In their excitement the handmaidens continued to make noise.

"It's an auspicious night!" one of them cried.

They all began to talk at once, their faces glowing with excitement.

"Be still!" Mira commanded. "Queen Arian is exhausted," she continued in a harsh whisper. "She needs quiet. Surely she's earned her rest."

The young women stilled, their eyes big with sympathy. Yes, indeed, Queen Arian deserved rest. After seven births of seven boys too frail to survive, the long-awaited healthy girl child had come! There would be time, when the Queen awoke, for her to view the baby and celebrate.

"Look, look!" one of the women exclaimed aloud, in the process of oiling the small body and wrapping her in soft garments. "This is no ordinary child. See her hair!"

Silver hair streaked with copper and gold sprang like a fuzzy halo around the tiny face.

"She's royal," another breathed, her voice filled with awe. "And special!"

A third gasped, pointing at the baby's face. She could hardly speak. "Look…see," she stammered. "There on her brow, just above her nose..."

All of the women bent above the cradle where the baby lay. They began to rustle and giggle and make such a commotion that Mira strode angrily across the tower room to quiet their fuss.

"I told you..." she began.

"But, Ma'am, look!" the boldest pointed out, her soft voice high with excitement. "She's marked with...could it be...a...star?"

Sure enough, between the baby's pale eyebrows, etched into her wrinkled flesh, was the tiniest mark. Could this child be the Chosen, the one described in the old, half-forgotten tale of Astraea?

"Someday Astraea will return to Mem in the body of a child," the tradition told. "You will know her by the silver, gold and copper of her hair and by the star on her forehead, just above her nose."

Could this fantasy possibly be coming true?

No rational human would really believe that once upon a time such a goddess as Astraea had actually existed. What modern could accept that a giantess, twice the height of the tallest human and as beautiful as the most fragrant flower, had moved gently among Mem's people many centuries ago, teaching and guiding them, showing them how to fish and farm and live with one another in peace and prosperity?

"I promise I will come back to you someday in the far future," the old story continued. "At my rebirth you will know me by the star on my forehead, just over my nose. I will be born of a Queen, to rule as a Queen, and from me will come a line who will keep

Mem in peace and plenty for all future generations."

"Could she be...?" the youngest handmaiden whispered, before quickly thrusting her hand over her mouth at her indiscretion.

"No more of this nonsense," Mira said in her most practical voice. "We must take her to the Prince-consort. One of you must stay with the Queen. I will bring the child."

Despite her best attempt at severity, Mira's voice broke on the last word of her speech. She stared down into the baby's face before turning abruptly away to change out of her birthing gown.

Once the child was ready, the maidens gave her to Mira, then nearly trampled one another in their rush to be first to bear the news to the Court waiting far below. One agreed to stay with the Queen. The others shot down turning stairs and through long corridors, jostling one another for position before flying through the massive doors of the throne room.

"It's a girl!" the first one cried, tumbling into the Great Hall.

"She bears the signs!" the second exclaimed, following close on her heels.

The other handmaidens rushed in, all talking at once, until the whole Court was buzzing with excitement. Eron, Queen Arian's High Mage, raised his hand for silence. He beckoned to Mira, who had suddenly appeared in the doorway, waiting silently with the newborn in her arms.

With great dignity she glided forward. The others stood back in silence, making a passage for her to reach the dais, where she delivered the child into the arms of Lor, her Queen's husband and consort.

"Sire, I give you your daughter," she said.

As she folded back the blanket from the baby's face, Mira pronounced her next sentence in the distinctive voice of power all mages could use when it was required: "As you can see, she is marked with the hair and what may be a star."

The whole room stilled. Even the air seemed to stop as Lor stood in motionless silence, staring bewildered into the face of his newborn child.

Finally he spoke, his voice puzzled. "Yes," he agreed, "what could be a tiny star seems to be forming on her brow."

"She has the star." The words traveled through the room, beginning in a whisper, erupting, finally, into a shout. "She has the star!"

News of the birth spread rapidly in all directions across the tiny planet. The people's new Queen had arrived on the night the tides had turned toward Spring. She bore the signs! Perhaps the old tale of Astraea was true after all!

CHAPTER 2

Despite these signs, from her beginning Atrid was difficult. As a small child she was unruly. Strong-willed, and determined to have her own way, she was rude to the servants, the mages and even her father, who found himself totally inept as a substitute for his Queen, who lay, high up in her tower, in what appeared to be an endless coma.

Soon after the birth, Lor began to soothe his grief by taking refuge in drugs and alcohol, encouraged and joined by many of the mage-priests who gathered around him. None of them had time for the child except to punish or exploit her. About the only thing Atrid was forced to do was visit her mother. Staring at the still body, kept alive by humming machinery, and at the screen that displayed the Queen's life signs, the little girl vowed that this would never happen to her.

"I won't let it," she whispered to herself at each visit. "Whatever I have to do, I will live!"

Growing up with no guidance, confined in a drafty castle where she was isolated and bored, Atrid learned to hide in corners, where she could secretly listen to the private conversations of mages and servants, many of whom blamed her for her mother's illness. "Surely," they would say, "it can't be true that this difficult child is the old Goddess returned. It's hard enough to believe she's been born to be Mem's future Queen!"

"But she has the royal hair," someone would always insist. "And what might be the star."

Others snickered derisively. How could anyone think Astraea would have chosen such a vessel as this nasty, disobedient girl? No, it was impossible. Yes, she had the royal hair, but look at it now! Just a matted snarl on her head.

One day while eavesdropping, Atrid overheard a mage say in her defense that she might surprise them all and be a great Queen someday.

"Yes," Atrid thought. "That's who I am, the greatest Queen of all."

"Ha, of course, she's obviously Star Woman returned," a male voice then joked derisively. "What a mistake!"

"That mark on her forehead is a scratch," another voice agreed. "Hardly noticeable."

"She's just an ordinary homely brat with a royal bird's nest on her head."

More derogatory comments, followed by guffaws, kept drifting back to Atrid as the voices disappeared down a corridor.

She knew they were laughing at her. "I'll show them!" she vowed. "They'll be sorry!"

The next morning, she went to the kitchen and pretended to beg for food. While no one was looking, she managed to take a small, very sharp paring knife, and slide it into one of her deep pockets. Standing in front of her own bathroom mirror, determined to do the job, she used the point of the knife to quickly cut the thin skin around her fading mark, strictly ordering herself to ignore the pain and think only of doing it right. Blood trickled down her nose and into her mouth, but she kept cutting, first a tiny circle, then rays surrounding it. After carefully wiping up the blood, she put a heal-patch over the wound. Probably no one would notice, but if they did she would simply say she had bumped the spot and was hiding an ugly bruise.

Tending the wound with great care over the next few days, she watched for the right moment. As soon as it began to heal, she took a minuscule emerald she had stolen from her mother's case, taped it at the center of the design she had cut, then covered the whole thing again.

Fortunately, there was no infection. Surely that was a sign it was meant to be! On the morning she took off the bandage and discovered the wound fully healed, she exclaimed with delight. Clearly revealed between her eyebrows was a glistening star. The mark of Astraea! Who could doubt her now?

"It's beautiful!" she thought, putting on a new patch before going out of her rooms.

She would wait for a special occasion to reveal the star. By then it would be so permanent no one would guess it hadn't just spontaneously appeared.

When her body began to change in adolescence, she decided she hated it, and vowed to reshape herself into someone thin. While eating far less, she began to secretly exercise, hiding her body from others by always wearing big clothes. Eventually she decided that by her thirteenth birthday she would be ready to reveal a transformed self.

Before Atrid was ready to make her move, however, her mother died. Immediately the mages planned the Queen's death ceremony. Arian would be sung to the Land Beyond the Stars.

Curious about the ceremony, Atrid decided she must go, so she cleaned herself up, washed her hair and brushed it till it shone, then put on a bodysuit that fit her developing form like a second skin. Knowing that her father was in too much of a drunken stupor to be approached, she went instead to Eron.

"My father must go to the ceremony," she reminded the High Mage. "You must sober him up and have him walked up the mountain. See to it that he has no alcohol or drugs until that day. I will go up to the ceremonial crater with you. Other mages will follow us with my father. You must see to it."

Not really looking up from his work, Eron replied tersely. "It will kill him."

"You know very well that he has to be there and he has to be sober."

Eron stood up but hardly looked at her. Atrid could almost hear his thoughts. He was wondering who she was to make such demands.

"Arian is gone," she told him. "I am now your new Queen." She paused to let the words sink in. With a puzzled expression on his face, Eron finally looked directly at her.

"You of all people know who I really am." Standing in the sunlight so her hair would glisten, Atrid pushed back the part she had let hang over her eyes, and revealed the star with its emerald center. "You and I can work together or we can be enemies. The choice is yours."

For long moments they stood, locked in silence. Atrid held eye contact with Eron as she waited. At last he spoke.

"Yes, my Queen," was all he said, before slowly backing away.

Three days later, they all climbed the mountain. It was obvious that Lor was very ill. Shaking, he leaned heavily on the two mages who half carried him as he gasped for breath, stopping every few feet to bend almost double with dry heaves.

Climbing ahead of him, Atrid didn't look back. The mages knew best how to deal with him. They knew what he needed. Soon the ceremony would be over and he would have his reward.

Once they reached the crater, the singing began. Expecting the harmony of plainchant, Atrid was shocked. The dissonance she heard was jarring. Sounding drunk, the voices kept wobbling off key. There was no power. For the first time in her life, Atrid felt sorry for her mother. How could anyone ride out on such wimpy, dissonant sounds? As she stood on the edge of the crater, she could hardly hide her disdain, wishing only that the stupid ceremony would come to an end.

"You'll never make it to that crazy place they call The Land Beyond the Stars," she thought to her mother. "Not with these voices."

Feeling impatient, Atrid pulled back from the crater's edge. As she did, something strange began to happen. For the first time since her birth, she felt her mother's presence surrounding her, pulling her into an embrace. It was as if the dead Queen were determined to hold her child at the last, even if the only way she could do it was to take Atrid along on her death journey.

"No!" Atrid shouted. "I won't go!" In a panic she threw herself at Eron.

"She's trying to take me with her," she yelled. "Doesn't she know that I'm Astraea, Star Woman, born to be Mem's Queen?" Clinging to the mage, she begged, "Don't let her have me!"

In an instant she felt Eron shaking her as he whispered, "Stop this nonsense. Arian is dead. Your imagination will make trouble for us all."

At that moment, Lor collapsed. The singing trickled to a stop. Freeing himself from Atrid's grasp, Eron rushed to Lor's side, leaving her to get herself back down the mountain alone. Her fright turned to fury as she made her way back to the castle. No one offered help. She was on her own. Didn't any of them realize that she was their Queen now? Where was the deference she deserved? Pulling her cloak around her, Atrid stumbled along, swearing that the moment she was crowned she would ban this ritual. In fact, she would ban all rituals. They were a useless waste of time and energy. She would show the mages—and all of Mem—who was Queen now!

That night, lying in her own big bed, she crossly ordered her maid to bring her a hot drink. She would talk to Eron the next day, reminding him that she must be crowned. Nothing could be allowed to postpone that final ceremony.

It was morning before she learned that her father had died on the mountain. Good. He was gone, along with his wife, to wherever it was the dead went. Into some black hole of nothing, she suspected.

"Well," she vowed, "I will never let it happen to me. I am born to be the best Queen ever, and I will be, even if I have to do it all by myself! And I will never go to any 'Land Beyond the Stars.'"

CHAPTER 3

Eron and the other mages kept suggesting a simplified ceremony for the crowning, but Atrid refused to listen, and ordered more pomp than Memmians had ever seen. At her instruction, invitations were sent out across the planet, and announcements posted in every available spot.

When the day came, the castle was filled, by her order, with processions of mages and officials, who circled the grounds for everyone to see, before stopping at an outdoor platform set high above Mem's marshes. In the adjoining harbor city of Syl, curious crowds gathered on dikes, boats and headlands to view the scene, some with binoculars, others with long-range scopes, in order to get better views. Many had staked out claims to their viewing spots days in advance, pitching colorful tents across the rice fields and marshes and along the edges of the royal mountain's greenery.

"Every citizen on the planet is watching," Atrid thought with satisfaction.

"Couldn't we have done this more quietly?" Eron protested. "Your parents just died."

Atrid simply frowned and dismissed him.

The ceremony was designed by Atrid. There was music and entertainment, and a few short speeches. Atrid had found and coached a young mage to speak in praise of her.

"Atrid is young, but she is intelligent and beautiful," he declared, spreading his hand over his heart. "She has great plans for Mem's future. I predict she will be Mem's greatest Queen!"

The crowd roared its approval.

By the time Eron came forward to reluctantly place the jeweled crown on Atrid's head, the crowd was worked up into a frenzy of happiness. The roar of their wild cheering filled the sky, from Syl's harbor to the plains, while the noise of fireworks echoed from Mem's mountain peaks.

Standing on her high platform, Atrid waved triumphantly as her people celebrated. All of her hopes and careful planning had brought this moment into being. She was the new Queen. Mem and its white city of Syl were hers!

The feasts in her court and among the mages in the mountain villas continued for days, while those in the city and crofts went back to work. Atrid swiftly made her next move. Giving Eron and the other mages no time to realize what was happening, she began to replace the old ways with her own new designs.

Her first royal announcement was made publicly from a balcony in Syl.

"As of today the old rituals will be discontinued," she told the city's residents, "especially those like singing the dead to the Land Beyond the Stars." Pausing for emphasis, she declared decisively, "There is no such place! It has all been a fantasy the mages have used to control you. I, your new Queen, tell you the truth. These old superstitions hold you back. It's time for them to fade and die. Let them go, and I promise you that together we will make Mem the center not only of the universe, but of a multiverse where a new day of plenty and peace will be our reward!"

Eron was upset. "How could you do this without consulting me?" he objected. "This decree will wreak havoc, mark my words. Mem has always been a peaceful planet. Why do you want to stir up trouble?"

"I have seen trouble most of my life," Atrid replied haughtily. "I am Mem's Queen now, and I know what must be done. Only I can make Mem strong again. You mages have kept us isolated and living in the past. I'm going to change all that."

"Every Queen has honored the old ways, and we've lived in peace," Eron pressed. "Why should we need to change anything? You must understand this and take back your decree. I will guide you as you learn what it is to rule this planet."

Atrid stared at him, her eyes cold. "I already know how to rule," she told him curtly. "Whether you believe it or not, I am Astraea reborn, and I am Mem's crowned Queen. I make the decisions, not you or your mages. Those of you who can't agree will have to suffer my displeasure. My decree stands, just as I do!"

Atrid could see that Eron was shocked into silence, now that she had taken on her authority. When she had been a child, he had hardly noticed her, and now that she was Queen he obviously thought she should depend on his advice. Why should she care that he disapproved? He was only a sad old man, useless to her and her plan. Annoying as tiny flies, the words he murmured in her ear could easily be brushed away. Arian was dead. That old Queen might have valued his wisdom, turning to him daily for counsel, but those days were gone. She had banished them.

Atrid's next move was to ban dreams and dreaming, along

with other frivolities like dancing and rituals. "A waste of our time and energy for which there will be severe penalties," she declared them to be.

When Eron tried to tell her of his dreams, in which the wild horses of old legends pounded down out of the western mountains to carry him off in wild exuberance to the Land Beyond the Stars, where Arian and Lor waited to greet him, Atrid threatened him.

Within months he was gone. She rapidly designed a simple funeral service, to be held in one of the small castle rooms. As a courtesy she asked Mira, who had been Eron's friend, to say a few words. "However, there must be no mention of either of my parents," she commanded. "This service is to be brief and only for Eron."

Mira disobeyed, and spoke at length about Arian and Lor, and their great love for one another and for the mage-priest who had worked so loyally beside them.

"Now they are all reunited in the Land Beyond the Stars," she ended, speaking the words in her mage voice.

The older mages sighed in agreement. A few secretly wiped away tears as a spontaneous chant began. Furious, Atrid jumped up to stop the chant and dismiss the gathering.

Mira died shortly afterward. No one spoke of the cause of her death.

One by one, any mage who disobeyed the Queen's orders or questioned her actions mysteriously disappeared. At first there were some weak protests, but only a short time passed before there was no one left who dared question Atrid's authority. By the time she, all by herself, took over supervision of an increase in taxes, not a word was spoken against it, or against the cutting of mage expenditures.

"I may be young, but I am not stupid," she told the mages. "There will be no more useless waste of time or money on frills."

Atrid took pride in her ability and appearance, working hard to perfect both as tools. She felt her power increase as she made new laws and ordered new services, new clothes and the continued reshaping of her body. Rapidly she proved her ability to achieve any change she desired, in her appearance or in the lives of her subjects. Surely it was her new beauty that finally made the mages grovel at her feet in admiration?

This also made some of them think of her getting married. As the months passed, many handsome mages tried to woo her. Having other plans, she simply waved them away. Instead, she began to visit the city of Syl, speaking to her people, more and more aware that her new beauty was a magnet she could use to draw them to belief in her plans.

"It is time for a new era here, one of accomplishment in science and expansion," she told them repeatedly. "We are threatened physically and economically by the species of other planets who wish to conquer us. We must conquer them first. For far too long our mage-guards have been here just for show. Under my leadership they will become skilled warriors who can keep us safe from the threats that surround us. I need your loyalty and your help. Mem has been weak. As your leader I promise you, we will become so mighty no one will dare to confront us!"

At first Memmians responded with uncertainty, but as time passed they began to agree with Atrid. Other planets and species were a threat. Only Atrid's warriors could protect Mem from the unknown dangers that lurked throughout the galaxy, waiting to pounce. Atrid would keep them safe.

"Life is serious," she told her people again and again. "There is no time for nonsense. We Memmians are at the hub of new worlds. It is up to us to create a new multiverse of peace and security."

"My empire will extend to the very farthest stars and beyond," she exulted, when she was alone. "It is my destiny."

CHAPTER 4

As decades passed and other planets in the Galaxy were conquered, more and more strange species joined her realm. Believing that she was a Goddess, some submitted peacefully. Others fought, but the strength of Atrid's armies eventually subdued them all. As years passed, her determination to enlarge and modernize a great Empire never flagged. What it cost in lives and money did not deter her.

"I am Astraea and this is why I have returned," she would explain to anyone who dared to question her methods as she sentenced them for insurrection.

In the early decades of her rule she knew she grew more beautiful with passing years. Many mirrors in her castle confirmed the awe she saw reflected in the eyes of her subjects. A day came, however when something happened that shocked her out of complacency. Climbing the stone steps up from her sunken fruit garden, she had to stop and lean against the balustrade to catch her breath and to realize that she was gasping, her heart pounding, her knees weak. How could this be? Wasn't it only yesterday that she'd skimmed up these steps as fast as her pet calico monkey?

Next she discovered that her mind had taken to wandering during court hearings. At first she told herself that she needed more sleep, but adding hours in bed only interrupted her sleep patterns and turned night into day.

Sitting in her great chair at the Judging Bench, holding her gavel, she found herself missing whole segments of testimony. To make an informed decision she had to ask the advice of one of her mages, pretending that she needed his input when really what she needed was a restatement of something she could not remember having heard.

In a panic Atrid increased her exercise, carefully creamed and oiled and pampered herself both inside and out, but the lapses continued. Age seemed to be creeping into her body like a sneak-thief, robbing her of her former acuity. How could this be happening? Astraea had once lived on Mem for three centuries. Why should it be different now?

Looking more closely into her hand mirror she began to observe new wrinkles around her eyes and mouth. How long had they been there?

"I don't recognize you," she told the aging woman she saw in the glass. "You're not supposed to be happening!" She tried denial, yet knew it was her image that was accurate, not her desire. Who was this stranger in the reflection if it wasn't her?

At night she lay awake fretting.

"I could grow old and die!" she realized. The thought filled her with dread.

"That cannot be allowed to happen." she told herself. "I am Star Woman, a Goddess born to rule forever."

Her fears began to jostle one another in her imagination. Perhaps she was not immortal. Oh, gods, perhaps she was not even a Goddess! Restless and worried she tossed and turned, pounding her pillows, throwing back her covers only to huddle under them again shivering. Her hands and feet seemed always to be cold.

When she finally consulted her court physician he told her it was simply a natural stage of human life that happened to every man and woman, all part of a normal aging process.

"I'm not supposed to age," she stormed. "I'm the Chosen. I'm supposed to live for centuries!"

When she asked for a remedy he told her with a smile that there was none.

Atrid tried to pray, but who would Astraea pray to? She could hardly pray to herself.

"If there's anybody out there with any control over this," she cried out in her panic, "you'd better make something happen!"

Of course no one heard her cries. The Alph had turned their attention to other planets in other galaxies, sending new dream seeds in other directions. If their attention had been on Atrid they would certainly have intervened but they slept and it wasn't long before an extraordinary opportunity came knocking at her door.

By then Atrid had completely forgotten her desperate prayer and didn't give a moments thought to the coincidence. It was only an unpleasant intrusion when one of her young laboratory scientists claimed an appointment with her. By the time he arrived she had forgotten he was coming and tried to send him away, but she was too tired and distraught to do more than gesture toward the door as she struggled to concentrate on the papers at her desk. When she finally looked up, she was astonished to see that he still stood there, patiently awaiting her attention. Catching her glance, he began to speak, telling her about some experiments he had been working on day and night.

She hardly heard his words but did notice distractedly that his brilliant dark eyes were filled with passion.

Atrid suppressed a yawn and wondered how long she would have to tolerate his presence before mustering enough strength to send him away.

Holding up a small vial of milky white fluid, he stammered, "Highness, I h ..h-have.. b-b..brought you the w..Water of Life!"

"What folly is this?" Atrid thought, watching him.

She was surprised to feel her body responding to his beauty. No man had interested her in a long time.

"What is your name?" she asked.

"Jotus."

He threw the name away as if it didn't matter. Leaning forward his eyes glistened as his trembling voice shot across her desk. "Highness, I have made a great discovery."

Atrid was fighting sleep. Even as she noticed the youngster, fresh and filled with life she could feel nothing but her own exhaustion. His stammering excitement irritated her.

Concentrating on his beauty she fought to stay awake. What would it be like to take him into her bed? Musing on his dark hair and eyes, on the sinew of his golden body she wondered if it might strengthen her. Could union with this boy help her forget that her hands had begun to stiffen? Would bedding him erase the wrinkles around her eyes and mouth and make her disregard the trembling of her legs when she stood too long?

No. He was too young. What would happen to her people, to

her golden Galaxy of peace, to all her innovations if she used herself up indulging herself with him?

Resignedly studying the boy she realized that she hardly wanted him, beautiful as he was.

"I'm too tired for this," she thought, and sighed, ready to wave him away.

He was still talking. Despite herself she began to listen. Immediately she recoiled, stunned to realize that the desire that made his whole being quiver was for his work, not for her. His passion was a need to make her understand the discovery he was offering.

Hurriedly Atrid shook her head, trying to shift her thoughts to his words.

"There is the chance of failure," he was warning. "You would have to take that chance if you try it."

He was suggesting failure! What could that mean?

"If it fails, your aging will escalate," he explained. "You will die."

Atrid sat up straight and glowered at him. He leaned forward toward her never shifting his gaze from her face as he continued to talk. His fervor was so intense that his whole body shivered as his voice softened almost to a whisper.

"Atrid, my Queen," he breathed, "it is my hope that if you open yourself to this elixir, you can take in the essence of youth, be rejuvenated, and live forever. My studies show that with it you will be able to take the energy and personality of anyone you choose and make them your own. My research shows that with it you may bring a total rejuvenation to yourself, body, mind and soul. You must make the choice of whether or not you are willing to try the experiment. If it works you could live forever as a young woman."

"You say there's a chance I could become a young woman again?"

He nodded vehemently. "Yes," he almost shouted.

"I could live and govern my Land for centuries to come?"

He nodded again, a smile beginning to creep from his mouth to his eyes.

Atrid studied his face. He was so lit up, so sure that he was giving her a great gift. She looked down at her hands. Blue veins traced a map of aging on them.

Was this an answer to her dilemma? If so she should seriously consider it.

"I will sleep on it", she told him at last. "Come back tomorrow and I'll give you my answer."

There was no sleep for Atrid that night as she weighed the possibilities the young scientist was offering her. Immediate death or centuries of life in a young body. The first would leave her empire in chaos. The second would give her years to enforce order and peace throughout the Galaxy. As Star Woman she was being offered this opportunity to expand and continue expanding her new Realm! Could she deny her destiny now that the possibility of such long service was offered?

Throughout the hours of the dark night she debated with herself, tossing and turning until her bedding was twisted into a snarl she no longer had the patience to undo. As dawn was breaking she dragged herself from her bed and dressed, noticing once more how much slower and painful her movements had become.

Coming out of her quarters Atrid found Jotus waiting in the corridor. He looked as if he hadn't slept either. Perhaps he had squatted in the hall outside her door all night? She motioned for him to follow her into her private dining room and had him served his morning meal. Only when color had come back into his face did she speak.

"I have decided to take the elixir," she told him firmly. "But you must agree to be the first to join me. If I succeed, you will be the first to live in me. If I die, you go with me."

The young man wept at her feet, his face filled with elation.

After two days of fasting and prayer to whatever power now ordered the universe, Atrid took him into her bed. When they had drunk their potions, hers from one bottle, his from another, she began to caress him.

It wasn't long before she realized that what was happening was different from anything she had ever experienced before. As she held him in her arms she felt his very soul permeating her cells. He did not have to enter her with his manhood. They were joined in a more profound communion, the kind every lover longs for but seldom achieves. Atrid could feel him becoming one with her as he lay beside her, his breath going into her mouth, his heart beating against her own. For a moment she wondered why the elixir pulled him into her and marveled that it wasn't the other way around. He could have tricked her, but he hadn't fought at all against her taking of him. Instead he happily lost himself in the ecstasy of joining her.

When it was over the beautiful young body lying beside her was an empty shell. The young scientist no longer lived in it.

For one moment Atrid felt upset. "What have we done?" she thought.

Would his presence get in the way of her ability to rule? What other marvelous accomplishments might she have made alone in her own body? Should she have taken him in? Had he tricked her after all?

"I am alive in you!" his voice told her in her mind. "I will help you achieve more than either of us could have done alone."

Atrid could feel his happiness throughout her inner core. On her tongue she was sure she could taste his triumphant joy. His elixir had worked even better than he could have hoped.

"You are Atrid," his voice seemed to say in her mind, "You are Queen of Mem, Daughter of the Blazing Star, Ruler of the Galaxies. We are One, living proof that you, our Goddess, can truly make any of us who takes the elixir a living part of you!"

For a moment Atrid recoiled from the rush of his sense of triumph and power, then made it her own, feeling his brilliance swell in her like a great wave pouring over the dikes of any last minute resistance and into the harbor of her new awareness. Everything he had been, his brilliance as a researcher, was now a part of her. She was now a scientist. Thanks to Jotus she could shape new elixirs, new creations and best of all, stay young forever!

Walking out into the sunshine on her balcony, she left his empty body behind on her bed, cast off like the shell of a beetle. Jotus was reborn in her! He had no need of any other body. His vigor glowed, strengthening her. She felt invincible.

Had her own body changed, too?

Looking down at her hands she saw them transforming, the wrinkles she had carried these last years disappearing. Her flesh was filling out even as she stared. Her whole body felt toned, changed, as if youth had entered and altered her flesh. She felt her breasts rise, her nipples firm. A surge of energy up her spine made her laugh out loud. She thanked Jotus within her. They shared the triumph. Now his knowledge of creating the elixirs was hers! Thanks to him she could create new potions, new science, a new realm. She could envision a time when the whole Galaxies would bend the knee to her.

As she looked at her hands, however, the thing she found herself celebrating most was his youth which seemed to be filling and expanding every cell of her body with vigor and health.
Watching her calico monkey leap up the steps to greet her Atrid felt delight. Her own reinvigorated body could now move just as fast and free.

Looking out over her land Atrid knew with surety that she would rule it for centuries to come. She would not die as her parents and Eron had. Thanks to Jotus' elixir she might well have become immortal. Hardly able to contain the joy she felt, she opened her arms and cried out to the mountainside and valley below, then beyond to the planets of her Galaxy, "I, Atrid, am your

Queen and I make you this pledge. You are my Lands. You are my People. I will take you into myself. You will live in me. You will join me and together we will rule forever!"

At first she kept the meld a secret, telling no one, not even the highest Mage. Jotus was hardly missed. Atrid saw to it that his empty body was quietly buried. Others remarked that she looked surprisingly young and lovely. She was most pleased to realize that she was also more brilliant than the mages realized. Thanks to Jotus her extensive knowledge of science was impressive. Eventually someone who had been Jotus close friend began to talk and rumors spread that the Queen had "melded" the young scientist who was now a part of her. At first people laughed at such outrageous stories, but as time passed and Atrid continued to show no signs of age, the rumor spread more widely. Word came back to Atrid that some people were horrified. Occasionally she overheard talk among the mages about the importance of integrity and the dangers of exploitation of others for a single person's benefit. She was amused that no one dared talk about any of this directly with her and decided the best choice was for her to ignore the gossip.

When twenty years had passed she knew there must be another joining if she was to stay young. The parents of the next youth she chose complained loudly saying, "The Queen is killing our children." Criticisms of "the meld" began to spread from Mem's new space station out to other planets. Many reacted, saying that the Queen was not only destroying peaceful planets but even worse, killing their children.

As a result, Atrid's next choice was an elderly priestess, wise with years but approaching death. The gossip died down. Soon Atrid realized however, that while she had gained wisdom from the old one, her body was not physically renewed. Within months she had to quietly set up another meld in which she took a fiery red haired teen-age girl who sought the melding in rebellion against strict parents with too many children. They were glad to see their difficult girl go into service with the Queen, especially when money changed hands.

When Atrid began to speak and act like the red head, those who had dealt with the youngster became convinced that the rebellious girl was alive and well within the royal body, proving that the meld was true.

Protests increased.

Atrid moved quickly, arresting those identified as gossips. The protests became whispers and eventually stopped.

"Atrid's ears are everywhere," the people warned one another.

Determined to make her melding acceptable, Atrid saw to it that the melding became a ceremony, a brief time when her subjects could celebrate their freedom from the increasing restraints she had to impose on their daily lives in order to keep the peace. Soon any last rag-tag remnants of old rituals either became part of melding celebrations or were firmly banished with stiff penalties. As a result, the meld became a boost for Mem's economy as huge multi-specie crowds gathered to celebrate and spend the new currency instituted by Atrid throughout her realm. Citizens of her growing empire began to look forward to the games and freedom she permitted on these holidays. Criticism of the meld lessened and eventually stopped. As her people, both Memmian and Alien, began to experience the extension of life that Star Woman could guarantee them if they melded with her, more and more began to offer themselves.

"How could anyone pass up such a chance?" Youngsters asked their parents. "Why would I choose aging and death rather than eternal life in the body of our Queen where I will be beautiful, eat well, and have a voice in ruling the whole Multiverse?'

Soon the only difficulty Atrid had in her renewal was choosing among the many who offered themselves. Occasionally she would take another elder, usually one of her mages, to gain their gifts. But youths were who she sought most, for they gave her physical strength and renewal.

The old rites of fires and dancing on the beaches were allowed once again, but only for the melding. Offerings of paper boats were a thing of the past replaced by the offering of a volunteer guaranteeing Atrid's own longevity as well as their own.

"I never have to force anyone to join me," Atrid assured her court. "It is always their free choice."

Decades passed. A new century began. Atrid remained amazingly young and vibrant. The management of her growing Empire demanded the skills of every Mage and half of Mem's citizens, plus high ranking leaders of other species, the best at managing their own. There was little time or energy to worry about the meld. Eventually enough time had passed that few could remember when the meld had begun. Some even thought it had been there from Mem's beginnings.

Atrid loved ruling her many species. It took strict measures to rule them well. Her variety of subjects were born, lived full lives and eventually either joined her or died, replaced by new generations. She and her staffs, both Inner and outer, were skillful at dealing with situations before they could become problems. Most of her subjects seemed content with her rule. Thanks to Jotus' brilliance it was not difficult to figure out how to cast out any of her Inners who couldn't fit in and do their part.

Atrid told herself that of course her loyalty to the home planet came first. She reminded Memmians frequently that she would do anything required to maintain Mem in its fullness.

Only on rare occasions would one or another of the mages in her outer court have the temerity to question the legitimacy of the melding.

"This is wrong," an over confident young mage who had briefly shared her bed exclaimed one day. "How can it be right to take the lives of so many just to lengthen the life of One?"

"Do you question my ways?" she asked, her voice stormy as she sentenced him to exile. "I give centuries of life to all who wish to live in peace in my Inner throng. We have brought prosperity to millions, improving and broadening their lives. Thanks to the brilliance of the scientist Jotus who now lives in me, I and those who have joined me can live for centuries, never aging, remaining young and vital perhaps even for eternity."

What fool would ask for more?

CHAPTER 5

Atrid was pondering taking on another new species from a planet that might bring increased trade and prosperity to her expanding empire.

"They look like lizards," her mage advisor told her, "but they are extremely intelligent and economically successful."

"I've heard that they are viciously cruel," she replied. "Is that just a rumor or is there truth in it? We don't need trouble."

"I've heard they kill whatever they don't like," her mage replied. "And often even what they do like, just for the thrill of it."

"Then perhaps we could train and use them," Atrid mused. "I don't want brutality among my subjects, but perhaps the threat might be useful?"

The rebellious lizard beings turned out to be harder to train than either she or her mages had anticipated. They boldly continued their brutality, profiting, cheating her subjects constantly while stubbornly refusing to join her realm. When it came to Atrid's attention that they were spreading rumors of the evil of her meldings like a virus across the Galaxy, she knew she must take action.

"We must teach them," she ordered. "Call out the troops and attack."

Atrid's mages tried to dissuade her. "The customs of other species are different," they told her. "Their DNA is too foreign. We really can't expect them to react as we would. Surely all this unrest will pass."

But Atrid was hearing more and more reports of unrest, even among Memmians who had always been loyal. Could the aliens persuade even her own humans to join them in rebellion against her? Would Mem allow itself to become involved in an interplanetary war? She knew from Earth history that such wars could be the end of whole civilizations. She would not allow that to happen.

"Little wars I can cope with," she told her warrior mages, "but a Great War must be prevented at all costs. All threats from this lizard species to the meld must be vanquished immediately."

"They blame the meld for every wrong," her high mage warned her.

Several attempts to assassinate her were narrowly averted. Atrid watched the increasing chaos and knew that immediate action was imperative.

Despite her daily attempts at a show of confidence, Atrid's old night terrors took over her sleep. No matter how she fought them, dreams of mass destruction, collision of planets and Mem turning into a ruin made her twist and turn, waking in frantic fear. Her Inner voices began to nag, begging her to make a move before it was too late. At first they gave only criticism, but when in desperation she asked for their advice, one voice in particular responded. It was the one she had long identified as the red head and who she had lately begun to identify as "Flame Girl."

"You must punish those who rebel against you," that young, strident voice kept insisting. "We are Star Woman. Would you let rebels destroy us and the magnificent Empire we have created?"

Waking from a particularly violent dream, hearing the terror in her Inner voices, Atrid rose, dressed and stalked to the throne room where she spoke with assurance.

"There can be no tolerance of unrest," she ordered. "You guards must round up and imprison these lizard instigators or kill them. Either way I am forced to sentence them to death!"

Despite this swift action the next year brought a series of disasters. Summer brought severe drought to several planets, including Mem. Two of the most distant planets began a new war with each other. One of the emissaries Atrid sent to straighten it out was murdered. Trading between planets became unbalanced and filled with problems. Mem's own economy suffered. For the first time Atrid could remember since she had been crowned the split between Mem's lowland and mountain people opened like a wide crevasse. Sylvans and crofters began to openly protest against exploitation by the mages and the wealthy mountain dwellers who lived in luxury supported by ever increasing taxes of the poor.

Throughout the planets of Mem's galaxy one small war after another began, each needing help from Mage troops. On the home planet anger kept exploding into violence. There were riots in the streets of Syl. Buildings and businesses owned by the rich were looted and burned.

"Atrid steals our young." What started as whispers soon turned to shouts, banners and web alarms that spread throughout the galaxy. "We struggle while she and her mages use the meld to feed her coffers and destroy the bodies of our young!"

Atrid was furious. Surely the meld was pivotal in the development of any future she could envision.

"More and more call the meld an abomination," her high mage reported when she consulted him. "They see it as an execution rather than a privilege."

When she looked through her old binoculars at the city of Syl it seemed to Atrid that the once sparkling white towers were dark with shadows in the setting sun. Was her own planet itself, on the verge of a civil war? The prospect terrified her.

It frightened her Inner throng, too. Some were furious and wanted immediate action. Others opted for peace and a quiet retreat from any threat. Was there unrest among her Inners as well as in the outer worlds?

"What can I do?" she asked her Inners. "What will stop this violence?"

They had no answer.

Atrid demanded more action from her guards, instructing them to torture and even kill if needed to maintain control.

"You give me no choice," Atrid coldly told those arrested. "Order must be restored."

But the crack-down seemed only to increase indignation and rebellion.

"Perhaps if I could increase prosperity among the masses things might calm down." Atrid thought.

That night the voice of a young mage she had recently melded spoke to her in her sleep.

"Doesn't Mem still have rich natural resources? Weren't

jewels like the one on your forehead excavated here long ago before an ancient ban on trade took place?"

Atrid liked it when those she had taken in the meld acted as advisors giving her positive suggestions. Often she felt guided far better by her Inner voices than by the mages who appeared daily in her throne room. This young Inner had planted an important seed. Atrid wondered how she might make it grow.

"Should we explore the mountains of Mem?" she asked her Inner court. "Is there a real possibility of gems and ores here that might be valuable?"

Their answer was yes.

Atrid's decision was made. "We must find a way to identify the old mining areas and send people to work there," she instructed. "There must still be some rich lodes left."

She felt elated. If the search was successful Mem's economy would grow accordingly and surely all of her planets would benefit. She could easily envision new trade across the galaxy bringing a constant financial stream into Mem's coffers. Then her people would live in peace again. All she and her Inner throng had to do was find a way to locate sites.

Long ago Atrid had melded an old seer-mage who was purported to have "the sight." She had dismissed his "gifts" as folly, but now turned to him for help. Together they located an ancient chart showing Mem's far Eastern mountains marked with forgotten mines.

When she thanked the old seer, he gave her an encouraging prognosis.

"Eventually something very precious will come to us from that region, a secret that will change many destinies," his frail voice informed her.

"Good," Atrid thought. "All we have to do is find these precious gems!"

"You could dowse for them," the old man suggested.

"I only know about dowsing for water," Atrid replied, "and I always thought that was a game. Who would believe in such foolishness?"

That night as she slept an image came to her. She saw herself using a three pronged branch from one of her garden fruit trees to search a map of the eastern mountains. As she took two of the prongs in her hands the third prong hovered over the map then suddenly dropped onto a certain spot. No matter how Atrid tried, she couldn't lift it away.

Should she put faith in a dream? Long ago she had forbidden dreams and dreaming. Weren't they superstition? Try as she might to dismiss the idea, however, like the struggle to lift the branch, her dream was impossible to forget. Finally in desperation she consulted the old Inner seer again.

There was a smile in his voice as he said, "Is there any harm in trying?"

Feeling foolish, Atrid hesitantly sent a few mages in air pods to the area of her dream. These explorers soon called back to report finding veins that sparkled with precious stones.

"Send miners!" came their jubilant request.

The mining venture was soon a success beyond anything Atrid

could have imagined. She began to teach selected mages her trick with the fruit tree branches so that more areas worth mining could be found. Their work dowsing maps in this fashion was so successful that they began to feel even more important than the miners and in jest to call themselves "diggers." The name stuck. Atrid was the best digger of all who soon needed no more than her index finger to point out a new site.

"It's a mind set more than a physical act," she proudly told her trainees. "You just have to concentrate all of your energy and all your mage skills on the task and we'll all be rich!"

A new guild developed. The men and women she trained became members and Atrid their obvious leader. Her own fortune increased tenfold as did the wealth of others who had either learned to "dig" or had made financial investments in the new mining enterprise.

At first the digging was secret, but before long word of the enterprise began to spread throughout the galaxy. Soon representatives of other planets came to barter and buy, increasing Mem's wealth. New mansions were built on the mountainsides. New businesses began to thrive in Syl.

Commoners who did the hard labor of mining were more comfortable as a result of their increased incomes but few became wealthy like the diggers and those who handled the trade. Whispers began about the inequality between those who labored in the mines and shopkeepers who made great profits on their sales. Instead of cessation of complaints among other species, resentment about Mem's increase of wealth drew new negative focus that centered on the meld.

Atrid was upset. Money that she had seen as a solution was escalating her problems rather than correcting them.

One morning she called her diggers to the throne room. They could dig maps. Could they do a different kind of digging? Standing on her dais before her throne she asked the question.

"Do you think it might be possible for you to use your skills as diggers to probe minds?" she asked. "We need to identify the trouble makers."

The answer was yes. Without a doubt they could use their new methods of concentration on the brains and hearts, not only of Memmians, but also of other species. It shouldn't be difficult now that they had learned the basic skills.

Many diggers soon developed their abilities to a point where they were able to read even the most alien minds as easily as they read a map. With others like the lizards it took longer, but in the end the new diggers succeeded even with those whose minds were carefully cloaked. The protests continued but trouble makers were easily identified. Some had merely whispered an objection to the gap between rich and poor. Others, more daring, continued to criticize the meld.

"How is it possible that they would challenge such a thing?" Atrid demanded again and again, pacing nervously. "Can't they see that I, Star Woman, am doing all I can to make their lives better?"

"Your subjects yearn for equality," one of her confidantes told her. "It's understandable. There are those who think your expansion happened too fast. Others feel ceremonies like the meld are abominable and that your decisions have only widened the schism between rich and poor as well as between aliens and Memmians."

"But the digging has increased all incomes," Atrid insisted.

"Equitably?"

Atrid stared at him. Voices had started to speak in her brain.

"Get angry!" the flame girl hissed. "He can't speak to us this way! We are the Chosen!"

"Calm yourselves," the Inner old seer-mage advised, "Anger isn't going to help."

"Just be quiet, all of you," Atrid commanded silently, "I need to think about how I can solve this dilemma and you're confusing me."

"We want to help," a tentative voice murmured. "You must know that there are those who think your new ways have become too restrictive. Many advocate for a return to the old days and ways of past Queens."

"The old days didn't satisfy them either." Atrid told him angrily. "Thanks to me the old, worn out past is gone, and thanks to me the wonders of the meld and the "digging" have brought my whole empire into an exciting new era of productivity and prosperity. The complainers must be dealt with swiftly so peace can return."

That same day a Mage spoke to her about the same topic. "You must know that objection to the meld continues to grow. Many say that if you were truly Star Woman you would never allow such an abomination."

"And you agree with them?" Atrid could feel her anger reaching a boil again.

"I fear the spreading fear and denial. Some of us believe that it might be better to discontinue the meld at least until things calm down."

"You mages are suggesting that I die!" Atrid's voice was frigid. "I could have you killed for such treason."

"Atrid, you must know we are loyal to you. I'm only trying to tell you the truth as your subjects see it."

"We already know how to handle this," Atrid replied. "We must discipline any who disagree. And my diggers will find them, you can be sure!"

CHAPTER 6

By the next morning arrests were escalating. Atrid sent the High Mage into exile in the far off mined out mountains. Joining him were those identified as having made complaints about the meld. All their sentences were for life.

"That should put a stop to this nonsense!" Atrid declared.

Like the rapid growth of fire in a dry landscape, however, the protests increased. Suddenly new demonstrations began to spring up jumping all of Atrid's barriers as they spread from one planet to the next. Riots and wars grew rampant throughout the Empire, with fires, looting, maiming, torture and death between species. Everything Atrid tried seemed only to increase the rebellion. Criticism of her rule and especially of the meld continued to spread.

"Your empire is turning against you," her diggers and guards warned her.

"We give them their lives if they behave," said a stony Inner voice, "and if they don't then they deserve to die!"

Atrid believed the words and spoke them aloud. The response in the throne room was stunned silence. Digging their thoughts, Atrid was shocked to realize that more than one of them secretly agreed with the protesters! If this was so, she was in danger and so were they. Soon the whole Galaxy would erupt. She must find a way to regain control.

"There has to be something we can do," Atrid told her many

Inner selves as she tossed and turned that night. "I cannot give up the meld. The consequences of that would be too terrible to even consider!"

She thought of herself as a girl being crowned. Citizens had truly supported her then. In the first years of the meld they had continued to honor her, giving themselves gladly to have eternal life as they renewed their Queen. What had happened to create such chaos?

"I haven't changed," she thought. "Like Mem I've just become more. Where would any of us be today without the wealth of the mines or the ability of my diggers? And how could any of this have come into being without the meld?"

Flame girl spoke in Atrid's mind, "They want us dead," she insisted, her voice cold. "Can't you see that? It's clear to me what we need to do. The Lizard rebels are traitors. They must be banished!"

"That would take a prison planet that is inescapable and so terrible that even the worst would tremble at the thought of imprisonment there. That sounds impossible," Atrid said.

"Can't you see the solution? You must find a planet you can turn into such a prison. You are not only Star Woman, but also a great magician. With the help of your best mages we should be able to create a prison planet so horrible that even the threat of it would make all species behave, even the lizards."

Other Inner voices began to agree.

Atrid was intrigued. "Could there be such a planet? And if so how will I find it?" She wondered.

The next day she began by searching the old castle library for maps, looking first at planets nearby, then spreading out toward the edges of the galaxy. Those that belonged to her Empire were inhabited. She had never before looked for one that wasn't.

"We could create such a place," the familiar Flame Girl voice said. "See that outer planet, the one named Zetti? It's obviously uninhabited and wildly overgrown, a jungle of plants and waters we can't transport or market. There doesn't seem to be any animal life except for snakes and such. Take a look at the old texts and see if there's anything useful there. If not couldn't we wipe it clean and make it anything we want?"

"Yes," Atrid thought, "all I have to do is figure out how!"

That night she awoke moaning in fear. It took her several minutes before the wave of panic receded and she calmed enough to realize she'd been having a dream. A dream of Zetti. Thinking about it, letting it come into awareness, she felt again how in the dream her body had been caught by coarse vines that entrapped her like huge snakes slowly squeezing life out of her. The more she struggled, the tighter she was held. All she'd been able to do was scream herself awake where she lay sweating and moaning for some time. When she was finally able to calm herself and to ponder the horror of what she had experienced she began to wonder what, if anything, the dream meant. What was strangling her?

"It's the perfect place!" The Inner voice claimed. "We could leave the vines and the serpents and wipe the rest. Doesn't the dream tell you to do this? Otherwise something represented by the vines will strangle you and those of us who live in you. Surely it's a danger to all of us if you leave Zetti as it is. Unless you change it, this planet will destroy us."

No matter what Atrid did, for the next few nights she was back in the dream. During the day she could hardly function. Her whole body was filled with aches and pain as if the vines were still squeezing her when she was awake.

"Atrid listen to us!" the voices began to chorus within her. "It's time to take action!"

The dreams grew worse. Not only were the snaky vines squeezing the life out of her, but gigantic trees were walking toward her and rushing waters threatened to drown her. When the sky above came crashing down, hurtling stars and planets around her as they fell, Atrid began to fight back, frantically waving her arms in a desperate attempt to fend off destruction.

As this happened a new voice, deep and self assured, spoke. "This mess is a symbol of your realm. Only you can fix it."

Yes, she must fix this terrible chaos and save her Empire. In her dream she began to shout, making strange guttural sounds as if she were she spitting out comets and fireballs. In desperation, unable to awaken, she forged the chaos into a weapon, hurling it at the greenery which began to sicken and die, then burn until the whole planet seemed to go up in flames and quickly become nothing but black ash. A strong wind came and blew the ash away revealing cliffs, outcroppings and wide expanses of shining flatland on which there was no color, no movement and no apparent life. Looking around all she could see in any direction was black glass-like rock. In her dream Zetti was barren. "I've killed it!" She said triumphantly.

Her words woke her up, panting like a terrified animal.

"It's just a stupid dream," she scolded. "Ignore it," she told her Inners.

Yet as daylight arrived she realized that the bleak, sterility of the dream had somehow entered, perhaps even melded with her. The image of shining black cliffs and flatland clung to her. She kept seeing the images just behind her eyes, a Zetti where there was no sound and nothing moved. Yes, in some strange way she had killed it. The planet was dead.

Shouldn't she be horrified?

Atrid spoke aloud, asking herself questions. "Which is worse?" she asked, "Overgrowth that would strangle my whole Realm, or creation of a dead planet that would be a perfect prison for all infidels? Zetti is a danger to all of us. I haven't hesitated to destroy those who threatened my rule. Why should I be so afraid to take action like that in the dream?"

"All we want is Peace," her Inners responded. "Surely together we are a Goddess who must destroy in order to create!"

Atrid agreed.

"We have great work to do!" she instructed her best Magediggers as they gathered in her throne room, "In our galaxy there is a planet called Zetti, so overgrown with noxious plants and tainted water that it begs for transformation. It looks pure but my dreams tell me it is foul. The animal life is grotesque. Zetti's wildness is untamed, like that of our rebels. It is like a cancer in the midst of our Empire, threatening to spread its malignancy throughout the cosmos. We will tame it by stripping it of its profusion. It will become barren and be a perfect prison planet!"

She could taste triumph on her tongue as she spoke.

For the next five days neither Atrid nor any of her best digger-mages ate, drank or slept as they psychically dug and transformed a planet, sending fiery word spells that shot like laser beams from their mouths across the Galaxy to transform Zetti's green mountains into peaks of a substance that looked like black glass but was harder and more impenetrable than any substance known throughout the Galaxy. Atrid named it "Extrine."

When they finished, Zetti's wide oceans were deserts of black sand. The only vegetation left anywhere on the planet was a fuzzy grey lichen that blanketed the tops of the Extrine mesas. Threads of narrow, sluggish streams covered with grey slime replaced the rushing green waters of Zetti's over abundant rivers, lakes and oceans. Where a sun had shone in terrible brilliance there was now a sky of ominous gray clouds that dropped more ash than rain on the planet below.

No animal or bird life was to be seen other than sinewy mountain creatures Atrid named Tak who were huge goats with terrible curling horns that looked as if they could pierce any challenger. These animals, totally untamable and wild, clambered sure footed over projections sharp as glass on the black cliffs and ravines. Their mating calls echoed from the heights like blood-curdling human screams. Their hides were tough and their sinewy meat barely edible. They were allowed to survive the purge only as a token to those who would be imprisoned, perhaps useful if anyone could figure out how to catch or kill them.

Also there were still huge black underground snakes left in the holes of the planet's cliffs, seldom emerging but ever present. Perhaps their flesh might be food, despite the fact that for centuries Memmians had seen serpents as holy and refused to kill or eat them.

"Starving prisoners can't afford to be fussy about old religious taboos." Atrid told her diggers with great satisfaction. "The only source of food will be shipments that we control."

The strange albino fish in the planets slime-covered streams were designed to have intermittent and irregular periods of spawning during which the tiniest fragment of their flesh became deadly poison. Fish ingested at such times created convulsions of pain followed by certain death.

Atrid had some difficulty persuading the mages that the cycles of fish were compassionate acts.

"If a prisoner is lucky he or she may find release through eating them and move on to death," she pronounced proudly.

One of the diggers referred to the planet as Zetti.

"The name now is Zed," Atrid told them.

By then all participants in changing Zetti into Zed knew that the prisoners would all be in constant danger of death. This would be true for aliens even more than humans. Most of them required very different diets from the supplies Atrid intended to send. Aliens of many other species might choose to eat the fish hoping to poison themselves.

When the mages reported this fear to Atrid she scoffed.

"After awhile they will learn that even Death is not kind to Atrid's discards," she told them. "Why should there be ease or relief for those who defy our laws?"

As more and more rebels were identified and shipped out on old, rusting spaceships, fear mounted in those left behind on their home planets. When they discovered that each prisoner was being sterilized before passage to Zed the small protests that sprang up were swiftly stopped.

Everyone soon learned that there was nothing they could do but accept Atrid's rules. Her digger spies were everywhere. When sentences were meted out in every city, village and colony Atrid's subjects, both at home on Mem and among the species of other planets, fell into a kind of helpless torpor. Atrid gave them no choice. Those who felt that she had finally gone far beyond the limits of reason quickly learned to bury their dangerous thoughts and behave like model citizens.

At first the guards who delivered prisoners to Zed came back with gruesome tales, agreeing among themselves that it was cruel and inhumane to sentence anyone, even the most evil, to such a mean existence. Banishment to Zed of any guard who spoke out set an example for others who rapidly learned the price paid for telling stories of the prison planet even in the privacy of their own homes. Atrid was determined to have order throughout the Galaxy. When people began to go about their lives much like automatons, Atrid celebrated her ability to rule without incidents, calling the new way "peace" and declaring what became known as "The Change" of

Zetti into Zed a huge success.

"This is some of the best work we've ever done," she assured her mages. "This Change is the beginning of a whole new era of peace, not only for Mem, but for the whole multiverse."

CHAPTER 7

The energy of the Change silently swept, at first in a slow wave but building as it sped toward the outer reaches of the Cosmos into an energy tsunami of seismic shock. Dark energy poured through each planet, moon and star, sinking into black holes only to emerge reinforced, leaving chaos wherever it touched. Strange storms added to the thunderous churning. Red lightning flashed incessantly. Outer stars imploded. By the time the force reached other galaxies far planets were plunging from their orbits. All the Heavens eventually felt the thrust of the devastation.

Turning a blind eye, Atrid refused to acknowledge any of the destruction.

"There is no connection," she insisted.

Finally the fury reached the outer rim of the known Multiverse. The stasis cocoon containing the Alph burst open and their incredible but formless mind energy scattered. With their penetrating wisdom and the clarity of their rapid intermingling they quickly regathered into a new great pool of knowledge in which each was a separate nano entity. All of them knew at once what had happened. They had sent Atrid a cautioning dream in hopes of showing her the overwhelming danger of her own expansive hubris. Atrid had totally misinterpreted their dream. Instead she had taken the images literally as a mandate to create havoc.

"It was always a human frailty," the Alph sadly agreed.

"Unless they are Shapers, human beings frequently see only the surface rather than the multi-layered meanings in the depths of the dreams we send them."

The Alph themselves understood the mistake they had made. Before Atrid's Change they had always lived with the hope of someday evolving into a multi-faceted entity able to take form. Now with the Queen's actions, that hope was dashed forever. It was as if the Change had imprisoned their scattering in an invisible extrine, similar to the change of Zetti's beauty into the black extrine of Zed. In one terrible moment their many brilliant minds had been spewed from containment as a single organism of pure thought and inner dreams out into a tumultuous star field of aftershocks and separation.

During an extended time of trying to regain their oneness, they accepted their plight and struggled to rectify at least some of the damage. At the same time they began to think about the future, not only for themselves but also of the cosmos. Might this Queen as she grew ever more powerful eventually do something far worse?

How might they intervene? At first there seemed to be no answer. Obviously she either rejected or totally misunderstood any dreams they sent her. Over time however a dream came to them with a solution. They each began to dream of a shaper human with the mind and talents of an Alph. Wouldn't such a being be capable of changing and tempering even a Queen as troubled as Atrid?

But where could they find such a human? No Memmian alive today would suit their needs. All were under Atrid's strict control and she had forbidden dreaming.

Long, long ago they had turned to the Nus and Las Shapers for help but no matter how they dream-searched the Alph could find no trace of either species. Without the aid of those dependable friends who had long ago shaped the Great Experiment and given human life a new start on Mem the Alph must find a way to handle the problem on their own. Whole galaxies must be saved from Atrid's future folly.

"Surely with our pooled energy we can create something even if it's merely a Light Being with human abilities." The thought came to all of them at once. "We need a human body with the mind and soul of an Alph to counteract Atrid's destruction."

All agreed, they must somehow create a human who could achieve such a task.

But how could they hope to accomplish such a shaping on their own? As invisible dreamers, they were unable to take shape themselves except as Light and then only in a crisis. How could they hope to create a human with the mind of an Alph?

A question came to them in a dream. Wasn't there still a trace of Earth human DNA left over from the Great Experiment's completion? Could they possibly find and dream it into being?

The Alph pool began to transform as it dream-searched, dividing once more into the singular dreamers they had been after the Change. Many Alph died flowing in dreams over the multiverse in their search. There were failures. At last they had to accept that while they were able to mind meld their energies to cling like atoms to the old DNA, there was no way they could dream a human with the mind of an Alph who would be visible and functional for more than a few hours at a time.

"Will the human DNA temporarily give him all the physical abilities of a human male?" they asked themselves. "If he coupled with a human female might he shape a human child with our mind?"

Considering the destruction Atrid might cause in the years it would take for such a child to reach maturity they temporarily felt defeated. Yet there was no other choice. This was a chance they would have to take even if they failed.

After several failures the Alph finally had their result: an Alph Light Being who had enough human DNA to take form for two or three hours at a time. Only after time in stasis could he be regenerated appearing and hopefully functioning as a human male.

Zari, for that was the name they gave this Being, was more than half Alph. For most of the time he was wholly Alph, invisible and wise beyond anything a human of Mem could possibly imagine. In his brief periods of embodiment he had every physical ability of a human man. This included the ability to engender a child. He also would retain all Alphian wisdom and hopefully pass some of it on. Their dreams told the Alph that this was the best they could do and would have to be enough.

They had already done dream exploration of a place in the Far Eastern part of Mem where the mountains that rose out of a desert had been abandoned when mined out. Most were now considered uninhabitable. Mind- searching the area, the Alph discovered a mountain where a few families had chosen to stay and eke out a difficult living from the rocky soil. After several generations there was no one left but one young woman whose parents had recently died leaving her alone. She knew of the rest of Mem from family books but was reluctant to leave and set out by herself into an unfamiliar landscape. Instead she chose to stay on her family farm. In her isolation, she perfectly suited the needs of the Alph.

At first the Alph sent her dreams of Zari so she would welcome him when he actually arrived. Then, reminding him that he would have only a few short hours with the girl each day before losing his form, they sent him to her with the understanding that during the brief periods of his embodiment he must somehow father a child with her. When this was accomplished, as they were sure it would, his human form would fade completely. He would once again be an invisible Alph. At most he would have two to three human months to achieve his task.

Zari understood. Like all Alph, he knew what he had been created to do. It was his destiny to serve such a purpose. He accepted his task gladly knowing he was part of the solution created in response to the Change of Zetti into Zed. If he succeeded, the girl child conceived might save Mem and other planets of the Galaxy. Who could ask for a greater task than to create such a child to eventually replace the destructive queen?

When Zari appeared on her doorstep Tessi had already learned from her dreams to love him. In the first week during the few hours they had together they were friends. Each time he became ill she tried to care for him, but each day after one or two precious hours he would disappear into the mountains. Though she searched, she was never able to figure out where he went.

By their third meeting they were lovers. When she discovered herself with child she was ecstatically happy, but as soon as the child was conceived Zari left, knowing he was losing form for the last time. If it hadn't been for the child growing in her and for dreams in which her lover came to her, Tessi would have been inconsolable.

The baby was a boy rather than a girl. Talin was their son.

The Alph accepted this change in their plan even though it would take far longer than they had hoped. They also gave Zari permission to stay nearby and invisibly help Tessi with the child, instructing them both in dreams and watching over every moment of the boy's early life.

Talin's childhood was everything the Alph could have hoped. Born with the silver hair inherited centuries ago from the Las and now a sign of Mem's royals, the boy had his own special ways. Thanks to Zari's dream instructions, Tessi gave her son great freedom, allowing him to play alone in the mountains and the meadows. He never told her that during these jaunts he was often accompanied by an invisible friend who would plant thoughts and images in his mind in the same way she planted seeds in their garden. The wonder of plants and tiny creatures glowed for him all through his childhood, a wonder shared by his invisible friend.

He never knew of his father whose name was not spoken. It didn't occur to him to be curious until years later when one of the students at the monastery in Lubin questioned his parentage.

"Was your father around when you were small?"

"Father?"

"Your mother's husband?"

Talin pulled at his chin, pondering. "I don't think she had one," he replied.

"Oh," one of the boys laughed, "she got you all by herself?"

Talin replied with dignity, "I suppose she did," and wondered why all the boys laughed.

In his early years Talin had never felt the need for another person. His mother and his invisible friend were enough. She had her own life caring for their croft and she let him have his. The rest of the time he was taught and helped by his invisible friend. When he needed either of them they were there to care for him but neither ever intruded if he needed time alone. Sometimes his mother would ruffle his silver hair and tell him he was special. He would let her hug him and would hug her back, laughing.

"I'm just me, myself and I," he would say.

"Yes," his mother would answer, fondly rubbing his silver hair, "And that's enough for me."

She never made him feel that anything about him was unusual or out of the ordinary. All he felt was her constant love and the freedom she gave him.

They were very poor. The Alph were unable to change that. Later in life Talin realized that his mother could have eased their common needs for better food and less hard work by taking both of them to the monastery at Lubin while he was still an infant. He was half grown before she told him of the instructions given to her in dreams. "It's important that you grow up here in the mountains," she told him one morning as she gave him his breakfast. "I had a dream about it."

Because of the power of her dreams, she kept Talin on the croft until he was ten. That year a terrible drought brought them to the edge of starvation. All meals became meager. Supplies were running out and new crops died of thirst because there was no rain and no water. When she was forced to cook the meat of their animals in her struggle to keep herself and Talin alive, both of them weeping over their loss with every bite, Tessi had to face the reality of their plight. They must leave or die.

One morning after waking Talin, Tessi told him he must pack his things. Struggling to stop her tears, she announced, "Tomorrow we'll be leaving and we won't be coming back."

Talin had that last day to roam, saying goodbye to each plant and tree. He tried to memorize every part of the familiar landscape. Finally exhausted with grief and starvation, he lay down in the soft grass and cried into the earth until there were no more tears. Then he fell asleep. In a dream his invisible friend came and held him and said good-bye.

"You won't return here again," he whispered in Talin's ear, "Or to me. But wherever you go there will be invisible friends looking after you."

When Talin returned home at dusk he felt as if his childhood had been left in the mud made of his weeping. His face was stained but he was ready.

They set out at dawn, making the long trek on foot. Living on herbs and berries they staggered along until they finally reached the town of Lubin and its monastery of cloistered mages. Knocking at the gate of the monastery one late starless night, Talin's mother hoped only that when the gatekeeper lifted his lantern and caught a glimpse of Talin's hair he would take pity on their skeletal bodies and give them food. At the gate she pulled off her boy's knitted cap so that his silver hair sprang into view. The man who admitted them took one look and immediately ushered them both to the kitchen where they were fed. After an interview with the Prior mage they were bathed and given places to sleep.

The next day Talin was called into a large hall where many mages sat in their silver robes at a great table. To Talin it was an amazing sight, for they seemed to shine with an inner light. The mages began to question him. Answers came easily to him. It felt as if he were playing a game. Some responses came from the books his mother had read to him, others from the dream stories his invisible friend had shared. Some came from what seemed like a deep pool of knowledge inside him.

"This is fun!" he thought until they asked if he had any animals.

"We had to eat them," he sobbed, unable to hold back his tears, thinking about the loss not only of his pets, but also of his invisible friend. He didn't mention the latter. That relationship he wanted to keep for himself.

After that day he saw his mother rarely. Soon she was given housing in the nearby town. Talin was given a small cubicle off the room of the mage who was to be his teacher. His training had begun.

From that time on he was always with one or another of the

mages. Other students lived together and ate together. Talin took part in some of their classes and in their organized games but most of the time he had his own tutors and his own schedule. This didn't seem odd to him. He was used to being separate. In fact he craved time alone.

Coming into "civilization" had been a shock. Almost at once Talin began to see his own differences. It wasn't just that he was shy. He was a stranger to others and they to him. When other students insisted that the only sentient beings in the Galaxy were those of Memmian blood Talin tried to protest.

"But I know a sentient being who has no form at all!" he insisted.

Even the teachers laughed. After that the other boys called him names and teased him unmercifully.

His own teacher tried to be helpful. "Too much imagination can get you into trouble," he told the boy.

"There are others who don't look like us or act like us," Talin insisted. "Some are far wiser than even the wisest here on Mem. How is it you don't know this?"

"You are only a boy," his teacher told him sternly. "A boy with too much imagination. If you keep spouting this nonsense others will see you as a fool."

By the time he left the monastery and came to Syl, Talin had learned the importance of silence. Only to himself did he wonder how it was that intelligent scholars could be so blind to a reality he had experienced throughout most of his life in the mountains.

He missed his invisible friend but never spoke of him.

Sometimes even the presence of a quiet teacher wasn't what he needed. Then he would find a way to steal out alone into one of the orchards where he could lie on the earth and study the clouds or the stars and reconnect with his former self. What he really sought was his invisible friend, but he never came now, even in dreams.

"Wherever you go you will always be looked after by invisible friends," his friend had assured him as he had lain weeping in the mud. Talin wondered if one of them would ever appear.

When the monks told him it was time for him to move on, Talin was told to say good-bye to his mother. He begged her to come with him, but her dreams had told her she must stay. With an escort of mages the boy was sent on a long journey by horseback, visiting monasteries along the route they took, always heading west.

Stopping for months to learn from the mages in one monastery after another they slowly crossed the country. At last they reached the city of Syl where they rested and swam in the sea and ate good food until Talin was strong and fit. By then he was fully grown.

On the day of his seventeenth birthday he was taken from Syl to the mountains and the court of Atrid. He was impatient, hoping to get the court appearance over quickly so he could begin his studies nearby with access to the castle's famous libraries.

CHAPTER 8

On the morning of his first meeting with Atrid, Talin stood for nearly an hour with the court mages waiting in utter stillness for their Queen. During that time not one of them so much as twitched or coughed.

Having been taught at Lubin to stand in such a fashion, he forced himself to stay motionless, controlling his impatience and increasing resentment at the delay. Who was this Queen to make them wait so interminably?

Suddenly the doors swung wide. As one the whole entourage fell to their knees. Later Talin learned that this was never demanded. It didn't have to be. Allies and foes alike were so well trained to the Queen's entry that their knees buckled without volition the moment she appeared.

In one instant he was the only person standing, frozen in place by the shock of seeing her for the first time. Moving only his eyes he watched her stride down the aisle toward the magnificent seat awaiting her on a dais at the front of the vast throne room.

Here was Atrid, whose body, clad in a skin of glittering fabric, appeared to reflect golden light. Her silver hair streaked with copper and gold flashed with energy. As she passed him her perfume drifted across his face. Her youthful body moved with such beauty and grace that the sight of her made it almost impossible for him to breathe. She was the most beautiful being he had ever seen!

Truly she was a Goddess. As if a bolt of lightning had struck his innermost core, he knew himself marked as Hers. Here was his Queen, his Destiny. Passion burst forth in him. In that moment he changed from boy to man, immediately knowing he had just found the woman of his dreams, the mate of his soul.

Struck deaf and blind to everything except this magnificent woman, at first Talin was unaware of the whispers around him. Only when sound like a gust of wind filled the room did he finally hear. Suddenly aware that everyone else was kneeling while he stood, he realized that what he had mistaken for wind was really the barely suppressed snickering of all the mages as they observed his lack of decorum.

On the periphery of his vision he could see the High Mage glaring as he silently gestured for Talin to kneel. Unfortunately that was impossible. Talin, caught in his own thrall, couldn't move. All he could do was stare in awe at the extraordinary woman, his Queen.

Feeling his gaze Atrid stopped on the steps before her throne and turned to see what had caused the noise. Her eyes widened as she saw the handsome young man who stood so visibly among her kneeling subjects looking directly at her rather than bending his legs or bowing his head. She was astonished to see tears filling his eyes. When he blinked one ran down his cheek!

Her own eyes widened. Then to Talin's utter astonishment, she opened a layer of herself to let him in. He instantly fell into what seemed to him to be the wonders of a galaxy in her depths. It was as if a night sky shone with every planet and star singing its own harmonies.

Talin did the only thing he could do in response. He opened himself to give her entrance into the very center of himself, allowing her to claim him as her own. He could think of nothing he wanted more than to serve her, to be of use to this wondrous being whom he already loved more than life itself.

At that moment the High Mage stepped forward. Putting out his hand he touched Talin's back. Trained to respond instantly to such a command, Talin's body released and he fell to his knees.

Nothing was said. No one spoke to him about the incident, though much later it was recorded in all of Mem's histories.

In one awestruck moment Talin knew for sure that his life had changed forever.

At first the Alph were disturbed. Though they had designed him to mate her, they hadn't anticipated that Talin's Memmian naiveté would give Atrid such power over him or that her beauty, enhanced by the youths and maidens she had melded, would affect him so profoundly. They should have known, but they were immune to Atrid's charms. Half human, Talin was not.

The moment Talin saw her he understood why Atrid's people all found it the highest honor to be chosen to join her in the ceremony in which their cells, as the source of her renewal, were melded into every cell of her mind and body. He would gladly have offered himself on the spot.

For a time the Alph feared that this might happen.

Instead of melding him, however, Atrid responded by falling in love with him as she took him into her bed and her daily life. He was the only partner she had ever considered. After a brief time in which she did most of the courting, Talin became her husband-consort.

In this way it eventually turned out close to what the Alph had hoped and planned. The difference was that Talin became Atrid's Shaper rather than theirs, so infatuated with her that for a long time he was blind to the negative traits and qualities of her personality.
The only fault Talin saw or questioned was one Atrid shared with most Memmians. From the beginning of his exposure to a world beyond the isolation of his childhood Talin had begun to question how a society like Mem's that had developed in so many sophisticated ways could be so blind to other realities than their own. How could the mages and people, including Atrid, be so blind to valuable differences in species? The more he realized Mem's rigidity the more difficulty he had with the Memmian view that theirs was the only truth and anything that differed was an aberration. How could the people of Syl and especially the mages and the court, especially the Queen, think that only what they could see, hear, taste, touch or smell was real? Though he had already experienced this limitation among the monks of Lubin monastery, he was nevertheless surprised when he tried to talk to Atrid about his experiences of an invisible friend and she dismissed them, along with his dream life, as childish naïveté.

At first Talin was frustrated, but soon he began to question what he had always seen as reality. Was he truly as delusional as Atrid, teasing him, insisted? In the beginning Talin was puzzled, wondering how a society that had developed something as sophisticated as "digging" and "the meld" could be so blind to differences in form. Slowly, however, as he absorbed the life of the court and the city of Syl he began to think like other Memmians. His childhood insights and hopes began to seem like foolish folly. The mages had long accused him of delusions. Perhaps they were right. He needed to grow up and accept the limitations of real truth about the nature of things.

Caught in his desire to please Atrid, Talin was determined to do everything he could to make her happy. If this meant giving up his old views about differences, or even dreams, so be it. He was completely hers. Pleasing her was his greatest desire.

A year after their marriage, in celebration of the 2nd century of her own melding, Atrid encouraged him to use the meld elixir and meld with a volunteer of his own choosing so that he, young and vibrant as he was, might never grow old but live forever at her side, the mate of her soul and body. No Memmian questioned this, least of all Talin. By then only a crazy minority ever thought of questioning anything Atrid did. These rebellious ones were soon ferreted out and banished to Zed where they became the living dead, known among themselves, according to the guards who delivered them, as the "Survivors," as if that were some kind of honorific.

Just as it was considered a privilege to be absorbed into the Queen's Royal Being it soon became a matter of respect to be chosen for melding with Talin. Even the wealthy and some of the mage caste offered themselves or their children to him in a kind of begging submission. None seemed to care that they lost their own bodies. After all, weren't those who joined given eternal life in the bodies of their Royals?

As Atrid remained young, so did Talin, thanks to the offerings of those who dwelled within them.

Atrid seemed to love him wholeheartedly.

"You are my better half," she told him again and again. "My inspiration. I never thought I could care like this or love this way. You've brought me completion."

Fortunately for Talin, her Inner throng seemed to agree.

As time went on Talin was recognized by the other mages as Atrid's right hand. Legends about them took form and grew. Everyone agreed: a part of Atrid's self, dormant from birth was now embodied in Talin. He was the peoples' mentor, their mediator, their trusted champion. It was he who brought their requests to the Queen. She seldom refused him.

Talin's melds along with Atrid's became major rites, celebrated by both rich and poor with feasting. Babies conceived at those times born with silver hair were considered especially sacred. As they grew these girls and boys were dedicated to either the magehood or the meld. Most hoped to be chosen for the latter. Atrid ruled her realm with Talin as her chosen consort. All was well.

Occasional rebellions were easily handled. Threat of life on Zed controlled Mem's general population. Offenders on all planets were rapidly tried, judged and if found guilty of insurrection shipped off to the prison planet so that peace was rapidly restored. Order ruled throughout the Galaxy.

Though they detested the meld and what Atrid had done to both the beauty of Zetti and the order of the multiverse, the Alph took no more action. It was agreed in their dreams that the love Atrid shared with Talin would slowly soften her and a day would come when Talin could persuade her to have a child. Years passed before the Alph accepted that this was not going to happen. The Queen had won. Atrid had made herself if not immortal, close to it. Everyone on planet Mem, including Talin, needed no future Queen. She would rule for generations to come, with a transformed Talin at her side.

At last the Alph realized that a new plan must be dreamed. They must help Talin recover his initial purpose.

CHAPTER 9

At first when night scenes began to bother his sleep and produce a restlessness in him, Talin wondered if perhaps he had melded a heretic by mistake.

"Why am I having these crazy dreams?" he asked himself. He thought of discussing them with Atrid, but she had long since outlawed any talk of dreams, making it a law of the land that dreamers would be severely punished. Finding his nights repeatedly filled with images so real he had to fight himself awake to escape them, Talin would get out of bed and go outside to pace the palace balconies trying to keep them at bay.

Nevertheless a strange desire began to grow in him as night after night dreams of a toddler who looked just like Atrid but had his eyes appeared in his sleep. Trying to stay awake, he tossed and turned in the great royal bed and eventually dozed. As if waiting for the opportunity, the dream child would immediately appear and climb into his lap. He began to anticipate her visits even as he avoided sleep. The dreams continued. Voices sang him children's songs. The child would twirl before him but as soon as he reached out for her she would dance away and vanish.

"Are you real?" he asked her in one dream.

"Only if you want me enough" she responded..

Talin grew thin and haggard.

"You don't look well," Atrid scolded. "You need to eat more and get more rest."

His temper grew short. New voices sounded in his dreams, urging him to make the child a reality.

"You long for her," they told him. "You can have her you know. All you have to do is persuade Atrid."

Talin tried. Atrid was furious.

When he pressed her, she exploded. "Don't ever speak to me of this again!" she commanded. "I am Queen of Mem. As Star Woman I am immortal. There is no need for a child!"

Talin tried to let it go, but the dreams grew more and more insistent. Plots began to unfold in them. He wondered if he might be going mad.

A careful plan was slowly taking form. Hard as he fought them, strange ideas poured into his sleep, He stopped sharing Atrid's bed, knowing how much his restlessness disturbed her sleep. Without his presence, however, she, too, had trouble sleeping and begged him to return. The next meld was coming. Tension was mounting. How could either of them be ready for another meld if they were sleep deprived?

"I miss you, too," Talin told her. "I'll come back, but we must both take a sleeping draught and get some sleep."

Atrid agreed.

At first he was unaware that he was preparing to make the dreams a reality. When they drank a sleeping potion together it was simply to give them rest. Atrid slept deeply, oblivious to commotion anywhere in the castle. She called the potion his gift to her and praised him for it.

One night he couldn't resist making love to Atrid while she

slept. In her drugged sleep she opened to him and responded with delight, but in the morning she remembered only that she had had a pleasant dream. The Alph had seen to that.

"I dreamed we made love," she told him at breakfast. "It was wonderful."

"What would you do if it were real?" Talin asked. "What if you found out it really happened?"

"As long as you make sure I don't conceive," she teased, laughing.

He knew she trusted him. He had always taken care of her. It had always been that way, but his dreams were now more and more insistent. There must be a child. The toddler kept coming to him in his dreams, sometimes doubled as if to stress her importance. He would waken longing for a daughter. Each day his arms felt emptier without her.

At last Talin's longing for his dream daughter was so intense that one night he gave in and did as the dream instructed. That night while Atrid slept as if she had fallen into unfathomable depths he wept as he impregnated her. Immediately she conceived. The next day he tried to confess his infidelity but the words wouldn't come out.

Soon, on a night of her further drug-induced sleep, Talin carefully followed dream instructions, removing the fertilized egg from Atrid's body. Carrying it in a sterilized container, he immediately took it to the chapel where the dream had told him one of the kitchen maids slept after several wakeful nights of prayer. The Alph had chosen her carefully as the surrogate mother, a virgin who longed for her family and home. Just as the mother of Talin had been, the woman was a good and obedient person who had grown up far from Syl, brought up to honor her dreams and follow them religiously. The Alph were sure she was the right one to carry out their plan.

That night the maiden went to the mages temple to pray because she was so lonely. While there she fell asleep and dreamed of a god who came to the altar where she slept and after giving her a potion to drink, did some sort of medical procedure. Waking in the morning she tried to remember her strange dream, but finally decided it had been caused by the cramps she was now feeling in her belly.

After carefully following his own dream instructions, Talin returned to Atrid's bed trembling with exhaustion and fear, wondering how he could have allowed himself to perform such a crazy act of betrayal. Would it work? He rather hoped it would be forgotten, like a bad dream fading in the morning sunlight.

The next morning Atrid told Talin she herself had had a dream.

"I was with child," she reported. "We made love and I conceived."

"I thought that was impossible," he replied. "What would you do if the dream were true?"

"I would abort it," she stated firmly, "along with the dream."

"Perhaps you should see the healer," he suggested. Atrid agreed, but at that time her schedule was particularly busy and she kept postponing the visit. As the voice in his dreams instructed,

Talin gave the kitchen girl money and permission to return to her family. He watched as she packed and left to return to her parents home far from Syl. Only then could he breathe freely. Soon she would be far from the prying eyes and minds of palace Diggers. Only then would he able to sleep, feeling safe at last, his task accomplished. What he had needed to do to achieve peace in his soul was done.

When Atrid finally kept her appointment with the healer it was reported that yes, indeed, she had conceived, but had obviously miscarried. That night Atrid and Talin drank wine together. Thanks to the Alph who helped him hide his misery and guilt, Talin managed to keep quiet and composed as she happily prattled on. It never occurred to Atrid to do any digging of him. It wouldn't have mattered if she had. The Alph barriers were firmly in place.

Talin was happily surprised to find himself able to smile, even laugh with her as she celebrated.

"When the child is a toddler we will help you find her," a new dream voice assured him. "Until then you must live your life as if nothing has happened. We will see that the child is safe just as we did with you when you were young."

But safety was not to be. Three months later catastrophe struck. The Alph could not prevent it. Despite all their best efforts things went awry. After completing her journey home, the kitchen maid began to fret. Eventually she turned around and came back returning directly to the Queen where she excitedly told her miraculous story. As Atrid listened, the char woman told how she had gone to the temple to pray for solace because she was so lonely.

"I fell asleep," she reported breathlessly, "and that was when the miracle happened."

Atrid was bored. "Yes, yes," she urged, "get on with it."

"While I slept!" the char woman exclaimed, her eyes wide with excitement.

Talin struggled to stifle his gasp. His stomach seemed to be spinning between his ribs. Fear rose like bile in his throat.

"I dreamed that a god came and placed a child in my belly," the woman reported, her whole face lighting up with joy. "I have never been with a man, but now as any digger will surely confirm, I am truly with child!"

Her whole countenance seemed to glow with gratitude and joy.

"Your consort gave me permission to return home to my family," she continued, "but I had to come back. I had to thank you for this gift that you, Star Woman, have given me. It's a miracle. I knew you would want to know that it was a success."

Talin groaned silently at how sadly mistaken she was. He wanted to grab her and run, but there was no chance of that. Atrid called for her diggers to probe the woman. Not only was the pregnancy confirmed, but the whole plot was uncovered.

"It is our child she carries," Atrid accused when she and Talin were alone again. "Yours and mine! I know this is true. How could you do this to me?"

Thus, against all Talin's carefully laid plans, he was identified unmistakably as the "god" of the woman's visitation.

Atrid was more than enraged. Livid with anger, she meted out punishment to both. Others expected her to take them in the meld. Instead Talin was tried, found guilty, shaved of his mage beard, stripped of his mage powers and banished like a common criminal to Zed along with the surrogate mother. Both he and the kitchen maid were sterilized. This was the fate of all prisoners before they departed. Zed could contain no possibility of new life.

Talin was tried at an outdoor court attended by mobs of Atrid's people and told that he could no longer be allowed to pose a threat to the security of Mem or the safety of the Queen. He was given no counsel. There was no possibility of defending himself, for he was not allowed to say a word or to protest in any way, either before, during or after sentencing.

Atrid's was the only voice. "So, my Soul, you would bring me down." A mage voice came from the darkest depths of her being. "You have managed the ultimate betrayal!"

Like a fierce beast of prey, she looked down on him from the rock where she sat on her makeshift throne, her eyes feral, her hand, stretched out like a great claw, emphasizing the illusion.

"Now you must pay the price,." she decreed. "And the woman with you." There was no pity, no love in her face, only rage. "I would meld you," she snarled, "But a traitor within is even worse than one without."

Her face was twisted, distorted, her eyes flashing as she proclaimed his sentence.

"Talin, High Priest of Mem, sharer of My throne and My will, I your Queen strip you of all you have been and cast you out." She flung out her arms, her fingers making an ancient ritual gesture of banishment. "You are unworthy to live on Mem, unworthy to be a mage, unworthy to share in My Being through the meld. You and the woman you chose to bear this abomination will be cleansed of any ability to repeat such folly. After that you will both be transported to the prison planet of Zed where you will live out whatever unnatural days may be left you. I, Atrid, Queen of Mem and the Planets, have spoken!"

She stood looking down at him from her throne platform, erect, beautiful, filled with the power of anger, her green eyes spitting venom into his like those of the golden serpent she wore as her signet. Drawing herself up, standing at full height, the power of hate seemed to fill and enlarge her whole being. "For Me and for Mem you no longer exist."

At the last minute she stepped down and stood directly in front of him. Looking deep into his eyes, she instructed, "Hear this last thing before you go; It is useless to cross Me." She took his newly shaven chin in her hand, emphasizing the loss of this last mark of his magehood.

"Do you hear Me Talin? I will never be replaced. I am Mem! The melding is perfected. I will live forever, rule forever, be Queen forever! None shall come after Me."

He was seeing her for the last time, the one who had shared his life and ruled him for so many years. Those years of sharing her bed and her arms, her body and soul, were ingrained in his bones. He had betrayed her and though he had been her consort and supposedly her greatest love, she had now cast him out into a living hell. There was no turning back. It was done.

She dismissed him. Trying to stay upright, he turned from her and staggered off between his guards.

As he moved toward the castle cells, he could feel her eyes angrily watching him from where she sat once more in her great seat, rigid, furious but determined, driven by the circumstances of his betrayal into a place where she would truly be the Ice Queen. The time when he would have run to take her in his arms and warm her back to pleasure was gone.

CHAPTER 10

On the third day out from Mem, the shuttle hit a dark-out storm. Almost immediately the ancient Supply-Spacer started to buck, creak and groan as if every seam was about to tear apart.

Panicking prisoners began to mill in circles like traumatized animals, clinging to anything they could clutch, frantically grabbing at one another as they tumbled and fell.

Ignoring them, Atrid's guards, used to such asteroid attacks, calmly strapped themselves into the safety of thick leather harnesses bolted into the strong struts of the cabin walls.

Talin was tossed about along with the other prisoners but unlike them he had heard and read stories of dark-out asteroid storms and knew they were an ordinary feature experienced on every crossing to Zed. From the way the shuttle maneuvered he was sure that the usual meteor shower was swirling throughout the space they were crossing and would only pass when the ship went into hyper space, yet when the storm seemed to increase in strength he too began to worry. The ship repeatedly climbed, dropped, swerved from side to side then dropped abruptly again, tumbling anyone not strapped to a wall like papers in a gusty wind. Prisoners and guards alike began to wretch and be sick.

Over the intercom came a barked order. "All guards to the safety pods, NOW!"

Unbuckling their harnesses, the guards slid and crawled as rapidly as they could to the forward hatch. In a moment the hatch door closed with a clang and they were gone.

It didn't surprise Talin that the captain cared only for the safety of his men. Atrid would demand the safe return of her trained crew and guards. He was sure that to her the prisoners, including him, were no longer her concern. What good were any of them to her now?

Talin could almost hear the captain growling to his first mate, "Atrid won't give a damn if we abandon these jokers. If I had my way we'd just dump 'em all."

There was no extra noise or movement outside as the crew pods separated and sped off. Sensing their departure Talin felt sure that the ship was now on auto-pilot. Surely the captain would have left with the others, abandoning his motley collection of prisoners to the storm. Obviously the gravity regulator had been turned off, for bodies, including his own, were suddenly weightless and out of control, tumbling, crashing, desperately trying to steady themselves with anything they could clutch.

"Why didn't they just eject us?" a rough alien voice yelled.

Something solid hit the outer wall of the ship. In the hold bodies were everywhere; on the floor, in the air, against the bulkheads, on the ceiling, sprawling, rolling into one another, banging, crushing, crying out in pain. Tiny objects the prisoners had given precious bribes to hide away in their clothing scattered like gravel. Covers in which all of them had huddled to keep warm were torn away and flung in every direction until the air of the hold was filled by a panic like mad birds swooping on the attack. The ship tossed and lifted and dropped, its metal skin shrieking under the stress, drowning the screams of injured prisoners. It was as if a dark force had entered the hold, filling it with terror, shaking its victims, throwing them about, exulting in their pain.

Talin knew he had to act. Surely he had been stripped of his mage powers, but he must try. What sounded was unmistakably the Voice of a mage, a trained voice used for control. Talin tried to see if there was another mage present before he realized that the voice had come from him! How had this happened? Had need brought back one of his lost powers? It must be true. The sound had come from his own throat.

"Use the guards straps and belts," his Voice commanded, "Strap yourselves in and save yourselves."

Though in recent years none of them had ever heard any mage voice except Atrid's, prisoners responded instantly. No one disobeyed or hung back. Since the beginning of Atrid's reign, this response had been bred into their bones.

"For what?" the rough alien gulped and bellowed, blood pouring from a wound on his cheek. "We're all dead anyways."
At the same time he was one of the first to fasten himself into a guard's harness.

"Put two in each harness." The Voice resonated above the chaos, possessing Talin. There was no time to wonder how the Voice had returned in this moment of crisis. Later he would puzzle about it. At the moment he could give only a fleeting thought to wondering if Atrid had missed something when she took and then threw away all he had been? What other gifts might she have overlooked in her anger?

Talin tried to stay calm as he watched the prisoners fasten themselves against the walls where the guards had been buckled. Finally he turned and found an empty harness for himself. With shaking hands he drew a figure from the floor, scooping her up, holding her tight against his body, her face against his chest as he placed the straps around them both, pulling them taut. He turned her face so she wouldn't smother. She was a dead weight against him but at least she was alive.

She was a plain young woman, sturdily built with wide hips and heavy thighs wearing the rags of what had been the uniform of a kitchen char. As Talin felt her belly pressing against him he nearly recoiled in horror. He knew who she was! He was lashed tightly to the very woman whose naiveté had betrayed them both! She was the kitchen char, the very one who had carried the seedling-child he had worked every miracle to conceive and transplant into what he had thought would be the perfect hiding place. He had underestimated her loyalty to the Queen. Against his most explicit and strict instructions she had turned back and begged audience with Atrid, insisting that her story be told because it was so miraculous.

The poor char woman had never realized that the pregnancy was not her own. Even in her dreams she had never guessed that the child given to her for safe keeping was the child that Talin had deliberately fathered on her Queen. Here in his arms was the very woman who had carried his daughter, conceived to change the fate of Mem, bringing new life to her people. Yes, and here was the woman who had ruined it all by telling Atrid. As a result of her action the increasing fear and disillusionment among present day Memians would never be replaced with security nor the melding with natural cycles of life and death. There would be no new Queen, no child to replace Atrid. Thanks to this woman in his arms, the future he had worked, plotted and risked his soul to bring about had been ripped from its surrogate and discarded. That was the bitterest punishment. The threat of banishment and stripping of his powers seemed nothing in comparison to the loss of his child and her future, a future that now held only a bucking prison ship, where a former mage and a kitchen drudge, strapped together like lovers, scourged of their past and banished, were now being brutally tossed across the Galaxy to Zed, the most dreaded planet a mortal could imagine.

Now in the hold, strapped against the storm, Talin was abruptly called back to his present situation when he felt the woman stir against him. She moaned, trying to lift her head.

"Of course," he thought. "She is suffering the pain of losing the child she thought was her own. This must be her true pain, more than banishment, more than physical wounds, more, even, than the terrible fate that awaits her. This uneducated, simple being may die of sadness long before she succumbs to the deprivations of Zed."

Freeing his arms, he placed his hand on her chest. If the Voice could still speak through him, remnants of his healing powers might be present, too. He felt the familiar warmth spread across his palm, weak, but enough to send her into sleep. At least he could do this much for her. He no longer felt anger toward her, only compassion for her pain. As he touched her, her body went limp again, her systems shut down in the total rest only healer mages could give.

Holding the sleeping kitchen woman in his arms Talin felt a faint stirring against him. In a moment it came again, stronger this time. Was she ill? No, she was deeply asleep. Yet something was moving in her belly! Something that seemed to be trying to mind meld with him! Without stopping to think, he opened himself to it. Could it be? Suddenly everything he had thought he knew shifted. He let himself empty. When the emptiness settled and cleared he felt a great leap of joy fill the space. At once he knew with certainty what had happened . The woman carried a child! His daughter! He knew with certainty that this was true.

By some miracle the original egg had divided and become twins. While one twin had been discovered and destroyed, the other had found a safe hiding place, a hidden womb where, despite the Queen and her Diggers, she had survived!

Talin wanted to hold his own head as he tried to get a grip on the idea but his arms were full, holding the woman. "My daughter!" he thought, wondering how he had ever managed to spawn such a child, so amazing she had somehow found her own place in which to hide and become. Surely a miracle had happened!

The chaos of the ship was nothing compared to his own chaotic ecstasy at what had transpired. She had survived! His child. His effort. His trickery. It had not all been in vain!

With all his strength and stamina Talin began to pour healing energy into the area where the child was gestating. He knew it might cost him dearly, perhaps even what was left of his sanity, but in that moment he could feel nothing but elation as he gave himself totally to his own semblance of a partial melding. No elixir. No ceremony. Just the giving of himself. All that was left of him was for this child. The final remnants of his magehood, his dwindling sense of self, his sanity, all that he was or ever had been given gladly to sustain her life. He felt a leap of joy as he offered himself to this new being, holding back only enough to stay alive so he could participate in her upbringing. It might not be a complete meld, but he had done his best and was giving her what he could.

"I am yours," he vowed silently to the child. "I pledge you my soul for whatever it's worth. I will live for you or die for you. If life is the choice, I vow that I will live to serve you and bring you to your destiny."

For the first time since he had turned rebel, he understood the emotion that led people to offer themselves gladly to the melding. It would be a triumph to join with this child, to leave his body and give himself totally to this new being.

His body was in no danger of dying. The Alph saw to that. Instead they dreamed a dream that filled him with an energy he hadn't felt since his first joining with Atrid. They knew that Talin had been faithful and deserved this reward.

Talin held the char woman close, rocking her and the baby she carried. He could feel power build in him as he gave himself up to a future he had so foolishly assumed lost forever. He wanted to laugh aloud at his new understanding. Compared to the force that had guided him he was less than a cypher. There had been a miracle. What was banishment from Mem in comparison? Perhaps his daughter, his princess was meant to grow up on a strange and barren planet. If that were so, he must accept his circumstances.

"Oh, great Dream Senders, whoever you are, please accept my gratitude," he prayed. "True Star Woman of old, how can I thank you for saving this miracle child. I vow to love and prepare her, my daughter, for her future destiny."

As if in answer, abruptly the storm stopped. Soon Talin felt the nudge as pods rejoined the ship and the journey toward Zed continued.

His last thought as he slipped into sleep was, "I am merely the tool. Something far greater than I is the Master/Mistress Mind." Comforted, he relaxed, the woman carrying his child safe in his arms.

CHAPTER 11

After arrival on Zed both prisoners and supplies were rapidly dumped. With no help given and no pause or instructions the guards quickly refueled and left on their return to Mem. None of Zed's "survivors" helped the newcomers. It was immediately clear that here on Zed it was every being for him or her self. Finding a safe place and getting the char woman settled took most of Talin's skill and energy.

At first they both slept in the large cavern where old crates revealed that supplies were stored. When Talin began to urge the new prisoners to bring in what had been dumped from the ship and left in the open, he found an empty space at the back of the supply cavern where it curved into darkness. Protected there from wind and wet he helped the woman who carried his child bed down, and was happy to sleep beside her, sharing her large woolen cape and the warmth of his body with her. Later he was able to construct a hovel for her out of old supply crates. After that, sure that she was safe, Talin, curious about the strange lifeless planet, began little explorations of the terrain around the compound.

Going up and down the dangerous cliffs, he found jagged "trails" where nothing grew. On the tops of great plateaus he found that a moss-like fuzz covered the surface. The sides of the black glass cliffs were dotted with caverns where huge black snakes slept as did the large horned goats called tak.

Determined to see that she was fed so that the babe in her

womb would get enough nourishment, Talin kept the char woman under his protection. He learned that her name was Magdalene. He called her Mag and covered the hut he had built for her with skins of several tak he had chased into arroyos where he could spear them with an extrine shard tied to a sturdy pole he found.

Their first months on Zed slowly passed as they struggled to adjust to deprivation and despair. Mag grew heavy with the child. As time passed Talin found himself trusting her more and more. She was not the simple char woman he had thought, but had her own amazing skills. She had been raised to be an herbalist and a healer. From the beginning of her stay on Zed she was able to give aid to those prisoners willing to accept her help. Gradually trust built among others and soon many came to seek her help.

To Talin's surprise it turned out that the woman, before their departure from Mem, had been amazingly resourceful. In each seam of the clothing she wore for the crossing to Zed Mag had painstakingly sewn herb seeds, so tiny they had apparently been undetectable to Atrid's most sophisticated diggers.

Once they were settled on Zed Mag persuaded Talin to help her climb up the cliffs to gather dirt from roots of the lichen that grew there. Over time she made compost from ash and whatever she could salvage of food and waste, then took the dirt mix to one of the flat areas that overhung the compound and planted a tiny garden of medicinal herbs. Talin was sure they would never grow. The dirt was too sparse and dry.

"They'll just blow away in the first wind," he told Mag.

She smiled and went on planting. Each day afterward she

climbed the short distance up to the "garden" lugging bags she had made with a bone needle and tak pelt filled with water from one of Zed's black streams.

"I was raised to be an herbalist like my mother and her mother before her," she told Talin as he helped her. "It was all I ever wanted to do. That would have been my destiny if Queen Atrid hadn't chosen me as a char for her kitchen."

One day she looked up at Talin from where she sat in the dirt. "Look, Talin," she laughed in delight. "I told you they'd grow!"

Sure enough, tiny sprigs of green had appeared.

Each day after that Mag studied the minuscule plants in silence. Talin suspected she was praying. When she was ready to rise he had to help her. She had almost come to term. He watched her wipe her hands on her skirt, patting her burgeoning belly.

"Now I'm an herbalist," she laughed. "This could never have happened if I'd stayed on Mem. It only shows that sometimes the twists and turns of fate take you just where you need to be!"

That night she made a tisane of a few of her seeds and went into labor. Talin was there. It was his hands that freed the tiny shoulders and lifted his daughter from her surrogate mother's body, holding her naked and cowled against his own heart, knowing her in a way he would never forget. It was his hands that tenderly removed the cowl, oiled the tiny face with its almost invisible star, and his fingers that spread tak oil over her tiny body and, with a lichen pad for a diaper, wrapped her in a blanket Mag had made from a piece of her woolen cape. All the while the child seemed to study him with wise violet eyes like his own.

Feeling almost reluctant, he finally gave her to Mag to be fed.

As all these things happened, Talin knew himself to belong to this child. It was different than what he had felt for Atrid. This love was filled with tenderness and simplicity and the promise to protect her as long as he lived and beyond.

Her beauty took his breath away. He gasped because he seemed to be looking into the infant face of the woman he had once loved and betrayed. Indeed she looked so like Atrid it frightened him. His newborn daughter had the same silver hair striped with copper and gold, the same skin, even a similar tiny star etched between her eyebrows. Her face was her mother's, but her violet eyes and long lean body were his.

Later when it was time to give her a name he made a suggestion and Mag agreed. He knew it had to be a soft name, a sibilant name. It was important that there be something soft about her from the beginning. Life on Zed would toughen her enough.

"Aricia." He knew the name was right even as he said it aloud. Decades before, back in Syl's library, he had read about Aricia, an ancient who had ruled prophetic visions experienced in wild places far from civilization. Remembering now, it seemed appropriate to give his daughter such a name to carry as she grew up in the desolation of Zed.

How Atrid had hated her own name! Despite his growing disillusionment with the Queen, he couldn't help remembering her endless groans and moans about it.

"Atrid," she had said to him many times, making a wry face as she held up her ebony hand-mirror to study her reflection. "Do you think that name suits me? "

"Of course it does," he had answered at first. "It's your name."

"But I hate it," she protested. "Why would parents give a child such a hard name? I don't care if it is traditional. It sounds horrid."

"Your parents probably didn't choose it," he reminded her. "The mages and astrologers did."

"I wish they hadn't!" she pouted. "It doesn't suit me at all. I should be called something lovely and soft like Sylvia, or Oceania; something that slides on the tongue so you can almost taste it. But Atrid!"

She would come into his arms, looking up into his face with a pleading smile. "Couldn't you call me something nice? Something sibilant and soft?"

To please her he and her staff had tried other names, but none lasted. She was Atrid. Whether she thought so or not, the name suited her. Perhaps she would have been a different Queen with a softer name. Talin tried to imagine a soft, compliant Atrid, but the memory of her flashing eyes and sneering scorn was too strong. Whenever he let his guard down he would feel increasing despair over his role at Atrid's side. How could he have given her so much power over him?

He must keep the baby safe! No matter what sacrifices he had to make or what he was called upon to do, Ari must thrive and Atrid must never know there was a child born to someday replace her.

CHAPTER 12

The game that would keep Ari safe was an Alph design, a thought they had reserved for an emergency. It began when she was an infant. By the time she was talking in sentences she had been told the story so often by both Mag and Talin that in telling it herself she saw it as clearly as if each detail were her own memory.

"I was carried by Mama from our hut to the back of the supply cavern," she told. "It was dry way back there and Mama was sorting out the lichen she'd collected up on the mesa so it could dry out. I was crawling around playing with a toy made out of tak pelt. Sometimes I would stop and chew on it for awhile because I was teething."

"Talin was with us, but he was in one of his moods that day and seemed very nervous. He kept getting up and pacing around. Finally Mama told him to settle down, so he sat on one of the old cases and watched me play, but he still looked frightened, as if something bad was about to happen. I crawled over and tried to comfort him but I was too little to figure out what was bothering him the way I can now."

"All of a sudden there was a noise outside. A ship was landing! Then there were voices, loud and scary, not like the Survivors."

"Mama looked at Talin and whispered with hardly a sound, "Do something!"

"We couldn't see the men come into the cave but we could

hear their boots. Talin jumped up, grabbed me and raced to where the cave bends at the very back, but there was no place to go, so he started to climb up a wall, hugging me against his hip. That was how he found our secret place. Or maybe it found him. He tried to flatten us against the wall behind a ledge, hoping we could stay hidden there. The next thing I knew, we were sliding on our backs headfirst down a hole! Only the hole was like a slide that went winding down and down and it was all shiny and we just went faster and faster until we came out at the bottom, kersplat! Then I guess he was still scared, so he put me into mage sleep. I can't 'member the rest, but Talin can."

They had landed in one of the largest caverns Talin had ever seen, so far underground it was like waking in an enormous dream hall deep beneath a mountain. More vast than a palace throne room, its rugged walls seemed to be pocked with black facets that shone like mirrors.

"You and I were huddled at one end of the space." Talin added. "The hole we had come through was almost invisible in the jeweled black extrine wall behind us. Up high toward the ceiling were other openings, perhaps small caves. I've never been sure because there is no way to reach them"

At that point he always stopped for a moment as if seeing what he remembered. Then he would continue the story.

"The cavern was almost as high as it was wide, and at the very top were what looked like tiny holes where light came through. The light seemed to bounce off the facets of the walls, magnifying as it fell so that in places at the bottom it was brighter than Zed's dull daylight. Oh, and I suddenly realized that it was warm in there! Not like the damp chill of the planet above, but comfortably warm!"

On that first visit he had put the baby, sleeping soundly, down on the extrine floor so that he could explore the area. Walking the parameter, he had come to a large pool in which the water was warm when he tested it with his fingers. It must be that Zed had some kind of natural heat underground. The water was so clear he could see it bubbling up from the bottom and sense the current moving out from the pool to exit with a splash under a massive overhang.

He soon realized that this was the only possible exit from the cavern. For a moment he thought of leaving Ari and testing the exit himself, then returning for her. Immediately, however, he realized that he couldn't leave her alone. If anything should happen to him she would die a slow death of starvation. He would have to find a way to swim both himself and the baby underwater, carried out by the current deep enough to go safely under the massive overhang. They would either live or die together.

But not yet. They must stay here until the guards left.

The first time they tried to swim out of the cavern Talin was terrified. Holding the baby in one arm with the fingers of his other hand clamped on her nose and mouth he slid down into deep water. The strong current took only seconds to shoot them past the overhang but to him it seemed endless. Could the child survive that long without breath? Surfacing on the outside he came up to shout with joy as he saw the sparkle in her eyes. Ari had loved it! Talin couldn't stop smiling. The cavern was perfect for their needs.

Within days he had designed and made the first of many small baskets of the waterproof skin of a large serpent, spreading it carefully over the bones of a newborn tak who hadn't made it into life. Filling the little vessel with soft lichen, he added a rounded cover that sealed tightly but was domed enough to let Ari breathe as he swam her underwater.

Before long she could swim her own way out without help. One simply had to jump in and ride the deep warm current for the instant it took to be carried swiftly below the overhang. She never made a mistake. It was almost as if she had an inner guidance system of her own.

By then Talin had learned how impossible it was to enter the cavern through that exit. He had tried just once to swim in against the current. Only the strong outgoing current had saved him from being smashed to a pulp. He was never foolish enough to attempt entry that way again. It was much easier to climb up and take the slide from the supply cave.

When Ari outgrew the little caskets, they used them to carry supplies.

At first the long arduous climb back up from the deep river valley was too difficult for Ari's tiny legs so Talin would carry her on his shoulders. As time passed, however, his last meld began to fade and he felt all the signs of aging.

Exhausted he would yell at the taks where they stood watching from the ledges above.

"Here you lazy good for nothings" Feeling his sweat and his

hair all wild, he would struggle under Ari's weight. Thanks to Talin and Mag she ate well, often with their shares. Talin kept trying to get the tak to give her rides but they would have none of it.

"You, carry!" he would command in his mage voice. The big goats simply ignored him and wandered away.

Sometimes Talin did peculiar things that frightened Ari. Suddenly in the middle of a sentence he would put his hand over her mouth. "Shh" he would whisper, "Go Blank! Go Blank! There are diggers searching for us."

Ari would beg him not to do it. He would promise, but seemed to have no control when it happened again.

Talin started their "Game" right after their first adventure. On stormy days he would play at going up the wall to the ledge, creeping behind the boulder to reach the slide. Holding Ari on his lap, he would flatten them both on their backs and slide feet first down the chute. Not even Mag knew where they went or how they got there.

"I don't want to know," she told him, "If I did a digger-guard might dig it out of me." Knowing that Atrid forbid any sign of new life on Zed, Mag worried always that if Atrid learned that Ari had survived the child would be taken from her.

Sometimes the secret cavern was a fun game in which Talin and Ari simply played, enjoying themselves as they took supplies like food, lichen and tak pelts down the slide. At other times Talin's voice would be urgent, rushing her for reasons she understood as a warning that the guards were coming.

It was frustrating for Ari that she didn't yet have the ability to judge how often the guards would make a run or what supplies they might or might not bring. Having discovered Atrid in her dreams, Ari blamed "the Bad Queen" for anything that went wrong. Occasionally when the bad Queen slept Ari could enter her dreams, but most of the time she found no thoughts of Zed there. Once or twice she tried to plant an idea in Atrid's mind, especially when a long period of hunger had robbed many survivors of their will to live. The whole process made her shudder and she hated it, even when she knew the survivors had already waited through many hungry months, barely existing on lichen and tak, before the awful queen would remember to send supplies. When Talin discovered what Ari was doing and told her to stop, she was relieved to obey.

Always Talin as well as Mag feared that the child might be discovered. She was so much the image of Atrid it made Talin worry that she might be seen by someone who would guess her origin. What if one of the Survivors mentioned her to the guards when they came with a delivery?

Fortunately Talin knew that expansion of her empire and the meld were the things Atrid cared most about, yet he couldn't stop worrying that this would only make the Queen destroy her own daughter to keep both intact. As long as he thought this, he couldn't afford to take a chance. Atrid had not hesitated to wipe out one child in Mag's womb. Would she hesitate for a moment if she discovered Ari wandering around in her dreams?

If he had realized that the Alph had imposed a dream sanction to insure that no one would ever speak of Ari to the guards perhaps

Talin would have been reassured. The Alph had never shown him what they had done to protect her, having seen to it that while the prisoners were able to speak to her and she was able to understand and eventually speak even the strangest of their languages, the "survivors", both human and alien, were never capable of speaking of her to anyone else.

Not sensing any of this, Talin could never drop his guard or let go of his assurance that he alone was responsible for Ari's safety.

"Surely" he thought, "I am the only one in the whole Cosmos who can protect my child from Atrid's wrath."

CHAPTER 13

Mag was not a worrier. She simply loved her child and cared for her, seeing that she had enough to eat and tasks to keep her entertained. Before she could walk Mag carried her baby from hovel to hovel to care for the sick. As a result Ari was exposed to many species and their languages and by the time she could talk in sentences she understood and spoke even the oddest most guttural alien tongues.

"I don't know how she does it," Mag reported to Talin, "She seems to understand all those grunts and clicks and snuffles. I think she even asks them questions and they answer her. Sometimes she can even tell me how they feel and what they need."

When Talin questioned Ari, she told him that she wasn't sure how but she understood each survivor. "They tell me stories about themselves. I like their stories."

Many of the storytellers were telling their stories for the last time. Their gratitude for someone who could listen and understand seemed to ease their way into the death world. Ari particularly liked the stories of rites and celebrations. When she asked Talin why there were no rites for the dying anymore he tried to explain that such ceremonies had been forbidden by Mem's Queen.

"But wouldn't they feel better if they knew we cared that they are dying? A lot of them love music. Couldn't we sing them to sleep or something like that?"

Talin was reminded of some of the lessons he had learned in

the monastery way back before he came to Syl and met Atrid.

"There was a time when the dead were sung to a Land Beyond the Stars," he told Mag and Ari. "By the time I came to know the Queen, all rites like that were strictly forbidden. I don't even know how they were done!"

"Couldn't we try?" Ari asked eagerly.

"You mean make it up?"

"Yes!" Ari's voice was excited now.

Mag protested. "Wouldn't that just get us into trouble? What if someone found out and told Atrid?"

"There's not much she can do to us that hasn't already been done," Talin mused.

"Oh, please let's try it!" Ari begged.

"It would mean a lot to the survivors," Mag gave in. "We could do it on the highest mesa where we take their bodies to be burned. What harm would it do to sing?"

The next death was an alien. Sitting with him as he died, Ari told him of the plan to sing him to the death world. "I'll sing in your language so you'll understand," she assured him.

That night Ari and Talin slept in the cavern. In the morning Ari told him that she had had a dream of someone planting music in her head.

"I dreamed my head had dirt in it and someone was planting seeds of music there like Mama does on the mesa with her seeds," Ari told him in the morning. "I think we're supposed to just sing it over and over."

At first Talin was amused, thinking the description of his own dream teaching was strangely accurate. But he had not planted the music. Yet when Ari sang it to him in her little girl voice, it sounded familiar. Perhaps he had dreamed the same dream? He wasn't sure. He only knew they had to try it.

Talin was silent, appreciating his daughter's gifts and imagination. She seemed to pluck knowledge from the dream world like fruit from trees back on Mem. Already her knowledge from dreams was beginning to surpass his own considerable abilities. Her intuition sharpened every day. Often she knew before Mag was summoned that one of the prisoners needed the healer's help.

As their times in the cavern continued, Ari was so tuned into Talin's ideas and moods that he began to wonder just how long it might be before she shared every thought he had. When that happened, she would surely pluck out the truth about him and thus about herself.

He had told neither mother nor child about Ari's true parentage. As far as he knew, Mag had no idea that Ari was his child with Atrid. Such knowledge would only endanger them all. Like all of the survivors, Mag had forgotten some of her own past, but she remembered vividly what it had cost to reveal her former pregnancy to the Queen. It was obvious now that she would do anything to protect the child who had survived, yet Atrid had methods that negated even the strongest will to resist. For that reason even Mag could never know her child's true identity.

A day came, however, when Ari had her own questions. There were stories some of the new survivors told her. She brought this up one day when she and Talin were in their cavern because it was raining and Mag had gone alone to help one of the new human survivors who was ill and might be contagious.

Ari and Talin sat on the cavern floor across from one another, with a weak moss fire between them. He suggested that they play one of the many word games they enjoyed.

"No," Ari said. "I want to talk."

There was a long pause as he waited, aware that she was growing up fast, maturing beyond her years,

"Mama says, I'm the only one ever born on Zed." She looked up at Talin with a quizzical glance. "I guess that's what makes me different."

"Yes," he agreed, "That makes you different."

Ari's voice trembled as she asked her next question, "Talin, am I real?"

He assured her that she was very real indeed.

Restlessly jumping to her feet, Ari looked at him in distress, her expression somber. For a moment Talin thought she looked more like a full grown woman than the eight year old she was.
"Then why do I have to hide when the guards come and why can't anyone see my hair? Am I supposed to be invisible?" Pausing she stiffened her back and glared at him. "Tell me the truth, Talin" she demanded. "What's wrong with me?"

She looked so much like Atrid, Talin's heart ached for her.

"There's nothing wrong with you," he insisted, trying to sound calm.

Could he tell her that she wasn't supposed to exist and help her understand why she was so special? How could he explain this to her except to say that many of the survivors around her were dying while she was growing and changing and becoming more and more herself? No wonder she thought herself different. In a death culture she was life.

Thinking about this as he watched her so serious and puzzled, Talin was overwhelmed with guilt. Should he tell her who she was now or wait until she was grown? The question burned in his mind but no answer came.

Mag had tried to keep the child protected and innocent. Talin wondered if he, himself, had colluded with Mag in trying to keep Ari safe. Surely she was still too young to learn the strange truths of Mem's Queen and the meld?

Again Ari seemed to be picking up his thoughts and emotions.

"About that thing called the meld," Her voice was determinedly casual. "Is it true?"

Talin forced his mind to go absolutely still. How could she know about the meld?

"Does Mem's Queen really eat people?" Ari's voice shook as she held out her hands as if in some ancient ritual of self-protection, then stared down at them, her face wrinkled with worry.

"The newest survivor told me she did it to stay young," she gulped, her chin almost on her chest. "Is that true?"

Talin didn't know whether to laugh or cry. Ari's face was pinched and serious. The tiny star mark above her eyes stood out like a scar. Talin realized that she'd given time and thought to her question. He could only sit in stunned silence. There was no answer that would make her understand. He began to sweat.

Ari waited as the silence grew. Finally she heaved a great sigh of resignation and stood up, walking toward the pool.

"If you're not going to tell me I might as well go," she said. "The cliffs talk to me better than you do!"

For a moment Talin felt relief. The subject had changed.

Ari continued, "They tell me they are an ancient species trapped in the rock."

The cliffs talking to her? Talin tried to hide his concern at what Ari was saying. What horrible fantasy was this? What was she telling him?

Turning to face him as she stood by the pool she looked as if she might burst into tears. "Oh Talin, the cliffs are so sad. They were trapped because they refused to leave with what they call their Others who could see a Great Change coming. They want to cry all the time, but it can only happen when it rains and that almost never happens here."

Talin began to worry. Should he confront her? Or should he listen carefully and try to puzzle out why she was making up such a tale.

"Sometimes when it rains I run and sit down by their cliff and cry with them. I understand how sad they are. They're lonely, too."

Was Ari so desperate for companionship that she imagined friends in the cliffs? Had he really failed her this badly? He must take care to spend more time with her.

"It's worse for them," she told him. "I'm free to move about and I have you and Mama and the Survivors. The cliff Beings are locked up in Extrine and can't seem to do much but mourn."

Talin tried to think of something reassuring to say, but could find no words. The silence went on and on as he struggled to think of words that would bring her to her senses but the harder he tried the more he felt only the blank emptiness of his mind.

Finally with a big sigh Ari spoke again.
"The guards have gone by now," she said. "We don't have to hide anymore. I might as well go." She began to take off her clothes. Not looking at him she added, "You don't seem to want to tell me anything. Maybe if I ask them the cliffs can tell me what I want to know."

"Stop!" Talin managed to blurt out. "There's more to be said."

He looked around attempting to calm himself. Ari came back and sat across from him, scowling.
"The Queen doesn't eat bodies." Talin stared down at his own hands, slowly finding words. Ari was completely still, obviously waiting for more.

"Then what IS the meld?" she finally asked.

Talin tried to tell it like a story.

"Once upon a time there was a Queen whose name was Atrid. She was a great ruler who loved her land and her people. But a time came when she was getting old and knew that soon she would die and have to leave her people with no Ruler."

Talin paused, realizing all that he wasn't saying. How could he hide the truth and yet make his child understand? She knew death, he was sure of that. Many prisoners, especially those of other species, had not survived the hardships of Zed. Ari had joined many times now in singing the dead to the Land Beyond the Stars.

"One day a young scientist came to see her. He was all excited because he had discovered an elixir that would keep her young and vital. Whoever took it with her would join her, become part of her, live in her body, leaving their own body behind.

Ari was listening attentively.

"In human years Queen Atrid is a now a very old woman who has lived for several centuries" Talin explained ."In order for her body and her mind to stay strong and vital, so she can rule not only Mem but most of the planets known today, young people have offered themselves over and over again to meld with her and give her new life."

It was obvious that Ari was shocked. Her voice trembled when she spoke. "What does that mean? How do they meld? Why would anyone think that was right? All those people sacrificed just so one woman could stay young? It's wrong!"

Solemnly Ari vowed that she would never allow herself to be melded, to be taken in and made part of such a Queen no matter how important she could make her people believe it was for her to stay alive.

"It's cruel and unjust!" Ari proclaimed, standing up defiantly. "I would never agree to be taken." After a pause she added, "And if I were ever given the chance I certainly would never meld another into me. Never!" she vowed, "I'd just go search and find a new Queen."

Talin was shaken. Perhaps he should have told it differently but how could he explain the meld to an eight year old when he was still struggling to understand his own participation? How could he have let Atrid have so much power over his life and his decisions? Was it Atrid's claim to be the re-incarnation of Astraea that had given her such power? Or had it been his own weakness in blindly loving her and accepting all of her instructions as if they had come straight from the Great Goddess Herself?

There was a long silence as he and Ari both got up to get lichen for the fire. When they were settled back beside the flickering ashes Ari sat looking at her hands then held them out to the fire and asked the question Talin dreaded most.

"Has anyone else ever melded people?" Picking up a tak bone poker kept nearby she jabbed at the meager fire, head down as if afraid to look at him. "Have you?" she asked.

How could he tell her that he had been over one hundred years old when she was born? How explain that he had worn a young body when he came to Zed only because he had been repeatedly rejuvenated by the meld? Now, of course, without another meld, he was beginning to age. Already she must be able to see the evidence.

Talin knew that no matter what it cost him the time had come when he must tell her the truth. But how? What words could possibly justify his decision to take the meld in service to his Queen?

Ari's words rang in his mind. "It's wrong!"

Yes, it was wrong. It had always been wrong. Here was an eight year old child simply learning about the meld and responding with the very revulsion and questioning he should have felt long ago. Why hadn't he refused the meld? He felt as if that question would haunt him for the rest of his life.

Talin felt his throat closing. His voice came out in a strangled gasp.

"Yes, I took the meld several times."

Ari looked horrified. Her whole body seemed to recoil. "But they DIED." she complained. "Their bodies died."

"Yes," Talin replied. "Yes, their bodies were of no use to them anymore. They were in a new body, the one who had melded them. I still talk to many of those I've melded."

Ari began to cry. "But can't you see, Talin? They're just like the giants in the cliffs. They can't live their own lives because they're captives. It's wrong!"

Talin wanted to weep with her but his response was too terrible for tears. Ari was a captive, too! That was horror enough. She was more of a prisoner than any of the tattered corps of survivors, living in this terrible place where she had to invent fantasy friends living in the cliffs because she was so lonely. How would she react if she found out who she was? How could she do anything but reject the evil queen and her consort who had done such horrendous deeds? "Eating people" was surely a more accurate description of the meld than any he had used.

Overwhelmed by the depth of his own despair, Talin sat in silence as he chastised himself. In taking the meld he had failed his child before she was born and now they both were paying the price. What ever had given him the idea that it was up to him to train her to be Mem's next Queen?

For a long time he was silent. Finally Ari spoke.

"The guards are gone," she said. "We might as well go back. Mama might need us."

Talin was exhausted. He agreed and together they returned to the compound.

From then on Talin's mood swings increased along with fugue states in which he was mute and lost. Filled with shame he was terrified that Ari would soon discover the truth of her own birth. Without any training she was becoming a "digger" whose powers would soon exceed his own!

Hardly able to sleep, he grew increasingly impatient over unimportant issues and found himself scolding Ari and Mag without provocation. The only thing that seemed to help was walking, so he began to take long excursions each day. But as soon as he stopped moving and sat down, his mental state worsened. Perhaps, he thought, if he went away and was by himself for awhile, he might return renewed? Supplies had just been delivered. The guards would not be back at any foreseeable time. It was as good a chance as any for him to be gone.

CHAPTER 14

Without saying good-bye or causing any fuss, one morning he simply left. Starting from the pool outside his and Ari's cavern, he followed the river, sometimes wading, other times slipping and sliding along the extrine ledges beside the water.

In his wandering he came to a place he hadn't seen before, a narrow rift between towering black cliffs that looked as if they had been eaten away by the churning flow of dark water falling between them. Finding no way to slide past, he decided to camp there for awhile. That night he slept on the extrine surface by the river. In the morning he caught a fish and after testing it with his digger senses found it safe to cook and eat. The rest of the time he just chewed on his store of dried Tak meat. It was simpler that way.

As the days passed, he missed Ari. The black bleakness of his surroundings had its own beauty, but the lack of anything living made him sad. There was no companionship, not even a tak. Everywhere he looked were black cliffs, black water, black extrine ledges. As he studied them, he found himself filled with questions.

Was all of this bleakness the result of the Change? Could he imagine what Zetti might have been before? Had there really been a wild profusion of plants and animals or had Zed always been as it was today. Atrid had told him that Zetti had been a bad dream. Why had he believed her? Why had it taken the cruelty of her rejection to shake him out of his thrall? Ari was right. The meld was wrong and the Change was too.

Often he had to sit down and rock himself trying to shake out his guilt. Nothing helped. The very landscape around him was a mirror reflecting his despair.

Trying to escape his feelings, he crawled in on a wide ledge behind the waterfall hoping to find solace in the flow of water. Instead what he found was a small opening that appeared to lead into the cliff. Seeking the comfort of enclosure, he crawled in. Within moments the space he'd entered expanded into something like a thoroughfare where he was able to walk erect in a kind of milky light that seemed to come from the walls themselves. In the stillness all he could hear was the hesitant shuffle of his tak skin boots. The farther he went the more aware he was of their noise as if sound expanded in the emptiness. Coming to a vast cavern he gasped in awe at the giant formations of rugged extrine growing like pillars up from the floor and down from the ceiling. Choosing his way carefully among them he continued on. Gradually his feelings of despair began to leave him and a sense of being comforted took their place. Knowing it was crazy, he had the sensation that the walls themselves were embracing him in a warm welcome. He began to feel that he was where he was meant to be. Moving a little faster he went on.

Some of the tunnels he entered reminded him of the mining mazes on Mem he had explored as a boy, though these were far cleaner and much more vast in their proportions. Increasingly he felt a sense of familiarity. It was as if he had entered one of his dreams.

As he went farther and farther, he realized that time had little meaning for him anymore. He was living on his own. Momentarily there was pain in his heart as he wondered if Ari was all right. As much as she mattered, however, something else had a grip on him now, a kind of quest he couldn't quite name. All he could do was keep on going deeper and farther. Sometimes he wasn't sure whether he was awake or asleep. Perhaps he was really dreaming in his lichen bed back in the compound? Or was he finally going mad? Perhaps he should turn back?

He had about decided to do just that when the new passage he had entered brought him to a sudden stop. He could see the way ahead, but there might as well have been a solid wall just before him. He was stopped in his tracks. An invisible barrier refused to let him pass. At first he was puzzled, but after studying it for a bit he began to recognize it for what it was. Back on Mem he had read of such things. He even vaguely remembered a dream in which he had knelt before such a web. He had always assumed that such things as webs of power were fantasy, but now here one seemed to exist, and it was blocking his way.

Remembering something he had read long ago, Talin got to his knees and bowed his head in silence. As if in response the web began to glisten. Tiny diamonds of light appeared and there was a soft hum like the sound of Mem's bees. Without volition Talin found himself reaching out to the softness of the curtain, feeling desire to touch it flood his being. As his hands made contact, energy seemed to pour into him until he felt as if all the tiny lights were coalescing and filling him. He felt exultant and strangely healed, wanting suddenly to jump up and wrap himself in the ecstasy of the lights. At the same time intense fear urged him to run back as fast as possible to the surface. Torn, he stood up, stumbling against the web as he struggled for his balance.

The net vanished as if it had never been. The way was cleared. Trembling, Talin stepped forward..

The tunnel he followed kept narrowing. At last he could barely squeeze through and ended up contorting himself into an opening too small to hold him until he scrunched down and made himself as small as possible. It occurred to him only afterward that he might very well have been stuck there slowly dying a long lingering death!

Hardly able to use his arm, he put out a hand, trying to get his bearings in this profoundly dark space. Immediately he touched a ledge, an opening in a wall he couldn't see. To his surprise his whole arm followed his hand and he was reaching into a kind of pit. He touched something and recoiled. It was serpent skin! Had he come all this way to waken one of Zed's great snakes? Trying to withdraw his arm, it got stuck.

Nothing moved. Slowly his fingers reached out and touched the skin again.

Calling up all of his courage, he slowly grasped and was able to withdraw something from the depths of the stone shelf. It still felt like a snake yet there was no movement and no life in it. Doubled over in that small dark space, Talin struggled to bring the object to his chest so that he could squirm out and find light enough to identify what he held. As he backed the walls that had held him slowly released and he turned and hurried to find the milky cavern light.

It was a parcel, a large bundle protected by the thick skin of an ancient snake. The skin, though darkened with age, was green, not black like the creatures of Zed. Trembling, Talin carried it as he raced to find more light. Reaching it, he sat down with his back against a wall and with trembling fingers untied the knotted leather thongs that held the snakeskin closed. Slowly he unfolded the skin, laying it back until he could see the contents. Something was wrapped in a substance he had never seen before, translucent and strong as a pelt. Through this "skin" he could see great pages of a similar strange, unknown substance, rather like paper, but this time opaque. Unwrapping the protective cover, Talin took out one leaf, handling it with extraordinary care. To his delight he could neither bend nor fold it! It was covered with writing but he couldn't see it clearly enough in the dim light to know whether or not he might be able to read it. He only knew with absolute certainty that he was holding a very great treasure, one for which he had been led on a search far beyond his limited human capacity to understand. He was also sure that the treasure had lain hidden here for centuries, perhaps even before humans existed on Mem.

Gasping with awe, he realized that despite the scourging of Zetti by Atrid and her mages something wondrous had remained, tucked deep into a hidden crevasse far down in the planet's core. Talin carefully rewrapped the packet, tying the thongs, and carried it against his chest back through the maze and into daylight. The surface of the leaf he chose to study was covered with strange archaic writing. At first Talin stared at it in bewilderment, but slowly he began to decipher a few words. Soon he realized that he had seen something similar in the display cases of the monastery library back in his youth. Feeling excitement rise in him like a flood, Talin was sure that he was seeing an ancient predecessor of the esoteric language from the time of Mem's beginnings. At the monastery where he had trained as a boy he had studied ancient books written in more "modern" versions of such a language. Excitement leapt higher in him as he foresaw a time when, with a lot of work, he might manage to decipher what was written on these pages.

Returning to the compound, Talin showed the leaves to Ari, calling them folios because that was the word that came to his mind.

"Do they say anything about the Lost Garden?" Ari asked in breathless interest. A favorite story was one of many he had made up to entertain her. Talin was sure the garden story was totally imaginary. He smiled at her enthusiasm. "Probably not," he told her. "I haven't managed to read any of them yet. I've only just found them."

"But you will be able to read them, won't you?"

"I hope so. Time will tell."

"And then we'll go search for the Gardens!"

Ari touched one of the great pages with the tips of her fingers then snatched her hand back. "They feel holy," she told him.

"I suspect they might be. They were carefully hidden and I believe have lain there protected for more centuries than you or I could count."

"They must be very important," Ari replied, her voice filled with awe.

Talin began to spend most of his time in the cavern working on the leaves, sweating and struggling over each word. He found a spot where a beam of light came directly down from a hole in the ceiling. This made his task easier,. Nevertheless, he had to put aside the work periodically because his eyes hurt and his head pounded. Occasionally he was able to push past the pain and keep working, but often he fell asleep if he didn't rest willingly.

Ari was busy helping Mag care for the sick, but whenever she could she appeared and urged him on in his work. She was almost as excited as he was about his find.

"Anything about the gardens yet?" she kept asking.

Talin had deciphered enough to guess that the folios had been scribed long before time was marked as they knew it today. If that was true, who could possibly have written them? What beings had scribed them so far back in such a timeless time? Every word he managed to decipher fascinated and captivated him.

He began to remember repeated words and to translate new words more easily as his familiarity with the style grew. Many of the words seemed to be predecessors, bearing the roots of words he had learned in the monastery. As months passed he became more and more certain that the folios were a record of some ancient fantasy or allegory.

"It's a myth," he explained to Ari, "An ancient tale of how humans were redesigned in a dream so we wouldn't make the same terrible mistakes Earthlings had."

What was written was wonderfully imaginative. As he read, Talin felt as if he had found new friends in the fertile minds that had dreamed up such a tale. It was almost as if it had been preserved so that someday it could comfort the despair of a half crazed outlaw like himself. The fantastic imagination seemed to lessen, even sanction, his own periods of despair.

Reading the leaves of the folios gave new meaning to the hours he spent sharing them with Ari. Repeatedly he had to remind her that the folios contained fantasy, not reality. It was a myth of re-creation.

"It's not real," he would explain. "It's a made up explanation. A tale."

"But it truly happened," Ari would insist. "I know it did."

In his life before banishment, Talin had been trained to sort out the difference between real and fantastic imagination. Phantasms of the mind might occasionally be true, but more often they were illusory. He had been taught this from boyhood, warned frequently by older mage-teachers that history was filled with fools trapped in their own inflated stories.

For a long time he read the leaves as fiction, products of a wonderful, wild imagination. He was amused by his daughter's insistence that what they described had actually happened. Soon he would have to teach her how to tell the difference between real and illusory, just as he had been taught by the Lubin mages and Atrid. Realizing how much their views had changed his, he was startled, puzzled and a bit dismayed.

As he worked on the folio leaves it slowly became apparent to him that he was beginning to recover some of his lost abilities. His old mage skills, stripped from him by Atrid as she sentenced him to Zed, were slowly coming back. At first he felt that this, too, must be a fantasy, part of the madness of Zed, but as the words on the leaves became more and more clear, so did his mind and his old abilities.

Hadn't he betrayed himself, letting Memmians convince him that only what could be experienced by one or more of his five senses could possibly be true? In his heart of hearts hadn't he always known that his invisible friend was real? When and why had he blinded himself to the different realities he had known as a boy?

His daughter saw the folios as truth. Perhaps it was her influence, perhaps it was running from his own craziness but one day he realized that something was changing. He found himself wondering idly if Ari might be right. Could the tales be a true report? Was their wisdom fact rather than fiction? The Memmian mage in him scoffed at such a notion. It was his own madness that gave him such irrational thoughts. Why couldn't he accept that the folio stories were nothing more than an incredible myth?

But what was myth if not a way of trying to tell a truth too large for any words or images?

He was never sure just when the turning point came, but one day he realized he was beginning to accept what he was reading on the leaves as an historical record that had been dreamed by invisible beings like the friend of his childhood. Those the folio leaves called "The Alph," invisible Beings who dreamed big dreams and sent them to "Shapers", both human and alien, for actual creation.

As Talin deciphered the folios he became fascinated by their stories.

Before Time began the ubiquitous Alph dreamers existed in the depths of non-being as invisible nanos of luminosity, unable to take action act except in their dreams. As Time began, however, they were able to send their dreams, like urges from the darkness, into the minds of those who came to be called Shapers because they could give form to the images they received in night visions. Some who received the calls were mages and scientists, advanced Beings called the Nus who appeared from another dimension to aid the Alphian dreamers in what came to be called their "Great Experiment." Another species, beautiful giants called Las, also heard the call and agreed to help. Together these two species slowly gave form to the Alph's dream of an improved human species, replacing those so tragically wiped out in the nuclear explosion of planet Earth and all her beings.

At first he had thought he would never decipher what the Nus were writing in their strange archaic script, but eventually a time came when he could read the leaves as easily as he had read books back in the castle overlooking Syl.

When he first started accepting the stories as true, he felt strangely astonished and delighted.

"How did you know the stories were true" he asked Ari. "What made you so sure?"

She shrugged. "I just knew," she said. "When I touched them I knew. Won't you read them to me Talin? I want to know all that they say."

CHAPTER 15

Through the next years Ari and Talin spent many hours together in the cavern as he slowly taught her the archaic language of the leaves.

"I feel like a little child learning to read for the first time," she told him laughing at her growing self as she struggled to make sense of each marking.

"That's the way to learn a new language, like a two year old," he replied with a smile. "You've already learned many languages of many species. The language of the Folios is especially strange to us because it comes from another dimension and we must translate it into something our more limited minds can begin to comprehend. The Shapers who gave form to the Great Dream of the Alph were brilliant."

By the time she was fifteen Ari knew many of the stories of the folios by heart. She knew about the progenitors. Together she and Talin had studied the folios until she could read them as easily as he. One by one Talin brought each folio forth from its hiding place so that Ari could learn from its contents. As a result she now knew that the Light Being who came to teach her in her dreams might well be one of those the folios described as an Alph dreamer. She had also read of the Nus, those early scientists with their enormous laboratories, archaic by present day standards, but very up to date and sophisticated for those early days.

The stories that really enthralled her, however, were those of the Las. She had immediately leapt to a conclusion that Mem's early mentor, the first Star Woman, Astraea, had been Las.

"It's obvious," she told Talin when he questioned her. " Your stories describe her as a wondrously beautiful woman over twelve feet tall with skin the color of milk or honey."

At first Talin had difficulty explaining honey to Ari since there was nothing on Zed to use for comparison. Ari's dreams had helped, however, and she soon began her own description of Astraea with skin the color of moonlight and cheeks pink as flower petals.

"Hair an almost white silver streaked with copper and gold, glows around her face like a halo," Ari read. "Talin, what is a halo?" she asked, giving him another task as he tried to tell her it was like her own, a kind of aura of light given off by the body.

"Oh," she nodded, "like yours."

"Is that why we have to keep our hair covered?' Ari asked him, touching her own head and its covering.

"We do it to protect ourselves. She may have done the same. I suspect she may have been more than Las, perhaps Alph, and Nus as well. When I think of the sea walls of Mem and the architecture of Syl's earliest buildings I realize that she was brilliant as a scientist and also at creating beauty in her surroundings that was functional and long lasting. If we Memmians have traces of any of her qualities we are certainly lucky."

"No wonder she was considered a Goddess," Ari said. "Whatever she was, she was certainly special and a great teacher, a wonderful gift to the earliest Memmian humans." Then she added decisively, "And there's no way Mem's Queen could be her!"

Talin could think of no reply.

Using pages of the folios he taught Ari about the progenitors, including the primitive Sar whose DNA had been taken without permission in hopes of giving physical strength, stamina and resilience to Mem's new humans.

When Ari read that the Sar DNA had been taken without permission while they slept she was upset.

"Was that why the Sar died out?"

"No," Talin replied thoughtfully. "I don't believe they died. I think they evolved into an intelligent species and are living on one of the planets in one of our galaxies today. Perhaps Memmian explorers will find them in some far off future. Whether or not I'm right about this, thanks to the folios we know that the strength of the Sar has been in every generation of Memmian humans and is in you and me today. We can certainly be grateful for that."

He paused, wondering what he could say that she didn't already know from her own reading.

"The folios prove," he told her, " at least to my mind, that thanks to the brilliance of the Alph, and the skills of the Nus and Las, the DNA of Earth humans who finally died out from one catastrophe after another was used as a basic model for an enhanced, peace loving species. Every human of Mem, including you and me, are descended from the results of the progenitor's Great Experiment.

"Am I Memmian?" Ari asked. "I was born on Zed."

Thinking of how to answer, Talin was silent. When he finally spoke it was from the depths of himself. "Yes," he told her. "Mag is Memmian and so are you."

"I think I'd rather be a human of Zed," Ari said. "Not one like the terrible Queen. Are there others on Mem like her?"

Again Talin thought carefully before he replied. "Until Atrid became Queen I believe all Memmians lived in peace. They settled their differences among themselves and were quite content. The Dreamers and Shapers became mages or crafts people. They all respected one another."

"So what happened to change this? Why did Atrid start the meld and use Zed for a prison?'

"Atrid was different. Perhaps she carried too many remnants of traits that have been dormant in Mem's humans for centuries only to take root again in her so that, like earthlings of old, she was determined to be the richest, most powerful person in the multiverse and to have eternal life in a young body. As she did this, the people reacted and the easy peace that had always one of the Memmian gifts was lost."

"Does she really believe that she's Star Woman?"

"Yes, and she has persuaded most of her people that this is true. As a result most of them serve her without questioning anything she does. Those who don't are severely punished."

"So they accept that she created the meld," Ari said sadly, "And made Zed a prison."

Stopping she looked at Talin, then asked hopefully, "Or are those just stories you made up?"

Reluctantly he had to admit the truth.

"But that doesn't change the facts of who we are and where we came from." he assured her. "You've read all this in the folios and I've told you before we were designed to be strong and peace loving, And now we know that thanks to the Sar we are also physically strong."

Ari was intrigued by the thought of having Sar qualities. She knew that those beings had been chosen for their strength, their assertiveness and yes, for their ability to fight and survive. Reading about them she began to celebrate her own Sar qualities.

He didn't tell her that she was too lovely to be seen as Sar. Ari had not only learned from the folios, but during the years of study she had also grown beautiful.

"Both inside and out," Mag told him when he mentioned this to her. "She is a great help to me now, speaking every language. She's learned everything I can teach her about healing. Sometimes it seems as though she knows more than I do. When I ask her where she learned to do something I never knew she says she dreamed it."

"Do you ever worry about her among the aliens?" Talin asked..

"No. They treat her almost as if she were a goddess. Some of them would kill any survivor who didn't treat her right and the rest of them know it. The new survivors learn right away that she is protected."

Mag looked at him carefully as if to see his reaction as she spoke again.

"She is special, Talin. You must know that. The survivors are not her only protectors."

Yes, he knew and was glad that Mag did, too.

"Now I can see myself as Sar and know I'm a Survivor just like the others," Ari told Talin one day. "I feel as though I can survive any challenge."

"Yes," Talin agreed, laughing as she flexed her muscles and stamped about. "But be glad you don't have their skin and multiple eyes!"

"Ugh," Ari grinned. "Then I'd be all slimy and scaly like one of the black serpents and one of the Survivors might try to kill and eat me!"

Many of the alien survivors did eat snake when they could catch one, ignoring the fact that Mag forbid it. On Mem, thanks to the original Star Woman, serpents were considered holy icons because they lived both underground and on the surface and were thought to be repeatedly reborn by shedding their skin. As a result, they had always been creatures protected by Astraea who had forbidden the hunting of them much less the eating. Atrid had not been able to change this.

Talin wondered as time passed if he, Mag and Aricia might be forced to eat snake meat before this winter was over. No supply ship had come, though it was long past due. Food supplies were rationed and would soon be gone.

He had tried to kill a tak but those creatures, too, were now mostly bones. The survivors had eaten up most of the lichen and fish the tak lived on. Lately the screaming animals didn't appear to be eating fish. Talin wasn't sure whether this was because it was spawning season or just that the goats were too exhausted to make the effort. He himself was beginning to be too tired to hunt, fish or find out.

Talin suggested to Mag that she come with Ari and him to the safety of their hiding place but she refused, giving him two reasons. The obvious one was that the survivors needed her. The other was that she still didn't want to know where he and Ari went.

"If diggers ever come I don't want to know where you are," she reminded him.

Unable to abandon either of them, he stayed on the surface.

While Ari spent her time helping Mag, Talin often huddled in a corner of their hovel, trying to warm himself with worn lichen blankets and a weak lichen fire. Occasionally he would manage to slip into mage meditation, but most of the time he could do little but suffer the cold. Lately he had taken to wondering if he might die of starvation before his task as Ari's father-mentor was fulfilled. Would he live long enough for her to be old enough to learn who and what she truly was?

It was one of the worst winters he could remember, blowing in with a blast to stay unrelentingly bitter through Zed's dark months. Ice on the rivers was so thick it took hours for those survivors who still had remnants of strength to break holes hoping to catch a fish. The older men died first, many from hypothermia. At first they were burned and sung to the Land Beyond the Stars by a trembling, coughing group. Soon bodies of the dead were simply left for the Tak. No lichen could be spared for a fire. Most of the survivors were too sick to leave their huts. Sleet and snow seemed endless, following themselves day upon day and night after night. Trips to the ice coated mesas for lichen were terrible misadventures of fatal falls or broken bones.

In the midst of all this shaking starvation Ari seemed strangely content. Talin knew part of this was that they were all three of them together and Ari felt little threat of a supply ship arriving soon to separate them again. The bitter winter weather held them all captive yet with Ari's help Mag somehow managed to continue her rounds of the sick. How long that could continue he wasn't sure. Both Mag and Ari were showing signs of depletion and ill health. Both were noticeably thin, their legs like sticks and eyes large and dull over sunken cheeks.

There was plenty of time during the frozen days that Talin could have used to work on one of the folios but he had returned them all to their nest and the thought of trekking to recover one exhausted him. The little energy he had was fading daily.

"Why don't the Alph intervene" Ari asked Talin one day. "I thought you said they wanted to help us."

"I don't know," Talin told her. "All we can do is keep praying for them to wake up and realize what's happening here."

Ari confessed to him that she had tried sending out pleas to the Alph. There had been no answer, even in her dreams.

"You'd better stop," Talin advised. "Atrid's diggers might pick up your thoughts."

"And save us from starving to death? Wouldn't that be too bad!" Her voice was weak but ironic.

When hunger became illness, Talin finally solved his

starvation by leaving his body for longer and longer periods. All three of them now lay immobile on their lichen mats most of the time. The cruel winter should have ended by now, but seemed to linger on and on.

One day Talin was off in meditation on one of his mage journeys.

"Too bad he never taught us how to do that," Mag said weakly.

Ari, curled up on her lichen mat, knees bent over her aching belly, didn't tell her mother that she knew the trick but was staying around so Mag wouldn't be left alone. She could feel herself going in and out of consciousness, however, though she fought to stay present.

When she saw Mag sit down on a packing case seat and watched her stare into melting snow in a bowl on her lap, Ari wasn't sure whether she herself was awake or asleep and dreaming. Was it her imagination or were there truly pieces of fish in the bowl?

Ari closed her eyes, knowing she must be hallucinating.

In her dream she could see that the fish was a tempting white and looked edible.

Watching, she saw her mother reach out and take one bite of broth. It seemed to taste all right. Obviously tempted, Mag took another mouthful, this time with a piece of fish. The soup seemed to satisfy her.

Ari was sure she was dreaming. She tried to wake herself up, but the dream continued.

It wasn't long before Mag began to retch. Soon Ari saw her go to the door and stagger out into the snow.

"It's poison," Ari thought, fighting frantically to waken herself.

Instead she found herself watching her mother take the pot outside and pour its contents deep into a snow bank, clawing at the icy snow to cover and hide it. After that Mag crept back in and fell onto her bed. Ari woke up and tried to go to her but could hardly crawl off her own thin mat.

"Water," Mag whispered.

Somehow Ari pulled up the strength to crawl and get the tak skin water bag hanging nearby. But as soon as Mag took a swallow she began to retch again.

Wanting to nurse her as she'd been taught, but too weak, after only moments Ari could do nothing but hold Mag, wishing her into sleep. She was relieved when the moaning stopped and her mother slept. Somehow when that happened, Ari managed to stand up and stagger outside. She needed to gather snow and let it melt so that there would be more water when Mag wakened.

The cold hit her with a blast. Falling to her knees she began to gather snow into the water sack. It took some time, but when she returned to the hut the bag was full.

"I'm back," she called as she entered, then stopped and stood perfectly still, listening. Inside the hut there was only silence. Her mother's rasping breath had stopped. Ari fell onto the floor beside Mag, putting her head on her mother's chest. Already her mother's body was stiffening. The fire had gone out.

"I must build it up," Ari thought. "I need to warm her."

Instead she began to cry.

"Don't die!" she whispered. "Oh, please don't die!"

But it was already too late. Mag was gone and unlike Talin she wouldn't be able to return. Her mother was no longer in the body that lay there, emaciated and empty. Ari threw herself across her mother, her face against Mag's cheek. What had happened? Why had Mag died? She was a survivor. She was strong. Surely it wasn't her time yet.

Ari began to sob. As she sniffed and wheezed she suddenly caught a whiff of something that smelled like fish. Putting her nose to Mag's mouth she realized that what she had thought she was dreaming had actually been happening. She had seen it all in her half aware state. Now she was sure of what had occurred.. Mag had finally caught a fish through the ice hole she'd been working on for weeks. Oh, Goddess, why? And why would she eat it without waking Talin to test it?

There was only one answer. Unable to wake Talin she had tested it herself! As a result, she was dead! Grief came up in Ari like a great hot wind. Racked with sobs she stood up and lurched over to Talin's body. Falling against him she beat at him with her fists. Talin didn't respond in any way, not even with a twitch of his cheek. He was gone on one of his dream journeys..

"Come back!" Ari rasped. "I need you." Sobs shook her but she had no tears. "I'm dried up," she thought. "There's nothing left of me."

Ari tried to cry out but her voice had no power. "Mag is dead!"

"Why can't I die, too?" she asked. "Why don't we all die? We're no good to anyone. Talin, wake up, I need you."

It was Mag who had kept them all alive. It was Mag who had cared for the survivors.

Ari tried one last time to shake Talin back, but her attempts were too feeble., She began to sob, but even her sobs were like whispers.

"Mama's dead!" She had to make herself believe it. "Mag is dead and it's all your fault!"

If he'd been present none of it would have happened. But he was off who knew where so Mag had eaten the fish and it had killed her. If he had been there he would have known with one smell that it was bad.

"I hate you," Ari whispered "It's your fault."

Leaning toward him she hissed in his ear, "I hate you forever."

His eyes opened.

"Mag is dead," Ari recoiled from his look.

As Talin began to comprehend his eyes showed his horror. Slowly he turned to look at the mat where Mag's body lay.

"It's your fault!" Ari repeated.

Somehow she found the power to turn away from him, her whole body bent with grief as she moved.

"I will never forgive you," she threw back at him as she stumbled toward the doorway.

Talin reached out after her, his face contorted with emotion. She ignored him. Pushing aside the tak pelt covering of the door she staggered out into the snow and stumbled against the wind toward the mouth of the supply cave. Several times she fell into the snow, but somehow managed to get up again and go on. She must get away.

Once inside the supply cavern she let herself collapse on the extrine, shaking with cold.

"I can't lie here," she thought. "I'll die if I do."

Talin had long ago taught her how to breathe in a way that would keep her warm even in coldest weather. Breathing that way now, she recovered enough strength to crawl to the back of the cavern where she slowly and painstakingly began to claw her way up toward the opening. Once she had been able to leap to it in seconds. This time it took what seemed like the rest of the day, stopping to rest every few breaths. When she finally reached the ledge she had to force herself to stay awake long enough to get into the slide. At the bottom, met by the warmth of the cavern, she immediately fell into the deep sleep of starved exhaustion. When she awoke, however, it was to misery and despair. Mama was dead and it was Talin's fault.

"He didn't do a thing to save her, " her mind stormed. "He deserted us when we needed him."

He had only returned when it was too late. Grief shook her followed by anger that filled her with fury.

"I'm never going to need you again Talin," she vowed. "You hear me, old man? Never again. Don't come after me. No more crazy folios. No more dreams. No more planting stupid ideas in my mind. I want you out of my life!"

Surely Talin must feel some of what she was feeling. He must be able to sense her disgust with him. Exhausted with weeping she fell asleep once more.

Much of the time she slept in a dark dreamless sleep. When she awoke the anguish would start again and she would talk to Talin in her mind.

"I don't trust you anymore. I don't love you anymore. I wish you'd died instead of Mama. What good are you, anyhow, just sitting around as if you were dead, too? Go, and take your stupid folios with you!"

What would she do if he came after her?

She would leave.

Ari realized that she'd better eat some of the sparse food they had left in the cavern for emergencies. When Talin came she would need enough strength to swim out into the cold and find a new place to live, far away from him. It took a long time to build a tiny fire and heat up some lichen in water. At first she could eat very little of the soup, but each time she tried it was easier. Several times she went and sat in the heat of the pool until she was warmed. Afterward she slept, then awoke to sip soup again.

Only when she began to feel stronger did she realize that time had passed and she had no idea how long she had been in the cavern. It was as if a blanket of fog covered her senses. When she came awake she felt disoriented and unsure not only of where she was, but who she was as well. Occasionally she would open her eyes to light coming through the tiny openings in the vaulted ceiling. Was it still winter outside?

Her anger at Talin began to abate, changing to puzzlement. He hadn't followed. Surely time had passed, but he hadn't come. Had he died too?

The next morning she awakened from a vivid dream. She immediately took a notebook from one of the ledges and began to write the dream down as Talin had taught her.

I am following Talin up a mountain of black glass. He keeps getting farther and farther ahead until he disappears. I try to run after him, but there are no ledges and no footholds so I keep slipping back at each step. Looking upward I see Talin reappear. In horror I also see that Memmian guards are waiting for him. I try to warn him, to call out, but my voice is frozen in my throat. I realize that I have no control over the dream. I am an invisible cloud with no dream reality, only there to observe. Disoriented I try to go straight up to where he stands but cannot get a foothold. I struggle to see a ledge or a path I can use to get to him but there is none. Instead I look down at my feet and see in horror that there are huge and very beautiful living beings caught and frozen mid-motion who have somehow become part of the cellular structure of this vast mountain I must climb, as if it is my duty to climb on their bodies, their very souls. A voice tells me to circle, to spiral my way up on the outer perimeter.

As I climb, the mountain changes. I discover that the mountain I climb has become the body of a gigantic woman who is part human and part one of the black serpents. Her top half is a woman, and from the waist down she is snake.

Everything grows dark as if a great storm is gathering. Talin appears high above me. His body seems to be made of light which reveals a way for me to go to him. As I hurry toward him he vanishes again.

Now the scene shifts. I am in the compound, wearing my mother's clothing. Taking a tiny book out of her apron pocket, I open it to a recipe for poison fish. I must cook it and serve it to the woman in the mountain. Suddenly I'm back on the glass mountain, slowly circling as I climb, carrying a large black cooking pot. The mountain is filled with faces with open mouths, eagerly awaiting the food I have cooked in my mother's pot, but it is not for them. It is for the snake woman so she will stop killing and eating the beautiful beings around her.

Ari woke from the dream in horror. Her grief for Mag was still heavy in her chest, but as she finished writing the dream, shame for the way she had treated Talin began to wash over her. Was he still alive? She felt no more anger, only remorse and fear. All her life Talin had been her companion, her teacher, the one who had always lighted her way. Had he believed her terrible angry words? Was that why he hadn't followed her? Surely several days had passed, but he hadn't come. Was it because she had screamed that she never wanted to see him again?

She must return to the compound and find him!

CHAPTER 16

On Mem the Queen only remembered Zed when a sudden whiff of unexpected imagery flew into her mind with one breath and out on the next. Something kept ghosting through her, vague images that came and left. She had to struggle to keep out wispy thoughts of the prison planet that threatened her ability to work or sleep.

"I believe something is happening on Zed," she told her court mages. "I don't know what it is, but I'm sure it has something to do with Talin."

The mages had gathered in the throne room as they did each day awaiting the Queen's instructions. Hearing Atrid's words, they simply stared at the pattern in the tiled floor, wondering where this new idea would lead them. Was it a new obsession or simply a good reason for another crack-down? They no longer allowed themselves to openly question anything she said or did. They had long since learned the folly of asking. It was suicide to ask, especially about Zed.

Atrid alternated between pacing the floor and throwing herself onto her throne, only to rise and pace again.

"Yes," she mumbled aloud, "Something is happening on Zed and Talin is involved. I'm sure of it."

Perched momentarily on the edge of her throne she drummed with her fingertips on its golden arms.

"We must bring him back out of exile," she pronounced at

last. It was a command not a request. "I sense that Talin has a secret," her voice was filled with anxiety, "and it has to do with me!"

In the big room there was utter silence.

Winter was ending. The first thaw had started. Every Memmian including Atrid and her troops knew that Spring Tide Turning was the most dangerous of all perilous times for a crossing from Mem to Zed. Few attempted it and for those who made it back long periods of rehabilitation were often necessary.

"I must have Talin back!" Atrid declared.

Not one person dared protest. Atrid's decisions were final

"I cannot go to Zed so he must be brought to me. Together we will dig this secret out of him!"

That same day Mem's fastest spaceship left at top speed for Zed. When it returned, not only the ship but most of the crew were battered, wounded and half crazed.

"Fierce storms almost did us in," the captain reported, barely able to stand he was so beaten by the trip.

With him was an old man who with a drooping head and listless body stood before her.

Atrid was shocked. Who was this aged creature? Had they made a mistake and brought her someone other than Talin?

Ready to pounce on the captain for his folly, she recoiled in shock as the old man raised his head to look at her. His eyes were ancient in his gaunt face, yet she knew them. Though pale now, they were still the violet ones she had known and loved. Eyes that once had loved her back and without hesitation obeyed her smallest command now looked at her filled with despair, then quickly looked away.

She fell back onto her throne.

"He is like a shell of himself," she exclaimed to the captain. "What did you do to him on the Crossing?"

"We had to drug him," the captain said weakly. "He was a wild man. You said we could if...."

Atrid turned on him with a gesture that told him to leave immediately or be destroyed by her anger. He left abruptly, his staggering footsteps echoing as the great doors opened for him.

Atrid moaned in disappointment, then rose and gave an order, fighting to control herself. She had hoped to welcome Talin's return but there was nothing to welcome about this wreck of a man. Was there any hope of recovering either him or his secret?

Straightening her shoulders she took a deep breath. "Find someone to meld with him and give him strength! You must make him young again and then return him to me," she commanded. "Take him away and get him bathed," she ordered, "I can't stand to look at him."

When they all left her she began to pace, trying to ignore the empty place within her that she had been so sure Talin could fill again. Her desire for his return had unleashed an old craving. Somehow he must be persuaded to do her will and take the meld again. Mem must have his story, the secret she was sure she must learn if she was to keep both Mem and her galaxied Empire safe. Once she had him back in her bed she knew she could riddle it out of him, but first he must take the meld.

CHAPTER 17

Wrapping her clothes in the water-proof basket, Ari lowered herself into the pool and let the hot water carry her out under the great black ledge. The river outside was filled with floating ice. The Spring thaw must finally have come as she slept! She had to get back to the compound. She jumped out of the water, took her lichen shift from the coracle and rapidly rubbed her shivering body until it was dry and warm, then she put on the rest of her clothes and boots and began to climb back up the face of the cliff, moving fast through the chill air in hopes that her body would stay warm, thankful that Talin had taught her how to counteract the cold.

Eager to see him and make sure he was all right, she reached the edge of the compound. Only then did she realize that something unusual had happened. In the cold Survivors were outside their hovels, hunched in clumps, hugging themselves as if in pain and among them were new prisoners who stood back looking disoriented. At the same time, crates of supplies were scattered around the space pad lying untended where they had been dumped. Ari knew at once that a supply ship had come and gone while she had been in the cavern.

There was no sign of Talin.

She went to one of the aliens. "Where is Talin?" She asked in his language. "Do you know where he's gone?"

He sat motionless, his many eyes lidded, as if he were deaf.

"You must know what's happened to him," she insisted giving

him a gentle push. "Tell me!"

No response, not even a blink. Was he in shock?

Walking among the survivors both human and alien, she began to shake them but it did no good. All of them simply sat in mute misery.

Not one of them had touched the supply crates. They all just sat silent as if they, too were in shock. Was it her mother's death that had pushed them all over this last edge? How long had they been sitting here like this, starving while surrounded by food?

At last Ari turned and began to open crates, taking out various foods that didn't have to be prepared or cooked, forcing each of the mute ones to eat whether they wanted to or not. She found a great container of water and poured it into a tak skin cup and made them drink. Slowly they began to sit up a little as life came back into their bodies. Humans were the first to recover.

While she waited, Ari began to search the hovels for some sign of Talin. Perhaps he was ill?

The compound was as empty of him as if he had never existed.

The last hut she searched was her own. Her mother's rag bed was empty. Mag's body was gone! Ari ran back outside.

"Who took my mother to the cliff?" she screamed. "Was it Talin? Where is he? Has he gone to the caves?"

One of the new prisoners spoke. "Mem," he said.

Ari stopped abruptly, her whole body shocked into utter stillness. "Mem?" What did he mean?

"Mem," other voices began to echo, each in their own

language. All of the old survivors began to rock their bodies. Someone started to hum. Others joined in until the whole area filled with sound. Ari covered her ears, trying to shut out the noise so she could think. A terrible possibility occurred to her. Maybe Talin was dead, too. Was that the meaning of her dream? If he was dead, where was his body? Was he up on the cliff with her mother, their ashes joined in death?

Where had she been when all this was happening? Sulking and skulking in her secret hideout. Ari tried not to sob out loud. Had she killed Talin with her grief and anger so that he had gone to join her mother? No doubt many human survivors saw Mem as a place they might return to in death.

"Where is the mage?" She begged again. A few began to waggle their hands in front of their faces, staring mindlessly into space. Others whispered almost silently to themselves. No one spoke aloud. She could feel fear circulating through the group. They continued to rock, crooning a kind of crazy rendition of a song, one she slowly began to recognize even in their twisted, tormented style.

It was a song of rejoicing. Why were they singing the rejoicing song? That was not a funeral song. It was a song sung after the guards had come and gone, a celebration that there was food and supplies again and relief that the terrifying arrival of new prisoners and old guards was over. Looking around she scanned the new faces, still standing, trying to look as if they didn't belong here.

"Where is the old man?" she screamed at the new ones. "The

mage, what has happened to him?"

One of the new men lifted his head and stared at her. There was still sanity in his face, though his body looked crooked and maimed. The music stopped. In the silence he spoke.

"They took an old man," he said, his speech slurring, "On the ship."

Ari stood there staring, her mind spinning. Someone began to sing again, a strange, haunting melody, different from the last. Others joined in. Listening, Ari slowly began to recognize some of the notes. She had learned them in her dreams, but had never heard this tune sung in the day world. It was the blessing for a long journey. No one spoke. No one moved. Only the music lifted in the silent twilight air.

Ari stood frozen, paralyzed by her own despair, her mind blank except for pain. Then slowly, inevitably, sense began to return .

Twilight had come. She realized that the new supplies needed attention. The guards never carried them to shelter. Turning away, she quietly gathered herself, then turned to the task at hand. If the supplies weren't brought into the storage cave before night fell, the presence of food would call the starving taks down from the mesas to forage and pillage.

Ari began to pull people to their feet, goading them to lift and roll barrels into the protection of the cave. This was activity their bodies remembered even when their minds were numb. They began to cooperate, but without sound. The strange singing had stopped and silence was broken only by their ragged breathing and occasional moans.

When the work was done, she gave them each their share of food, then saw them all to their hovels. When that was done, she went into her own lonely hut.

What was left of her mother's clothing hung on a bone hook by the door. Looking for comfort, she took off her own clothes and began to put on Mag's as she had seen herself do in her dream. Taking off her own familiar cap she covered her hair with Mag's bonnet. With the remains of her mother's fire she darkened her face and arms. It was the only way she knew to mourn. As she tied on the big pocketed apron Mag had always worn, she thought about her healer mother. In some way she must live her mother's life now, taking on her identity. She would become Mag. How else could she survive and maintain her own sanity? Who else was there in all of Zed who could take care of the survivors? This might well be what the dream had tried to tell her, that she must feed and care for them now as if she were their healer.

That night she slept in her mother's bed. The next day she took a bit of their precious new store of fuel and cooked on what she thought of as Mag's fire, then went on Mag's rounds of healing. As time passed, this became her daily routine.

Survivors began to call her Mag, her mother's name. For most of them the girl Ari had never existed. In some way it was as if it had been Ari who had died and Mag who survived. For much of the time even Ari managed to convince herself that she was Mag who cared for the others as if they were her children. She affected the walk and movements of an older woman, serving the mad and the sick as Mag would have done, feeding them all from her pot.

The rest of the story of her dream lay in storage, hidden in the forgotten labyrinth of her soul.

It soothed her grief and kept her protected to become her mother, but the space where Talin had been remained empty and never stopped aching. She tried to comfort herself with a folio only to discover that they too, were gone. Had Talin taken them or had he managed to hide them again? Why had he been taken?

Talin had been abducted. She was sure of it. He would never have agreed to leave her or to desert the survivors who needed him now more than ever. She would now have to be both her mother and Talin, taking his place as well as Mag's among the survivors.

"All I can do is try," she thought. "I may not be a healer or a mage, but I'm all they have and I'm here."

Each night with that thought, she would finally fall into exhausted sleep.

And so the days passed and time went by. To the survivors she was their Mag who had also become their leader. Most of them forgot that Talin had ever existed.

Ari never forgot.

CHAPTER 18

As days passed and turned into weeks of failed attempts by Atrid's diggers, frustration threatened to overwhelm the Queen. Where was the answer she sought and how was it that none of her diggers could find what she sought no matter how they probed the old man's mind? All they found was his determination to get her to read the folio fantasies he claimed to have discovered on Zed. How could that be true? She and her mages had destroyed everything on that misbegotten planet centuries ago. She would have to dig him herself. She continued to sense some threatening truth that had nothing to do with anything so trivial as old folios from Zed.

At first she tried to pressure him to take the meld. She could have tricked him into it, but knew he had to agree if it was to work properly. Talin smiled at her as if she were a recalcitrant child.

"I will never participate in it again," he told her repeatedly. "I'm an old man now and have only the folios to offer you. Since you don't want them I am no good to you. Why can't you just let me be? Or better yet, send me back to Zed?"

Atrid could barely control her anger. Who was this horrid old man who kept insisting that his only secret was the folios? The more he refused her, the more convinced she became that he did carry a great secret, one that could endanger her whole Empire, one that he stubbornly refused to share.

She felt now as if she had known from the moment she banished Talin to Zed that something was amiss. Her dark dreams had begun about that time. In her dreams Talin was plotting the death of Mem, sometimes by mass poisoning, other times by war, more recently by opening her chest and tearing out her heart. This last had come right after she'd sent her guards to bring him back to her.

As the digging of Talin continued Atrid's nightmares worsened. Night after night questions seethed in her mind until she wondered if she, too, were going as mad as those she sent to Zed? Had Talin's exile also been her own?

Perhaps she should have melded him, she thought, rather than banishing him. Yet how could she have lived with one among her Inner throng who had betrayed her?

Though he was an old man, and for now his body a broken shell, she could see that he was getting stronger. Even so, he was adamant about one thing. He would under no circumstances consent to another meld. Soon she heard rumors that his refusal had become the gossip of Syl. People were laughing at her and at the news that Talin was refusing to give her what she wanted!

She knew she must find a way to control him. Just as she had controlled Zetti making it Zed she must find a way to bring him back to her. Their old ways of joining were impossible as long as he refused. Somehow she must find a way to bend him to her will. Twisting and turning in her great empty bed, questions continued to plague her. Was there truly a secret? She wasn't sure. The only thing she knew with certainty was that what she sensed was definitely not his crazy folios. She didn't give a damn about that fantasy.

When she couldn't find the secret herself she sent more diggers to search each nook and cranny of the prison planet. When they returned to report having found nothing, she sent her best diggers. They, too, found nothing to support her intuition. Most of them claimed that there was no danger.

One of her best diggers did report, however, that there might have been something just out of sight.

"I sometimes had the feeling that something lurked in the shadows of the caves," he reported, "And a vague uneasiness among the prisoners. As fast as I felt it, however, it was gone."

"Aha," Atrid cried. "Just as I suspected. There is a secret and I will have it! There will be no rest for any of us until this is accomplished."

Immediately she sent another airship back to Zed, this time with specific instructions.

"I've had enough of this Zed difficulty," she stated. "Wipe it clean.

CHAPTER 19

Struggling to write his memoirs, Talin sat at his old desk by the open terrace doors. His eyes were dim now but he could still look down past the green treetops and across the miles of paddies, interspersed now with space platforms filling in the old marshland, to the distant view of the white city of Syl. Though its splendor was blurred to him now, he began to remember how its towering elegance had looked in his past, white against Mem's dark stone dikes and purple sea.

Daydreaming, he would scan the semi circle of mountains remembering a time when, in his imagination, he had seen them as the arms of a huge being holding its enormous green belly, while its head, the dormant volcano at the skyline high behind him, rumbled and grumbled like a being with a belly ache. In the days of his youth he had taken it all for granted. Now he saw the land as it had been centuries ago and imagined the old rites taking place as they had before Atrid banished them. Long ago Memmians had danced on the beaches in celebration of Tide Turning. They had also sung their dead to the Land Beyond the Stars. Was it old age that made him long for that now? Or was it for something or someone else that he wanted it done? He couldn't remember. He only knew he felt love for the land he surveyed.

"Mem is the home of my heart," he thought. Zed was nothing in his mind compared to this. What was it then that kept calling his mind back to the prison planet? Could there be more folios? Atrid dismissed what he told her of them as sheer nonsense. Again and again he had insisted on their importance as historical documents. She wouldn't listen.

"You are deliberately blocking me," she accused "The folios are a ruse."

Talin tried to tell her that he had nothing else to give her. His protests only increased her anger.

When Atrid and her mages urged him to write of his time on Zed, assuring him of the inviolability of his words, he knew they were lying. All too frequently Talin felt her presence in his mind and knew she was still digging him. This was hard to bear. Her "visitations" plunged him into despair, causing him to lose himself. He found that he needed solitude if he was to regain sanity, otherwise his thoughts vanished like wraiths engulfed in a maw of empty darkness.

He sent word to Atrid that he could do the work she demanded only if she stopped trying to dig him. She must leave him completely alone.

Atrid sent word back that she would honor his request.

If not the folios, what was it she wanted so desperately? They were the only clear memory he had of his time on Zed. Occasionally he could still feel the excitement of finding them. Why didn't they excite Atrid too? Their contents were stupendous! The history and biology of Mem would be rewritten if they were ever accepted.

Only when Atrid finally left him alone did the fragments of the person he had been, the life he had lived long ago on Mem begin to appear in his memory. As he wandered through his own past on Mem he came upon more and more broken bits, like shards of the ancient pottery he had collected when he was a boy in the mountains. Putting the pieces together gave him a renewed sense of his old self, the boy, the young man, the one who had loved Atrid and been her consort. At the same time he remembered himself with shame as one who had taken the meld not once but many times, the man who had been his Queen's Consort, mage and digger, never protesting anything she asked of him. The intense pain these memories caused finally made him physically ill. When he realized what he had done as her consort he wondered how he could possibly go on living with himself.

Along with Talin's memories of the meld came the realization of something he found equally unbearable. He, himself, had been a digger of minds and hearts and he had taught many of the mages all his clever tricks. Now Atrid and those he had taught were using those same skills to dig information out of him!

The deeper recesses of his battered mind he left alone, fearing that memories of Zed might be more of the same, so terrible to recall that they would simply increase his pain.

To counter-balance his horror at his past, Talin began to search the old, abandoned library for all the old stories of Mem, recalling knowledge from his early training as a mage. He read of ancient times, when Memmians had led lives filled with ceremonies with singing, dancing and constant celebration of life. In those far gone days there had been a ritual in which the dead were sung to a Land Beyond the Stars from which they would eventually be reborn. For days after he read of it he was haunted by a chant he was sure had been sung, wondering why it seemed so familiar. Perhaps he himself had been sung into death in such a fashion far back in Mem's history?

Immediately he thought of those he had melded. They had never been sung out! For them there was life only in his body. How long was it since he had given those he had melded any attention or care? He hardly remembered they existed as parts of him. The bodies out of which they had been born were simply abandoned and shot out into space to burn to ash on re-entry. There was no singing for them and no rebirth.

Were his Inners all as tired as he was? Did they feel the same shame? Talin began to read aloud to them, sharing Mem's history and the days long ago when they had lived in their own bodies. At first it was as if they all slept, then one or two stirred but it was as if their memories and abilities had been wiped clean. Everything he read was new to them. He became their teacher. One day he shared with them the story of a legend from the past about wild horses who sometimes came galloping down out of the rugged mountain heights to run through meadows that bordered the marshes, "a sight which thundered in the mind long after the horses were gone." This shard of history gave them all great delight.

That evening Talin spoke of this to his servant, the young mage Caz who was moved to retell the old legend passed down to him from his own father who had it from his grandfather, son to son.

"In the days before the meld," Caz told Talin, "Memmians

knew that when we died we lost only our bodies, not our souls and that there were wild horses who came down from the mountains to run in the meadow and offer themselves to the dying as transport. Often they came first in a dream so the person would be ready. In those days the dead were still sung to the Land Beyond the Stars. Every Memmian knew that this would happen when their time came. To most of them it was a great comfort."

Hearing the emotion in Caz's voice, Talin was sure that both of them had a silent longing for those old times and rites, for days when every transition was celebrated and Star Woman had been a mystery, an icon, a source of help and solace, not a power hungry Queen named Atrid determined to rule her expanding Empire forever, no matter what it cost in both human and alien lives.

Talin saw Atrid more clearly now, not as Star Woman but rather her antithesis. He had loved and obeyed a delusional woman! He felt sympathy for her but also fear. He must be careful not to ever be caught in her thrall again.

Atrid came one day to tell him she was sending another ship to Zed. Her visit was brief. As she was leaving she looked back at him over her shoulder, her green eyes sparkling with determination.

"I've learned that there truly is a Secret on Zed." she told him. "If you won't share it with me I will have to deal with it in my own way." Opening the door to leave she added triumphantly, "I've sent a ship with a crew who will destroy any possibility of threat to me. If there is Secret it will be purged."

Talin felt a great leap of fear, then nothing. In his mind there was a great sound, as if enormous iron doors slammed shut in his soul.

He opened his mouth to protest but discovered he could no longer form a word. The room began to spin. He tried to move his fingers and noticed that they wouldn't respond any more than his voice. Slowly he fell to the floor. As he toppled into blackness he saw Atrid move in slow motion toward him.

They told him later that a healer came immediately and probably saved his life. Even so, his voice was gone, lost behind those huge doors, cut off by a force far greater than anything he had ever experienced, a force that made the power of Atrid seem puny in comparison.

His recovery was slow. Caz told him he had had a bleed in his brain. All Talin knew was that he was mute. His speech centers were paralyzed.

He dreamed of the ancient Star Woman and remembered that once, far back in a forgotten time and place, he had made a promise and offered Her his life. In a new dream it seemed that this beloved Goddess was once again claiming him. At first he thought she was asking for the death of his body, but as he recovered physically he began to accept that his body was to live. What the Goddess needed now was muteness of his voice and soul. Why this was true he couldn't guess. All he knew for certain was that he was Hers and must accept Her design, whatever that meant for his future.

"It will all work out," she told him in a dream. "Have no fear."

He knew that his silence enraged Atrid. Trying to cooperate, he was relieved to discover that there was no way for him to communicate. His fingers would no longer work on a keyboard, nor would his mind give any thoughts to a machine. It was useless to try. Sitting on his terrace with Caz beside him, hearing occasional comments about the weather and the scene below, Talin began to relax. Only his eyes functioned. The sight of Mem's cloudless sky and brilliant sun warmed him. As he looked at the familiar landscape below, space stations stretching all the way to Syl, he could feel his heart opening. A strange sense of peace began to rise in him as he looked at the clutter of this planet that had birthed him, nurtured and initiated him, where he had swum in the purple seas and loved a woman with joy until she had thrown him away. What had he done that had brought such ruin? No matter how he tried, he couldn't remember. Nor did he know why he had been forced to return. Atrid claimed she knew that he carried a secret that threatened her whole empire! Yet no matter how hard he searched himself he found nothing. Finally he stopped trying. For now it was enough that Mem welcomed him home.

CHAPTER 20

Twice Ari hid in the safety of her cavern, sensing the departure from Mem of supply ships headed for Zed in unusually short intervals. Only when she was sure they had come and gone did she return to the compound, relieved when she could return to her patients. Sleeping in the hovel Talin had built before she was born, she listened for any call from those who were ill. For awhile she was able to establish a routine, doing the work as Mag had taught her. Each night she slept the deep sleep of exhaustion.

The call when it came was not from a survivor. One night she was wakened by a strange light in the corner of her hovel sending her images of another airship leaving Mem and speeding rapidly toward Zed while a strange Voice urged her to hurry and hide. It was a stern command with authority in it. Ari knew she must respond immediately.

Suddenly wide awake she jumped up and began to rapidly put on Mag's familiar clothes then quickly made her way to the storage cave, taking food stores as she passed until her apron bulged, but trying not to take more than her share. Others would need what she left.

Ari was sure that the Light Being had been warning her of grave danger. Until she entered the supply cave she could feel a protective presence moving beside her. This had never happened before and seemed like a more serious urging than any she had experienced in the past. Yet suddenly as she turned the corner at the back of the cave the guiding presence was gone and she was on her own. Tying up her apron full of supplies, she let it go down the slide, then got inside the opening to the chute and onto a narrow ledge where she managed to lean out and use every ounce of her considerable strength to move a nearby boulder just enough to hide evidence of the opening she had squeezed through.

Had Talin set wards of protection around this entry long ago? It gave her comfort to imagine that he had. Now if only his wards would hold.

Still feeling a sense of urgency and fear, Ari squirmed herself onto the slide, letting it carry her spiraling down into the cavern below. In the two times she had been in the cavern she had felt no serious danger but now she felt terror. What could be that bad?

The moment she reached the cavern she began to pace. Terrible images had begun to flood her mind, images of slaughter, mayhem, blood that made her stumble and almost fall. Her mind raced. Memmian guards in bright red jackets were searching every hut in the compound, roughly dragging survivors out into the open. Then, as if she were dreaming, she saw a brief glimpse of laser guns drawn and fired as her survivors emerged. Not one of them fought back or ran.

"It can't be true," she thought. "I'm just crazy with fear." She wanted to rush back to her people, but instead she began a walking meditation Talin had taught her, convincing herself that the only threat to the survivors was her own terror.

"Why would anyone want to hurt them?" She asked herself. "Their lives on Zed are punishment enough." The Light Being had told her she must hide. She mustn't let panic make her do something foolhardy.

Despite her determination, however, the pull to return to the compound didn't go away. Was something trying to trick her into exposing herself? After all, the survivors were now her responsibility. If they were in danger she must return and protect them, especially now that they thought she was Mag. Couldn't she swim out and go along the cliff to look down and make sure they were all right? As soon as she thought this the Voice in her mind commanded, sternly, "No! You must stay!"

Ari had no choice but to obey. It was awhile, however, before the nightmare images stopped and she was able to sit down and rest. It was even longer before she could force herself to swallow food. Eventually she managed to drink water from the underground spring and eat a few bites of what she'd brought from the supply cave, but hours of fretting went by before she could sleep. Marking the nights in her hidden notebook was the only way she could count the hours that went by at an agonizingly slow pace.

On the fourth morning the Being made of Light appeared again, this time to tell her she must return to the surface. Aware of a great sadness emanating from the Light, Ari swam out of the cave and climbed toward the compound. Immediately she noticed a profound silence. Almost at once she was aware that heavy smoke clouds hung like a shroud over the landscape. No tak jumped or screamed. No wind stirred. No serpents slithered. It was as if all of Zed had gone completely still in her absence. Feeling chilled and numbed through she forced herself to climb up the narrow, hidden path toward the community, anxiety building with every step. The terrible smell of smoke grew stronger, cloying in her nostrils. Ari tried not to sneeze or cough. It seemed important to keep silent as she moved.

Near the compound she heard sharp, strident voices, completely different from the languages of Survivors. Avoiding the turn that would take her down into the village she kept on climbing, determined to remain hidden. The guards must' still be present. Why? They never stayed this long.

Once she reached the ledge over the compound she cautiously crept toward the edge, sheltering behind a boulder, to peer down and view the huts below.

There were no huts! The compound was empty of everything except smoldering ashes! The only movement below was that of four men dressed in bright red jackets. She knew those jackets! They were the uniforms of Memian troops. She had seen them once before from this same spot on a day when she and Talin, caught outside the cavern, had lain here hiding as they watched a supply delivery. She could still remember Talin's distress and his strange frightened talk about "diggers."

Where were her people? What had the guards done with them? And what was creating this noxious smell?

Once again she heard the strident voices. This time she could make out words.

"Well," a rough male voice proclaimed, "This job is done. Now we can get back to the comfort of Mem and leave Zed behind."

Fear gripped Ari's chest making it hard to breathe. What had happened here? Could her vision have been true? No. The thought was too terrible.

Another guard voice spoke, "Let's go. Our job is done. We need to get off this foul planet."

Cautiously Ari lifted her head again, daring this time to take a quick look around. As if struck, she fell back, gasping. Not only were there no huts, but near the space port pad at the center of the compound there seemed to be a great pile of charred bones! It wasn't just the burning of dwellings that had created this noxious smell! The pile was the remains of her companions, her survivors, the ones she had tended and nursed with such care.

Were they now all dead, their bodies lying stacked in a charred and blackened, half burned mound, still smoldering, still sending out the stench of burning flesh?

Ari suppressed her sobs, letting herself slide down into despair, still within earshot, hidden behind an outcropping where her black tak cloak would blend in with the landscape should the guards look up. She should have been here to protect her people! How could she have abandoned them?

Now here she was, still alive but trapped. Her access to the cavern was cut off by the soldiers below. If she moved from this spot in daylight they would see her, and where could she go even if she did move? For a moment she thought of the possibility of turning herself in, but the instant the thought came she banished it. Giving herself up would mean certain death. It was all too obvious that there were to be no survivors. It was as if she could hear Talin's voice inside her head telling her again that the most important thing for her now was to keep herself alive.

Why had the guards done this? Had the Evil Queen ordered it? She must be mad. No sane person would keep prisoners all this time only to eventually destroy them. The Queen had Talin, wasn't that enough? Ari held her head, suppressing a sob. Was Talin dead, too?

Dizziness began to overwhelm her as she continued to listen.

The second rough and cocksure voice she'd heard before queried, "Hey, Cap'n, you think maybe we did 'em all a favor to give 'em a swift death? It must've been horrible to live here. Myself, I think I'd rather be dead."

A third voice sounded then, young and shaky but strong, "It seems a terrible waste to me, all this slaughter. Why create this wasteland and put people here to live on the edge of starvation all these years, then without any explanation or warning laser them down?"

"It's the Queen's will and don't you forget it," The ugly first voice Ari had heard spoke again. "You don't have to understand it. Just don't you let nobody hear you question it."

"Even if it's wrong," the young voice was bitter.

"Atrid ain't never wrong."

Ari huddled where she was, trying to control herself before she did something stupid like run down into the compound screaming.

The first voice again. Was it the captain who sounded so rough and cruel. "Are ya' sure we didn't miss nothin' in the caves?"

The second replied, "Where could they hide? We've combed every inch of this place, a real labyrinth. Scared out some guys who tried to hide and a couple of them skinny horned beasts. Only other thing is huge black snakes and nobody in their right mind would mess with them."

Ari knew she had to find a way back into the cavern before they discovered her. There must be a witness to this horror. Atrid must pay. Ari began to feel anger rise in her like one of those black serpents unknotting itself. She would atone. She would see that the evil Queen was punished.

"Nobody in their right mind," the young voice scoffed. "You think any of these folk could still have been in their right minds after a turn here?"

"Shut up," the captain ordered. "You're gittin' on my nerves. Most of em was just freaks, good for nothin."

"Oh, it's okay to kill but to talk about it gets on your nerves?" The young voice was cocky, but with an edge of reckless hysteria.

The captain's voice was like a whip. "Just becuz you're one of the Queen's chosen don't give you no right to question my orders ....or hers! I've a good mind to leave you here."

"Atrid wouldn't like it."

"I can handle that. Tell her you asked to stay you loved the place so much."

"She'd never believe you."

"But she'd believe me if I said you needed discipline. Yessir, I think a turn here would do a lot for your character, Boy. We'll just leave you and old Bim here to deal with any stragglers." He laughed a mean, snarling snort. "We'll even leave you the extra pod to live in. You can use the supplies we brought so's you won't starve or freeze." He snorted again. "It's for sure nobody else ain't gonna be needin' em."

"I don't see any point in anyone staying." the boy voice protested.

"Well I do!" There was silence.

Ari peeked up just long enough to see a big, swaggering creature pointing a laser gun at a very tall, slender young guard. Both wore uniforms, but there the similarity ended. The captain looked as if he had slept in his clothes for months, seedy and ill kept, almost as ragged as the survivors. The young one's uniform looked brand new. His laser gun was still in its holster. She wondered if he'd ever used it.

"One way or another, you're stayin'. Alive or dead, it's up ta you."

Silence. Aricia cautiously lifted her head again. It was like a moment frozen in time. Nobody below moved. No one spoke. The two just stood there staring at each other. It seemed forever before the young one lowered his head to stare at the ground. She could see him mumbling.

"What's that? Speak up! I cain't hear ya."

"I'll stay. Old Bim needs someone to look after him."

The boy lifted his head again. Ari could feel his hatred pour toward the captain. She wondered that the captain himself didn't feel it and shoot the young soldier on the spot.

As Ari watched, lifting her head, then ducking back again and again, she began to shiver not only with fright but also with the cold of twilight falling. Smoke still swirled from the spot where bones lay half-burnt, but it was lessening now. Two of the guards were preparing to leave. She could see the spaceship on its landing ramp preparing for take-off. Soon only two figures were left beside a fat little white pod that hardly looked big enough to sit in, much less sleep or eat. Even with that shelter, how could an old man and a boy survive alone on Zed? Somehow she knew they had no experience of this kind of survival. The old man was not strong enough. She could tell that from the way he moved. If he lived to the next round it would be a miracle. And the young one? He looked to be about her age, yet his wild, naive belief in doing the right thing made him seem much younger.

Ari watched the ship depart, sure that the two left behind had been left to die. There wouldn't be any more shipments or returns. Zed was now abandoned and they with it.

Ari wondered if there were any way in which she could help without getting herself killed, then questioned her thought. Why would she want to help a Memmian guard?

She must get back to her cavern where she could ponder what had happened and decide what to do next. Pulling her mother's heavy cape closer around her, she hunkered down, her body and her spirit stiff with grief and fear. From below she could hear the voices, but couldn't make out the words, old one reassuring the young. It washed over Ari, there was no one left to do that for her.

CHAPTER 21

On Mem Atrid was growing impatient.

"Bring Talin to me!" she commanded one day. She must make one last try to dig his secret out of him.

He sat in his old seat in her quarters looking uncomfortable and out of place, his cane at his side. It was painful to see how much he had aged. Atrid walked around her mirrored room, observing the youthfulness of her own reflection as she touched one familiar object after another. Many were gifts Talin had given her long ago. Most had been stored during his exile, but this morning she had had them put out again, hoping the sight of them might jog his memory.

With tapered fingers she touched the ancient vase he had rescued from one of his digs in the ruins of an old civilization in the far western regions. Scientists had studied it. Even Jotus agreed that it was from a time before the meld and depicted scenes from forbidden dreams and rituals, scenes of death and rebirth. She remembered the day Talin had given it to her. She had seen it only as a relic, something to be discarded. He had liked it, however, so she'd kept it hidden away. Now as she looked at it, she realized he had been giving her a clue to his growing desire to bring the old world of dreams, intuitions and death rituals back into their lives. Why hadn't she noticed his interest back then? She could have intervened and saved them both years of grief. Had his idea to replace her with a daughter come to him from a dream?

Moving slowly away from the vase Atrid was aware of Talin watching her. When at last she turned to face him, she had the strange feeling that neither she nor these familiar gifts had much meaning for him anymore. He simply looked at her and to her surprise she found herself forgetting she had planned to dig him once again. Instead she began telling him of the progress of her new air vessel and her plans to go to Zed. As she did, she could feel her own excitement.

"I've had the same image in my mind for weeks," she told him. "It seemed that I must give it reality." She could hear the energy in her voice. "I finally knew that I had to build a very special space vessel, a rocket unlike anything ever built before, so that you and I could go together to Zed."

Talin stared at her. His eyes seemed ageless. She felt as if his look penetrated deep into the core of her being.

Atrid turned away and mentally shook herself. After all, who was doing the digging here?

She closed herself and began to move carefully toward the edges of his mind. Immediately she was filled with his sad weariness. He did nothing to repel her, but simply turned his head and looked away as he let her in.

"Perhaps you must go to Zed to understand what you have become," his voice said in her mind.

She wanted to laugh, to scorn and berate him, but as he turned his head again to look at her, his eyes suddenly held her. She could only watch as two tears slowly rolled down his leathery cheeks. It frightened her to see his aging and feel his sadness. Why couldn't he accept her offers of the meld? He would feel so much stronger if he did it. Why must he continue to refuse?

"You will come with me," she told him. Even as she said it she knew that he would never survive another crossing without a meld.

Only his tragic eyes moved, looking away from her.

"Neither of us would have to go if only you'd tell me what happened on Zed." Atrid eyed her old lover with half closed lids, caught by an impulse to enter him fully, to dig once more for his secret. Her best mages and seers had failed, but she was Queen. Surely she could find what they had missed.

As she shot into his mind she heard him gasp. For one instant she felt triumph, then found herself in a profound silence. It was as if she had stepped into a landscape of black ice and snow. The inner fire she had sought in him so often in the old days was gone leaving only frozen darkness. She shivered with the cold as she moved through him. Where was the old spark? It had to be here. Her intuition was never wrong. Surely there was an invisible something just out of sight, endlessly eluding her. Was it simply an ember of his old being that hid like a whisper just out of sight? Or was it something more real, more carefully hidden? Why couldn't she reach it?

Suddenly she could hear Talin's voice in her head, thin, weary, like that of a ghost coming from the far spaces of himself.

"It's no use," he said, "I am closed even to myself. If there is anything here, I can't find it either."

She knew this was true, yet her frustration made her want to shatter the frozen world of his being. She wanted to punish him, perhaps even kill him. How could he have let himself become this wintry wreck?

She could feel him smiling and abruptly came out from her search, aware that it was she who had brought about this impasse. She had sent him to Zed, the planet of the living dead. The Talin she had known and loved was gone. Why had she ever thought she could bring him back?

"He looks like a corpse!" she thought in horror as she stared at him. "Where is the man I loved?"

Could this wreck of a man ever have truly been the most favored consort of the woman she had just seen in the mirror?

Talin looked up at her from what seemed a thousand years away.

"Yes," his eyes agreed. "I am very different now. You are kept at the peak of youth, but I am dying."

Slowly he closed his eyes and slumped deeper into his chair as if dismissing her.

Atrid stood before him wondering what to do next. Should she shake him awake so that she could dismiss him? Somehow she didn't want to touch him. Nor could she stand there staring as his despair slowly invaded her senses. The despair was not for his death. She was certain now that he looked forward to that release.

For a moment she felt rage. He was smiling now. She could read him still. He thought he would die before she learned his secret!

Then something new entered her mind. For one moment he opened his eyes and seemed to look into her soul. Atrid recoiled. Talin's despair was not for himself. He despaired for her!

"Perhaps you will discover what you have become," he spoke in her mind.

She knew what she had become. She saw it in the mirror. She saw it in the awe struck faces of her mages. She saw it in the lifted, eager faces of her people. This old man was dying, but she would be reborn, again and again.

"I know what I have become!" she spoke aloud, her voice insistent and shrill even to her own ears. "I am your Queen!"

She began to back away from Talin, stopping abruptly as she realized that she was retreating like a supplicant before royalty. With that, she tossed her silver hair, smoothed her skin tight suit over her hips, turned her back on him and whisked out of the room. She was on her own now. She would go to Zed and find the secret for herself. She would have her ship and go on her own quest. She was, after all, Star Woman, the Queen of Mem.

As she strode down the long corridor to her quarters a thought suddenly struck her. Suppose she forced a meld on Talin, making him young again? She could slip the elixir to him secretly. It would be hard, but in his weakened condition he wouldn't be able to repel her. She would join with him and then bring in one of the youngsters who served her to join them. When that was completed, she would withdraw. Once Talin was young again and her ship was completed she would take him with her to Zed. He would be strong enough to make the crossing. Surely once they arrived she would discover the secret. Yes, Talin was the key and soon she would use him to unlock the mystery.

Left behind in his rooms, Talin discovered he was not alone.

Either he had fallen asleep and was dreaming or there was actually one of the Light Beings in the corner. Talin heard its voice clearly in his mind though he was sure there was no sound in the room.

"You must take the meld." The voice in his head was gentle and very calm.

"I can't," Talin replied in his mind, "For one thing, I'm dying."

"No, it is not time for your death, only time for the death of this phase of your life. Though you despise it, you must take the meld one last time so that you have the strength to go back to Zed. You must go with Atrid. Only you can protect what is hidden there, waiting to be revealed."

"I can't!" The very thought of the meld made him weaker. He wanted to cling to the arms of his chair, wringing them in his hands as if they could strengthen his refusal but found himself unable to move.

"If you don't, the Future will be lost."

The words didn't make sense to Talin, yet his stomach clenched and heaved as if he had just heard the ruination of everything he held most sacred.

"Look at me!," he thought, "That's already happened,"

"You are wrong," the Voice in his head said firmly. "You have forgotten. We saw to that. Now it is time to begin remembering."

With that word, pieces of Talin's mind, those shattered shards, slowly began to fit together. He could feel this happening, but couldn't see yet how they would shape. He only knew that something in him was coming together to form a whole.

Inside his head it was as if he could feel a nod of agreement. "Yes, but only as it is safe. The Secret must still be guarded, even as it begins to reveal itself."

"But I cannot take the meld," Talin protested, speaking aloud for the first time in months, astonished by the sound of his own voice.

"You must." The voice was fading now, the light in the corner dimming. "The Secret must be saved."

For one instant Talin saw a girl with a cloud of silver hair shot with copper and gold. He reached out to her, his heart open. She turned and looked straight into his eyes, and he saw in hers the violet of forest pools, his own eyes in Atrid's face. Was this Atrid as a young girl, before the Change, before he had known her? Why, then did she have his eyes?

In a flash she was gone along with his memory of her.

Talin was puzzled yet knew he had no choice. He must take the meld one more time. For some reason he must return to Zed and only with the meld would he be strong enough to do so.

The Light in the corner was gone. Feeling was coming back into his body.

"It's an abomination," he said aloud. "How can I do it?"

Yet he knew he would. Not only were there powers greater than Atrid's. There were powers far greater than his own as well.

CHAPTER 22

On Zed days passed for Ari as she made herself a temporary shelter in the cliffs where she could remain hidden and spy on the ruin below. Leaving her hiding place only long enough to climb and gather lichen or catch fish, she cooked in daylight on one of the highest mesas knowing the smoke would join Zed's dark clouds and be unnoticed below.

Any hope of returning to the cavern was dashed when she saw that the pod had been moved and was filling the opening of the supply cave, obviously placed there for protection from Zed's storms. Thin as Ari was, she suspected there was no way for her to squeeze past its bulk without revealing her presence.

Each day Ari watched the boy soldier wander around the outskirts of what had been the compound. He was obviously exploring but never wandered far from the periphery. Apparently he didn't want to get out of earshot of his companion. As days passed the old one came out less and less. Each time he seemed more ill until he stopped coming out at all. Ari could feel the boy's worry. With winter coming soon the weather could only get worse. Could the old man survive?

Would she?

Knowing she had to find better shelter for herself before winter's sleet began, she climbed down a hidden way to where the river emerged from her hidden cavern. Hoping to swim back in under the rock shelf, she stood looking down into the rushing stream. The power of water roaring out from under the huge rock overhang brought an immediate image of her battered body lying in the rapids below. Ruefully she faced the fact that even with her considerable swimming skill she would never make it back into the cavern in this perilous manner. Sick at heart she turned and retraced her steps back to her temporary shelter. At least she could keep an eye on the pod from here. Her only hope was to find a way to get past it into the supply cave and there wasn't much time left before winter struck.

She awoke the next morning to a clang of metal on rock. Peering cautiously through a crevice she saw the young soldier struggling to chop through the black floor of what had been the compound. Battering and bashing with a great pointed tool it looked as if he was trying to dig a hole through the planet itself. Ari could have told him it was hopeless. She knew from her own experience that only great storms and quakes could penetrate the obdurate solidity of Zed's surface. She vividly recalled a time when she had tried to shape one of the storm stones into a comfortable seat for herself. Talin had sat cross legged on the ground silently watching her struggle. The extrine had proved to be impenetrable. She hadn't made even a scratch. Soaked with sweat and aching with strain, she had finally accepted that there were some things that could not be changed.

As she watched the young guard he suddenly threw down his tool and collapsed, shaking with sobs. Only then did she notice what lay in front of the pod, a dark bag the size of a body, but just partially filled. He was trying to dig a burial hole for his friend's body! Ari had seen something similar to this in her cave dreams of Mem, a thing Talin had called a "grave" when she described it to him. She still found the practice hard to believe. On Zed no such thing was possible. Here on Zed bodies of the dead were burned in ritual fashion and their souls sung to the Land Beyond the Stars. This guard boy was attempting a hopeless task. No wonder he wept.

As she continued to watch, he sat up cross legged, rocking himself back and forth. Feeling his grief and terror, the desire to comfort him pulled at her but she forced herself to hold back. She had her own loss, her own loneliness and fear. Knowledge of her perilous situation made her teeth chatter. Each night was colder now. The old man had died. Wouldn't she die, too, before Spring? If she couldn't get past the pod and into the shelter of the supply cavern, how could she hope to survive?

Perhaps she should walk down into the compound, approach the boy, and talk with him? The only other two legged left alive on the planet, he was young, probably with fewer years than she had. What harm could he possibly do?

He sat up, and as he lifted his head from his lap, his hood fell back. Astonished at what she saw, Ari jumped, almost hitting her head on an overhead crag. The hair that sprang wildly out from under his hood was silver! He had hair like hers! She had never seen anyone other than Talin with that hair and he had it because he was a mage. Otherwise it was, like hers, something to hide. What did it mean that the boy guard had this hair?

The urge to go to him grew stronger along with her

curiosity. At the same she was sure she must stay hidden. It was as if all Talin's warnings had become part of her. Touching her own head she felt Mag's bonnet and was reassured that her hair was safely hidden. Her hair had always been a secret,. Yet here was a boy from Mem who had the same hair. Was that the real reason why he had been left behind?

Watching him more closely, Ari was surprised by her desire to know him better. Ideas jumped into her mind. Why not join forces? Could either of them survive the coming winter alone? He had access to food and shelter. She knew the planet and its ways. She could show him what to do with the old man's body and warn him about the fish.

Ari shivered through two more nights before making up her mind. That morning she left her hiding place taking a long circuitous route down into the compound.

The half empty body sack was still lying in place. There was no sign of the boy.

She was sure that there was a sledge in the cavern. If she could retrieve it and get the body bag onto it, she could drag the old man's body up to the Death Mesa. There she could sing the death ritual, not only for the old man, but for her survivors as well. Perhaps in chanting out the old man she could even say goodbye to her mother as well as those doomed by the massacre. She alone could sing them out, freeing their haunted spirits from the terrors of their lives on Zed.

Deciding to take action, Ari knocked tentatively, then louder on the hatch of the pod. There was no answer and she had no idea how to gain entrance. In desperation she decided to wriggle her way past the pod and into the cavern. Squeezing and struggling, she managed to contort her body enough to shimmy her way past the fat pod. It took all her strength and agility but she did it. Once through, she was tempted to flee to the safety of her hideout. No, the dead were calling her. Who would free them if she left?

The sledge was near the entrance. Made of old crates, it wasn't heavy, but the pod took up too much room. She tried pushing but it wouldn't budge. Struggling to turn the sledge on end, she tried with all her might to force it through the narrow opening where she'd entered. At her first shove it jammed and wouldn't go either forward or back.

"Hey, what do you think you're doing?" The yell came from across the compound.

Ari couldn't see past the sledge but was sure the boy couldn't see her, either. The temptation to turn and run back to her hideaway cavern nearly took her. Instead she stood still, waiting.

His voice was close now. "I know you're in there. Identify yourself," he ordered.

Ari stayed silent. Then she heard the pod hatch open and close. A motor started and the vessel began to move forward, out of the opening and into the cleared space where only the ashes of huts and bones remained. As the pod released it, the sledge clattered to the ground. She had to leap out of its way.

Without thinking about it, she protested, screaming, "What are you doing? Are you trying to kill me, too?" She could see the pod as it stopped abruptly and the boy shot out of the hatch to stare at her in disbelief.

"Great Star of Heaven, you're a WOMAN!" he exclaimed. "What are you doing here? Where did you come from?" He looked terrified, as if seeing a ghost.

"Are you real?" he asked finally.

Ari had already assumed the stance of an old woman, hiding her face, glad that her hair was covered with Mag's bonnet. She pulled the hood of her cloak closer and tried to move into the shadows so the boy wouldn't be able to see her clearly. She needed time to decide what to do. Could she keep up the pretense of being Mag? Would that keep her safe?

She made her voice tremble as if with age. "I live here." she mumbled. "I need food."

"Nobody lives here except me," the boy burst out. "I'm the only one left on this godforsaken planet." He seemed on the edge of hysteria.

"Well," Ari replied in a shaky old woman voice, "I guess that makes me nobody."

He came up closer to the sledge which lay between them, peering into the dimness of the cavern as he struggled to see her more clearly.

"Come out of there," he commanded. Ari could sense his struggle to regain control of himself and the situation, but he was obviously frightened.

"Let me see you," he ordered.

Slowly she began to climb over the sledge, pretending age and a bit of infirmity, yet remembering how strong Mag had been right up to the night she had eaten the fish. Keeping her face down, Ari slowly moved toward him, staring at his heavy guard boots, so different from her own tak pelt sandals. The boots reminded her that while he might be young and lonely and scared, he was still one of the guards from Mem, one of the dangers Talin had taught her to avoid. Though every cell in her body urged her to flee and hide, she slowly crept out into the open. The boy now knew she existed. Somehow she must convince him that she was an old healer-herbalist.

"Who are you?" He asked again.

"I am all that's left," she replied, rasping her voice in her throat to make it sound more like Mag's.

He stared at her in disbelief. "How did you escape? They searched everywhere." His voice caught as he remembered. "No one escaped. No one. They killed every single one."

Ari could tell he was struggling to be brave.

"And now I'm alone. Old Bim is dead, and I can't even bury him!" The boy's voice began to rise. "You can't be real! I must be hallucinating."

"I'm real," she assured him. "You can touch my arm if you want to. And then I can show you what is done to honor the dead on this planet. That's why I was getting the sledge."

Ari turned back to move the sledge. Once it was out of the cavern, she had to move the body bag out of the way. She could easily have lifted it alone but wasn't sure the boy would accept her as an old woman if she did.

"Hey, what are you doing?" The boy jumped toward her,

trying to stop her.

"I'm moving him so we can begin the death ceremony preparations," she answered crossly. "Would you rather leave him here to rot? You might help me, you know."

Instead he stood staring at her, obviously wondering whether or not to trust her.

"Where would you take him?" he asked.

"There's a place up on the mesa where bodies of the dead are burned and their souls are sung out." She pointed at the center of what had been her village, now a heap of ashes and sooty bones. "We don't treat our dead like that."

"Nobody should treat their dead like that," he agreed decisively and moved forward to help. Ari took a tool from the cave and began to shovel up ashes and bones from the mound left at the center of the village, piling them on the sledge.

"What are you doing now?" the boy asked excitedly.

"I'm collecting the remains of the dead to take to the death site," she explained. "You don't want them here, do you?"

He began to help her. When the sledge was heaped high, they each took one of its dragging poles and began to move slowly forward, the boy following her lead.

It took many trips to complete their task. The body bag and its contents went on the last load. By the time everything had been transferred to the ritual place on top of the largest mesa the boy was pale and worn out. Swaying, he looked as if he might collapse at any moment. Used to the heights and the labor of life on Zed, Ari was unaffected and wondered if she should seem more depleted than she was, yet once again remembered Mag's strength.

"The height usually bothers new people," she told the boy. "You'd better sit down and put your head between your knees."

"I'm young and strong," he objected. "If you can do it at your age I certainly ought to be able to do just as much."

Ari felt relieved. Her disguise was working.

Shrugging she turned away.

"I was the village healer," she said, "You can either trust that I know what I'm doing or ignore my advice. It's up to you."

Obviously exhausted, the boy slowly sank down to squat on the ground with his head on his knees.

Standing apart, Ari shivered feeling the cold wind warn of snow tonight.

Thoughts went through her mind as she gathered more lichen for the fire. The boy would be in his pod. Where would she sleep? Should she simply abandon him once this job was finished and slip back into her cavern? If she hibernated there, he would be alone but she would be safe.

The boy finally recovered enough to assist her. Together they stood by the hill-like mound they had made of bones, ashes and dried lichen. Ari started to use the slow traditional method of making fire. Immediately the boy took something out of his pocket. Instantly a flame shot forth and the pyre started to burn.

When flames had risen to the height of the old man's body, Ari began the ritual chant, her voice joining the wail of the wind. After her third repetition, the boy began to sing with her. Once he settled into the chant, his clear tenor cut into her soul, releasing her sadness. She felt tears coursing down her cheeks. Trembling, she watched through the blur as sparks spun into the sky, spitting and dancing on the wind. The flames leapt higher, and as they did she felt herself deepening, opening, spinning into the chant as if she, too, were caught in the strengthening wind, riding the sparks, guiding the old man's spirit out of his body toward the beyond. Suddenly she was aware that the boy was soaring with her! The surprise of this brought her momentarily back into her body. Then it was as if he reached out and pulled her out to rejoin him. Together they guided the old man out, and the chant seemed to swell and fill the skies as the voices of dead survivors joined their own. Ari saw her mother, filled with joy, leading the others. In that moment all the hardships of life on Zed seemed to be released in a kind of ecstatic annihilation as the dead transformed.

Longing built in Ari. An overwhelming desire to plummet after them into that joy, to join her people took her and she began to move after them as they entered a black hole that was opening in space.

"No!" a voice cried.

She felt herself grasped in strong arms and held, pulled back into her body, back onto Zed, back into life. For a moment she fought to be free, but she was held fast. She felt a heartbeat pounding against her own, and something else, too, a gentleness in the heave of his chest. The boy pinned her to his body as if he thought he could give her life by holding her fast.

"You can't leave me!" he shouted in her ear.

Her body collapsed against him. Everything went black.

CHAPTER 23

When Ari awoke she was lying in a strange place on a strange bed. Looking around, trying to orient herself, she saw walls that were white and seemed to be made of a strange substance she'd never seen before. Under her head was something soft that conformed to her head and neck. She reached up to touch her head wrapping and sat bolt upright in shock. Her bonnet was gone! Her hair was springing wildly, freed from constraint. Looking down at her body under the shiny fabric that covered her, she saw that she was naked. She drew the cover up to her chin, huddling as she tried to figure out what had happened and what to do next. Just then the hatch opened and the boy came in.

"Oh," he pronounced cheerfully, "you're awake!"

Ari could only stare, her mind racing.

As if able to read her thoughts, the young guard smiled, "It started to sleet right after you passed out," he told her. "By the time I got you back here you were soaked, so I stripped you and rolled you up in that blanket."

He seemed about to laugh. She clutched the coverlet closer.

"I'll have to admit you gave me quite a surprise," he grinned. "Why did you pretend to be an old woman?"

She began to seethe with anger. No one except her mother and Talin had ever seen her naked. Only they had ever seen her hair released like this. She felt disgraced. No matter who this young guard was, her taboos had been broken and that was not funny!

"You black serpent!" She spat out the words, wondering wildly how she could get out of the pod and escape to her cave. "How dare you?"

"What did you do with my clothes?" she demanded, her voice cracking with fury. She wanted to get away.

"You mean your rags?" He began to mess around with something in a pot that he placed on a surface that seemed to have some kind of heat in it.

"I'm making you some food and some tea," he told her, his back turned to her as if to reassure her that he wasn't going to stand and stare at her. "You'll find some things I laid out for you on the foot of the bed. They were issued to old Bim back in Mem, but he never got around to wearing them."

He banged around on the cooker for a moment, then said in a choked voice, "There wasn't much occasion to dress up around here."

Clutching the coverlet around her, Ari peered at the pile on the foot of her bunk. They were a man's clothes, but looked as if they might be about the right size. Since she didn't have much choice, she pulled a long sleeved soft grey shirt over her head, then wriggled under the covers into some long, grey, stretchy pants that immediately molded to her body in a way that felt warm and comfortable. The next layer she eyed with disgust. It was the uniform of a guard.

"I'm not wearing this thing!" she exclaimed, holding black pants up with a thumb and finger as if they might contaminate her if she brought them closer.

He turned to see, then snorted and replied, "How else are you going to stay warm? Of course I don't mind if you walk around in your underwear and get frost bite. You might not realize it, but winter has come and it's bitter cold out there."

"Where're my clothes?"

"I put them in the sonar cleaner. They're just rags. The only things that stayed intact were your cape and that's pretty old and beat up and a big old apron with seeds in the pockets that I didn't clean because it wasn't dirty."

She looked down at her body. She couldn't go outside without more layers. Reluctantly she began to draw on the pants. At least they were warm. With trembling hands she picked up a quilted red vest, the clothing of the enemy, trying to overcome her disgust by thinking of the importance of being able to leave the pod. She had to get away. The boy kept intruding in her mind. It took too much of her strength to keep him out. Somehow she had to get to the cavern and hide long enough to find herself again.

With two fingers she picked up the guard jacket with all its braid and put it aside. How could she dress like the men she had been taught from babyhood to fear and avoid? It might be ragged but her old tak skin cape would do. The hat the boy had supplied was a black toque, stretchy and soft. Stuffing her hair into it, she yanked it down over her forehead and ears and immediately felt more like herself. Ari couldn't remember a time when she'd gone with her head uncovered except alone in the cavern with Talin.

Talin was gone. All she had for companionship now was this strange boy who didn't seem to understand any of her ways. He didn't seem a bit concerned that his hair was a wild silver aureole around his head, or that it was totally visible to her. Ari wanted to ask questions, but felt shy about pointing out his flaw. Even though he showed no shame, he must have some sensitivity about this aberration.

"What's your name?" he asked suddenly. "I can't keep calling you 'hey you'." He started to laugh. "Especially now that I've seen you naked."

Ari glared at him, but answered. "I'm called Ari. And you, who are you?"

"My name is Jonce."

He gave her food and watched silently as she ate. She could feel him studying her, probing, but kept herself closed. The food was good. Her strength was returning.

With her mouth half full she blurted out, "Are you a digger?"

He looked astonished, then amused. "If I were, you wouldn't be able to keep me out," he laughed.

"Then stop trying to get into my head!" she commanded. "If you're not a digger, what are you, anyhow?"

"I'm a student mage," he replied. "Do you know what that is?"

"I know what a mage is." Talin had been a mage and a digger. Even at his craziest she'd never been able to keep him out. What was the difference, she wondered, between Talin and this boy?

"That means I'm in training for magehood." His voice was proud.

"So how come you're wearing a guard uniform? How come you're here?" She swung her legs over the side of the bunk. Sitting on the edge, she continued to eat. Until now she hadn't realized how hungry she was.

The boy Jonce began to move dishes around, turning his back to her. His voice was muffled. "This trip with the guards was part of my training. I was sent by the Queen." He blew his nose loudly. Ari wondered if he might be crying. Did soldier mages cry?

"Why did that captain leave you?" She put her hand up to her head, eyeing his hair as she did so.

"He thought I needed discipline."

Remembering how the boy had objected to the killing, Ari felt a twinge of sympathy but immediately tried to bury it. He was one of Atrid's soldiers. Didn't that automatically make him her enemy?

Eyeing him cautiously, she studied her hands where they had abruptly stilled halfway to her plate. "Don't you ever cover your hair?" she blurted.

"Why should I?" He turned to face her, looking puzzled. His face was red, but he had himself under control now. "I'm proud of my hair."

"Proud?" she could hear the astonishment in her voice.

"Sure," he seemed surprised at having to explain this to her, "If I didn't have this hair, how would anyone know I have royal blood?"

"Royal?"

"Oh, I admit it's pretty well diluted in me, but my hair brought me to Queen Atrid's attention. Without this hair I probably wouldn't have been selected for mage-hood. In fact, I'm sure I'd be working in a shop someplace. Why are you asking? You have the hair, too. You must be royal too. Why do you hide it?"

Ari stopped eating, feeling shy and confused, her old fears rising. He had seen her hair. He had seen her body. Feeling stripped she wanted to run and hide.

"You even have a star on your forehead," he continued, oblivious to her fear and confusion. "Sort of like the Queen. I saw it when I took off your hair covering. You look like Atrid. Are you a relative?"

The question made Ari's head ache, almost as if she'd received a clout from a tak bone on her skull.

"Yes," the boy mused," I expect you're somebody pretty special, so what in the name of all that's good are you doing in this terrible place? How did you get here? How did you survive the massacre? Who ARE you?"

The questions came at her like snake fangs. Ari felt as if they were killing her brain cells, destroying everything she had ever thought or felt. Somebody pretty special. What did that mean? Was she truly the monster she had once feared herself to be? Or was she something else? The pod felt stifling . She couldn't get her breath. Maybe the food was poisoned? Something terrible had gotten into her.

"I have to get out of here!" Spilling the last contents of her plate on the bunk and floor, she reeled to the hatch, then couldn't figure a way to open it. The mechanism was unlike anything she'd ever seen in either outer or dream reality. Ari could felt feel tears of frustration rising in her throat, in her nose, and throbbing behind her eyes.

"I can't breathe," she managed to rasp out.

Quickly the boy opened the hatch and she tumbled out, falling into a light layer of snow, scrabbling like an animal attempting escape. The boy followed and put his hand on her shoulder.

"I'm sorry," he spoke softly as if to an injured beast. "I didn't mean to frighten you. I want to be your friend. We need each other. I can't make it here alone."

Ari could feel herself starting to cry as she shook him off. Great silent tears rolled down her cheeks. All the grief of the long past months since her mother's death and Talin's disappearance seemed to be rising to pour out of her eyes. She breathed deeply, as Talin had taught her in her dreams, but the sobs came anyhow and she could hear herself keening and moaning. There was no stopping it anymore.

The boy tried to put his arms around her. With all her strength, Ari gave him a huge shove to get him out of the way as she bolted for the supply cavern. Looking back she saw him lying on the ground holding his head. There was blood. He must have hit his head on something as he fell. The healer in her told her sternly to go back, but her fear drove her on into the darkness at the rear of the cavern. She struggled feeling pulled apart on what to do.

All that mattered was getting away. But he was injured. He might die. He wasn't a digger, he'd never find her. If Jonce was unconscious, he would freeze, too. Ari slowly let herself realize that he was the only other human on the planet. Was she going to let him die? Could she survive alone? Wasn't he better than no one? He had saved her from death, though she wasn't sure whether this was a gift or unfortunate interference. Regardless, she couldn't let him die.

She couldn't move the boulder! Putting her leg under it, she tried to pry it up so that it would roll out of the way. Suddenly it lifted, then fell. She heard a crunch as a bone in her ankle broke. The pain was intense. Ari began to cry, sobbing helplessly. There was no way now that she could budge the boulder. She wasn't sure she could even stand. All she could do was lie here sobbing as the cold seeped into her body. It was hopeless. She beat her fists against the surface of the ledge, obdurate, impermeable. There was no safety, no place to hide from the cold or the boy. If she stayed here she would slowly freeze to death.

With a last great effort she extricated her leg and managed to drag herself back down from the ledge to hitch herself with great difficulty back to the entry. Outside the cave darkness had fallen, but she knew the way without sight. Pulling herself from one supply crate to the next, she slowly made her way back to where the boy had fallen beside the pod.

The spot was empty. Obviously he had recovered and gone back into the warmth and safety of his pod. Now her choices seemed to be either to join him or lie in the snow and slowly freeze to death.

She began to slap with the flat of her hand on the side of the pod. After a long time the hatch opened and she pulled herself in. The boy had obviously dragged himself from bed to answer her repeated banging. She saw blood on the cloth he held to his head and noticed more blood browning on the bunk where he had lain.

Acting disoriented, he was struggling to keep his balance. Was his wound really serious? Ari felt panic rising in her throat and jaw. What if he should die? What if she had killed him when she shoved him out of her way? Her ankle throbbed with intense pain as she forced herself to help him back onto his bed.

He seemed to be dreaming already. Half asleep he obviously didn't have the strength to protest as she forced him down on the bed and covered him with the strange shiny fabric folded at his feet.

Ari felt the pulse in his neck. It was thready and irregular. His face was ashen, the pupils of his eyes noticeably enlarged. His breathing sounded like a fish out of water, gasping for air.

"You have to stay awake," she told him, making an effort to keep fear out of her voice. "You have a head wound."

"Sleepy," he muttered. "Wanna sleep."

"You can't," she commanded. "I won't allow it."

She wrapped his head with bandages she found on one of the shelves. From the pocket of her apron she took seeds and made a tisane using water from a tube in the wall and, after a struggle, heated it on the surface he had called "cooker," experimenting with buttons she had seen him push earlier. All the while her ankle made her double over with pain. Determinedly she tried to ignore it.

Forcing him to take sips from a spoon, she could only hope that the drink would stimulate him enough to stay awake.

"I'm not going to let you slip away," she told him. "I need you here."

He opened his eyes. "Not dying," he mumbled.

"Promise?"

He tried to nod, then grimaced in pain. She could hardly understand his ragged speech. He kept trying to fall asleep. Each time she forced him to open his eyes and look at her. Talking to him she found herself saying inane, stupid things as if the nonsense might somehow stimulate him back into consciousness. Each time he stirred he seemed ready to speak but would slide back with little more than a garbled mutter. At last he murmured words she could understand. It took her a few minutes, but slowly she realized that he was telling her to get a patch from the shelf where she had found the bandages and that she should put one on his forehead.

"Green," he slurred, "for m' head."

Ari carefully stood up to search, holding back the pain in her leg.

Soon after the green bandage was in place the boy's pupils went back to normal and his breathing became steady. At last she let him sleep, though every few hours she woke him again to make sure he was all right. She herself did not sleep. She spent the time tending to her own injury. When the pain finally subsided to a dull ache she was able reach into Mag's healer bag the boy Jonce had saved to retrieve strips of tak hide and lichen and wrap her ankle.

For two days and nights she sat dozing on the bed opposite the boy. When he finally awoke, weak but hungry, she fed him, then fell onto the other bunk and into a deep sleep. Her fear was gone. She knew he would live. She wasn't alone.

CHAPTER 24

As Jonce slowly recovered they began to adapt to living together in the pod. Ari continued to have intense pain until he persuaded her to use another of his green patches. Soon after that her ankle began to heal.

She was grateful that the space in the pod was so small. Often she could reach things she needed without much movement. The luxury of the pod was an endless source of amazement. At the front, under a huge wrap around window was an instrument board so complex she had never seen anything to match it in her most exotic dreams. It seemed impossible to her that anyone could know how to manage all the dials and buttons, especially a boy as young as Jonce. When he told her he was sixteen, she nodded, hiding her surprise. She had thought him much younger. He was only a year behind her and yet he knew nothing of survival on a place like Zed. He did, however, claim that he could fly the pod, assuring her that he had had many hours of training and could easily fly anyplace she wanted to go as long as they stayed within the atmosphere of Zed.

"I don't think we could make it back to Mem in this," he told her regretfully. "It's not designed for more than emergency trips. Besides, I don't think the fuel pack would last to go that far"

"I have no desire to go to Mem," Ari sniffed. "Zed is my home."

She looked around the pod. It was still strange to her. Two

bunks came out of the walls with the touch of a button. When both were open, they took up most of the space in the cabin with only a narrow walkway between. When not in use, the same buttons folded them up so that there was enough space to move about. Just beyond the bunk area was a tiny area for cooking and cleaning up. Ari marveled at that. Before living in the pod she had never known any cooking except over the weak and smoky lichen fires of Zed. Nor had she ever seen water that hadn't been hauled from the river in a tak skin bag. Water that came out of a thin metal tube controlled by yet another soft touch button delighted her.

At the rear end of the pod, in a space that Jonce called "aft," was a small closed off area with a seat that puzzled Ari until Jonce discovered that she was periodically crawling out into the snow to take care of her personal needs. After he had explained the use of the seat, Ari limped out only long enough to show Jonce how to collect water from one of the frozen streams to replenish the storage tank in the pod. She also taught him to ignore Zed's fish and replenish their food supply from stores in the cave.

Storms raged. The cold made her leg ache. As soon as Jonce was strong enough, he did most of the work, urging her to stay off her feet. Eventually he was able to start the pod and with her guidance back it into the cavern once again so that they could go in and out sheltered from Zed's fierce winter winds and sleet.

Most of the time they stayed quietly inside so that they both could slowly heal. He taught Ari to play chess. Both of them slept a lot.

"Like hibernating bears," Jonce told her, then had to explain as well as he could what a bear was.

At times Jonce would start to pace the open area between their closed bunks, muttering and kicking against confinement. To pass the time they began to tell each other stories, Jonce about Mem and Ari about her life on Zed.

"At least you have people back home," she complained one day, "What's left for me? The guards destroyed it all."

"You have someone on Mem, too," he insisted. "Talin is there. I met him before I left. Speaking of Talin, what about the lost Gardens?" he asked. Jonce had been fascinated when she told him of the fantasy that she and Talin had shared that someday they would find a pocket of the old Zetti left like a secret amid all Zed's blackness.

"Oh, that's just a dream he made up," she replied despondently.

Jonce looked up from the game board where they were playing. "The weather is improving," he told her. "It must be almost Spring. Soon they'll be coming back for me. When they do, you can come with me to Mem and be with Talin."

Ari stiffened, panic rising in her chest taking her breath.

"Do you really think they'll bother to come back?" she asked, trying not to show her fear. "They knew old Bim would never make it, and what's one boy? Don't you know they left you here to die?"

"Well," he answered stubbornly, "I didn't, did I? And neither did you. Whether they come back or not, we're still alive."

Ari sat hunched over, fighting to quiet the fear spreading

through her back and chest. She felt as if she were gasping for breath. It was hard to talk. "So?" she finally managed to blurt out.

"I guess we wait." His voice was firm.

Ari could only whisper. "I'm as good as dead," she rasped.

Jonce stared at her. "You?" he questioned. "With your hair? You've got to be crazy. Nobody would hurt you. They'd take you to the Queen right away."

Ari jumped up, wincing as pain shot from her toe to her hip. "So she could kill me!"

She had to run. Turning to flee her leg banged into the bunk and she found herself huddled on the floor panting with pain.

"They mustn't find me!" She could hear the panic in her voice. It was as if she could hear Talin's voice saying, "Game, Princess. Hide." Why had she let this boy guard know she was here, alive? She should have stayed in the cavern. She could feel the pulse beating in her throat. It seemed to say "danger. DANGER."

"I've got to get out of here." She began to crawl toward the hatch. Jonce jumped up and barred her way.

"Don't be ridiculous. What's the matter? Come back to the game."

"Something's going to happen," she protested, pushing at him, feeling like a caged wounded animal. "I can feel it. They'll kill me. Let me go!"

He began to talk to her softly as he blocked her way. "You said yourself that they're not going to bother to come," he reassured her. "It's only us. Just you and me."

Jonce put his hand gently on her shoulder. She could feel his strength. It seemed to pour into her, giving her courage.

"I could work on the pod." he said. "Maybe I could even make it fly again at least enough to look around. We could explore. Don't you think it might be worth a try?"

Ari was silent, her body taut with fear. Tears came to her eyes. She grabbed her leg wondering how she could do anything now that she had re-injured it. The pain was intense.

"I can't do that," she said. "I think I've broken my ankle again" She could feel the sound of her voice echoing in her head as if it belonged to someone else.

"Besides," she heard herself say, "There isn't time."

Someone like Talin was warning her. Or was she just warning herself? All she knew for sure was that she must hide, yet if she did, there seemed to be no other choice than to take Jonce with her. A digger would discover her in his mind no matter where she hid.

"They're coming," she told him. "I feel it in my bones. We have to hide. They will kill us both if they find me."

He shook his head as if trying to get a new thought into it.

"Why would they do that?" he asked.

She frowned in exasperation. "Do you think they could leave either of us alive to tell the tale of what went on here? Would they let you go back to tell your own version to the people of Mem?"

"But why you?" he insisted. "What have they got against you?"

The words began to tumble out of her mouth without volition, almost as if someone else had taken over her voice. At the same time she could feel her own horror at what she was revealing but there seemed no way to stop the flow.

"I was born on Zed where there is supposed to be only death and despair. My mother was cleansed before her passage, but somehow I survived in her womb. I grew up here, but my life is a secret. No one on Mem can know I exist, least of all the Queen or her guards. If they knew they would have to kill me. Always when the supply ship comes I must hide."

Jonce looked puzzled. "But there is no place to hide on this forsaken planet," he exclaimed. "The diggers would find you in a flash."

"There is one place," Ari told him. "Even diggers haven't found it yet. I don't know why. Perhaps because Talin put some kind of psychic protection around it. With this injury I can't get there without your help. But before I show you the way, you have to decide: are you with me or do you want to wait here and take your chances of getting back to Mem?"

Jonce turned away, looking around the pod. "They'll never believe I did the death rites all by myself," he muttered. "They'll know there was someone else."

He began to finger the eating utensils they had used, lining them up in rows on the table. "They'll dig me and find you in my mind."

Suddenly he turned to Ari. "You're sure they're coming?" he asked.

She nodded. "I'm not sure when," she frowned, "but I see them making plans. I think they're building a new ship."

There was silence as Jonce stared into her eyes. Then he nodded decisively. "I'm with you." His voice was firm.

Slowly Ari found she could move again. Standing up, she winced with pain, then held her leg up and shook herself like a tak coming out of the river.

"We need to prepare. You'll have to do the work. I'll show you." Her voice seemed to echo in her head, but determination was strengthening her. She knew now what they had to do.

With Jonce's help she managed to leave the pod and move slowly back through the supply cave, pointing out supplies for him to collect once he managed to get her up the cliff to the opening. Now that their task was clear, her need was overriding her pain. Another green patch helped.

"You'll have to make several trips gathering supplies before we send them or ourselves down," she told him. "I don't know how long we'll need to stay hidden."

It was a struggle for both to get Ari up to the ledge. Lying there, her arms were still strong enough to push and with Jonce's strength added, they managed to roll away the extrine boulder that blocked the entrance to the chute. After he had collected the supplies Ari showed him how to send them, then sent him following down the slide. His astonishment kept circling back to her like a bellow from every twist and turn as his body flew down into the depths. She would have to warn him about the noise his mind could make.

Next she went herself, backwards down the familiar passage, slowing herself toward the bottom so that she landed softly, protecting her leg. Jonce stood nearby as if stunned by this new adventure and the vastness of the space in which they'd landed.

"It's like a temple," There was awe in Jonce's voice.

"I suppose it is," Ari replied. She felt a mixture of pain and joy, of missing Talin and pleasure that Jonce could sense the sacredness she and Talin had always felt in their sanctuary.

"It's beautiful," Jonce said.

After he had explored the space, she instructed him about swimming out and climbing back up to the supply cave.

"We'll have to wait here until the weather outside warms up," she told him. "The river ice is too thick." Ari was surprised at the relief she felt when he agreed. He wasn't going to attempt anything foolish.

"It's warm in here," his voice was surprised.

"Yes", she said. "It's always been this way, even in the worst winter storms."

"There must be heat in the planet's core."

"Yes," she agreed. "Talin thought perhaps something called a volcano?"

"More likely hot springs," Jonce mused.

In the days that followed, Ari taught Jonce how to make a fire at the center of the cavern so that smoke would go aloft and disperse in the high reaches before it could escape to be seen or smelled by anyone on the surface. After they felt enough time had passed, Jonce swam out and following Ari's directions, went back to collect the chess board and more supplies. No troops had landed, but Ari still felt a sense of warning. Her leg was healing, but it was slow. They needed to stay put.

One day Jonce looked up from their chess game, his eyes deep with new thoughts.

"We can't stay here forever," he said. "We don't know when they might come, tomorrow or years from now. I don't want to spend my life cooped up in a cave. Do you?"

Ari looked around. The cavern felt like home to her.

Jonce stood up and began to pace. "I have an idea."

Ari touched her Queen, pretending to ignore him as she contemplated her next move.

"Let's go exploring," Excitement seemed to explode out of Jonce. "We can pack up our supplies and take the pod and just go."

Ari sat very still.

"There's nothing to hold us," Jonce reasoned. "We can get far away from here."

Ari studied the chess board as if that next move were the most vital thing in her life. Finally she murmured, "But the Diggers?"

"We'll be on the other side of the planet."

"You think that would make a difference to them? No, we can't go. They'd find us."

Jonce began to pace more rapidly. "So you want to stay in this hole like a frightened animal? I can't do this anymore. You can come with me or you can stay, but I'm going." He stopped and turned, trembling, to face her. "I've got to go." He began to shed his clothes, running to dive in to the pool. As swiftly as that he was gone, swimming out under the barrier. When Ari tried to follow him, something stopped her. It was as if a protective screen of energy was between her and the pool.

"Not now," a voice in her head told her. "Not yet."

Later that afternoon Jonce came back. He'd been working on the pod. While he had he'd made plans. The weather had definitely changed he reported. For a moment it had almost seemed as if there might be sunlight in the West. They should head that way as soon as the pod was ready.

"We can't take the pod," Ari argued. She had been thinking about it for hours. "If we did they'd know right away to search all over the planet for you."

"There's no other way," he insisted stubbornly.

"Yes," Ari insisted, "there is a way. It won't be easy, but if you can't stay here, it's our only choice. We'll have to wait until my ankle is healed and we can go on foot."

They argued about it for several days between Jonce's trips to the surface to work on the pod. He was unwilling to wait. Finally they compromised. They would take the pod to a place where there was a cave to give Ari shelter. She had found the place on one of Talin's maps left in the cavern. It appeared to be a treacherous place to land, but Jonce could lower her and her supplies in a tak skin pouch. She would show him how to kill a tak so he could bring her both the skin and the meat. She could dry the meat and make a pouch while he worked on the pod.

"After you let me down by the cave, you can fly back to the compound and leave the pod," she told him. "Then you can hike to where I am. By then I should be able to walk again."

They talked about the pros and cons of burning the pod, but

finally decided that a time might come when they would need transport again, especially if the troops never came.

Ari gave him the map, warning him not to eat the fish in the streams and to watch out for the serpents who could so easily remain hidden, their black bodies a match for the iridescent obsidian of the cliffs.

"You can eat dried tak and the lichen that grows on the heights," she told him. "To you it may not taste good, but it's nourishing. Don't try to build a fire. It would be like a beacon leading the guards right to you."

The night before they finally left Ari dreamed of something or someone invisible in one of the cavern crevices that lifted her out of her sleeping body and took her far from Zed to a large white area where a great air ship was under construction much larger than any she'd seen before.

"There is time." she was told. "It is important that you two take this journey."

The next morning Jonce flew Ari to the little spot where she would wait and heal. Because he got lost several times, it took him a month on foot to reach her after leaving the pod back at the compound. By that time she could walk without pain. As she healed, she spent the time gathering lichen, exploring the area in wider and wider circles planning the next step of their route. They would leave the cliffs and start out across a flat plain of extrine. This would take them west to a part of Zed that even Talin had never explored.

Ari seldom minded being alone as she waited. At night she

could hear the screams of the tak on the mesas high above her head. In a strange way those screams were a comfort, reminding her of nights with Talin and Mag when she was a child. Most mornings she bathed in a pool she found deep in the cave where she slept. Unlike Zed's sluggish streams, the pool seemed to be spring fed, deep and clear

At last a day came when she felt Jonce coming and was able to walk to meet him. He looked ragged and exhausted. Reaching her cave, Ari insisted that he rest for several days before they set out together on a route she had chosen as the easiest. Finally both were strong and ready.

Packing up their gear they started out.

CHAPTER 25

On Mem the day of Talin's meld was set. Once more wanting a great Celebration, Atrid had made the preparations elaborate. Talin knew that when his meld was complete she expected every one to stand in awe as she and her rejuvenated consort, accompanied by chosen mages, guards, diggers and crew boarded her magnificent new space vessel, Shikari. With fanfare and glory the rocket would then depart on its mission to Zed.

Caz told him that invitations to the ceremony had been sent out to all the usual dignitaries and colorful flyers summoning all Memmians to the festivities were being displayed in every public place. People were already beginning to gather in and around Syl for the great event. Every guest house on both the mountainsides and in the city would be filled to overflowing.

On the seashore, close by Mem's latest space station, a grandstand had been erected with a view of the private pavilion where the meld would take place.

"Can't it be done quietly without all this fuss?" Talin begged. Atrid knelt by his chair, taking his hands in hers. She was still tentative in her dealings with him as if remembering her shock when he sent word that he had changed his mind and would accept the ceremony.

"The people deserve to be included." She told him. "They need to know that their Prince has returned to the fullness of youth."

As if of minor importance she added with a dismissive wave of her hand, "Of course they will all want to watch my new vessel ascend."

"Who has been chosen to meld with me?"

Previously he hadn't wanted to know any details of the meld but as the event grew closer it seemed necessary to have an idea of what kind of person he was going to take into himself.

"So many offered it was hard to choose." Atrid told him, then added, "Talin, are you sure this isn't some kind of trick on your part?"

How he wished it were, but the Light Being had insisted. He must obey, so he simply grunted, watching Atrid move about, touching objects he cherished, her face mirroring distaste.

"Talin," she complained, "Why do you keep these shards? They are old and useless."

"Yes," Talin thought, "Just like me."

In the years of his banishment Atrid had changed in ways that had little to do with her meldings. In the years of his absence she had cleared out all reminders of their old life together along with any remnants of the past. Only what was new, innovative and young was part of her present existence. Except for the meld, all the old customs were gone. Everything that showed signs of age had been banished or destroyed as if no past had ever existed. Talin felt deep sadness about this.

Now the elder he had become was about to be purged as well. Atrid was determined to make him young again. Would she insist on sterilizing his life and his surroundings, as well as his body? He shuddered thinking of it, wondering why in the name of all that was good and holy he was being required to go through this terrible act one more time.

Atrid's voice brought him out of his reverie and back to the present.

"Many fine boys have offered themselves," she was saying. "Everyone knows what an honor it will be to meld with you."

He studied his hands, bones visible under mottled skin, blue veins extended in knotted traceries. Yes, he was old. Any effort made his heart race and flutter. In his present state he would not last long here at home, to say nothing of on a Crossing. Despite all the comforts of Atrid's new rocket he would never survive the stresses of the trip in his present condition.

Talin sighed, distressed by the thought of taking the life of another young man. Was it truly necessary? Why did he have to return to Zed? Couldn't the folios be verified in some easier fashion.

The Light Being had spoken clearly. It was Talin's destiny to take this meld. There was no alternative.

"I think I would prefer death," he muttered. Yet he knew he would go to the pavilion and allow the ritual. He would do it because the luminous figure had told him he must.

All too soon the day arrived. Atrid came to accompany him. Holding out her hand she pronounced triumphantly. "It's time to step into our future!"

Reluctant and sad, Talin followed her out to the waiting hover car. He was quiet as they traveled the distance across the expanse of landing pads and space vessels to the beach and the launching pad where Atrid's magnificent ship lay glistening in the sunlight. To Talin it looked like a beautiful sea creature standing erect, out of its element, on the black sand of Syl's beach. Nearby, nestled against the dikes, was the melding pavilion covered with waving flags and banners.

Talin felt ill. He could barely breathe. When a roar of approval went up from the crowd he was comforted by knowing that Caz was close behind him, ready to catch him if he should start to fall.

Atrid preceded him to the door of the pavilion and turned to watch as he crept forward. He could see the anxiety in her face as she wondered whether or not he would make it over the last few feet. Determined, Talin struggled to reach her.

As he reached her, Atrid turned to face the crowd, raising her arms and stretching her lithe body to its fullest height. Instantly there was silence. As Talin half fell toward the pavilion, she turned and opened the door to where the youngster waited to receive him.

Fighting tears, Talin stumbled forward.

The meld started with smooth efficiency. His decision had filled Atrid with obvious delight. The boy she had chosen for the meld was superb, glowing with health, unusually strong and filled with passion and a desire to please.

When she started to join them on the melding bed Talin hastily waved her away. Forced to stand aside she was restless and kept inching forward. Each time she took a step he stopped her. Wishing he could reprimand her, Talin turned his back and concentrated all his attention on the boy she had chosen, aware of the youngster's desire to please him.

As the meld was completed, Talin kept telling the youngster. "I am so sorry! I thank you for your sacrifice and promise to honor you. Together we will..."

Atrid's voice in his ear was angry. "Stop this maundering, Talin," she commanded. "The meld is a success. Let others tend to the boy's body. We must go!"

Feeling bottomless anguish he turned to look at her, seeing her fury. Grabbing his arm she began to pull him up from the bed. Silently, with great dignity, he rose and let her lead him out to greet the crowd, knowing that Atrid was determined to show him off to her people as a sign that her will had triumphed. He had accepted the meld. She thought she had won and he was hers once more.

The crowd roared its approval. Atrid glowed with pride. Talin stood silent at her side. He didn't move or wave to the people no matter how she nudged him. The celebration went on around him. After a short time she led him away, into the new rocket she had designed where her crew awaited orders.

He tried to speak to the boy he had melded, reassuring him. There was no reply.

Talin was tired. There was always a period of exhaustion after the meld. He knew he needed rest.

The journey to Zed was about to begin.

CHAPTER 26

The take off was even smoother than planned. Atrid was exultant, pacing the control room, hardly able to contain her excitement. Her ship had surpassed all expectations. The ride had been so smooth it was difficult to believe they had actually launched. As she paced she talked with the crew, her words spilling out in triumph. She had created the perfect rocket! Everything was under control and going just as she had planned.

Everything, that is, except Talin.

She had thought he would join her. But the moment he arrived on board, Talin cloistered himself in his quarters and stayed there.

"He will come round," she told herself. "He simply needs time to adjust."

Yet the invitations she sent asking him to join her at meals were ignored. He wouldn't come out or interact in any way, nor would he allow anyone in. Food trays left in the passageway outside his cabin lay untouched.

At first the pique she felt at his rejection was mollified by her awareness of what a radical change this particular meld had been for him. One moment he had been a very old man, ill and near death. In moments, thanks to the meld, he was suddenly young, viral and desirable. In the first days of the trip she had told herself she could forgive his rudeness but as they passed the midpoint of the Crossing she found her anger peaking.

She dreamed that Talin held her in his arms, only to wake up and find herself alone in her luxurious bed .

She tried to distract herself by concentrating all her energy on running the ship, but it ran so smoothly and her staff was so efficient that there was nothing for her to do except pace and fret. She told herself that she could wait. Eventually Talin would have to come around.

Nevertheless, when Shikari landed on Zed, Talin was still locked in his cabin.

Atrid went by herself to tell him they had arrived. Determined to be present when he first stepped onto the surface of Zed, this place where he had lived all the years of his banishment, she wasn't going to let him out of her sight. Surely seeing Zed would stir his memory and as soon as the Secret came into his mind she would have it!

"Talin," she called, knocking on his stateroom door, "We've arrived. Come. It's time to disembark."

Nothing happened. Moments went by. She rapped again. This time she raised her voice. She was just lifting her foot to kick the compartment hatch when it opened. Her foot stopped just short of Talin's shin. His younger face looked haggard, unshaven, his clothing so tattered he looked as if it had come out of a rag bag. He had lost weight. Obviously he hadn't eaten throughout the trip. Had he even slept?

"I wasn't hungry," he told her, reading her mind.

His arms were crossed over his chest. Atrid studied him, realizing that he looked just like the pictures she'd seen of Zed's Survivors. On his feet he wore tak-skin boots. Where had he found them, she wondered.

"They're mine," he told her. "I was wearing them when I was returned to Mem," He strode past her and started down the corridor to the main cabin. "Come, I'm ready."

Atrid was astonished at his arrogance. No one preceded the Queen! Her arm went out to grab him but stopped when she caught the smell of him. He stank! Obviously he hadn't washed for days. What was he up to? Had he gone over the edge into madness?

Trying not to recoil she grabbed him by his shirt. "You look like one of the Survivors," she scolded. "You smell like one, too."

"I am simply one of your prisoners," he reminded her as he hurried forward. As she followed Talin onto the foredeck Atrid was aware of the startled puzzlement on the faces of her crew. They too were shocked by Talin's appearance. This rag tag creature who showed no respect to the Queen was not at all like the handsome young man who had come aboard at the spaceport on Mem. Standing in silence, eyes on Atrid, the crew waited for her instructions.

"Report!" Atrid commanded them sharply. She stood very straight, her back rigid with anger. Talin was the only relaxed person in the space. Slouching against one of the foredeck seats, he smiled and nodded, first to her, then to the troops. Atrid's fury increased. Anyone might think he was a king and a very spoiled king at that.

No one spoke. This time Atrid shouted in the Voice, "Report!"

The captain took a step forward nervously but quickly regained control as he gave his account. The two older space vessels sent on ahead carrying Atrid's foot soldiers had already arrived and swept the area. They declared the planet uninhabited. It was now safe for the Queen to descend.

"There isn't much to see," the captain added. "Black cliffs. Everything else was burned by the last troops. One must, however, watch for great black snakes and strange beasts called Tak. Also your people must be warned again not to eat the fish. "

"Talin knows all this," Atrid announced. "He will lead us."

Without a word Talin turned, went rapidly past her to the open hatch and strode down the ramp. Hurrying to follow him, she paused in the hatchway to observe his curious behavior. The moment his feet touched the planet's surface he knelt and kissed the shining black. The only place Atrid had ever seen this action before had been when one of her mages who had spent half his life on the other side of Mem had been flown home to end his life in Syl where he had been born. He had kissed the ground and when he had stood up, his face had had the same mixture of anguish and joy that Talin's showed now. It was as if he'd come home. How could that be? Mem was Talin's home, not this desolate planet. What was he trying to prove?

Atrid stiffened her shoulders, and stomped down the ramp to his side. This ridiculous behavior had to stop. She took his elbow and began to usher him forward away from the others.

"What are you doing?" she asked in an angry whisper. "Are you trying to shame me?"

He turned to face her. His words began to pour out as if everything he had repressed during the journey was bursting forth.

"Why should it shame you?" he asked. "This was my home for many years. Did it shame you when you sent me here? I am only what you've made me. I can't remember much about my years here, but today, right at this moment, I know that I'm back where I belong. There is peace in knowing I am home."

Talin looked around, his eyes sweeping the cliffs and the grey skies over their heads. Slowly his eyes returned to Atrid's face.

"Do you ever wonder about where you belong Atrid?"

She refused to answer such a strange question. Instead she asked in a tight voice, "What do you remember Talin?"

"I know that there was a whole village here. I lived here in one of the huts." He looked around, his eyes filled with sadness. "What happened here?" he asked, his voice raw. "What did you do? Where are the survivors?"

"I didn't do anything," she insisted. "My old captain did it. He purged the planet."

"Oh," Talin said. "I thought you had already done that when you changed Zetti into Zed. I suppose he was only following your example? Only this time it was my people."

"They were only survivors," Atrid told him defensively.

"I am only a survivor," he replied. "Why couldn't you have let them kill me, too? But no, you had to make me into this ridiculous parody of myself. You had to be the all powerful Queen who can change worlds and change people but can only change her own character from bad to worse."

Atrid recoiled as if he had physically struck her, then drew herself up to her full height and spat at him. "How dare you!" she hissed.

Talin looked at her as if he couldn't believe what he was seeing. Finally, without another word, he turned away and began to circle around the space where the compound had been. Atrid's eyes followed him but she didn't move. Breathing deeply she tried to calm herself. He was distraught and it was making him crazy. She reminded herself that she must try to be patient with him.

At last he returned to the spot where she was standing. When he spoke it was as if his heart was breaking.

"Was no one left?" he asked.

She pointed to a cave and the space pod that lay there just inside the opening.

"Two of my guards. One an old man. The other the boy I had planned to meld next. He was the real sacrifice. I'm told there's no sign of either of them. The supplies are gone so they must have hung on here for awhile. I suppose they could not survive without more supplies."

"Has the whole planet been searched?"

"I'm told every nook and cranny." Atrid kept her voice carefully modulated, grateful that he had given her time to regain her composure. Then she couldn't resist adding, "But they found no folios!"

She watched in silence as Talin circled again. When he came to the pod now just inside but not blocking the opening, he paused to look it over, then passed it into the cave itself. Atrid followed.

"Where are you going?" she called.

He came back toward her. "I'm trying to remember," he told

her. "That's what you want, isn't it?"

She drew him out of the cave and back toward the spaceship. He resisted, following her unwillingly.

"I must try to see if there are more folios," he explained, struggling to get out of her grip.

"Forget the damned folios." Her hand tightened on his arm as her anger escalated.

He turned and looked at her. His eyes were sad. "Atrid," he said slowly, "You don't understand. They contain our earliest history. They are the Secret."

Atrid looked at him with disdain. "I didn't come here to seek out that craziness," she scoffed. "We have work to do. Tomorrow you and I will begin our own exploration of the planet, every cavern, every cave, every inch. Something is here and with your help I am going to find it."

"And you will help me, Talin" she added, "Or suffer the consequences."

CHAPTER 27

That night, Talin lay awake, tossing and turning in his narrow bunk. Everyone else on the ship slept, relieved to have made landfall. Everyone, that is, except the guard Atrid had posted in the hall outside Talin's door, placed there to "ensure his safety." Talin knew what that meant. Atrid intended to keep him a prisoner until he agreed to her demands.

He cursed his own restlessness. His memories of Zed gave him no peace. Flashing through his mind like ephemera, they were gone as soon as they came. Mental pictures rose up continually, like waves in an open sea, only to crash again into spume on the barren beach of his brain. Again and again he tried to grasp them, but each image vanished as it appeared.

Eventually he gave up all hope of sleep. Restive and miserable, he rose from his bed and left the ship, determined to walk around outside. The young guard tried to stop him, but with a wave of his hand Talin dismissed him, as he would a minor irritation. He was used to being watched, guarded, detained. On Mem he had behaved. Here on Zed he was a survivor. Brushing past the guard, Talin continued on, his young keeper having no choice but to obediently follow him like a little dog.

Soon, Talin found himself climbing up the highest mesa, to a place he recognized as an ancient site of rituals for the dead. The images that had eluded him on the ship began to return. He remembered those who had been his people for so many years.

Human and alien alike had vanished without a trace. Where were they now? Had there been no one left to sing them to the Land Beyond the Stars?

One image was particularly sharp. He kept envisioning a middle-aged woman, dressed in a ragged apron and bonnet, caring for the others. Slowly Talin recognized her as one who had been special to him. He was sure she had cared for him as well as for the community. As the memory of her grew, he knew that he had lived with her. She had been an herbalist. He could see her making tisanes out of the herbs she grew in the scrabbled dirt of the mesas. If only he could have said goodbye to her, and thanked her for...what? He couldn't remember. All he knew was that he felt deeply grateful. Perhaps he could send a message out into the death world to tell her so. Was this wish simply a trace of his old madness? He didn't care. He would try to do it.

As Talin faced the west, and stretched out his arms to the night sky, he noticed the new strength in them, and simultaneously felt ashamed that he had taken the meld. He almost pulled back when he saw the guard watching him. His every move would be reported back to Atrid. Talin knew this, but decided to continue. He tried to block out awareness of the youngster's presence, or at least to render it insignificant. The only thing that truly mattered was remembrance of the old rituals. If he could enact this service for the dead, something might be laid to rest in him as well.

One star glowed brilliantly just above the horizon. Wasn't that unusual in this cloud-covered land? Talin was moved to pray.

"Oh, Great Star Woman," he began, his mind reaching out into the cosmos. "I am here, back in this black world, slowly remembering myself, and You, and the survivors who shared my fate for all those long lost years. Did I promise myself and my life to You? It seems to me I did. There was also a woman who gave me a great gift. Please help me to remember."

Images began to appear in his mind. He saw a ragtag group of males and females of every species. One of the human women he knew as Magdalene, the herbalist. Talin felt a rush of affection, and then profound sorrow. All of them were dead! They had already gone, but they seemed to be gathered now to reassure him that he was still alive. Had he been responsible in some way for their deaths?

He was struck by an overwhelming desire to join them in the death world. They were his people. A memory of soaring out to usher the dead toward the clouds pulled him out of his body, as he imagined star energy shooting into his chest, spinning him into the night sky. He felt himself flying free, riding out in search of the others. A sudden burst of joy carried him forward in a rush of emotion.

"Here I am!" he called. "Coming to join you!"

There was no happiness in remaining on Zed. The people he loved were waiting for him in the cosmos.

"No!" An Alph voice he had almost forgotten rang in his mind. As if a hand had reached out and grabbed him, he was pulled back. "Not yet!"

Talin plummeted back into his body, and immediately dropped to the lichen-covered ground. He began to sob with long, dry gulps. He had no strength, no will to keep living. All he wanted to do was die and join the others.

"There is more to remember." The familiar voice entered his mind, nestling there.

The young guard was hovering over Talin. "Are you all right?" he asked. "Do you need help?"

Talin motioned him away. For a while longer he lay still, his face in the moss. "Oh, Mag," he thought at last. "I hope you know that I loved you. Why can't I join you?"

"Now is too soon." It was her voice he heard now. "You have work to do."

He began to weep. "I think I was responsible for your death. Oh, Magdalene, I'm so sorry."

Again he heard her voice speaking in his head.

"It was necessary. I needed to go first so that I could help the others when they were killed."

In his mind, Talin could see her in the hut they had shared. Had there been someone else? Mag turned and pointed at the tak skin flap that served as a door. It opened, and someone entered.

"She lives," Mag said.

With a shock of complete recognition, Talin saw who it was. This time he knew her. Instantly, before he could claim her, he shut down his mind. There must be no realization that he had remembered. All images vanished as he stood up and started to walk, forcing his mind to stay only in the present moment.

But he could not get the words out of his mind. "She lives." Mag had said it!

"I must find a place to hide," he thought. "I must get away where I can't be probed. Oh, Goddess, help me!"

Hurrying his steps, he passed the young guard, and made his way back down to the plaza where the spaceship lay asleep. Were there diggers awake? Would they know what had appeared in his mind? Perhaps Atrid would awaken from a dream and pursue the Secret once again. He must leave immediately!

As he entered the supply cave, he motioned his guard to stand at the opening. The boy obeyed. Atrid's people had explored the cavern. No other exit had been discovered.

Remembering, Talin went deep into the cave, past where it turned to the left, and continued on. There was no time to take supplies. He would have to survive on his own. When he reached the ledge, he scrambled up, releasing the protective wards, repeating what he had done so many times before. When he discovered the boulder blocking the hidden entrance, he was glad for the first time that he had taken the meld, and that the boy he had taken had had almost superhuman strength. It took every bit of that strength to push the boulder aside enough to squeeze by, and then to replace it behind him. As soon as this was done, he plummeted down the chute, landing in the familiar cavern.

Just below his consciousness, his memory was flickering. It took all his discipline to keep her image from forming.

To his surprise, there were a few supplies in the cave: a little lichen, and some dried tak meat. Not much, but enough to sustain him for a day or two. There was also a bone knife, carved from a tak horn. Talin recognized it as his own, one he had made long ago and had put here for safekeeping. This knife, and one that matched it, had always been kept here together, meant to be used only if predators appeared. Now the second knife was gone. Seeing this, Talin felt a surge of excitement. It was as if a message had been left for him.

"I live."

Once more, against all odds. Just as in Mag's womb, she had survived.

It was not safe to stay here, so close to Atrid and her diggers. Others might have missed this cavern, but he knew Atrid would ferret it out as she searched for him and for his Secret. Her passion would be her compass.

Gathering the meager supplies, he put them, along with his bone knife, into one of the old miniature coracles that still lay on the ledge where he had placed them long ago. He stripped off his clothes and added them to the pile, before slipping naked into the pool, then swimming to where the tide would carry him under the overhang. It was all as familiar to him as if his return to Mem had never happened. The only difference was that, thanks to taking the meld, he was strong and sane. Once more he thanked the boy who had given himself to make this possible.

The night was still dark, but Talin knew dawn would come soon. Carrying the coracle, he stepped out of the water, in a hurry to get away from the area. Following the river, he passed the rapids, finally coming to where the stream widened and slowed. Here he slid into an underwater channel, where the extrine had been smoothed and the dark water was deep. The current carried his body for some distance before the riverbed grew shallow again, and he was forced to walk.

Though he was cold, Talin wore only his tak skin moccasins. They gave him better traction on the slippery riverbed. There wasn't time to open the coracle and get his clothes. He needed to reach his destination before daylight.

At last he came to the area he sought. He climbed onto a ledge, where a narrow and treacherous path lay hidden in the twists and turns of the cliffs, behind a slim fall of black water. He kept climbing, jumping from one broken ledge to another, until he reached it: the opening he had somehow been led to find during his explorations years before. Was it his madness that had brought him to this underground maze of caverns descending deep into the planet? He remembered this place, despite the intervening years. He had never shown anyone the hole where the Folios lay hidden in the planet's deepest core. There was only one other on Zed who had ever read them. Fortunately, he had never told anyone where they were hidden. The area was under protection. Talin suspected its ancient safeguards were stronger than anything even Atrid could breach. It still seemed a miracle that he had been allowed to enter.

As he descended through the tunnels into the heart of Zed, Talin was certain he would be safe now, until he could figure out what to do next. Only when he had reached the deepest cavern, however, could he allow himself to relax. This was where he had found the Folios lying wrapped in their nest, undisturbed for centuries. Here, at last, he could allow himself to remember how he had read them with Ari, his daughter, bringing them one leaf at a time to the surface. He had carefully replaced them in their nest after reading them, sure that he could return to them whenever he wished, but there had been no time to rescue any before his abrupt abduction. All he had had on Mem was the vivid memory of each leaf, but he had totally forgotten the ways he had used them to prepare his child for her future.

Talin began to smile. He was finally safe enough to let memories of Ari return. What a miracle she was. She must be a young woman now. Was she truly alive? How had she escaped the holocaust?

"She lives." The words echoed and re-echoed like a joyous shout in his mind. Still retaining some of his caution, however, he tamped them down.

When he had slept and eaten just enough to give him a little more strength, he set out again, exploring first one then another of the many passageways that stretched out from the Folios' nest like spider legs. At last he found one that appeared to continue indefinitely. It felt like the right way, so he kept going, stopping only to sleep or to nibble at his food supplies, just enough to satisfy the worst of his hunger. He knew that time was passing, but he had to move with care in the utter darkness, keeping his hand on the wall and following it wherever it took him. Occasionally he came across a spring, and he stopped briefly to refill his water bag. Sometimes he entered caverns where dim light, teeming with dust motes, spilled down from an unknown source that seemed to be as far above him as another galaxy. Standing in one of these showers, he called Ari's name, using the Voice, then abruptly stopped. A digger might pick up the word and be led right to her. It was too dangerous.

He was absolutely certain that, someplace on Zed, Ari was alive. Atrid must not find her. He must find her first.

CHAPTER 28

Ari counted twenty days since they'd left the cliffs and entered the unrelenting desert. She knew her count was accurate, because Jonce had made a ceremony of marking his tak bone walking stick each night before they slept, one mark for each day.

Jonce, exhausted, stopped frequently to lean on his stick. Once, he managed to give Ari a crooked grin, rasping out between parched lips, "Know...what I...miss?"

She simply raised an eyebrow, too tired to speak.

"Birds," he croaked.

They had started playing this game while moving through the cliffs, before reaching the horrors of what Jonce called "the flatlands." When he had first mentioned birds, Ari had had no idea what he meant. Even in dreams she couldn't remember having seen such a creature. As far as she knew there were no birds on Zed. Jonce had spent days describing every bird of Mem: their plumage, their colors, their habits.

Back then they had been able to laugh, talk, even sing together. When Ari looked back on those carefree days she was struck by their contrast with the dreadful present. She wondered why she had ever felt led to this terrible trek. Could they possibly survive it?

Ari only shook her head in response to Jonce's attempts at levity now. Speaking took too much effort. It was obvious that he was trying to lift her spirits.

"Fine," she managed to grunt, trying to reassure him.

His face was a question.

"Fine," she stated again, knowing full well that neither of them could last much longer without replacing more of the liquid they'd lost to the heat.

Each day the desert heat was like fire. The nights brought bone-chilling cold. Huddling together to share whatever heat was left from the day's scorching, they fell into the depths of dreamless sleep. In what seemed only moments, the next day's sweltering heat woke them up again. Exhausted, they forced themselves to push on.

Struggling across the slippery extrine, Jonce fell and hurt his knee. Despite Ari's urging him to hurry, he moved more slowly.

"Oh, taks!" Ari swore. She was struggling too. "This is hopeless!"

It was clear to her that the only possibility for saving themselves was to keep moving toward the distant horizon. They had come too far to turn back.

The tasteless lichen that had sustained their energy was gone. Their tak skin water bags hung limp from their shoulders, each containing less than a cupful of precious water. Ari knew they could struggle on without food, but when their water was gone, their lives would go with it.

Each time she stopped to wait for Jonce, Ari tried to fall into meditation, to give herself some rest. Her pauses became longer and longer as her mind drifted.

Once she thought she saw Talin beckoning to her, another

time her mother. Finally she had a vision of Mag taking two walking sticks like the ones she and Jonce carried, sticking them into a crack in the ground and covering them with a tak skin, making a kind of lean-to shelter. Ari came out of her meditation, puzzling over the image.

"I'm in a dream," she thought. "This is not real."

As she watched Jonce approach, she could see visible waves of heat all around him. His face, half-hidden under the hood he wore for protection, went first scarlet, then ashen. His bright eyes had faded to a washed-out grey, their old sparkle gone. The thing that worried Ari most, however, was how gaunt he looked. He had opened his shirt. The bones of his chest stood out, looking as if they'd outgrown his withered skin.

"I must look the same," she thought, feeling under her shirt for her own rib cage.

As she continued to wait, she noticed something new. Fissures punctuated the surface of the extrine. Starting as tiny cracks, they widened and deepened as they extended forward in the direction she and Jonce were traveling. This gave her an idea. Couldn't a fissure guide them? For days now, changes in the light had been their only assurance that they weren't going in circles or retracing their steps. As she followed the longest crack with her eyes, she realized that with the little lights Jonce carried, they might use the cracks to travel by night. Then they could sleep through the heat of the day.

That night, after having borrowed one of Jonce's tiny lights, Ari persuaded him to follow the longest fissure with her. At the first sign of daylight, they used their capes and walking sticks to make a shelter, into which they fell, exhausted. When they wakened, it was night, and they started out once more, wearing their capes against the chill and leaning on their sticks.

By the next dawn, every drop of their water was gone. Again they slept. As black night fell and they were taking down their shelter, Ari looked up to see the unchanging grey cloud cover suddenly open. For one moment, she could see lights in the sky. She had seen them only once before in her life. Talin had told her that the lights were stars and were a message of hope from Star Woman.

As she looked up, Ari felt a thrill run down her spine. Surely Astraea was giving them her blessing, lighting their way.

"Come," she urged Jonce. "We need to go on."

He groaned, trying to fasten his cape.

Gathering their things, they began to stagger forward. Ari tried to hold the memory of the stars in her mind, but she found herself continually imagining both their bodies lying dead on the empty plain, the relentless wind blowing all the flesh from their bones.

It was only when Jonce spoke, breaking the silence, that Ari realized they were walking on opposite sides of a fissure. The crack was widening.

"Hey," was all Jonce managed to say, but it was enough to break the spell of her thoughts.

She reached out her arm to touch him and found that he was several feet away. After she had gone a little farther she realized that the crack had widened considerably, and if she didn't cross it immediately they would be irreparably separated.

Ari willed her legs to stumble over the gap. Once across, she clung to Jonce. They struggled on together. Jonce was first to fall; Ari was dragged down with him. Huddled on the extrine, they lay face down in a stupor. Ari wanted to comfort Jonce by telling him that at least they were dying together, but she couldn't rouse herself enough to speak. When she finally managed to pry her eyelids open, she realized she was lying face down above the fissure, looking into a deep space. For a moment she thought she smelled water far below, then she realized she was hallucinating. She knew they must move on. If they continued to lie here in a stupor they would both die.

Ari tried to get to her knees, but immediately the world began to tilt and spin. She found herself flattened on the surface again. All she wanted was sleep, but a voice in her head kept commanding her to stay awake. With her head hanging over the opening, she found herself imagining that she was hearing her own voice calling down into the crack, listening to it echo back as it fell far into the depths. She began to spin after it into the darkness below. Was this death?

She must have fainted, for the next thing she knew was a feeling of coolness, a splash, and a welcome wetness on her head. If this was death she would accept it gladly! Turning to face the wetness, she immediately woke up to the reality of water drops gently falling into her mouth! Sweet water!

A tiny voice, soft as a musical whisper, spoke so close it seemed to be inside her ear.

"Ah," it said softly. "We are in time. They live."

"Lucky she's an empath," a second little voice replied.

Ari opened her eyes, but all she could see above her was a faintly lit grey sky. It was dawn. Day was coming.

She tried to lift her head, but it was too heavy. Suddenly, just above her chin, a tiny face appeared. A body no larger than her thumb hovered in the air on whirring wings right before her eyes. Was this one of Jonce's birds? He had never told her they had human faces, or that they could mind speak her language!

Beside her, Jonce was moaning. When Ari turned her head she saw that another of the tiny creatures was with him. Was she dreaming? Were they both dead? She wanted to speak, but no words would come.

"Don't try to speak." The voice was inside her head. "Think your speech and we will hear."

Ari felt a great surge of emotion. The water the creatures had given her seemed to be turning to tears. Tiny drops wet her lashes, and more found their way into her mouth. The flavor was strange but delicious. She licked her lips and opened them for more.

"Sweet," she heard Jonce say.

"It is juice of a healing fruit," the second of the small voices said in her head.

Jonce must have heard the voice, too. "More," he begged.

"Wait," the voice twittered. "Let your strength grow. You must be able to move. Day has come."

Ari's body felt like a withered vine, all fiber and no life. She tried to imagine moisture infusing her, but even her blood seemed to have turned to ash in her veins.

"Can't." Jonce spoke aloud, his voice a rasp.

"Then you will die." The mental trill was soft, but firm.

Ari turned her head to see him, realizing how important he was to her. She could lie here and die, but Jonce must be saved. He must move. But how? These tiny beings could never carry him. She started to pour the little strength she had into him, imagining his blood beginning to pulse through his veins. As she did, she began to feel her own strength building. The little bird people were strengthening her even as she worked to save Jonce.

Soon Ari was able to move her legs, then her arms. At last she sat up. Finally she stood, looking down at Jonce as he, too, began to stir and come back to life.

She began to hear a hum in the air and to feel joy. If she had been able, she would have leapt up and danced. All she could manage were a few awkward steps. As she moved, the humming swelled. Suddenly, she and Jonce were surrounded by tiny beings who were herding them forward and down into the fissure. There was a chute! It was not unlike the one that spiraled and plummeted into her cavern at home. Ari let Jonce go first. This time he slid down in silence as she followed.

They emerged into a canyon. A shallow stream ran at their feet. Immediately they tumbled into it, letting its coolness flow over them. Only then did Ari realize that the landscape here was like that of her home compound. The cliffs were extrine, the water dark. How was it that the landscape of home was suddenly here, in the midst of the endless black desert they'd been crossing?

"Did we die?" she questioned again in her mind.

"No." The tiny voice was reassuring. "You have reached safety."

Soon they were shown to a dim cavern, where they were encouraged to sleep. When they awoke there was food, and more of the healing drops, which immediately made them sleepy. They slept again. Ari dreamed of conversations among the little bird people.

"We can't keep them here," a tiny voice protested. "We've done what the Alph asked. We've saved them."

"The Alph?" Ari thought, beginning to wake, but the words vanished from her mind before she could speak or puzzle over them, and she was back in her dream.

"But what can we do with them now?" the little bird voice was saying. "We can't just leave them here."

"We could take them to the shadow people, the hidden ones."

There was a long pause. Ari sensed fear, mixed with sorrow. Finally another little voice asked a hesitant question.

"Will the shadows help them?"

"We can only hope so. They have no more trust in humans than they do in us, but they can help them if they will. We're too small to protect these two. We either have to abandon them or take them deeper into the Shadow lands. They are not safe here. Their own people hunt them, and they are in serious danger if they are caught. The Evil Queen will destroy them."

"We promised the Alph we'd save them. We must do what we can."

Upon waking, Ari's mind was filled with questions. "Who are the shadow people? And why is the Evil Queen searching for us?"

As if they had heard her thoughts, the bird people began to twitter and fuss.

"She hears us!" one exclaimed.

Instantly there was silence, but when the discussion eventually resumed, Ari could hear distress in their voices. She wondered about the shadows. Why did they arouse such distress in the tiny bird people?

"They must choose to go," a new voice twittered. "We cannot make the decision for them."

After much humming and fluttering, an agreement was reached. Ari and Jonce were given a liquid that strengthened them and lifted their spirits. When they had foraged some lichen from the banks of the stream, they were told by the birds that their only hope was to go into the depths of the planet, where beings known to the tiny ones as the "shadow people" resided.

"It will not be easy," a voice that Ari could now identify as the leader's spoke in her head. "It is a dark region filled with dark forces. Most of the shadow people are good, but others are full of hate."

"And if we don't go?" Ari asked.

"Eventually those who seek you will come. None of us wish that. We are here because the Alph sent a dream to us, asking us to rescue you. Now we must leave. If Mem's Queen finds us, she will capture us and we will die."

"And if she finds you she will..." another twitter began, but it was abruptly cut off by a flapping of wings.

The leader's tiny voice spoke again, sweet, but firm. "You really have no choice. If you stay here we must abandon you. If you agree, we will take you, but it is a perilous journey for us and must be done quickly. We must not be seen by the shadows, especially in their tunnels."

Without hesitation both Ari and Jonce nodded their agreement. They would go. With the bird people flying around them, showing them the way and urging haste, they followed the stream into a side canyon and through an opening. The path took them into the depths of the planet, going down and down a gradual slope through cool caverns of black extrine, some containing great pools of water, others resembling ornate throne rooms. All the while, the bird people continued to herd them rapidly forward, as if time were short.

"Don't dawdle," Ari heard them say in her mind. "There is still a long way to go."

Ari's curiosity kept slowing her steps, as she tried to take in the strange landscape. Finally, Jonce took her arm and began pulling her along, in obedience to the birds' pleas for haste.

After a long time, they emerged from a tunnel into a cavern. The energy here was completely different from anything they'd experienced before. The pulse of the planet beat in this place as if it were a heart chamber belonging to gigantic beings. Ari turned to Jonce, her eyes wide with wonder. He appeared to be listening so intently that he hardly noticed her standing beside him.

As their bird escorts prepared to leave, they caroled, "Wait here. The shadow people are near. Hopefully they will help you." Forming a "v" shape, they soared back into the passageway through which they had come. In an instant, they were gone. Ari could feel their desperation to be away.

"I wonder what frightens them so much? Is it the Evil Queen, or the shadow people?" she asked aloud.

Jonce didn't reply. He stood absolutely still, frozen to the spot.

Ari tried to conquer her fear, but she knew, just as Jonce did, that they had been abandoned, with no idea how to either return or go forward. Taking his arm, she clung to him, feeling his fear as well as her own. The booming sound in the cavern grew louder, until the walls were shaking. There was no place to run, no place to hide. Was the whole planet about to explode?

"What's happening?" Jonce asked in a shaking voice.

Ari could barely answer. The whole cavern seemed filled with cold terror.

"Something is coming." She managed to choke out the words.

Jonce's hand tightened on her arm. He pulled her closer, as if to protect her. "Why did the bird people leave?" he asked.

"They were terrified."

"They abandoned us."

"Yes. They had to. They don't belong here."

Suddenly, all sound stopped. The silence was even more terrifying than the deafening beats. Ari felt her mind filling with a dark invisible presence. It pressed in on her, tormenting her. Frantically, she clung to Jonce, only to realize that he was having the same feelings. Terror had arrived.

CHAPTER 29

As soon as she was told of Talin's disappearance, Atrid realized that she had no time for displays of temper or punishments. Talin must be found quickly. He was her only hope of finding what she sought. Her obsession with her ship, her extravagant spending on its creation and her decision to turn Mem over to others as she traveled across the Galaxy had all brought her to this point. She could not let him ruin it.

Suddenly one of her Inner voices spoke to her, "Or he will destroy us!"

"Hurry," Atrid instructed her captain. "Gather everyone. The search must begin immediately."

Pacing as she waited, she tried to imagine where Talin had gone. Obviously he had planned all along to get away from her. He must be determined to escape her surveillance, but where could he hide in this forsaken landscape?

"What's taking so long?" she fumed as she paced. "Don't the men realize that time is against us?"

Her guard-mages were the first to appear. They were a bit disheveled, looking as if they had just tumbled out of their bunks.

"Listen to me." Atrid's voice was harsh. "Thanks to your ineptitude Talin has escaped. It is imperative that he be found!"

The mages glanced at one another, bewildered. What was the crisis? Talin had kept to himself in his cabin, useless to anyone on the trip across from Mem. Why the rush now?

Atrid grimaced at their stupidity, then barked her orders. "Get yourselves awake," she commanded. "And use your powers to relay an urgent message to Mem. Tell them to send another legion of guards immediately."

The mages looked puzzled.

"Talin has become a danger to us all," she told them. "He plots against me, against all of us." She paused. "May I remind you that he knows this planet well. If there are any places to hide, he knows them. He must be found at all costs. I, your Queen, command this. Do you understand me?"

Furious at their continued lethargy, Atrid glared at them.

"Oh, damnation," she thought. "What has happened to my mages?" In the old days, when she had changed this planet, her guard-mages had been brilliant. Often they had known her needs before she had. Now, the mages were nothing but simpletons, for whom she had to spell out each command.

Impatiently waving her hand, she sent them on their way. There was no time to explain. They didn't have enough intuition to begin to understand, and she knew that they obeyed only because they feared the consequences of failure. Let them go. She needed to focus on organizing her digger-mages to once again sweep every inch of the nearby area.

Would they do any better?

"You missed something," she scolded the group when they had gathered. "There has to be a clue. Even Talin with all his skill is not invisible."

Like the guards, the diggers looked exhausted and bedraggled.

"Great Queen, this is a terrible place," their leader dared to say. "All of us have been on duty for twenty-four hours straight. We've had no sleep. Perhaps we could be excused from the hunt long enough to..."

With one look Atrid silenced him. Such insubordination!

"There will be no rest for any of us until Talin is found," she told them all through clenched teeth. "When you find him..." She paused. "...And you will find him!" she emphasized, glaring at them. "Remember too that he is also a digger. Be careful to have your barriers in place to keep him out. Remain hidden. He must not guess we're on to him. Instead, trail him. Find out where he's headed and what he's up to, then send a message back to me."

The men went off obediently. Some grumbled in whispers. They knew it wasn't safe to complain. There would be no rest for anyone until Talin was spotted. The sooner they got this over with, the sooner they could topple into their bunks.

Atrid joined one of the teams that was scouring the area adjacent to the landing pad. It was she who discovered the opening high in the wall beyond the back curve of the old supply cavern.

"How could you have missed it?" Her voice was icy.

Obviously Talin had left it warded against everyone except her. He had never been able to keep her out! The moment reminded her of a time long ago, when the two had often played a game with each other, trying to break each other's wards. Now Atrid smiled a tiny grimace of satisfaction. He must have known she would find the opening eventually, no matter how much time he wasted protecting it. He knew her strengths well. And she knew his. Suddenly she felt like a player in a war game. The hunter and the hunted. Was this their old game? It almost made her smile.

Atrid waited impatiently while her men, one after another, slid down through the opening into the cavern below. By the time they returned they looked half-drowned. They reported finding only a huge space that contained a few meager old supplies. Her temper reached an explosion point. Crossing her arms and tapping her foot, she waited for the leader's report.

"There's nothing of significance," he told her wearily. "Just some old objects that show that the space was used a long time ago."

What, then, had taken them so long?

Slowly the leader explained that they had had trouble finding an exit, until they realized that the only way out was through a pool of water. One of the group had struck his head on an overhang as he swam, and had been saved from drowning only because his friends had managed to yank him out while a swift current tried to sweep his body downstream. If Talin had come this way, he had left no sign, either in the cavern or beyond. No blood, no footprints, no trail. The black glass rim of the river showed no evidence of his passage. Nevertheless, three diggers had been directed to follow the murky stream as far as they could, just in case he had gone that way.

Muttering to herself about the hazards of incompetence, Atrid spun on her heel and stormed back into the rocket, slamming the hatch door after herself. Her men had not been dismissed. They continued to stand, shifting from one foot to the other. They tried to rest in place. Not one thought of bolting. They knew their Queen's temper too well.

At the end of the day the three who had gone downstream returned.

"We're sorry, Ma'am," one of them reported, shamefaced. "We didn't find the slightest whiff of him."

Another spoke up. "Or, for that matter, any other living thing."

It seemed that Talin had evaporated into thin air.

"He must have used his mage skills to hide his trail," the first digger continued. "It's as if he vanished without a trace. He obviously knows how to hide, even from us."

Atrid strode about, her anger mounting. How could she expect to find him when her guards and diggers were so incompetent? Calling the mages again, she commanded them to resume the search.

"But we found nothing," one of them said.

"I think this planet has addled your brains," Atrid stormed. "You are all worse than a bunch of schoolchildren. Not one of you has the ability of a gnat."

The mage named Caz spoke up then. "It is not our lack of skill," he told her. "It is Talin's superior ability."

Atrid knew he spoke the truth. Caz was the grandson of Talin's oldest friend. He had grown up hearing tales of Talin's prowess. Though he was a digger mage, he had chosen to be Talin's caretaker and servant when the old man returned from Zed. Atrid knew they had become close friends. Caz had cared for him all through his illness. Surely he, of all people, had first-hand knowledge of how Talin's mind worked. If anyone could discover Talin's whereabouts, it would be this young mage. He might succeed where others had failed so miserably.

"Take me into this underground place," Atrid ordered after she had pondered his words. "I will do the digging myself, and Caz will help me." She turned to the others. "I know there's something you missed. You will follow us down."

At first there were objections. The mages tried to tell her how dangerous the exit was.

"It's the only way out," Caz warned her, the others loudly agreeing.

Atrid scoffed at their fears, calling them cowards and fools. They followed her obediently as she strode toward the supply cavern. Caz climbed through the opening first, then Atrid. The others followed. One by one, they slid down the spiral into the cavernous space below.

Atrid was immediately struck by the energy of the place. It had been used in some sanctified way over a long period of time. Sniffing the air, she was certain Talin had been here before. She could detect his lingering aroma.

And there was something else! Or was it someone else she sensed? A surge of expectation flooded her as she began to explore the cavern.

Was this where she would find the Secret?

Atrid thought the ledges were empty, until she reached one where something had been tucked away under a protruding slab of extrine. Reaching into the space, she retrieved a nest-like structure, about the size of a cradle. Slowly she inspected it, then held it to her breast, mimicking what she had often seen mothers do as they comforted their fretful children. Immediately feeling disgust, she thrust the thing back under its eave. There had never been a child in need of comfort on Zed. She had seen to that. Probably the thing had been an animal's nest. Perhaps a container for the young of the black serpents.

Though she found nothing more, Atrid couldn't rid herself of the feeling that she was missing something. She tried to banish the thought as she finished her inspection and swam out of the cavern with the others, feeling impatient at their instructions to dive deep and only surface when she was on the other side of a giant overhang. She was a strong swimmer and had no trouble staying underwater as the current carried her. It was exhilarating to be flushed out of the cave in this fashion. For a moment she let that feeling stay with her, and then she turned her mind back to something that had eluded her in the cave. A wisp of awareness flitted just outside her full consciousness. She kept shaking her head as she climbed back up to the spaceship, trying to get her thoughts in order. By the time she reached camp she was in a foul mood again. She began to berate her troops.

"You'd better find Talin soon," she threatened, "or someone is going to suffer!"

That night she had one of her hated dreams. In her dream, the nest from the cavern had become a coracle, a small lidded boat. As she opened it and looked inside, Atrid saw a sleeping baby, with silver hair streaked with copper and gold spread like an aureole around its head. Staring, Atrid realized that she was looking into her own face! Instantly she awoke, gasping for breath, feeling as if she were inside that lidded basket, suffocating. It was several minutes before she could calm herself and begin to breathe normally again.

"Am I going mad?" she asked herself.

The dreams didn't stop. When she slept again she dreamed that the coracle was beside her, closed, as she squatted on the black floor of the supply cavern. Slowly, tentatively, she began to open it, knowing this was forbidden but determined to satisfy her curiosity. As she did, she kept scanning the space to see if anyone was watching her. All she could see were great shadows on the walls. She finally lifted the lid, and immediately jumped to her feet, recoiling in horror. Exploding from the coracle was a host of inhuman black shapes, both large and small, spewing terrible guttural sounds. They were neither alive nor dead. Immediately they were all over her, diving at her like birds, nesting in her hair, swarming on her skin, trying to get into her as if in a meld. Atrid cried out and awoke, bathed in sweat, shaking with fear and nausea, her heart beating wildly. She had banned dreams. Why then was she dreaming?

Sitting upright in her bed, she fought sleep until dawn.

At daylight she ordered the nest to be brought out of the cave and burned. While it was burning, she summoned one of the pods from her own spaceship, one that had been designed to go long distances without refueling. Aside from the pod's pilot, she allowed only Caz to accompany her.

"If we find Talin, we won't land or try to intercept him," Atrid instructed. "We will simply order more troops to converge on the route he is taking, and then lie in wait for him until we can trail him to wherever he's headed."

Though they flew from dawn to dark for three days straight, they found no sign of the missing mage. After searching endless cliffs and high black mesas, they reached an open, barren desert of flat extrine, where there was no sign of life. Finally they returned to the spaceship, defeated.

"Could he have traveled underground?" Caz asked, sounding exhausted. At first Atrid dismissed the idea. When Caz brought it up again, however, she took the time to rethink her earlier response. Without a single sign of Talin on the surface, where else could he have gone?

"Where would he have gone underground?" she asked, tilting her head as she waited for an answer.

"There must have been a place other than the supply cavern," Caz replied. "The young guards found many small caves as they searched. Perhaps they missed one that leads to a hidden underground area."

"How could they have missed one?" Atrid bit her lip in frustration. "They were trained to search. None of them found a way under the surface of the planet, except for the small caves where serpents nest. We closed every orifice at the time of the Change."

"But there was a large cave only you could find. The diggers missed that," Caz reminded her, referring to the supply cavern.

"What if there are more, under the same protection?"

"You're right," Atrid agreed. "It would take a spell far stronger than anything Talin could conjure to repel me." She was sure of this. She knew all of Talin's spells.

"Where did Talin find the Folios he kept talking about?" Caz raised this touchy subject with caution. "I seem to remember Talin saying he'd found them hidden in the depths of Zed. Has anyone discovered their whereabouts?" He stood before Atrid with downcast eyes, submissively waiting for her response.

"Oh, those damned Folios!" she scoffed. "Who cares about them? They were just the fantastic ravings of a crazy old man."

"Suppose they were more than that," Caz dared to say, lifting his head to look into her eyes. "Suppose they were real, and had been hidden in a place under such strong protection that Talin knew it would give him sanctuary if he went there again?"

Atrid glared at him. Turning, she began to pace. "They can't be real," she muttered.

Two days later, some of her best diggers returned, reporting that they had discovered a hidden opening under a waterfall in one of the cliffs farther downriver. Entering, they had found a crawl space that had widened and taken them a long way into the planet. However, something invisible had brought them to an abrupt halt. No matter how they tried, they had found no way past the barrier. Atrid sent more diggers, but they returned to confess the same failure. The barrier was unlike anything they'd ever known. They had neither skills nor spells to breach it.

"It seems I have to do everything myself!" Atrid stormed.

"Come, Caz, we will see what can be done."

This time she took her guards with her as well. As soon as she crawled into the cave, Atrid was sure she sensed a whiff of Talin. Positive that he had come this way, she eagerly led the others forward. They had walked quite a distance through a wide tunnel before they reached the barrier. At first it was invisible, but as soon as Atrid waved her hand its form was revealed: a gigantic white web of gossamer threads that covered the passageway from wall to wall and floor to ceiling. Atrid put out her finger to touch it, and immediately recoiled from the shock. Her finger turned red and began to swell. Caz took her hand in his and tried to heal it.

"I feel that we should send the others back," he told her softly. "There are too many of us here. Perhaps just you and I could stay?"

Atrid looked at him, puzzled. Was he about to betray her? Why else would he want to be alone with her? She tried to enter his mind and ascertain his intention, but he had defended himself against her.

"I have the intuition," he explained calmly, "that the wards are set against anyone who is not an advanced mage. Order your guards back, my Queen, and see whether or not I am correct."

Reluctantly, Atrid ordered the others to return to the entry and wait for her there. As soon as they were gone, Caz moved forward and knelt before the force field. He looked like he was praying. It had been a long time since Atrid had prayed. Declaring herself Astraea had made her a goddess, and prayers had become unnecessary. She stood back, unsure of what to do next, until Caz motioned her to his side.

"It will take the prayers of both of us," he told her. "Yours especially."

"Let us through," Atrid commanded the barrier. "We must find Talin."

She seemed to hear a voice in her head that asked, "What will you offer in payment?"

Atrid felt a flow of determination surge up her spine. Leaning forward, she opened her mouth to speak. Instantly Caz's hand was on her arm, restraining her. "Don't!" he commanded.

She turned in astonishment to look at him. He was commanding her? She turned back to face the web, feeling her anger increase her power.

"I am Atrid," she mind-spoke. "Queen of thirty-seven planets, ruler of galaxies. I am Astraea, Star Woman of ancient tales. No web commands me. I command you to open."

"And what do you offer in return?"

Atrid jumped to her feet, her mind blazing. "It was I who changed this planet into Zed. I do not bargain. You will treat me with respect. My command is all you will get from me."

"If your command is what you offer, oh Queen, we accept."

Instantly the web fell.

Atrid strode forward. Caz followed, fussing over the promise she had made. Immediately the web closed again behind them. Atrid could feel the vibration of its recovery as she led the way down a new passage, a tunnel where they could walk erect. Caz was still muttering about her having paid too high a price. Was he crazy? She had paid no price at all. Rather, she had simply demanded her right to pass. Whatever force maintained the web had capitulated to her command.

Soon they came to a branching. The tunnel on the left was narrow and dark and led downward. The tunnel to the right was wider. There she and Caz could walk side by side. The right-hand tunnel seemed like the obviously superior choice, though Caz wanted to go the narrower way. It seemed safer to Atrid to have Caz at her side rather than behind her. His response at the web had made her distrust him. Why had he wanted to stop her from using her power to force entry? Such insolence! How could he possibly think she had paid too high a price?

The wide tunnel gave them unobstructed passage. Also, some kind of light source gave them enough vision to see a few feet ahead at all times, so that they were able to move rapidly forward. Only when they stopped at a spring to drink and rest, and eat a bit of the rations they had brought with them, was Atrid aware of shadows on the walls.

"Don't you think it's strange that shadows are accompanying us?" Caz asked.

"I think your imagination is working overtime," Atrid scoffed, but she began to watch the walls more closely as she and Caz moved on. Surely it was a trick of the light, an illusion created by their own shadows, thrown onto the shining black, that gave the appearance of movement.

When they tired, they stopped and slept, each of them rolled in the warmth of the bags they had brought with them from the ship.

This time Atrid had no dreams, though when they woke Caz complained wearily that he had dreamed of shadow beings trying to redirect them from the way they were taking. Atrid ignored him.

At the end of a second long trek they slept again. Atrid dreamed once more of opening the coracle and inadvertently releasing from it all the ills of the galaxy. Upon waking, she could hardly make herself get up and move. She felt angry at Caz and angry at herself, and to force her feet to keep going she had to repeat like a mantra. her litany of power. Was she only imagining that the hard black surface was getting more and more slippery as they continued?

She must find Talin. She must have the Secret. She insisted on taking the lead, despite the protests of Caz. She decided to ignore his repeated warnings that the shadows were increasing in number and size. He was being paranoid. Even if they truly existed, what harm could a shadow possibly do?

CHAPTER 30

The sudden silence sent a frightened shiver through Ari's body. She could feel a threatening emptiness pressing in upon her. It reminded her of Talin's description of the mind probing that was done by the diggers on Mem. Were she and Jonce being probed? She tried to shield her mind, but discovered to her surprise that she couldn't.

"Why does she struggle to keep us out?" A deep voice, soft as fingers brushing skin, sounded in her head. "Doesn't she know it's impossible?"

A drumming was going on in her mind! She was frozen into immobility, held fast by fear. Her ears heard no sound, yet her mind seemed to be receiving rhythmic speech. Was she going mad? Only her eyes were able to move, but all she could see were enormous walls that shifted and changed and seemed to shimmer as she looked at them. Was it a trick of the light that made her think she was seeing huge shadows there?

As she looked, the shadows began to grow. Soon they were enormous shapes on the cavern walls, grey against the black extrine. She knew about shadows. In her hut back home she had sometimes seen her own shadow cast on the tak skin wall. But what could be throwing such large shadows here? There were no solid forms present, except for herself and Jonce. He was tall, but even he was too small to cast such a large shadow. The cavern walls were at least as tall as one of the high cliffs back at the compound, yet the grey she was seeing towered along them from floor to ceiling.

The more she stared, the clearer the huge shadow forms became. They hovered like great monsters examining their prey. Ari sank to her knees and covered her eyes, shaking with fear.

"She sees us!" The drumming in her mind was filled with surprise. She was astonished to realize she could understand its meaning.

At once the cavern began to boom with the drum sounds. The shadows were yelling! The first drum sounds she had heard, back when the Bird People had left, had been steady as heartbeats. Now there was a cacophony of beats and tones, as if the drum voices were tumbling and thrumming over one another, until the noise became like the roar of a rockslide, with the voices crashing and crushing one another, pounding into her mind.

"Stop!" she cried out, covering her ears with her hands as if to shut out the invasion. "Oh, please, stop."

Abruptly there was utter silence. The shadows on the walls had gone completely still.

After a few moments, a tiny beat came into Ari's mind like a whisper, soft enough for her to understand the words.

"She hears us!"

"How can it be? What is she?"

"Let her speak. Perhaps she can tell us." This drum voice spoke firmly, with authority.

Again there was silence, now filled with anticipation. They were waiting for her to respond.

Ari cleared her throat, hoping to relieve its constriction. Could she speak? Would they understand her language, or must she think in their drum speech?

Hesitantly she began to imagine drumbeats in her mind, beats that said, "I am Ari. I am a human who was born on this planet." The silence continued, but now it was filled with puzzlement. The shadows seemed to be thrusting themselves out from the walls, attempting to surround the spot where she and Jonce stood.

"There has been no birth on this planet since the Change."

Ari formed an image in her mind of the tiny Bird People. Surely they gave birth.

"They are not born here," she was told. "They come from another dimension. They don't belong here."

"And all of you?" Ari asked. "Do you belong here? Are you born here?"

"Not anymore. Not since The Change."

"What does that mean?" Ari wondered, forgetting that they could hear her thoughts.

The drumming replied. "We are Shadows of who we were. Because we are no longer real we cannot fully live or die. We cannot be born anew."

Ari could feel their presence all around her. In some she felt a sweetness. Others had strange thoughts that filled her with terror. Wanting to make them more real, she reached out to them, trying to give them living shape, but no matter how she tried, she could see nothing but gigantic shadows.

Just then, Jonce spoke, for the first time since their arrival. His voice sounded as if he were slowly coming out of a trance.

"It's so quiet in here," he whispered. "It feels so empty, as if we're waiting for a catastrophe to happen. Do you suppose they'll ever come?"

Ari realized that he wasn't sensing the Shadows.

"No," an authoritative voice in her mind stated. "He cannot. We are astonished that you are able to perceive us. We try to remain invisible."

Ari put her hand on Jonce's arm. "The shadow people are here," she told him. "If you look carefully at the walls you will see them."

Jonce was staring at the walls. "They're here?"

"Yes," Ari answered. "I've been having a conversation with them. They're trying to figure out who we are and what we're doing here."

"You can hear them?"

"Can't you hear them?" she asked.

Jonce tilted his head and seemed to listen. Suddenly, the booming resumed, increasing until the whole cavern seemed to reverberate with sound.

"I only hear drums," Jonce said. "And all I can feel is sadness...and hate! We should leave, Ari. It's not safe."

Ari felt dizzy as drum words flooded her mind. She grabbed Jonce's arm and hung on, as if once more he might save her.

There was renewed activity on the walls.

"They're probing us," Ari said. "And putting pictures into my mind. Oh, Jonce, I don't understand what's happening. I'm seeing a memory of when I was a little girl and thought I was talking to Beings in the cliffs. I told you about it. I thought they taught me about rainbows, until Talin told me I was imagining them."

"I remember." Jonce's voice was bewildered. "But why are you wasting time on that? We need to get out of here!"

The drum voices were still booming. Ari put both hands on her head, trying to hold it steady as the beating exclaimed, "Ari has known our Others! They chose her!"

"Too loud," Ari protested. "My head won't stand it."

The noise immediately quieted, swirling gently down around her. Ari could feel the shadows' excitement and curiosity. At the same time, she saw herself as a child, sitting with the cliffs as rain fell down their faces like tears.

"They are our lost ones, our Others, caught in the planet's Change, trapped because they refused to flee. You spoke with them. What can you tell us of their fate?"

As if she were her child self again, standing below the cliffs, Ari felt the profound sadness of those great beings. It was as if she had opened a secret cavern within herself that still contained all the emotions she had shared with the cliffs. They had wept, sharing their loneliness and despair with her, a lonely little girl who thought perhaps she wasn't real. She felt old tears well up as she remembered.

"They were so lonely," she softly drummed. "I was lonely, too. They were my friends. They cared. We cried together."

Once more the drumming became a torrent of sound that filled the cavern. "She wept with them," the drums declared. "She shared their tears!"

Ari could feel their astonishment. "Yes," she mind-drummed back, "I thought they were alive, and they talked to me."

"They exist!"

The sound was intense. Ari could feel the joy in it, as if the warmth of the cliffs were wrapping around her once more.

She turned to share the joy with Jonce, and realized that he was still determined to leave.

"The whole place is throbbing," he told her. "Ari, I think there's going to be an earthquake! We need to get out of here. The walls are about to cave in on us!"

"What is this?" an angry drum voice boomed. "What is he saying?"

"He is my friend."

"He is from Queen Atrid!" The words were like a rat-a-tat in her brain. "He is the enemy!"

The voices' sudden change to intense anger frightened her. She grabbed Jonce and pulled him closer. They must protect each other.

"He is my friend," she repeated, before thinking of a better way to explain it so that they would understand. "My Other!" she exclaimed.

Jonce was trying to pull her away. "Please, Ari, we must run. There's going to be a landslide. We'll be killed."

"It's not a landslide," she told him. "What you hear is the speech of the shadows. They're upset because they think you are their enemy."

"Not you?"

"They know me."

"How come?"

"Because I knew their Others when I was a child. Do you remember, Jonce, I told you about my fantasy of the cliffs when I was small?"

"But that was just foolishness," he replied, his voice certain.

"No, they were real! The shadows say the cliff beings were their 'Others,' those who stayed behind when Atrid and her mages made the Change. They were mostly women and children and were trapped in the cliffs because they wouldn't flee. The ones here went into the tunnels and were turned to shadows. The drumming is their speech. They've been asking me to tell them what I know of their lost ones."

The drums were slow now.

"It sounds like a dirge in my head," Jonce complained.

"Yes, they are sad. After all this time they still grieve. Some blame you because you are Memmian and look like one of the Queen's guards."

Jonce protested. "But I wasn't even born when Atrid changed Zetti into Zed!" he exclaimed, flinging his hands down, before swiftly putting them back over his ears again.

"It hurts!" he complained. "You tell me that terrible noise is talk? Ari, that's crazy! We need to get out of here. The walls are booming. There's going to be a landslide. If we stay it's going to bury us!" He grabbed Ari's hand and tried to run.

Abruptly there was no sound. It was as if the cavern had

suddenly emptied. Had the shadows abandoned them? Ari cried out, "Don't go! We need your help!"

"Come on," Jonce yelled, pulling at her. "This is a terrible place. Hurry!"

Turning to Jonce, Ari tried to calm her voice. "No, Jonce, we have to stay. There truly are real shadow beings here and we need them."

He looked at her as if she had gone mad. "Beings?" he questioned. "Ari, there's nobody here but us, and we're in danger if we stay. Come on!"

Ari grabbed his arm and gave it a shake. "Stop it, Jonce," she commanded. "Just because you haven't eyes to see them and can't modulate your mind to understand their drum speech doesn't mean you can deny them. I tell you, these shadows are powerful and we need their help! Please tell them you're sorry for doubting them. The drumming you hear is their only language now. Try to listen!" She turned Jonce to face the wall, hoping he might see the shadows there.

"You want me to listen to a wall?"

"Yes, to the shadows there. Right now, or we're in big trouble. You need to apologize to them for doubting them, and you need to do it immediately, before they leave us."

"Uh...I'm sor...Oh Ari, I can't do it."

The shadow voices began to sound again, this time more softly.

"He is young," said a drumming. "She is an old soul, but he is a fledgling. We are searching him. So far we find no harm."

The soft drumming continued, as if in affirmation of what had been said. Jonce held out his hands, palms up, as if making an offering. "I didn't mean to insult you," he said, still looking bewildered.

Suddenly, there was great movement on the walls, and with it a feeling of shock, like a wind blowing through the space. Ari heard something like gasping. Could it be that the shadows were gasping in surprise? But if so, what could have astonished them?

"The boy is Las!" She understood the drum words, but what did they mean?

"No," another drumming corrected angrily. "He is human!"

"He carries strong strings of the Las," the first voice insisted.

"And Mem." This drum voice was louder, more emphatic. "He is Memmian and a servant of Atrid."

"But the Las is strong in him!"

Ari knew from the Folios that the Las were progenitors, the original Shapers. Everything they touched had blossomed into beauty. Like the Nus, the Las had disappeared many centuries ago. Why would anyone think Jonce was Las?

The drum voices grew louder still. Some sounded furious, while others kept drumming that the boy carried 'strings of the Las.' The angry voices boomed back that this was impossible.

Ari was puzzled. She knew that the Las had been giants, twelve feet tall. Did the shadows mistake Jonce for Las because he was unusually tall? But his height was only half of twelve feet! They must be mistaken. She kept trying to follow the drum conversation, even as she wondered what it meant. What else were they saying?

The noise continued. One voice was clearer than the rest.

"I have scanned them both," it drummed. "Ari is special. She is a Dreamer and a Shaper. But the boy has a Las ancestor." Suddenly the drum rattled, as if expressing shock. "They are both direct descendants of Astraea! He is one of our own! And so is she!"

Could Mem's original goddess from the stars, Astraea, truly have been Las? Was that who they were talking about? Ari gave her head a quick shake, trying to get her thoughts straight.
Suddenly clashing drum sounds began to fill the cavern. They sounded as if they were having an argument.

"That is impossible! Astraea never coupled with a human."
"How else can you explain the fact that they are definitely Las as well as human? They are our kin!"

The drumbeats seemed to echo and re-echo, like thunder shaking the walls.

"Our kin...kin...ours...our kin."

Some voices were filled with joy. The majority sounded furious.

"Kin?" Ari thought. "What do they mean? If we are Las as well as human, and kin to the shadows, could it be that these shadows think they are descendants of the long-lost Las?" She shook her head, as if to rid herself of this crazy notion.

"Ari," Jonce exclaimed, "I think I see the shadows! Oh, Ari, they're gigantic. Why can't I understand them? I feel as though I should be able to, but I can't."

Suddenly he seemed to panic. "Oh, they're moving toward a tunnel." Jonce's voice cracked. "Why are they moving? Something is happening. Are they leaving us? Oh, why can't I understand?"

"I don't know," Ari replied, "but I do know that we need to go with them. We can't stay here." She too saw that the shadows were on the move.

"Come!" commanded a drum voice that Ari had already identified as belonging to the shadow leader. "Hurry, there is no time to linger. Atrid's troops have found the tunnels."

The shadow forms were rapidly vanishing. Ari and Jonce ran to catch up with them. A single drumbeat kept all of them moving at a very fast pace.

Breathless, Ari's mind drummed out, "Where are we going? Why must we hurry?"

The drum voice that answered was again that of the shadow leader. "Finding you, the Alph have found us. Now they ask that we promise to lead you to safety."

"The Alph?" Ari was astonished. "They know we're here?"

"Yes. The Alph tell us that a ship has arrived from Mem and sits in your old compound. Queen Atrid is searching for what she calls the Secret. The Alph say that you are that secret and that her intentions toward you will not be good. Your only chance for safety is to come with us and do it quickly." He added, "Try to keep up."

It wasn't long before Ari realized that some of the shadow beings were slowing their movement so that she and Jonce could stay with them. Periodically, they stopped to rest. Ari knew they did not do this because the shadows needed a break. They were obviously tireless. She and Jonce were the only ones who were staggering with thirst and exhaustion.

At one point, they paused at a place where cold, refreshing ice water fell from a rock wall into a tiny pool. The youngsters were given time to drink their fill. As they did, the leader spoke to them again. "We still have a distance to go," he said.

"Where are you taking us?" Ari asked.

"We are taking you to a place no human has ever seen. We are taking you to our Home, the only place where you will be safe. We do this at great risk to ourselves. You could betray us, but we must take that chance. We have promised the Alph that we will save you."

For a few moments there was silence, as they rested beside the small spring.

"We ask you both to take a vow that you will never reveal our whereabouts. If you agree, you must swear on the sacred water in this pool."

An image came into Ari's mind of her hands clasped together, index fingers pointing so they would fit into the tiny pool. She showed Jonce how to make the gesture, and together they let their hands enter the water. Prepared for icy cold, they recoiled in shock.

The water was burning hot! Gazing down into the depths, Ari saw molten fire. Her hands were burning.

She had to struggle to keep them steady. "I swear," she promised. Then she told Jonce what was being demanded, and he swore, too.

After lifting their hands out of the pool, they both stood. They stared at their hands, expecting them to be scalded, even stripped of skin. The burning sensation continued, until they each spontaneously plunged their hands into the icy water that was pouring down the wall. The burning stopped.

"It will start again and destroy you if you betray us," Ari heard in her mind. As she turned to tell this to Jonce, she saw a look of wonder on his face.

"I know." He looked down at his hands, turning them over and over. His voice trembled. "I heard." Looking up, he stared at Ari as if he had just seen a miracle. "They say I am one of them. Ari, am I turning into a shadow?"

Ari shook her head impatiently. "I don't think so, Jonce. Maybe it's just because you're very tall for a human and because you have silver hair. They seem to think we are Las, and that they are, too. But how could we be? The Las have been gone for centuries."

The shadows began to move forward once more, flowing easily through a new tunnel.

"We are what is left of the Las," the leader voice drummed beside Ari. "Since the Change of Zetti to Zed, we have been shadows. No one recognizes us, therefore no human knows we still exist...until now."

Ari turned to reassure Jonce, but before she could speak, a new voice sounded, drumming with urgency.

"Come," it insisted. "Don't delay. We are almost there."

CHAPTER 31

The home of the shadow people was a vast network of burrows, an underground city. Jonce, holding his nose against the musty smell, described the place as "prison holes where they live like bats in the dark." However, the area where he and Ari were held was more like twilight than utter darkness.

"I think I might like the dark better," Jonce complained. "This light seems too artificial. It's unnatural. I can't imagine where it comes from."

"Don't complain," Ari chided. "It's a kindness that they've given us some light."

They had been given adjoining cells on a curving corridor. As their eyes adjusted to the dimness they became proficient at moving around, but they soon realized they were confined to the immediate area by the shapeless grey ghosts who constantly hovered nearby.

"It's hard to count the time," Ari complained. "The light never changes. I have a hard time remembering whether we're eating breakfast or dinner."

Each day food was left for them. It tasted good, but looked colorless and unappealing. At first Jonce refused it, remembering old tales of the dangers of eating food that was offered in the underworld. Ari had no such compunctions. While Jonce viewed their rescuers as captors, she was determined to see them as hosts. Eventually she convinced him to eat.

Often they were visited by the Shadow Leader, who came each day to instruct and encourage them. Though Ari could hear his drum voice more and more clearly as time went on, she saw him only as a shadow. Jonce, on the other hand, saw what he described as "the old one" in his dreams.

"What does he look like?" Ari asked.

"He is very tall, more than twice my height. I've always been considered unusual because of my height, yet I feel like a dwarf beside him. I keep wondering why I dream of him! On Mem dreams are forbidden."

"I know," Ari agreed. "Along with old rituals. They've never been forbidden on Zed. I've dreamed all my life and I've sung more Survivors to the Land Beyond the Stars than I can count."

"Atrid calls all of that abomination," Jonce replied. "She says it gets in the way of progress. Back on Mem I wouldn't have dared say I'd had a dream, but here the Leader in my dreams is wonderful, and very real. I think I'm seeing him as Las. In my dreams his hair is silver and streaked with copper and gold, much more even than yours, Ari."

Turning to her he added, "In my dreams his skin is honey-colored. He is very beautiful, Ari. His dream voice is like music."

Ari's voice was rueful. "Talin always said I was a natural Dreamer, but I don't dream of the shadows or their leader."

"I trust him," Jonce confessed.

"I do too," Ari agreed.

Soon they heard the Old One's name. He had been visiting with them when suddenly he was called away. "Melas!" a drum voice boomed. "Come. You are needed."

Later Melas told Ari and Jonce that he had been called away because of an uprising led by what he called "the renegades," shadows who were plotting against the captured humans.

"This is understandable," Melas told them. "There has been a split between us since the Change. Most of us want peace. Others say we should not protect humans whose Evil Queen destroyed our civilization."

"So there are good shadows and bad shadows," Jonce exclaimed. "How do we know which is which?"

"It's not that easy," Melas drummed. "Few can forget or forgive the cost of The Change."

"But no one on Mem knew you were here!" Ari exclaimed. "Everyone thought the planet was uninhabited."

"Many wonder how that could be," Melas replied. "Who did Atrid think had created such lush beauty? Zetti didn't become a place of wonder without Las Shapers. Why didn't the Alph tell her we were here?"

"You keep speaking about the Alph!" Jonce exclaimed. "Who are they?"

"Surely you must know of them, Jonce," Melas said. "They are the wise invisibles who send us dreams to shape. Ari, you must know them."

"Yes," Ari agreed. "From the Folios. They are those who send dreams, but Atrid had forbidden dreams, so how could they tell her?"

"That's true," Melas affirmed. "Unfortunately, we Las lost our ability to Shape after the Change. But if Atrid were truly Astraea born again, she would have known she was Las, and that we were here."

"So Atrid is not really Star Woman?" Jonce sounded bewildered.

"No Las has ever believed it." Melas's voice was sad.

His drumming paused. There was a long silence. The room seemed to darken around them before he resumed.

"Long before Astraea returned to us and was sung Beyond the Stars, the peace-loving Las were threatened by an intergalactic war. Word came that our original planet was to become a base of operations for a violent lizard species. Our leaders knew that the only way our people could survive was to leave. In those days we Las had transporters. Our ancestors chose what was then a barren planet, called Zetti. Nobody wanted such a place, so it was ignored. Being skilled Shapers, our ancestors slowly transformed Zetti into a paradise of beauty where our people lived, hidden and ignored, until your Queen needed a prison planet and made the Change."

Ari interrupted him. "She's not my Queen!" she objected. "I am not Memmian. I am Zedian. I was born on this planet."

Melas nodded, then continued. "Our ancestors' mistake was to make Zetti the most beautiful planet in the Galaxy. We would have been wiser to live in less noticeable conditions, but we had forgotten any necessity to stay hidden. No one bothered us for generations. As a result the Las flourished."

"So what happened?" Jonce asked.

"The Change," Melas replied. "About three hundred years ago, your Queen and her Memmian mages changed our paradise planet into its original barren form, or worse. I don't know why or how they did it, but it happened, and when it did we had to hide out in the tunnels, where we all became shadows of our old selves, unable to either fully live or die."

He paused, as if unable to go on. Finally he managed to drum again. "Is it any wonder that some of my people fear, even hate, all Memmians? It was your Queen and her mages who turned us into Shadow, and Zetti into the horror of Zed."

"But they didn't know you were here!" Jonce exclaimed.

"Perhaps," Melas told him. "Nevertheless, it's true that it was the Change that almost destroyed us. In the past our people were always sung to The Land Beyond the Stars after they died, to be reborn. To save ourselves from total annihilation in the Change, most of us fled to these underground burrows. Here, we are Shadow. We must stay in this hidden world, out of the light. For three centuries we have barely existed, unable to live or die, hiding out in this underworld, where, thanks to the Bird People, you've found us. You are the first humans to know of us. Is it any wonder that some of us are frightened and want you killed before your Queen finds you and discovers us?"

"Talin found the Folios," Ari said. "After that it was only a matter of time before someone discovered your existence."

"We saw the Folios in your mind when we probed you. We know that you learned of us from them."

"But I never learned that you still exist," Ari stated. "Nor that the Evil Queen had turned you into shadows! I never knew you were here! Talin didn't know either. If we had we would have searched until we found you."

"Now you do know." Melas's drumming voice was heavy with sadness. "And if Atrid finds you she will know, too."

The next day Melas came to them in deep distress. "Those who object to you are planning an attack." His voice was quiet, like the brushing of a whisk on a drumhead. "They want to destroy you first, then go to the compound and attack the Memmian Queen and her troops. It would be another holocaust."

"But it was your people who saved Jonce and me!" Ari protested.

"The renegades think that was a fatal error. They found an assassin to murder you. He has been stopped, but more dire plans unfold constantly."

"Aren't you their leader?" Jonce protested. "Can't you reason with them?"

Melas was silent.

It became clear to Jonce and Ari that they were in grave danger. The guards in the hallway were seemingly there as much for their protection as to keep them contained, but could they be renegades too, waiting to murder them as they slept?

"We should leave," Ari said.

"We should leave at once," Jonce agreed. "It's better for us to take our chances outside than endanger you."

"No!" Melas was adamant, his drum voice booming. "You are in danger from those here who fear you, but we would all be in far greater danger if Atrid's troops were to find you. Leaving is not a solution, unless I go with you and take you to a place where you will be safe from her probes."

"We can't cause you trouble!" Ari exclaimed.

"It is my task to protect you," the Old One assured her. "The Alph sent me a dream and made me promise. We three must leave and go to Sanctuary."

There was a long silence. All Ari could hear was the sound of Melas's heavy breathing.

"I don't understand," Jonce said finally.

Melas replied. "Sanctuary is hidden and warded. Few of my own people even know it still exists." He paused, then drummed again. "You two must talk it over and decide, but be quick about it. We must leave shortly, before it's too late."

Melas turned to go. Suddenly all three stood like statues, as they simultaneously became aware of an uproar of drum voices, moving rapidly toward them.

Melas boomed at them. "RUN!" he beat, racing out of the corridor.

Grabbing their capes, Jonce and Ari instantly followed him. Jonce was right at his heels, keeping pace. Panting, Ari hurried to keep up as they twisted and turned through narrow passages. She kept Jonce always in sight, knowing that without him ahead she would immediately be lost in the maze they were running through. Terrified, she pounded along.

"Oh Astraea, true Star Woman," she thought frantically as she panted for breath. "Please, please help us."

Instantly she remembered how to run the way Talin had taught her, timing her feet to her breath, letting her body relax and follow the rhythm. As she hit her stride, she let her mind clear. She didn't have answers, but surely she could manage her fear. Talin had taught her that, too.

Now she must trust Melas and simply let her body keep moving.

"Sanctuary." The word became a mantra aligned with her breath and her feet. "We're headed for Sanctuary!"

CHAPTER 32

Melas finally stopped. "Rest," he told them. "You've done well. We'll be there soon."

Heaving a great sigh of relief, Ari sank to her knees. Jonce was still on his feet. Instead of resting, he stood, gasping, as he stared back into the passage from which they'd just come. He reminded Ari of a tak she had seen in her childhood, a great beast caught in a trap, that had known it was doomed and had stood paralyzed, shaking with fear. Jonce had that same expression.

Disturbed, Ari nevertheless tried to keep her voice calm. "Jonce, sit down. You need to rest."

Instead of resting, he began to inch his way back toward the tunnel.

"What are you doing?" she asked, worry now evident in her voice. "What's wrong with you?"

Jonce ignored her and kept moving. "Someone's lost. Calling. Needs help! Trying...gotta find..." Suddenly, in one flapping motion, he lunged forward and began to race back into the tunnel. Ari leaped up, but Melas was there before her, surrounding Jonce with his shadow self, forcing him back. Jonce began to cough and sputter as if he were choking.

"Must go!" he rasped. "He's calling!"

Melas's drum voice was steady and strong. "Calling?" he queried. "Who, Jonce?"

"It's a...someone...don't know. Gotta go!" He pushed at

Melas's shadow, struggling to get free, but, strong as he was, he was no match for Melas, who held him fast.

Rushing to him, Ari grabbed his shirt. "Jonce," she ordered. "Wake up! You're tranced. You know we can't go back. There's nothing there."

"There is," Jonce insisted. "He needs to find us."

"Who?" Ari asked. "Who needs to find us?"

Melas interrupted. "The shadow rebels are seeking us," he told Ari quietly. "If that's true, we need to go quickly and reach Sanctuary before they locate us."

Abruptly Jonce stood still. "Ari," he said, sounding shocked. "He's calling your name! Someone is calling YOU!" He grabbed her hand and tried to step away from Melas. "We must go back!"

Snatching at Ari, Jonce tried to push forward, but the shadow held him. "We've almost reached safety," Melas insisted. "We must go on, not back."

"Who is calling me?" Ari asked urgently. It was not like Jonce to be so upset.

"It's...I don't know..." Suddenly Jonce straightened, his body going stiff with a new realization. "Oh, yes I do! Ari, it's one of the Survivors!"

Ari felt herself go rigid.

"That can't be," she cried. "They're all dead."

After a moment she added, "Unless it's a ghost."

"No." Jonce was definite. "He's alive. And..." He took a deep breath. "He has our hair!"

Melas's voice drummed more urgently. "We knew you would

be pursued by Memmian troops, but this is faster than I feared. Come. We must go on." He was pushing them now, forcing them to follow him.

"He's calling your name!" Jonce yelled into Ari's ear as he struggled to free himself.

"No one knows my name except the dead." She stopped suddenly, despite Melas. "Unless...Oh, Jonce, could it be Talin? Is it an old man?" She felt a thrill of excitement. Had Talin come back for her?

"No." Jonce was definite. "No, it couldn't be. This one is young."

Ari knew her voice sounded distraught. "Talin must have told someone about me."

She tried to move away, but was stopped again. "Unless...Oh, Jonce, do you suppose he took the meld?"

Jonce's voice was firmer as he replied. He seemed to be coming back to himself. "Remember I told you that before I left Mem everyone was talking about how the Queen wanted Talin to take the meld again?" he asked. "It was a secret, but everyone knew. Do you remember, Ari?"

She nodded. "I remember. He said no, he would die first."

She struggled to hold back tears as she began to follow Melas away from the tunnel, urging Jonce along with her.

Melas encouraged them. "Hurry," he urged. "We must reach safety."

Ari tried to face the truth. Talin would never return. Even if he wanted to, he was too old to survive another Crossing. Jonce was right. Talin would never take the meld again. They must go on. Whoever sought them, it wasn't Talin.

"Hurry!" Melas's drum voice was an insistent whisper of sound. "We must not linger here. If we do, we might lead others to Sanctuary. We are very close now."

After a few turns, Jonce was himself again, moving forward without Ari's help. Soon she felt his arm around her shoulders, and she gratefully leaned into him as they followed Melas. They picked up the pace, moving rapidly toward their goal.

It was only a short time later that Melas stopped and motioned for them to stand back. In front of them, blocking their passage, was a solid wall. Ari wondered if they had reached an impasse, but Melas stretched out his hand to splay it on the shiny black surface. Immediately, to her astonishment, the wall vanished! As a blast of brilliance spilled through what was now an open gateway, flooding the dark tunnel with dazzling light, Ari recoiled, covering her eyes as she turned her back.

Jonce kept moving forward, his voice filled with enthusiasm. "Look, Ari. It's your secret garden! We've found it and we're here!"

"Too bright," Ari exclaimed, waving her arms as if she could make it go away. "I can't see. What's that light?"

"It's sunshine, silly." Jonce took a few steps back toward her, reaching out. "Come on, it's beautiful!"

Melas flowed back to her.

"Come." His voice was gentle. "We've arrived. Keep your eyes closed and as soon as I shut this gate I will lead you. Trust me. This is the only entry. Once it's sealed again you will be completely safe."

Screwing her eyes more tightly shut, Ari let him lead her forward. There was no sound, yet she knew that a wall had closed behind her. Trying to relax, she went forward into a strangely welcoming warmth. The damp chill of the tunnels was gone. She tried again to open her eyes, but the light blinded her, and she quickly closed them again.

"What's this heat?" she asked, suddenly recalling the heat in the desert she and Jonce had crossed. "Is this a desert?"

"No." Melas was still guiding her forward. "Here the heat is pleasant. You may want to take off your cloak."

Ari realized that, along with warmth, she was also feeling the grip of a large hand on her arm. Squinting, she looked down to see long, graceful fingers, just starting to release their hold on her. Following the hand as it lifted, she looked up through slit eyes at a white-robed waist. Had Melas regained his original Las form? She wanted to see his face, but the bright sunshine blinded her. As she covered her eyes, she stumbled and went down on her hands and knees, falling on something soft and resilient. She peeked at the ground and saw tiny spears which seemed to be growing out of its surface, rather like lichen, but soft, and brighter. She stroked them with her hand, and was surprised to feel tears trickling down her cheeks again. Surely this was grass, the kind Talin had shown her in his picture memories of Mem. How did it get here on Zed?

"We're here, Ari!" Jonce interrupted her thoughts, his voice filled with joy. "Look, look! We've found it at last! Sanctuary is your lost garden of Zetti!"

Ari couldn't speak. Emotion filled her with wonder. There were smells she had never smelled before, sounds she had never heard, feelings she had never felt. Thinking of the great shadows imprisoned in the cliffs back at the compound, she understood in a new way why they had wept such endless tears over their loss.

"Is it beautiful?" she asked. "It's so bright I can't see."

The next thing she knew, Melas was tying something soft over her eyes.

"This will dim the sunlight until you become accustomed to it." Melas's voice was no longer a drumbeat, yet it retained a similar quality and timbre. He spoke gently, as if to a child. "You are safe now, so open your eyes. Come, there is shade under the trees, and water where you can bathe."

Ari blinked. Sure enough, the light appeared dimmer. She was looking through something grey that allowed her to see but cut the impact of the light.

"It's called 'netting,'" Melas explained. "Often those who are privileged to come here have to use it after they've spent too much time in the tunnels."

Ari slowly opened her eyes wider. Yes, she could see. There was a tall boy in a ragged Memmian uniform. She felt a rush of relief. Jonce was still with her. She could see him. There was also a giant, dressed in a white robe. She caught her breath. Melas was beautiful beyond anything she had encountered before. As he moved away from her, she was able to see all of him. His robe was of the softest white fabric that glowed from within, as if a flame were inside it. Under the robe his whole body was incandescent, as if a fire burned deep within his being. She stared at him, fascinated. His hair was amazing, springing around his head in a sparkling aureole of silver streaked with glistening colors. She knew somehow that she was seeing the original version of her own hair; hers was no more than a dim replica.

She touched the covering on her own head and wondered once more why she had always had to keep her hair hidden.

When she took off her cap, she expected Melas to react, but he showed no sign of surprise.

Melas was amazing. Why was he protecting them, even going so far as to share this garden paradise with two humans as insignificant as herself and Jonce? Even as she thought this, the boy was dashing ahead, rushing down to a large pool of water.

"Take off your blinder, Ari," he called. "The trees shade the lake."

He plunged into the water. Following him to the edge, Ari looked into liquid so clear that even through her veiled eyes she could see pebbles on the bottom. The stream was shaded from the sun by huge forms, some dressed in rough and ragged garments, others with shining skin. All had many arms, filled with something that rustled in the warm wind.

"Trees!" she thought in amazement.

She looked at Melas, questioning. He nodded. Slowly Ari unwound the netting from her eyes, then gasped in wonder. Talin had shown her images of trees in his teachings, but she had thought they existed only in dreams.

"They're real!" she exclaimed, realizing that the rustle she heard was made by small shapes called "leaves," which grew from arms called "branches." Reaching out to touch the bark of one of the largest trees with tentative fingers, she found herself wanting to fling her arms around them all, to sing to them, laugh into their rough exterior, sway in a dance with them and celebrate the wonder of their beauty. As she looked at the trees, she felt as if her eyes could hardly hold the emotions she was feeling.

Leaning down to look into her face, Melas nodded his approval.

"You should bathe," he reminded her softly. "We've had a strenuous journey."

Melas's whole body was radiant. Ari reached out a finger to touch him, and felt flesh and bone. He smiled. She jerked her hand back and looked at the ground.

"Yes, I am solid." His voice was amused.

"I-I th-thought you might be made of light," Ari confessed.

"In my true Las body I am very solid." He laughed, but then his voice grew sad. "But that can only happen here in the Garden. What you see now is all we have left of our planet's beauty." He added, "Jonce is swimming. Can you swim, child? It's time for you to get into the water."

Ari lifted her head to tell him with pride, "I've been swimming since I was a baby. Talin taught me."

Emotion took her again. Her hands became fists. Talin was gone. She would never see him again. She had lost them all, the Survivors, her mother, her home and, worst of all, Talin. How he would have loved this Garden!

"He was my friend and teacher," she finally managed to say. "He was a mage, one of the Survivors."

"So he was taken in the purge."

"No. He was captured and taken back to Mem."

Ari remembered how she had sulked in their secret cavern, selfishly angry, unaware of Talin's abduction. She began to choke.

"It was my fault. I failed him. I'm sure he could never survive another Crossing. He was too old."

"Was he the only one taken? Were there others?" Melas's voice was deep with concern.

"He was the only one. Later the guards came back and that was when..." Ari began to choke, unable to hold back her tears any longer.

Jonce was suddenly at her side, dripping wet.

"Come, Ari." She felt his hand on her back. "Come into the pond. The water is healing. It will help."

Still sobbing, Ari let herself be led into the pond. Jonce gently brought her to the shallows, where she sat, up to her shoulders in water. He tried to wash away her tears, but she pushed him away.

Melas stood on the grass just above them. "Let her be, Jonce," he instructed. "She has mourning to do. She's safe here."

After a bit, Jonce tried to take her hands and draw her into deeper water, out of the shade. She held back.

"Doesn't the light bother you?" she asked.

He laughed. "No. It's like home, like Mem. It's normal."

"Not for me."

"Just relax, Ari," Jonce instructed. "Let the water hold you. You'll feel better if you do. In a while you'll adapt to the light."

Ari let herself float on the surface, eyes closed. She could hear Jonce splashing nearby. Slowly she became aware of other sounds. There were birds here, and they were singing. Turning onto her stomach, she opened her eyes in the water. Below her she saw fish unlike any she'd seen before. They were not the white ominous fish of Zed, but bright fish of brilliant colors. She started to exclaim, then leapt up, coughing. As she spit out a mouthful of water, she was surprised to discover how sweet it tasted. Moving into deeper shade, she lay again on her back, floating.

"This must be what it feels like to be happy," she thought in astonishment. It was true. For this one moment in time, she was where she needed to be, held by the water, with Melas and Jonce nearby. They had survived and now they were safe. Talin and the Survivors were gone, but she was alive. Talin would want her to live.

"Jonce," she called. "We made it!"

She heard him laugh; delight bubbled in the sound. "Yes," he affirmed. "You always said you would find the Lost Garden someday, and now here we are."

From the edge of the pool Melas spoke. "It's not quite over yet," he cautioned. "There are renegade shadows searching nearby, and I fear they don't wish either of you well. You'd better get out of the water. I need to leave you and find out their plans, but before I do I want to take you to a more secure area."

"Surely no harm can come to us here," Jonce protested.

"Come." Melas's voice was urgent now. "Follow me. You must hide. There can be no confrontation in this place. If the renegades should manage to breach my wards, they must not find you."

Ari hurried after Melas as he left the pond, with Jonce just behind. After striding through the garden, Melas touched another wall. Again his fingers splayed against the stone. Again the wall disappeared, but this time there was dimness beyond it, rather than dazzling light. As they stepped through the opening, Ari saw that they were in a circular room. At the center was a table that looked as if it had been carved from one of the biggest trees. It was very high, and beside it were some odd structures that Jonce identified as "chairs." Ari couldn't imagine sitting on one. They were very large, and obviously designed for a person of Melas's size, not hers. On the floor was a substance that felt as soft as grass to Ari's bare feet.

"This room has been the sanctuary of Las leaders since long before the Change," Melas told them. "It will open only to my touch, and to that of a few gardeners I have chosen. There are coverings here to keep you warm, also food and water in the cupboard, and oil lamps you may light with the wands beside them." He indicated a structure against the wall.

Turning to Jonce he asked, "You know how to handle all this, don't you?"

Jonce nodded.

Hurriedly Melas instructed them, "If anything happens and I haven't returned by the time the food runs out, there is an escape door you can open at the back of the room that leads to a tunnel which will eventually take you to the surface. For the present, however, you must stay here. Hopefully it won't be long before I return."

"But..." Ari began to protest.

"I must go. Eat some food, then wrap up in the warm wrappings I've given you and sleep. Hopefully things will soon be resolved and you will be able to come back safely into the Garden, but you must wait for me. Right now the most important thing is for you both to remain hidden."

With that, Melas said good-bye. He stepped once more through the wall, back into the Garden. The wall closed behind him.

Shivering, Ari was glad to see that Melas had brought her cloak. She put it on. Jonce did the same with his, before lighting the lamps and taking out some food. He placed the food on a coverlet on the floor and urged Ari to sit down and eat. The food was cold but good.

"What is it?" she asked through a mouthful.

"It's bread and cheese," he told her. "They must grow the grain here in the Garden, and there must be goats somewhere."

"Of course there are goats, the tak are goats," Ari scoffed. "They are everywhere on Zed."

"But I doubt anyone ever milked one of them!" Jonce snorted. "That's what this cheese comes from, tame goat's milk."

Ari's mind filled with images of the wild tak leaping on the heights above the compound. The thought of trying to tame or milk any animal like them made her grimace.

She yawned. Starting to nod with fatigue, she could hardly keep eating. Images of her home and her mother and Talin came to her unbidden. Determined not to cry, she stopped eating, and rolled herself up in the puffy bedding Melas had left. As she lay down, she knew she would soon be asleep. She tried to relax, telling herself that the past was behind her.

The last thing she heard as she tumbled into exhausted slumber was Jonce clearing up the food and rolling out his own bedding nearby.

"We're safe at last," Ari thought, and then she slept.

CHAPTER 33

Atrid and Caz continued their hunt for Talin, but each time she sensed his presence, it immediately vanished. The search was making her feel leaden and lethargic. As she and Caz moved through the tunnels she kept sitting down to rest, waiting for her lungs to recover their ability to breathe. But as soon as she stood up she began to pant again.

"What is happening to me?" she wheezed. She was shocked when her usually powerful voice came out weak and strained.

A strange kind of paranoia began to grip her mind. Briefly she wondered if perhaps an occult illness had been secreted in the youngster she'd taken in her last meld. Was that what sapped her energy now? She stood and tried to force herself onward, but each time she moved her body seemed to grow heavier until, her face wet with perspiration, she could do nothing but collapse.

"Yes, we must stop again to rest," Caz reassured her, but his voice, usually calm, was tense with concern.

"Talin must be nearby," Atrid gasped between coughs. "We can't stop now."

Determined, she rose in order to stagger on, but immediately was gripped by another racking spasm of coughing. Barely able to breathe, she was forced to stop. She sank onto a ledge which jutted out from the wall of the small cavern they had entered.

"Don't sit there!" Caz cried out.

"Rest," she coughed, "a moment."

"But you're sitting in the shadows. They're all around you!"

He grabbed her arms and tried to pull her up, but she couldn't be budged! It was as if her body had adhered to the spot.

"I can't move!" she choked, beginning to panic. "Why can't I move?"

Caz put his arms around Atrid and pulled with all his strength, but it was useless. She was held fast.

"They've caught you!"

"What?" Atrid could barely get the word out. "Who?"

Was it a spell that held her fast or was it her own fatigue? Once again she tried to stand, but instead of rising she found herself feeling heavier and more weighed down, unable to lift even an arm.

"I'm caught!" She began to feel terror. Was her whole body turning to lead?

A new, even worse thought struck her like a bolt: was she rapidly becoming extrine like the walls?

"Caz, do something!" Atrid tried to shout but her voice came out in a breathless croak. "I'm not myself!" She could hardly hear her own words. Panic filled her.

Caz backed away and came to stand at the center of the cavern, staring fixedly at the wall behind Atrid.

"Let her go!" he commanded in a mage voice.

Sound seemed to explode from the walls like the clatter of hail beating on a metal roof. Was it laughter?

Atrid wanted to cover her ears, but couldn't raise more than a finger.

"Caz," she gasped. "Help...me!"

Caz was staring at the walls. He seemed to be listening to something, as if there were a message in the rattles that continued to sound. Every now and then he nodded his head. Sometimes he shook it as if he were saying 'no.' He seemed to be holding a conversation! And every time he "answered," the noise level increased until it seemed to beat into the very pith of Atrid's bones.

"Stop!" she tried to cry. "I command you!" No sound came from her mouth.

Truly frightened, wondering what Caz could possibly be hearing, Atrid struggled to speak but found she could not.

"At least my mind is still working," she thought. She would mind speak..

"What?" was all she could send. Her panic grew. Was her body turning to stone and taking her ability to communicate with it? Her mind raced, thoughts tumbling over one another. She could hear her Inners starting to panic, too. Their mind voices began a racket that competed with the outer noise. Atrid wanted to cover her ears, but her hands refused to lift.

Caz moved back toward her. "The shadows speak," he told her. "Can you hear them?"

Her Inner voices were yelling at her now, commanding her to move. She couldn't budge.

Caz's face filled with alarm. "The shadows say they are going to turn us into ones of them."

"Them? Who?" Atrid managed somehow to gurgle the thought to him.

"The shadows. Look at the wall. You can see them there," he answered.

It took all Atrid's willpower to lift her eyelids enough to glimpse the wall. Squinting, trying to focus, she began to see movement there, grey against the dark extrine. Shadows? More like giant birds of prey waiting to devour. They seemed to tower above her in malignant anticipation.

"Are we going mad?" she mentally asked her Inners.

Caz's thoughts reached her again. "They are the Shadow people. And they say we are evil, that you and your mages destroyed their planet. I am guilty, too, because I am your mage."

"No."

"Yes. Long ago. They say that it was you who changed Zetti into Zed."

Atrid could move her lips, but the moan she felt rising from the pit of her stomach wouldn't come out. Something was happening to her body, and to her Inners, who were spinning within her as if they were being forced out and taken!

Then she felt as if her whole being was spinning. Wanting desperately to hold herself and her Inners together, and to keep resisting the shadow pull, she tried to relax, but those melded within her were all being drawn out of her! She could feel it happening. She felt as if her whole body was about to explode, yet she couldn't move. Her mind kept running in circles, asking questions, even as she sat inert.

Who are these Shadows to accuse her of evil? There had been no people on Zed. She was sure of it. So where had these terrifying shadow "beings" come from, and why were they claiming that Zetti had been theirs?

Was Caz trying to trick her? Had he made up this fiction to frighten her? Was it his spell that held her fast? If that was the case, she should be able to counteract it. She must concentrate.

The activity on the walls increased. Now the drumming seemed to deepen. It was getting into her head. She began to think she was hearing words! If only she could shake them out, but her head, spinning frantically, was caught in a squeeze that was pulling her out of her body, along with her Inners.

"What is happening to us?" she thought frantically.

A distinct voice emerged from the drumbeats. "You are all transforming," it drummed. "Just as you forced us to do. Soon all of you will be like us. That is your punishment."

"I've fallen asleep!" Atrid thought. "This is a nightmare."

She tried to wake herself, beginning to be sure this was all a dream Caz had created to gain control over her. Dreams were forbidden. She had seen to that centuries ago. Caz must be punished!

Immediately there was a clatter like derisive laughter in the drums.

"She thinks you betray her!" Atrid heard them tell Caz. "That you are shaping her 'dream.'"

She wanted to protest, but she could no longer move so much as the tip of her little finger. Slowly it occurred to her that the shadows were reading her mind. She didn't need to send a thought. She only had to think.

"I am Queen Atrid," she began, choosing her thought words carefully. "Star Woman. You cannot treat us this way."

The drumming became raucous. Out of the cacophony of sound a "voice" emerged. It was derisive and seemed to snarl.

"Star Woman indeed!" the drum voice mocked. "A fantasy woven to suit the needs of your royal self."

In desperation Atrid cried out in her mind. "Who are you? Why are you doing this?"

"You call yourself the Chosen," the drum voice sneered. "No one chooses you here. You are the Evil One. Now WE choose your fate!"

Atrid grew even more leaden. Was she dying? No, it couldn't be. She wouldn't allow it! Caz could no longer help her. She needed someone far more powerful.

"Talin!" she cried in her mind. The words seemed to come from the core of her being. "Talin, I'm dying. Save me! If you ever loved me, help me!"

Surely if he were near he would come to her. She must not die. What would happen to her realm, to say nothing of herself? Hadn't she always done what was best? Everything she had done she had done to preserve her planets and her galaxy. Who could think otherwise?

The drums were laughing at her. Atrid felt fury, then despair. As the dark feelings took over, the drumming became stronger, its rhythm steady, repetitive, compelling. Terrified, Atrid felt it enter her body, and take over her will. They had already taken her Inner throng! Was this war? She tried to fight, and to tell her Inners to do the same, but she had no strength. One at a time each member of her Inner cohort vanished. Horrified, she discovered that she, too, was leaving her body! In a moment she found herself hanging on the black cavern wall, in a grey shadowy mist, looking down at the body she had lived in, which was now empty and dead!

Wishing she could cry out, Atrid clung there, terrified, unsure what to do next. Discovering that she still had eyes, she saw what she presumed was Caz's body collapsed on the cavern floor. Horrified, she watched as a grey wraith separated from his human form and flew up to take a place at some distance from her on the opposite wall. Beside him were multiple shadow bats.

"Your companion and those you have melded," the drum voice beat in her mind. "We have given them release."

Attempting to speak, the shadow who had been Atrid discovered that her voice was now a drum.

"I am Shadow?" she thought the question.

"Yes," another drum voice replied. "Now you and your throng are separated. We have made all of you into shadows who will aid us as we hunt for other humans to change. Your desire to find them will lead us like a magnet to where they hide. They, too, will join us. Eventually we will change all of you."

Against her will, Atrid found herself gathered up into the center of a collection of beings who looked like grey gauze, except for their eyes, which, when opened, were glistening black.

"Yes," the leader said. "When we want to remain hidden we keep them closed, but we no longer need to hide from you. You are one of us now. Come! You must join the hunt."

"Talin! Save us!" Atrid heard her own mage voice but didn't recognize it. She was a shadow, clinging to a high wall, surrounded by other shadows.

An authoritative drum voice sounded. "It's time to move on."

Caught up in the shadow surge, it didn't occur to Atrid to struggle or fight. As she disappeared into the mist of movement, her old self vanished.

The authoritative voice sounded again. Immediately everything was still.

"We will make war!" it beat. "Death to all Memmians!"

With those words, the whole entourage peeled off the walls and began to fly, like mythical horsemen. Mindlessly, the former Memmians joined them, caught inexorably in a gray stream that carried their new shadow selves through one tunnel after another.

"I am lost," was Atrid's last lucid thought.

CHAPTER 34

Talin had been captured as he slept, dreaming that Atrid was calling to him for help. Something had apparently followed her voice to him, surrounding him before he was awake enough to escape. He wasn't sure what it was that held him fast. Hard as he looked, he saw nothing in the cavern where he lay except huge, ominous shadows that hung like nearly invisible gray smudges from floor to ceiling on the extrine walls. He had dreamed that these shadows were what had taken him prisoner, but he knew that must be impossible. How could a mere shadow do any harm?

The only thing he could hear was drumming, but he couldn't figure out where it was coming from. Perhaps he was still dreaming? Hard as he tried, he couldn't wake up or free himself. Suddenly the drumming increased. To his astonishment, he discovered that he could hear words, as if the drumming were a language! He listened, trying to hide the fact that he could understand what was being spoken.

"We have the Queen, and we have changed her. This one we will keep in his human body so he can speak to the other humans when we find them. He will help us or die. Come, we have a long journey ahead of us."

As this was being said, it looked to Talin as if the shadows were dropping from the walls. They began moving into a tunnel. He was glad to see them go, but his relief turned to horror when he discovered that he was forced to run after them. Was he becoming shadow after all? He decided he must be asleep and dreaming, yet he couldn't wake.

The dream was strenuous. He had to keep up with the flow of shadow, which was much too fast for him. Touching his body, he was reassured to find that he still had a human form. Before long, however, he realized that if his human feet slowed even slightly, one of two shadows who followed hard on his heels would hurl him forward, like a ball thrown toward a goal.

How long would it be, he wondered as he gasped for breath, before his lungs, even though they had been considerably strengthened by the meld, would collapse? Already each breath felt like hot sand in his chest as his muscles creaked and groaned with pain. He must waken! Could even a dream body survive such mad abuse?

As he ran with the shadows he began to see them more and more clearly.

"I'm awake!" he thought. "This is not a dream."

Soon it all began to be real to him, real and dangerous. There appeared to be a whole contingent of the shadow beings, filled with purpose and determination. If the drumming had been right, they had captured Atrid! And now they had captured him, but what did they intend to do with him?

Periodically, the whole shadow group stopped to rest, clinging to the cavern walls like giant nocturnal creatures. As soon as they stopped, Talin would collapse into deep sleep on the cavern floor. In less than a few breaths, however, his shadow guards would kick him awake, and the race would go on. His keepers were obviously wasting no time in reaching their destination.

As tired as he was, Talin noticed that the shadows avoided light, even the dimness that occasionally filtered through cracks in the ceiling.

Though he tried, he found that it was impossible to make a map in his mind of the route they were traveling. All he could manage was running, in a heedless, mindless struggle to stay alive. After a while he began to lose any sense of time or space. In the beginning it had felt vital to him to keep track of patterns, but he soon found himself able to concentrate on only one thing: staying alive.

If the shadows ever ate, Talin didn't observe them doing so. Perhaps they ate when it was too dark for him to see? Occasionally they would make a brief stop at a spring, just long enough for him to lap up water like an animal. Once he found a chunk of something he recognized as dried tak meat. While he chewed the leathery substance slowly, taking it in tiny bites, he put the rest in his pockets to make it last.

Soon he lost all sense of direction. Even worse, he had also lost any sense of what he was searching for. Gritting his teeth to keep from falling, it took all his waning strength to stumble along, struggling to keep pace.

Each time he fell into sleep, Talin wondered if this might be the time death would come for him.

On the third night, he woke suddenly. He felt something gathering him up as he lay curled in the darkness of a tiny burrow-cell, while the shadows rested in a larger cavern beyond. Talin sensed no movement in the cavern. There was no sound, not even a rustle. His ever-present guards had vanished. He tried to sit up, but a soft brush of a whisper, just barely stroking his eardrum, stopped him.

"Don't move!" the whisper breathed.

Talin lay back, his heart thumping in his chest. Was it the voice of Death?

"Who are you?" he thought.

"Don't think." The words were soft but filled with authority. "They'll hear."

"Who ar..." Talin's own sibilant whisper was immediately stopped by something like netting over his mouth.

"Don't speak!" The breath in his ear was urgent. "Ari is safe." The whisper was only air wafting into his brain. "Come. Make no sound. Think no thought. I will carry you to her."

Talin felt his body lift, wrapped in a mist. There was no feeling of threat, no stumbling or struggle. Whatever had come, claiming it would take him to Ari, was simply surrounding him. It carried him to the next tunnel in a motion so fluid it felt as if he rode a breeze. Since there was no alternative, Talin decided he must try to relax. Wrapped in a cocoon of invisible thread, he was being carried rapidly forward, flowing through one tunnel after another, leaving the shadow hoard far behind.

At last the movement stopped. Talin heard a soft drumbeat and realized it was speech.

"Thank you for trusting me," it said.

"Who are you?" Talin asked aloud.

The drumming replied, "I am Melas. The Alph sent me to rescue you. I have already taken your daughter and her friend to safety. Soon we will join them."

"Why should I trust you? Aren't you just like those who held me captive?"

"They are my people, but they don't understand." Melas's drum voice was softer now. "They believe all humans of Mem are their enemies because your Queen and her helpers changed our home into a prison planet and all of us into shadows. They kept you in human form so you could lead them to your Others."

"And you?" Talin was skeptical. "Aren't you the same?"

"I am their leader, though these renegades no longer listen to me. They have chosen a different way. But I am a Shaper and must serve the Alph who send me dreams. I agreed to do all I could to help you and your miraculous daughter. For a long time I watched you, Talin. I saw you wander and search and find our lost Folios. All through that time, the Alph sent me dreams telling me that you humans were to be protected, especially Aricia, Mem's future Queen. Recent dreams have shown me that the future of many people and many species, including us Las, will depend on her. She and the boy she has chosen are our only hope. Together you and I must do everything we can to save them and bring them to their destiny."

As Melas spoke, Talin heard another voice in his mind, a familiar voice that had often instructed him in the past, a voice he had never doubted.

"Trust him, Talin. He speaks truth."

Talin nodded. Both Melas and the Alph voice had confirmed what he had always known, the purpose he had blindly served, from his first dream of his child to his terrible decision to take the meld one last time in order to come to her.

"Yes," he agreed.

"Hurry now," the Alph voice said. "There is no time to waste."

Obviously Melas had heard the voice, too, for he immediately gathered Talin up and resumed their forward flow. As they moved he instructed, his beat becoming stronger and more urgent with each word.

"We will keep silence now. Already the renegade shadows trail us. We must get back to the children."

Talin began to think of Aricia. "Oh, Ari, I should have told you who you are," his mind cried.

"Stop broadcasting your thoughts." Melas's whisper struck like a knife. "The renegades may not hear our voices, but there are those among them who can pick up any broadcast of thought, even from a great distance."

Talin tried to still his mind and his thoughts. Aware of the miracle of his release from the renegade shadows, he felt a surge of emotion. Quickly he dropped into meditation.

Without stopping, they flowed from one tunnel to another. It was clear to Talin that Melas knew every twist and turn as he carried him toward their destination. Again, he lost all sense of time and space. Occasionally he slept, safely wrapped in Melas's shadow. His exhausted body began to regain strength. He needed no food to do so. It was as if Melas were infusing him with the nutrients he needed for his recovery.

At last they stopped in a narrow passage. Cocooned as he was, Talin was barely aware when they flowed through a wall and moved forward into dazzling sunlight. Abruptly, he found himself on his own feet and separated from his carrier, who was already transforming into a giant.

Talin gasped in surprise. "You...you're Las?"

"Yes," Melas said. He no longer spoke in a drum voice. His voice had transformed into one of deep and melodious tones. "Now, here in the Garden, I am in my original form. This is Sanctuary." The white robe he was wearing fell back from his strong arm as he pointed. "This is all that is left of Zetti. You and Ari called it the Secret Garden. With others, I have protected it for centuries, even from most of my own people."

Talin realized then how fortunate he was to be allowed into this obviously sacred space. "Your people?" he blurted. "You are all Las? How can that be?"

"Until the Change we were all as you see me now. Zetti was our home. But three centuries ago your Queen found the beauty we had created repulsive and managed to spell a great Change. Thanks to her and her mages, all of Zetti became stark, with little life. My people were changed, too. Those who stayed above ground were captured by the horrid impenetrable darkness of extrine. Those of us who hid at the core of the planet thought we were safe, only to discover ourselves becoming shadows of who we had been, able to 'speak' only in the voices of drums. We have lived this way ever since. But the real danger for us is that anywhere on the planet, except here in the Garden, it takes only one moment in light for us to be trapped in rock. The moment we surface we turn to stone."

Melas paused, as if it was too difficult to go on. Finally his resonant voice sounded again.

"Do you remember the giants in the cliffs Ari befriended when she was a child, Talin? Those were our Others, the ones who stayed behind. Most were our women and children. All of them became part of the extrine walls. Years ago they befriended your daughter, but you taught her that they existed only in her imagination. Thanks to our probing of her, we know now that they still exist, though they are locked in a prison of stone. Like us they are half alive, unable to live or die, but their fate is even worse than ours, for they can neither move nor show themselves." Melas walked forward into the Garden. "The only time I can take my true form is here in this Garden. Anyplace else on the planet I am a shadow, like all my people, forced to avoid daylight and spend my years underground, coming to the surface only on the darkest nights."

"But why don't your people simply live here in the Garden?" Talin queried. "And retain your original forms? Why do you have to be shadows when you could stay here and be yourselves?"

"This Garden is like a dream," Melas told him. "It takes energy and care to maintain its beauty and integrity, but overuse and selfishness can destroy it. It can't support its own true form for long if we shadows use it to feel better about ourselves. To preserve it we have to stay away. Occasionally a few of my trusted staff who are gardeners come and take on their original forms here, just long enough to tend the growth, but even the best of them can't be focused on their own needs, or the landscape starts to change. Even your Memmian children could unknowingly be a threat. Consequently I have hidden them to keep both them and the Garden safe. Come," he added, "We must go to them."

CHAPTER 35

They took a path through an orchard where trees were heavy with unpicked fruit. Next they crossed a grassy meadow of blossoming wildflowers. Just beyond was a stand of ancient trees, gnarled and majestic. As they reached the top of a hill, Talin looked down into a flower garden with a large pool at its center. Suddenly he could sense Ari's presence. Had she swum in that pool?

"It is so beautiful!" Talin's voice was filled with awe. "Ari must have been filled with wonder at the sight."

"Yes, though at first the bright light was difficult for her," Melas replied. "But hurry now, time is short. We must go to them and make sure they're safe. Then we can figure out our next move. We can't stay here."

He led Talin through the garden and past a stone wall, straight toward a cliff face. Moving vines and overgrowth aside, he revealed a door. As he placed his hand into a handprint where a lock would normally be, he murmured a word, and the door began to open.

"It's Melas," the Las called out as they entered. "I've brought a guest. Don't be afraid. So far everything is fine."

There was a scrambling at the back of the room, and suddenly a boy appeared, carrying a lamp.

"Jonce!" Talin exclaimed. "Is it you? Is Ari with you?"

Holding the lamp up, the boy looked puzzled as he searched

Talin's face. "Do I know you?" he asked.

A girl came hurtling forward out of the darkness. She threw herself into Talin's arms.

"Oh, Talin!" she cried. "Oh, you're alive. I'd know that voice anywhere. It's you. It's truly you!" She leaned back to look into his face, then, puzzled, she stepped away from him. Tears began to roll down her cheeks. Talin reached for her to wipe them away.

"Ari," he said. "Princess...it's me. I know I've changed. It's because I took the meld so I could come back to you."

"But you're so young!" Ari cried in dismay. "And Talin said he'd die before he'd take the meld again. Jonce told me that."

"I am Talin," he assured her. "I was in the cavern playing 'the game' with you when you were a baby. I carried you out in a little basket when you were too young to swim. Do you remember?"

Jonce broke in. "You...you took the meld?"

"Yes." Talin stepped back, giving Ari room. "I was told by the Alph that I must."

"The Alph?" Melas sounded excited. "You've had contact with your people?"

"My people?" Talin had almost forgotten what the shadow beings had told him: that he was half human and half Alph. "Oh, that was simply a strange story your people made up, I suppose to try to intimidate me."

Jonce laughed. "Yes, like they tried to say Ari and I are part Las."

The air around Melas grew heavy. No one spoke. At last he said softly, "Both are true."

"What is true? That they made up the story?" Talin began to laugh.

"No." Melas's voice was stronger now. "You are indeed half Alph, and Jonce is half Las. He is one of us. Also, Ari is..."

Talin interrupted him. "Not now," he said sternly. "It's too soon."

"Also Ari is what?" the girl exploded. "Am I Las, too? Is that why the people in the cliffs talked to me? This is just getting too weird. Here is Talin, who says he's my Talin, but he's not an old man anymore, and now he's part Alph? And Jonce is not just plain old Jonce, he's part Las? And who am I? What fancy label are you going to give to me?" She shook her head. "It's all simply too much."

Talin looked at her. His child. His Aricia. But she was not a child anymore. She was a beautiful young woman. His heart thudded in fear as he realized how much she looked like Atrid. Only her deeply violet eyes were his, and at the moment they were filled with distress and disdain. Ari looked as if she had swallowed something bitter.

"All right," she spat finally. "I am listening."

Instantly a voice spoke in Talin's mind, the voice he had heard for most of his life in his dreams.

"It's time!" The Alph voice was stern. "Now you must all learn the truth of yourselves before the battle begins."

"Battle?" Talin repeated out loud. He was shocked. He turned to Melas. "The Alph say there is to be a battle. Is that true?"

"Have your people spoken to you?" Melas was excited. "Are

they here to support us?"

Talin shook his head. "I don't know what's happening," he said.

"If the Alph say there will be a battle, then it is true. But it must not be here on this sacred ground. It would destroy the Garden. We must meet your people someplace else."

"The shadows have the Queen," Talin said. "Their drumming told me that she is now one of them. If this is true, she may teach them her strategies."

"And they will teach her ours," Melas replied sadly. He turned to Ari and Jonce. "It is time you both accepted the truth," he told them. "Yes, Jonce, you are Las, descended from Astraea who was Las. I don't know how it happened, but she must have had a child with a human. You need to know your heritage, and you need to know you will be fighting against your own species if we battle the renegades. And Ari..." He paused, looking back at Talin. "Perhaps your father should tell you himself," he said.

"My fa..." Ari could not complete the sentence. She was suddenly pale.

Talin looked at his feet, clearly worried about what was to come next.

"It is time." The voice in his head spoke sternly now.

"I am your father," Talin confessed. "I was there when you were conceived. I delivered you from Mag's body when you were born. I lived here on Zed with you, and even at my craziest, every day was joy because I was with you, my daughter." Talin was weeping openly now as he lifted his gaze to meet the girl's.

"But why?" she cried. "Why would you pretend?"

"You had to be a secret," he told her.

Ari's eyes flashed. Her voice was bitter and filled with scorn. "All that hiding." She turned to Jonce. "He is not my father," she announced. "I don't think he's even Talin. This is nonsense."

She turned back to stare at Talin. When she spoke again her voice was icy.

"If you are my father you must know that you killed my mother!"

"Yes," Talin agreed. "I could not save Mag any more than I could save myself. But, Ari," he added, looking at her beseechingly, "there is more. Mag was truly your mother in every way except one. The mother who conceived you, the one whose genes you carry, is another, not Mag..."

He turned to Jonce. "Jonce, look at her. Can't you see who she is?"

"She is Ari," Jonce replied.

"And who does she resemble?"

"Herself?" Jonce sounded puzzled.

"Have you seen her hair? Have you seen the star above her nose? Who else has that hair and that star?"

Jonce was staring at Ari. Suddenly he realized who Ari looked like. "Atrid?" His voice broke. He reached out blindly, as if to grasp Ari, then dropped his hands. "She looks like..." He let his thought die unspoken.

"Yes. Atrid," Talin pronounced. "She is my daughter with Atrid." His voice cracked. He had finally said it! Turning to face

Ari, he added, "Mag was your foster mother."

"NO!" Ari flew at him, hands outstretched, as if she could dig the words out of him and stomp them into the ground. "You're mad. You've always been mad. You killed my mother and now you want to kill my memory of her. I hardly know you!"

Melas reached out and took Ari in his arms, holding her back, trying to calm her, even as she kept flailing, attempting to free herself so she could attack Talin.

"What Talin tells you is true." Melas's voice was deep and gentle as he slowly released her.

Ari began to sob.

Blinded by the tears running down his cheeks, Talin tried to speak. "I am your father," he said, his voice breaking. "Everything I've done I've done to protect you, to keep you safe."

Ari turned to look at him, her face full of emotions. Fear, shock, pride and despair all warred within her.

"I only had one mother," she cried. "She loved me. She protected me. Where was Talin when she died? Where was he when the Survivors were destroyed? He was gone. He disappeared. How can you say you protected me?"

She began to cry as she threw her words at him. "If you are Talin, which I don't believe you are, you were off taking the meld, getting young at someone else's expense. Talin was my hero, my best friend, my teacher, and he left me all alone."

Jonce moved toward her as if to intervene.

"If it hadn't been for Jonce I might have died." Her voice was shaking. "He protected me. The Bird people protected me. Melas protected me." She lifted her chin to look at Talin. "How have YOU ever protected me? I don't even know you. Where were you when we crossed the desert, when we struggled through all that blackness? Where were you when the renegade shadows wanted to kill us?"

Suddenly she began to sob, her breath coming in deep bone-racking gulps. "Oh, Talin, where were you? I needed you so much!"

Jonce interjected, his voice soft but sure. "The guards took him away," he reminded her. "He had no choice."

She glared at Talin. "But you had a choice about taking the meld," she accused. "And now look at you. You're not even someone I know!"

Talin started to reach out to Ari, then thought better of it and hung his head instead. "I had no choice," he mumbled.

Ari jumped forward with a fresh accusation. "There is always a choice. You could have said no."

Talin looked at her then. It was as if she had suddenly become Atrid. Fury and fear seemed to war within her. Eyes and hair wild, color high in her cheeks, she looked so much like Atrid it made Talin heartsick.

When he spoke his voice was filled with sadness. "You are Atrid's daughter," he said. "No one seeing you now would question that."

Jonce stared at Ari, his face suddenly pale. "It's true," he cried. "You look just like Atrid."

Suddenly Ari crumpled. She would have fallen if Talin hadn't caught her. Sobbing against his chest, she clung to him. "It's all too strange," she wept. "Everything keeps changing."

"But look where we are." Talin pushed her hair back from her face, stroking her cheek. "You've reached the place you always wanted to find, the Secret Garden of Zetti. It's not a fantasy. It's real, and we're here."

"But..." She broke off, stared into his face, then turned away, sobbing. "I can't..."

"Yes, you can," he assured her. "Remember how you learned to swim out under the ledge in our cave and how proud I was that you could do it? That hasn't changed. Look at all you've done. Melas has told me about your adventures. Oh, Ari, I'm so proud of you. That will never change."

Ari stared into Talin's eyes. He realized that she was attempting to dig him, so he opened himself to her, keeping nothing hidden. Suddenly she relaxed and let herself fall against him. "You ARE Talin," she sobbed. "Oh, Talin, I've missed you so. I thought I would never see you again. I tried to hate you or forget you. I tried to be strong."

She leaned back to look into his face once again. "Oh, Talin, I love you so much!" She lowered her eyes. "Are you...are you really...my...father?"

"Yes." He was smiling now. "Mad, crazy, sane, stupid, old, young...yes, I am your father and always have been."

"And you always knew it?"

"Well...except when I was mad. Then I forgot." His voice trailed off as he remembered the time after Atrid had recalled him to Mem. "Yes," he said thoughtfully, "I forgot everything then. The Alph saw to that. You were my secret. They hid your existence even from me. I didn't remember until I was back here and Mag showed me..."

"Mag?" Ari stood back. "Mother?" Hope blossomed in her face.

"In a dream," Talin replied gently. "Sometimes the dead can speak with us in dreams."

Melas cleared his throat then. He'd been waiting patiently to speak. "Come," he said sternly. "Let's go to the surface and be in the Garden. This is a place for hiding, not a place for decisions."

Leading the way, he took them back through the vine-covered door, carefully replacing the overgrowth after they had all come through. Then he pointed them to the pond where Ari and Jonce had bathed, urging them to sit on stone benches under the trees. In his true form, he went hastily to the orchard. When he came back, his arms were filled with fruit, which he shared with them.

"Refresh yourselves," he instructed. "We have much to plan." Talin took a bite of fruit, and felt pleasure as the sweetness slid over his tongue and down his throat. He was suddenly voraciously hungry.

"Talin, do you still have a way of contacting the Alph?" Melas asked once they were settled. "Time is growing short. We must prepare ourselves to meet the renegades."

Talin stepped back. "If I send a thought to the Alph will your people intercept it?" he asked after a moment.

"No need to send a thought," the familiar voice spoke in his mind. "We are already with you. The renegades can't hear us. We know how to block them."

Talin turned to Melas. "Did you hear?" he asked.

Melas looked puzzled, but Ari turned to Talin. "You mean the voice that said something about being here already?" she asked.

Talin began to smile. Looking at Melas, he said, "Perhaps you're right about our being part Alph."

Melas smiled back but still looked puzzled.

"She is my daughter." With his arm around Ari, Talin spoke to Melas. "The Alph message is that they are here already. You can't hear them because they know how to block their thoughts when they wish to." He paused and looked at Jonce before adding, "And I presume that means from you as well."

"If that is true," Melas pointed out, "then both you and Ari are surely Alph."

"Yes." It was Talin's turn to look puzzled. "But how can that be? The Alph are invisible. They cannot take form. Ari and I have tried many times to be invisible. It was a game we played when she was small. But we never succeeded. How could a human have mated with an Alph? No, it's impossible."

"Talin, there were times when you were only half visible." Ari's voice was soft, as if she were puzzling over a very deep question. "Your body was there, but you were gone. Like the night Mag ate the fish," she added slowly. "I thought you did it on purpose to get away from us."

"No..." Talin started to protest but was interrupted by the voice in his head.

"We engendered you," the voice assured him. "Yes, you and Aricia are both human and Alph. But right now there is no time to wonder about that. The battle will come upon you soon. We must make a plan."

"We?" Ari and Talin spoke together, looking at each other in surprise.

"In another day the renegades will be here," the Alph voice said. "You must decide what to do."

"Must we have a battle?" Talin spoke aloud.

Melas looked puzzled.

Ari explained. "The Alph are mind speaking to us. They warn that the renegades will be here in another day."

"Yes," Talin agreed. "The Alph are here. They want to help us make a plan."

"And will they take our part in the battle?" Melas asked, his face filled with worry.

In his memory Talin heard again the words that had been spoken to him long ago: "Ours is to help with the plan. It is up to you to carry it through."

"No," he said quietly. "It is our battle. They will simply give us their ideas. They can't take form to aid us physically."

The Alph voice was urgent as it instructed them. "You all must go through the tunnel to the compound. Then you must organize Atrid's troops and get the shadow renegades to follow all of you from the tunnels out to the planet surface and into the daylight. They cannot survive in the open."

"What about Melas?" Talin asked silently. "He can't survive

there either."

"Melas must turn back just before you reach the surface," the voice continued. "He must return and protect the Garden."

Talin and Ari took turns explaining the plan to Melas and Jonce.

"We know from experience that Jonce can survive on the surface," Ari stated. "It must be the strength of his human side." She paused as realization slowly blossomed on her face. "Oh," she said in surprise. "I suppose that can be said of me, too!" She looked thoughtful. "Are we all more than one kind? Not like the meld, but in a way don't we all have the DNA of many species in us?"

"You have grown wise," Talin told her proudly.

Melas interrupted. "We must leave immediately. The Garden is already starting to change. You must stop talking. We can get on with the plan as we go. The renegades must not find us here!"

"Will you show us how to get to the surface where there is a place we can defend?" Talin asked.

Melas looked worried. "I only wish this could be settled without a battle," he said. "I cannot bear to think of any more of my people held captive in the cliffs, not even the renegades. They too are Las."

Talin tried to reassure him. "Surely the Alph are wise. They will tell us what we need to do."

With some reluctance, he, Ari and Jonce followed Melas as he hurried through the trees and into a tunnel.

"No matter what happens we must keep the renegades away

from the Garden," Melas instructed. "It will be hard to make them leave their burrows and go out to the surface. They know full well what will happen if they do. They may decide to sacrifice some of their number in order to kill you, in which case you will have to hide long enough for them to meet their fate. I would hope, however, that a way can be found to negotiate and keep all of you alive."

Suddenly Talin remembered that Atrid, who thought herself to be Star Woman, was now a shadow herself, if what the renegades had said was true. Would this mean that she, too, would turn to stone if they forced her to the surface? Was there any possible way to save her? She was still Mem's Queen.

"What is it they want?" Jonce asked. "It must be more than revenge."

"I think they want to be returned to their true form," Melas replied. "And for Zed to be Zetti once more."

"You mean the whole planet would look like the Garden?" There was wonder in Ari's voice as she thought of the garden, the orchard, the meadows and the sunlight they had just left. "How could that be possible?"

"I don't know." Melas's voice was sad as he led them. "Many of my people have tried for decades, but nothing they tried could undo Queen Atrid's terrible work."

Talin spoke. "Atrid swore she would never give birth. She would rule the multiverse forever. For a long time I saw to it that she didn't have a child, but the Alph sent me dreams insisting that there must be a daughter to carry on the line of Queens. Ari, you are that daughter."

Ari's voice was sharp. "Does she know about me? Does she know that she has a daughter here on Zed, a child who has grown up in a prison camp?"

"No." Talin reached out to her. "You had to be a secret."

"Why?"

Melas reached back as if to stop his words, but Talin knew this was a moment for truth.

"The Queen wanted no daughter to replace her," he said as they hurried forward. "Mag and I were both sterilized and sent to Zed as our punishment when Atrid learned of my duplicity. She still thinks you were aborted, but miraculously, you survived."

Talin's face filled with wonder as he remembered that first Crossing, and the discovery he had made as he held Mag in his arms. "You were meant to be," he continued. "All these years it was my job to keep you a secret, to raise you and teach you all that a future queen needs to know, or as much as I could teach you here on this forsaken planet. That was why we hid in the cavern when the guards came. Princess, you are indeed Atrid's daughter, but she could never know of you, for she would harm you if she did. She is determined not to be replaced, sure that she will live forever!"

"So I have a mother who must never know I exist." Ari's voice grew strong. "A mother who would kill me if she knew! Oh, Talin, what have you done?"

"On my first Crossing to Zed, when I realized that you had miraculously survived, I promised Astraea, the true Woman of Stars, that I would serve her always. I know now that my promise to love you and teach you and keep you safe was also to the Alph. Exactly what dream they have for you I have only been able to guess. I think they have dreamed of a future only you can bring into being, and though I don't know the details, I do know that somehow you are to be a great leader and must live to fulfill your destiny. The dreams they have sent me have told me that much, and I trust them and your future with my life and my soul."

Ari was silent, taking everything in. Slowly she lifted her head, her eyes filled with determination. "The Alph say we must stop talking and hurry. In a short time the battle will begin. Melas, is there a shorter way to reach the compound before the renegades do?"

CHAPTER 36

Melas led and the others followed, climbing gradually upward through miles of dark, twisting tunnels. As she hurried along, Ari noticed that Jonce, who usually strode forward without a backward glance, was again dragging his feet and pausing to peer behind him. As he did, he seemed to be listening intently, cocking his head as if waiting for a message.

Ari shook herself and kept moving. "I must be imagining things," she told herself.

Jonce, who hardly ever complained, began to fuss about the pace.

"Aren't we there yet?" he grumbled. "How about a break?" He stopped to lean against the wall of the tunnel they had just entered. "I feel like I've been climbing forever," he protested.

Ari began to worry that he might be ill. It wasn't like him to behave this way. The only time she remembered him dragging his feet was when he had thought someone was calling. That time it had been Talin calling to her. Now Talin was here, just ahead of them.

"Come on," she scolded him. "Keep up. You're slowing us down."

"What's the rush? The battle can't begin without us, can it?"

Ari felt confused and a bit frightened. Was Jonce really tired, or was it something else? It was almost as if he wanted to stop and wait for the renegades!

Talin, ahead of her and close to Melas, seemed to be having the same thought. Looking back over his shoulder, he sped up. "Hurry," he instructed. "The renegade shadows could be right behind us by now."

"We're here," Melas said suddenly, pointing ahead to where light was visible around a curve in the tunnel. "And this is where I must take my leave of you. I must go back to make sure the Garden is protected."

It was Talin's turn to protest. "We need you," he said.

"No, Talin," Melas chided. "You know I can't live out on the surface, and my people need me. I must go quickly, but I leave you in the care of the Alph. Their thoughts will guide you from here."

Ari and Jonce both came to him. Melas touched their faces tenderly with the tips of his shadow fingers.

"Beloveds, it has been an honor to know and serve you." Lightly brushing their cheeks, he added, "I believe it won't be long before our paths cross again. May the Alph protect you both."

Turning back to Talin, Melas bent his tall body from the waist, so that his shadow head was in front of the Memmian's eyes. "Thank you," he drummed humbly, "for all that you and your species have done and will continue to do to correct the catastrophe that befell my people when Zetti became Zed."

"Yes," Talin agreed. "It is the Alph who guide the whole, not us meager humans."

Melas nodded. His shadow face grew brighter, and Talin knew he was smiling.

"Yes," Melas said, "I know that. I also know that you and Ari are Alph as well as human. Certainly you can begin to accept this now?"

Talin nodded slowly. "Perhaps I can begin to accept that this might be true."

Melas turned and knelt before Ari, so that her eyes were even with his shadow chest.

"My people in the cliffs have told me that our greatest hope lies with you," he said, bowing to her. "I will see you back in the Garden when you return."

Talin started to put out an arm to steady his daughter, who had moved up closer to him.

The voice in his head stopped him. "No," the Alph commanded. "Leave her be."

Talin stepped back and simply watched. Something was happening. Ari's face was becoming luminous in the half light of the passageway. Once again Talin tried to move to her side.

"Leave her be!" This time it was a command.

Talin saw Ari reach out to touch Melas's shadowy forehead with her outstretched palm. Then she spoke. "Promise that no matter what happens you will always be a guardian for Jonce and me," she said.

Melas nodded. "I swear on my honor that I will. You have my oath."

"Be blessed," she said. Her voice was strong; it echoed in the passages behind her, the ones Melas would take on his return. "You have our eternal gratitude."

She sounded so much a Queen that both Talin and Jonce

startled in surprise. Ari herself was puzzled by both the gesture and the words that had come from her mouth. They all stood in stunned silence. In the next instant Melas rose and was gone.

"You must all go to the surface while there is still time." The thought-voice of the Alph was urgent.

Ari looked puzzled. When she spoke she sounded irritated.

"Why are we still standing here?" Her voice was firm. "We need to get to the surface."

Sensing danger, Talin wanted to argue, but Ari turned and held out her hand to beckon him.

"We've had our orders."

Taking Jonce's hand, she began to lead him toward the surface. He looked dazed, but he followed. Talin came behind through the widening tunnel. Having reached the exit, they stepped through, and found themselves standing high up on a ledge of shining black. There was no place to hide. Talin drew the others back into the tunnel, motioning for them to get down. He flattened himself on the floor. Cautiously, he and Ari peered out. No wonder the area seemed familiar to them. It was the opposite side of the space that had been their compound. As they looked across the area they could see the familiar cliffs, and the opening in one of them that had been the supply cave and the entrance to their secret cavern.

Ari could see Talin struggling with his emotions. Obviously he was remembering. From here they could all see the whole big space.

Jonce spoke, breaking the silence. "The only beings in the

compound now are Atrid's men," he observed.

Ari was suddenly aware of uniformed men scurrying about, their bright red jackets clearly visible against the extrine surface. Less visible were the mages, whose pale grey robes barely contrasted with the black. Though all were moving rapidly, their tasks did not look like preparations for war.

"It looks as if they're getting ready to leave!" Jonce sounded relieved.

"I don't understand," Talin hissed. "They wouldn't go home without their Queen."

"Unless they think she's dead," Jonce replied softly.

"Why would they think that?" Ari asked, keeping her voice low.

"Perhaps she's been out of contact. Perhaps even the diggers weren't able to find her." Jonce let his words trail off into silence.

"I suppose that's possible," Talin said sadly. "I haven't been able to locate her since I heard her distress call many days ago."

"They look like they're leaving. We have to stop them," Ari said, beginning to move.

Jonce jumped up. Talin quickly pulled them both back down, hissing at them to stay hidden.

"Without the troops there are only three of us." Jonce's voice trembled. "And the battle is about to begin!"

"Yes," Talin agreed. "I know for sure there are at least two contingents of renegades, perhaps more. One is the large group that took me, and I'm pretty certain there were an equal number who captured the Queen."

"And made her one of them." Jonce's voice shook.

"Could they make us shadows, too?" Ari pulled her cloak around her face, as if she wanted to hide behind it.

"Only if we turn back to meet them in the tunnels." Talin's voice, too, was shaky.

Ari could hear his thoughts. "How can we keep the troops from leaving?" he wondered. "We need their help to lure the enemy out to the surface. We certainly can't do it by ourselves."

"If we stay on the surface they won't be able to take us." Ari found courage in the words as she said them.

Talin turned to her, then to Jonce. "Come," he said to them both. "We need to find a spot where we can hear some of what the troops are planning."

All three of them crawled on their bellies out to a nearby boulder. Reaching it without incident, they huddled together behind it, breathing deeply in relief. At Talin's signal they rose, still hunched over, and prepared to start climbing a slanted outcropping that would lead them to a ledge above.

Across the remains of the compound, the figures in red and grey were too engrossed in their tasks to notice the movement of the three. Reaching the ledge, they flattened themselves again behind an overhang.

"If we work our way around the perimeter, we can be directly above them," Talin murmured.

Inching their way to the left along the ledge, feeling at times as if they hung by their fingernails, they moved clockwise around the cliffs. It was frustratingly slow and painful, but finally they reached a familiar hiding spot directly over the opening of the supply cave, and Ari began to feel safe. From this vantage point they could easily observe all the activity of the camp directly below.

As they started to settle themselves, both Ari and Talin startled so abruptly that Jonce, stumbling, nearly pushed them off the ledge.

Ari had heard the voice of the Alph again. She was sure her father had, too.

"Stop!!" the Alph commanded. "Aricia must go alone and show herself."

Talin grabbed his daughter, steadying her as she turned to him.

"Why?" she gasped. "Why do they say I must show myself...alone?"

Jonce protested. "That would be much too dangerous. Whatever gave you such a stupid idea, Ari?" Suddenly he looked stricken. "Was it the Alph?" He stumbled over the question, his face full of fear for her safety. "No! Ari. You can't." Then he added, as if to persuade them both, "Aren't you the Secret?"

Ari looked helplessly at her father. "Must I?" she asked.
"Hurry!" The voice came again. "Time is short. Ari must show herself. There is no time to waste." The words were stern. Ari bent her head in submission.

"You must," Talin answered regretfully. "We have to trust the Alph. I think they are our only hope."

The Alph voice became more urgent. "There is a hidden pathway to the ledge just above. You know the place, Ari."

"Yes," she mentally agreed. "I hid there back when I saw Jonce for the first time."

She began slowly to sidle out from behind the boulder. Jonce leaped forward to stop her, but Talin grabbed him. With a quick glance over her shoulder, Ari gave a small wave of her hand and started along the ledge. Soon, she had vanished behind another boulder. Jonce jumped out of Talin's grip, but it was too late. Ari was gone.

CHAPTER 37

"Damn you, Talin!" Jonce exploded. "The Alph might be taking her right back into more tunnels." Tears of anger and frustration were in his eyes. "How could you let her go?"

"There was no choice." Talin's body cramped with grief. "We have to trust the Alph."

"Not me!" Jonce fumed. "I'm going after her."

He started forward, but Talin was quicker, and the older man blocked his passage.

"You would sacrifice your own child?" Jonce accused, squirming to free himself from Talin's grip.

"Watch." Talin pointed. "Look there."

Ari had emerged onto an open ledge far above and to the side of them. She stood there, revealed both to the two men where they hid, and to the scene below. Her silver hair with its streaks of copper and gold stood like an aureole around her head. Her bearing was regal. From this distance she looked so much like Atrid that both Talin and Jonce could only stare in amazement.

Suddenly, she called, and it was Atrid's signal that came from her mouth, the ululating warble that both men had heard many times on Mem, when Atrid had called for the attention of her guards. How had Ari known to make that sound? Was it the Alph speaking through her, using her voice?

On the ground below the troops stood utterly still, staring up at the figure on the cliff.

The wind was blowing Ari's cloak so that it billowed around her. She looked every inch a Queen.

As Talin and Jonce watched, Ari raised her arm. As if they had been swept by a gigantic hand, every man below fell to one knee.

"They think she is the Queen!" Jonce's whisper was a mixture of terror and awe.

Ari held out her arms and beseeched the troops, begging their help.

With clenched fists and a great roar they saluted her.

In the next moment, a mist blew across the ledge where Ari stood. When it cleared, she had vanished.

The men in the compound froze in place.

"The Queen needs us!" a voice bellowed.

With that, the scene exploded into chaotic activity, the men appearing like ants as they ran in circles, making their preparations.

Talin heard the Alph voice again, speaking in his head.

"Go down to them immediately, Talin. You and Jonce must organize the troops for battle before the renegades arrive."

Talin started to protest.

"Now!" the voice commanded sternly. "We will look after Ari and guide her to safety. Go! There is no time to waste."

Jonce looked stunned. "Someone is talking in my head!"

"Yes," Talin affirmed as he began to climb down, taking the lad with him. "It's the Alph. Come, Jonce, we have to trust them. It's our only hope, the only way we can protect Ari."

"Are you sure they can be trusted?" Jonce protested. "How can we be sure they'll take care of her?"

"They love her as much as we do and will keep her safe," Talin assured him. "Jonce, you must know they've given you a great gift. I suspect they haven't talked to anyone except other Alph in centuries. All they ask in return is that we follow their instructions. Can you do that?"

Jonce listened but did not reply. As they clambered down to the compound, Talin saw the youngster straighten his spine, as if he'd made a decision.

"What do we do when we get there?" he asked.

"The Alph will tell us. Hurry, Jonce, the renegades will be here all too soon."

Already the Alph were instructing them, telling them what they must do to organize Atrid's men.

"The troops must go into the tunnels in search of their Queen. Talin, you must lead the first battalion. You must show yourselves, but then instantly retreat to the surface. Timing will be crucial."

"And if the shadows don't follow my troops to the surface?"

"You must ready your troops for another try, while Jonce swiftly leads the second cordon in. You must alternate action in this way until they are in enough mindless fury to chase you out to the surface."

"What will happen to the shadows when they emerge?" Jonce's voice was tight.

"They will live like their brethren in the cliffs, hoping for rescue someday." There was a long pause. "Or perhaps they may look forward to release after all these years of captivity, and find the freedom to be born again."

"So they will turn to extrine." Jonce's voice was distressed.

"There are always sacrifices in any transformation." The Alph voice sounded deeply sad.

"And Ari?" Jonce looked back at the cliff face.

The Alph voice spoke again. "We will help her return to the Garden. She will be safe there with Melas, and with the Alph who have always watched over her."

"Will she have to go through the tunnels?" Jonce's voice was filled with fear.

"You forget that she is Alph! We will protect her. Time is short. You and Talin must hurry."

They had reached the base of the cliff. Talin led Jonce onward into the camp.

"It's Talin!" a mage voice exclaimed. "And Jonce!" said another.

Instantly men began to gather around the two, everyone talking at once.

"We saw a vision," one of the men explained. "Somehow the Queen sent her image to ask for our help. What do we do now? How do we rescue her when we don't know where she is?"

"Atrid is a prisoner," Talin explained. "She was captured by strange beings who hate her because they think she turned them into shadows. A battle is about to begin. If you want to rescue her you must stay and fight."

"So how do we do that?" The men moved in closer, eager to

hear Talin's reply.

"We will lead you," Talin declared. "Jonce and I know the shadow beings and we know their ways. Half of you will follow me," he instructed. "And the other half will follow Jonce."

A protest began, but Talin squelched it instantly.

"We are the ones who know the way," he explained, "but you must agree to follow our orders without question. Any delay in your response could cost the Queen her life, and many of you, yours." He added thoughtfully, after a pause, "Or worse."

After a few sullen grumbles the men began again to raise their clenched fists high in the air. Shouts went up.

"For the Queen!"

Talin, in his mind's eye, could see Ari, windblown and wild, standing on the ledge, looking every inch the Queen she had pretended to be. The men had been convinced she was Atrid, sending a vision of herself and pleading for their help. The Alph had been right to send Ari alone. Now he must trust them to keep her alive.

"All right," he shouted to the men. "Divide into two lines."

There was a scurry of activity. After giving Jonce instructions, Talin sent him and a few of the men off to collect weapons from the spaceship and the pods. He knew there would be little use for human weapons in what was to come, but he suspected it would give the men courage to be armed. It seemed wise to let them think this might be the kind of battle for which their training had prepared them. Talin began to sweat again as he realized how dangerously different this situation was from any the men could imagine.

Some of the officers and mages had started a small, smoldering lichen fire in the old fire pit. Talin knelt among them and gave instructions.

"Put the fire out," he ordered. "We must prepare to strike. Have your troops line up. You officers, scatter yourselves among your men so that if any of you are taken other officers will survive."

Talin picked up a large shard of extrine and, holding it like a knife, motioned to the officers to line up their men. Recognizing the young man who had been his guard on the night of his escape, Talin pulled him out of the ranks.

"You're with me," he ordered. The youngster raised his fist in salute and stood at Talin's side.

"We must all face the cliffs opposite," Talin began, but he was immediately interrupted as one of the officers bellowed an order. The men of both cordons spun on their heels to face the cliffs on the other side of the compound. On each side of the spaceship the men stood in ordered ranks, row after row lined up in perfect symmetry.

"Can this possibly work?" Talin asked silently, worried.

"Trust us," the Alph voice said in his mind.

As he and Jonce stood together by the spaceship, the young guard Talin had chosen as his aide stepped back slightly, out of earshot.

"Choose a man for yourself," Talin told Jonce. "Someone to watch your back."

"No." Jonce refused. "I want no one."

"Are you sure you can do this?" Talin asked softly. "Can you fight your own people? Can you remember that they are renegades who wanted to kill you and Ari?"

Jonce was tight-lipped, surveying the men he would lead. "How else can I protect her?" he asked.

Talin slapped the boy on his shoulder. "You are a good man, Jonce." He could feel the tears welling behind his eyes as he realized what a strong bond there was between his daughter and this lad who had been with her through so much turmoil. Were they soul mates? The thought made him remember his own early allegiance to Atrid. At that time he would have battled even the Alph to protect her.

He realized suddenly that Jonce had no gun. All the other men were armed.

"You know, of course, that our weapons are useless against the shadows," Talin told the boy quietly.

Jonce nodded.

"You could carry extrine..." Talin began.

"I will carry a gun," Jonce stated determinedly. "Like the men."

He left Talin and went around the spaceship to the hatch that opened into Atrid's armory. When he returned he had a weapon. Without hesitation he gathered four officers from his rank and took them to the fire pit where Talin stood.

"You need to talk to them," he told Talin. "They need to know what we're facing. It's only fair."

Talin nodded and turned to the men Jonce had chosen. He spoke quietly into the huddle they formed around him.

"We are asking you to risk more than your lives," he told them.

They looked startled.

"The ones we face are not like any species you've ever seen. They are shadow beings who believe all Memmians are their bitter enemies. They have taken the Queen and will try to take you. You will be able to see them only as shadows on the walls of the cavern or the tunnels. But be aware. They are not benign. If they get you within their grasp they will turn you into shadow and you will become one of them. This could happen to you or to any man who chooses to go with us in our attempt to rescue the Queen. You must explain to the men that they face grave danger. They must choose to go. We cannot force any Memmian to take this risk."

"If anything happens to Jonce or to me," he continued, "you will have to sound the retreat and get the men to safety. We are trying to force the enemy to the surface. Once they are out in the light they will turn to stone. On the surface you are safe from them, so try to get them to follow you out."

The Alph voice broke in. "Hurry! The renegades are almost in position."

This time both Talin and Jonce heard the words. They responded by quickly moving their men across to the far cliffs.

The battle was about to begin.

CHAPTER 38

Memories of showing herself on the ledge high above the compound filled Ari with apprehension. Every guard had seen her! She had called to them with a strange sound, as if some other being had been using her voice to make sure the message was delivered.

"What happened to me?" she wondered, upset at her loss of control. Why had she just stood there like an automaton, letting strange sounds come from her mouth?

"I won't have it," she fumed. "I won't be used this way. I am strong. I am perfectly capable of making my own decisions."

But where had her strength been when the Alph had used her for their own purposes? Her anger grew as she struggled to understand. Why had the Alph used her this way, putting her in a trance, giving her no choice as they forced her to serve their needs rather than her own conscience?

The spot where she had left Jonce and Talin was empty! They were gone.

The Alph voice spoke, soft but firm in her mind. "It is time for you to return to the safety of the Garden."

Did the Alph really expect her to flee like a coward? Could Talin and Jonce have agreed?

"Did you forget that I am a Survivor?" she asked aloud. Standing tall, she flung her arms wide so that her cape blew in the wind. "I have Sar blood in my veins! I won't be underestimated. Haven't I already proven myself against the renegades? Why did you make me show myself? Did you think I was too weak to fight?"

She thought about the game she and Talin had played all throughout her childhood. She had loved the secret cavern and the lessons she had learned. Always the most important lesson had been that she must stay hidden. Why then had the Alph used her in this fashion, and why had Talin let them? Most important of all, why would Talin and Jonce have used her absence as a chance to leave her behind?

"I'm being exploited!" she fumed. "The Alph did it. And now here they are again, telling me—no, commanding me—to run off to safety and leave the battle to the men!"

Where had Talin and Jonce gone? She wanted to join them, but they could be anywhere, in or out of the maze of tunnels and caverns that underlay most of the planet.

Feeling abandoned, Ari stood rigid on the ledge, fighting angry tears, stamping her feet in frustration.

"I will not hide!" she said aloud. "Not anymore. Talin knows I am loyal to Zed. And Jonce knows I'm strong."

She'd been with them every step of the way. How could they have left her behind with the battle about to begin?

"Zed is my planet. I have the right to protect it if anyone does. They have no right to exclude me. I won't leave! They can't make me go back to the Garden!"

Slowly Ari slid into a sitting position, then turned onto her belly. Pulling the hood of her dark cape up over her head, she wriggled herself forward until her nose was at the edge of the precipice. Peering down, she squinted, trying to figure out what was going on below.

From this spot, the whole compound was visible, including the area that had been her home. How had everything fallen apart? It was the Evil Queen! If Atrid had been turned to shadow so be it! Didn't she deserve punishment? Perhaps it would teach her to be a better Queen.

Ari recoiled then, thinking of the time when she had emerged from the cavern and returned to make peace with Talin, only to discover that he had been taken away by the guards, leaving Jonce and Old Bim behind in a burned out emptiness. Though she now understood that Talin had had no choice, and had been taken against his will, she still wondered if Atrid might have controlled him while he was there on Mem. Was that why he had taken the meld? Could he still be loyal to the Evil One?

No, this was his way of trying to protect her, his daughter. That was why he had left her behind.

Ari studied the compound, still a wasteland, but no longer barren. The flatland was alive with movement. At the center she could see an enormous shining space rocket, larger than any supply vessel she'd ever seen, even in her cave dreams of Mem. Surely it had been there when she'd shown herself, but she'd been too ensorcelled to notice. Scattered around the spaceship were dozens of small white pods like the one she and Jonce had lived in before their journey. Had she missed the pods too, in the spell cast on her by the Alph? All she remembered now was revealing herself to masses of guards who weren't supposed to know she existed.

The scene below was stranger to Ari than any dream. Yet, slowly, as she kept watching, she began to understand. Instead of preparing the spaceship for departure, as they had been doing before she'd shown herself, the guards were now preparing for war, a war she was supposed to retreat from, returning like a coward to the Garden! Oh, the fools! The troops obviously had no concept of what they were about to face. They served the Evil One, but they were human.

"Like Jonce," she thought, "and me! I must warn them."

Once again she tried to ululate, but this time her voice was lost in the wind that swept straight at the cliffs and right into her face. "They will all be taken," she thought. "The renegades will turn them into shadows to reinforce their own numbers. Oh, Goddess, what can I do?"

Suddenly she saw her father, unmistakable in his dark Survivor rags. A strong sound came to her on the wind, the familiar sound of his voice. Her whole body tried to respond, ready to leap up and run to him as his mage voice called the men.

"With Me!" The call echoed from the extrine cliffs.

A vivid memory came into Ari's mind like a flash. She was a child clinging to Talin's back as he yelled at the tak, using his mage voice as he tried to coerce the animals into carrying her. Despite her anger and fear, in the moment Ari couldn't suppress a derisive snicker. The mage voice had never worked on the blessed tak. In their stupidity they had simply ignored it. Talin had been forced to carry her himself. Determinedly she closed her mind to his call and hunched back into the cleft behind her. She could play stupid, too. She could refuse to let his Call work on her. Much as she wanted to stop him, she needed time to figure out what she should do before making her move.

It was obvious that the Call worked on the soldiers below. As she watched, she saw them run from every direction to gather around Talin. Ari guessed he was giving orders. Oh, if only she could hear what he was saying!

"I must understand what he's planning," she thought, but his voice was his own now, and the strong wind swallowed his human words before they could reach her ears. Frustrated, she could do nothing but watch as the men gathered and began to line up in ranks on the far side of the spaceship. Leaving an open space as wide as a tunnel, another rank formed on the other side. Soon Talin stood alone between the ranks.

"Oh, Talin," she said aloud. "You're just asking for trouble! You know the Shadow renegades. They had you. How can you even think about fighting them in this human way?"

"Hear me, you Alph," Ari shouted. "I'm not leaving! I'm going to stay and fight."

The only response she received was the soughing of the wind as it swept again from the compound into the cliffs behind her. Could the Alph hear her? The wind seemed to catch her words and throw them back into her mouth.

Where was Jonce? No sooner had Ari asked herself that question than he appeared from behind one of the pods to stand before the men in the second rank. He was dressed in his old red and black uniform. And he was carrying a laser!

Ari felt sick with horror. Didn't he remember that weapons were useless against the renegades? What was he thinking? And he was not the only one carrying. Each man in each rank seemed to be armed. Only Talin had no gun. What he carried looked like a large knife-sized shard of extrine.

On hands and knees Ari began to scrabble along the ledge toward the path that led down from the heights. She must stop them. Before she could move more than a few feet, however, she saw Talin wave his arm, urging his contingent forward. They began to march straight toward the cliff on the opposite side of the compound, straight toward the tunnel from which the three of them had emerged only hours before. Her limbs went rigid. Her heart seemed about to pound its way out of her chest as Talin and his men disappeared into the cliff face. Frozen with horror, she watched helplessly as they vanished.

"Oh Goddess!" Ari thought. "Do they have any idea what may be waiting for them?"

She could almost hear the angry drumbeats of the renegades. Would the Shadows swallow the whole army? Without knowing how she knew, Ari was sure that the renegades were waiting in those very tunnels, ready and eager to capture any who approached them.

Why would Talin do this stupid thing? Was he determined to precipitate a war? Was that what the Alph were demanding of him? Didn't they know it meant the destruction of both Talin and the Memmian guards? Could the Alph be determined to destroy them all? Ari began to shake with fear. What about Jonce?

"What can I do?" Ari cried out in desperation.

No answer came. In the silence, however, she began to hear a sound. It came from deep within the tunnels of the cliff behind her and made her spin to face the wall, panic filling her so that her heart pounded and her mouth went dry. Drums were sounding deep within the cliff she had turned to face. The renegades must have split their forces, so that some were in the tunnels opposite, and others were approaching right here!

Now on her hands and knees, Ari scanned the cliffs that encircled the compound. She knew that each cliff contained tunnels. How many renegade shadows waited there for their prey? Torn between a desire to scramble down the cliff shouting a warning to Jonce, and an overwhelming need to rush toward the drums in the tunnel behind her, Ari tried to move, only to find herself frozen in place, as if her legs had turned to stone and become part of the ledge. Had the Shadows taken her, so that she was turning into extrine out here in daylight?

"Let me go!" she screamed in her mind, but there was no answer.

Ari fought to stay calm. Only her eyes and thoughts seemed able to move. Her heart was beating; she could feel the pounding of it. Yet she was held captive where she stood. All she could do was watch and listen.

Drumbeats came from every cliff. Across the compound there was no sign of Talin or his troops. Had they made contact?

She tried to lift her legs, but they were held fast. Oh, why couldn't she move? All she could do was listen to the drums and try to understand what the Shadows were saying. Her heart thundered as she realized that there were no words. Drums from every direction were sounding a battle cry! Fear gripped her. Gulping, she tried to catch her breath. I mustn't faint, she thought. She felt as if the noise were pulverizing her bones.

Then, in one instant, the sounds were gone. All around her was profound silence.

In the next moment, Talin appeared below, leading his men as they raced out from the opposite cliff face, rushing at top speed toward the compound.

Relief flooded her. He was safe! Now she could move her feet. Once again her muscles could respond. She wanted to call to him, to ululate as she had earlier, but her voice wouldn't work. Standing there, Ari could feel the wet tears on her cheeks, tears of gratitude. Her father had survived. She looked down again, watching the men. No shadow emerged from the cliff. Talin and his men had not been followed. What would happen next?

Once again, she stiffened. Jonce was leading the other rank of men forward to the very place Talin had just left!
"No!" Ari screamed aloud. "No...no...no!!"

As she watched in terror, Jonce led his contingent of guards into the same cliff face. All Ari could do was stand helplessly silent as rank after rank of men followed him, disappearing into the darkness of the tunnel opening.

Throwing her body against the cliff face, she began to beat on the extrine with her fists.

"Talin!" she screamed. "How could you do this to Jonce? How

could you do it to me?"

Not only Talin, but the Alph. This must be their design. They had made her show herself. Had all that been a subterfuge to get her out of the way? She began to sob again. How could Talin have given the Alph such control? How could he have let the Alph use Jonce in this fashion? Jonce was untested. How could anyone expect him to fight his own kin?

With all the weight of her arms and her body she pushed at the wall as if it could give her an answer. Tears poured down her face. "If anything happens to Jonce..." She couldn't finish the sentence, even in her mind. All she could do was lean against the wall, sobbing.

CHAPTER 39

Time dragged as Talin paced. Where were the troops? Where was Jonce? At last soldiers began to pour from the cavern, retreating rapidly just as the first group had. But where was the boy? Those who emerged from the caves looked shocked and haggard. There was no sign of their leader. Feeling sick and defeated, Talin looked for the one who was so important to Ari. What if Jonce hadn't been fast enough?

Approaching the last of the men who had just returned, Talin recognized a Captain who had tried to befriend him before their Crossing in Atrid's ship. He was about to question him when the officer looked at him wild-eyed and choked out, "They took the boy!"

Talin grabbed the Captain's arm to keep himself from falling.

"He stayed and let them take him," the man began sobbing. "They let the rest of us go because they had him."

"That wasn't the plan," Talin barked. "Why didn't you save him?"

"What were we to do?" the man protested. "He ran right toward them as if he wanted to be taken."

"So now they have Jonce as well as the Queen." Talin wanted to hit the man. Instead he made himself turn away. It wasn't the Captain's fault. Jonce was Las. Obviously that part of him had taken over.

Thank Goddess Ari was safe, back at the Garden with Melas.

Yet Atrid and Jonce had both been captured and were probably Shadow now themselves.

"It's my fault," Talin thought. "I should never have sent him. Ari will never forgive me."

Already he could see the men grumbling and turning their backs on him. How could he possibly persuade Atrid's men to follow him into the tunnels once again, especially now that they had an idea of what they were up against? They were ignoring him. Why should he be surprised? They were finally remembering that he was the madman their Queen had decried and derided, the one she had cast out from her Inner circle to be exiled, imprisoned and finally hunted like a dangerous animal who needed to be caged or killed. Now that the guards had remembered all of this, how could he expect to lead them?

Talin began to hear sounds of rebellion, a mounting determination among the men to leave and return to Mem.
Wrapping his arms around his chest, he struggled to hold back the sob in his own throat. What had he done?

"What about the Queen?" He heard a mage voice ask the question.

"They've got her. It's hopeless." The impact of the words ran through the exhausted crowd like a wave.

"What about those the shadows got on the first charge? Shouldn't we try to get them back?" another voice asked.

Talin saw one of the men from the first charge standing atop a pod. Using a mage voice that carried to the very edges of the circle of resting men, the man shouted, "We need to get out of here before they get us all. Do you want to live the rest of your lives as shadows on this forsaken planet?"

Talin tried to think of a retort but his mind was in turmoil.

Why had Jonce done this terrible thing, wrecking the plan, destroying any chance they had of defeating the enemy? Now there was no hope except flight, and even that seemed impossible. Thanks to Jonce it felt as if the battle had ended before it had begun.

Where were the Alph? Where could he turn for help if they had deserted him? No matter how hard he tried to contact them, there was only silence. A miracle was needed, but there wasn't one available.

After sinking to the ground, Talin huddled there in utter despair.

"There's nothing I can do," he thought. "It's over. We've lost."

CHAPTER 40

Waiting in the Garden, Melas had to accept that Ari was not going to return. Had she met some ill fate? No, he would feel it in his center if she had. It was more likely that she had refused to leave Talin and Jonce. Whatever the cause, the time when she should have arrived was long past.

After taking a deep breath of resolution, Melas let it out in a great sigh, knowing he must leave the sanctuary to seek her out. Dreams had repeatedly told him that Ari was now his greatest responsibility. Her safety far outweighed not only his own life, but also the safety of all his shadow beings, and even that of the Garden. He knew with certainty that the future of not only his beloved planet, but also that of Mem and its realm would soon depend on her, though she obviously didn't know this yet. The Alph had shown him clearly in dreams that a future without Aricia might well mean chaos and destruction for every planet in the Galaxy. Whole galaxies had lost their Light under Atrid's domination. Greed and destruction were rapidly thrusting one planet after another back into the Dark. Three centuries had passed since the Change, during which Atrid and her Inner minions had gained more and more power, stripping planet after planet of beauty and individuality. Under Atrid's rule of "progress," not only had the Las been changed into shadows or extrine, but the whole of her realm seemed in danger of being permanently swallowed by a black maw.

In dream after dream Melas had seen what these two youngsters meant for the future. It was they who would shape a new dream, not only for humans, but for all species, including his own.

Melas made one last tour of the Garden, hoping against hope that the girl might have returned exhausted and fallen into a deep sleep in some quiet corner. He knew in his heart that the search was useless, but he had to try. It was no surprise to him when there was not the slightest trace of her anywhere within the sacred area.

At the gateway Melas paused, turning to survey what he was leaving. Would he ever return to see it again? Sinking to his knees, he felt the reality of his Lasian body, and wondered if this might be his last experience of existing in such a body. If the renegades found him, surely they would imprison him far from this garden paradise he loved so deeply.

"Oh Great Beings," he prayed to the Alph, "you have shown me in dreams what is asked of me now. Please give me strength to do what I must, to bear what comes, and to remain true to the task you have given me."

He finally rose, turned and went through the gate, accepting what lay ahead. As the gateway closed behind him, his form immediately became shadow, yet it was a shadow unlike any he had known before. As if something of the garden had come with him, he felt a radiance in his being that spread from him in the form of a blue and white light that showed him the path ahead.

"What is this?" he asked in wonder. There was no reply, but he had a strong feeling that he was now made of soft Light, rather than the familiar pale grey he had known for centuries. Starting his flow, he discovered that he could move more rapidly than anything he had ever experienced before. As if caught up in his own Light, he sped through tunnel after tunnel, glancing quickly into every cranny and side passage as he flowed. There was neither any sign of Aricia nor any sense of her recent passage. She had obviously stayed for the battle! Moving even faster, he shot toward the place where he had left his three friends.

Suddenly he came to an immediate halt. He heard drum voices ahead in what he knew to be a large cavern. It was the renegades! He recognized their chatter. Wondering why they had gathered here, Melas tried to think of what he should do. If they saw him in his new form they would surely stop him, perhaps even imprison him. He had to find a way past them without being seen. He must find Ari before it was too late.

Taking an enormous risk, he flew up to the high ceiling and flowed into the cavern, far above the group below. The band of renegades all hovered in a mass of dark shadowy stalks, encircling something on the cavern floor. Fortunately they were all so focused on what they held in the center of their circle that none of them noticed his presence high above.

A large, half naked human boy lay among the shadows, curled up in a fetal position on the black extrine floor, his hands wrapped tightly around his head. He was the only one who noted Melas's arrival. As if suddenly aware that something new had entered, he lifted his face to look up and, as he did, Melas saw with a jolting shock that the human was Jonce! How could the boy have let himself be captured? Where were Talin and the troops? And where was Ari?

Knowing he mustn't reveal himself, Melas tried to simply blend in with the ceiling. If the renegades identified him they would undoubtedly take him prisoner. They might also kill the boy. Perhaps the only thing that had stopped them so far was the knowledge that at the core Jonce was Las as well as human.

Melas was relieved that Jonce didn't recognize him or see him as anything but a blue and white light. Looking anguished and scared, the wounded boy was protesting, his voice becoming increasingly desperate.

"I am one of you," he kept saying. "I am Las. Would you kill one of your own?"

Drum voices began to speak. They began softly, sounding like twigs brushing on a drumhead, before growing into loud and definite drumming. "Liar," they accused. "Traitor...Coward."

"Take him," one voice drummed. "Make him one of us." This voice was immediately joined by others, all of the voices growing louder until the cave seemed filled with hatred.

"Quiet!" a commanding beat thundered. It was the leader. "Look at him."

The shadows surrounding the boy drew closer until the boy almost disappeared. Melas, truly fearful now, clung tightly to the extrine of the cavern roof.

"Does he look like one of us?" The beat thundered in derision right over the boy's head. "Can he talk like us? He is human. Isn't that obvious? He is from Mem. He is the enemy!"

More drumbeat sounds, now all filled with derision, echoed off the cavern walls once again. "Change him!" they demanded.

"He wants to be one of us," another voice spoke. "We took the Queen. Why not do the same with him? Couldn't he lead us to the other humans?"

The renegade shadows continued drumming, communicating with one another.

"Could he be Las?" one voice boomed. "I can hear his thoughts. He thinks he is one of us. He understands what we say."

Suddenly Jonce lay face down, perfectly still. Had he died? Had they killed him?

"He's fainted." Melas recognized the renegade leader's drum voice and felt a wash of relief.

"Then this is a good time to make him one of us." Melas knew this voice, too, a constantly challenging one. "While he's unconscious he won't be able to fight it. We have to go to battle and we certainly can't carry him with us!"

Someplace far ahead drums were urgently sounding the call to battle.

"No time." The renegade leader's drum voice boomed. "We are called to battle and to increase our numbers we need those the Queen ejected before she became one of us. Quickly now, go collect them from the walls where they hang so we can all start moving."

Melas hadn't noticed the tiny bat-like shadows that hung high on the cavern wall not too far from him. Several dark shadow forms began to flow toward them. Surely they would see him as they gathered the tiny shadows Atrid had left clinging there. Melas wrapped himself into a ball, trying to be totally still and undetectable as he hung in the dome just above the shadows' movement.

On the floor below, Jonce had disappeared into the press of shadows, who were shoving and beating at him. Melas wanted to go to the boy but didn't dare move. Then the renegade leader's voice sounded, like a pounding drum.

"Stop!" it commanded. "Leave him be. Can't you see he's dying and is no threat to us? Come! Hurry! The battle is about to begin again."

With that, the shadows fell in behind their leader, and in a great wide swirl they disappeared.

Melas watched the renegades leave. On the floor, the boy stirred from the place where he had fallen forward and hit his head on the cavern floor. Somehow he managed to raise his blood-drenched face and speak, but now a different voice came from his mouth. Though it spoke with the sound of a shadow drum beat, to Melas it was clearly the voice of a woman!

"I am Atrid," it said. "I have found a new host. They thought they could defeat me by making me one of them, but I am cleverer than they thought and I found a way to escape and survive! I am here in this boy's body!"

Melas recoiled in horror. Was it the Great Changer herself, the very one who centuries ago had wreaked havoc on the whole Lasian race? Had the renegades truly captured her and made her one of their band? How had she escaped and melded with the boy?

Was it truly the Evil Queen herself who spoke through Jonce's mouth?

Anger surged through Melas. "If I could kill her myself I would," he thought.

Yet if she truly was a part of Jonce in some weird version of the meld, the only way Melas could destroy her would be to destroy the boy as well, and he had made a sacred promise not only to the Alph, but also to Ari, that he would protect Jonce.

The boy was in peril, not at the moment from the renegades, but rather from the Evil Changer herself! He had promised Ari to keep the boy safe. Now he must get Atrid out of the boy and save him from her as well as from the renegades, but how?

CHAPTER 41

Ari was angry. Why hadn't the Alph chosen her instead of Jonce? She was a survivor. She had grown up tough and knowing how to survive. Perhaps Talin still thought of her as a little girl who needed to be protected, but the Alph must know how strong she had become.

With all the weight of her arms and her body she pushed at the wall as if it could give her answers. As she began to cry angry tears the soft whisper of a drum came into her mind. At first she thought it was her own sniffling, but in a moment words began to take form in the rustle.

"Ar...ie...ie... weeps..."Another whisper. "With us...sss."

Into Ari's mind flashed the image she had seen of herself in the cave where she and Jonce had first met the shadows. She had been a tiny girl standing at the base of the cliffs as water poured down them into a pool at her feet. She had known somehow that these were the tears of giants, and she had wept with them.

"Yesss..."

And now it was as if they were weeping with her once more. Was this only her imagination or were the giant beings she had known as a child still here in these cliffs?

"Yesss..."

As if the beings could soothe her, she leaned into the wall with all her weight, spreading her arms to take their comfort.

The walls responded. Ari sobbed, sure that the walls were

moving, softening, becoming pliant in their effort to hold her.

"Help me," she sobbed, unable to stop sounding like the small child they had known in the past.

"Yes...sss."

The wall she leaned into wrapped itself around her, holding her.

"Jonce is in the far tunnels," she told the walls, "The renegades will capture him. I know it."

"Yesss..."

"Your people," Ari began, clinging to the wall.

"Fool...isssh."

"They will turn him into a shadow!" Ari lifted her head. "He is part Las. We have to save him!"

"Sss...star Wo...oo...man."

What were they saying? What did Star Woman have to do with it?

"Hisss...an...cesss...tresss."

Star Woman was Jonce's ancestress? They couldn't mean Mem's Evil Queen! Did they mean the old Star Woman, the one of legends and myths, the giantess who had guided Memmians in their first days?

"Y...e...e...s...ss...As...tra...e...a."

"She was Las?" For a moment Ari forgot her grief. "And she mated with a Memmian and is Jonce's ancestress?"

"Yesss...sss."

"We must save him!"

Ari suddenly had an image of herself running as the renegades chased her! If she could get their attention, would they try to catch her?

"Why would they pursue a mere girl, a nobody like me?" she asked herself aloud.

The walls swayed and began to swing back and forth in a dizzying sweep.

"Mohr," she heard.

"Re...e...e...deem...e...ers...Ari...Jonnncce...save La...s...ss."

Ari sobbed harder. "Redeemers"—was that what they were saying? Was that what they believed!? Could they have some strange impossible belief that she and Jonce could save them and release them from the extrine?

"Ye...sss."

Did the beings in the walls think she could work a miracle just because she had cried with them when she was a child?

Ari suddenly knew the truth. The people in the walls thought she could save them! Perhaps she believed it, too, deep in the recesses of her childhood heart. But what about Jonce? The renegades had him. How could she save him?

"We...call...renegades...will...come. Follow Ari..."

Could it be true? What were they saying? Could they call the renegades from every tunnel to follow her? Did they want her to run into the tunnel? If she ran to meet the shadow renegades would they spot her and follow her out to the surface? Could she possibly run fast enough to lure all of them out into the open before they caught her?

"But then the extrine will take them!"

"Our only h...ho...pe is...s dea...th...re...bir...th."

"You think you can all be reborn?"

"Ma...n...y."

"I'm only one ordinary human being," Ari thought, "but I am the last of the Survivors. I believe in you. All I can do is my very best. Pray Goddess that's enough!"

"YESSS...SSS...SS!"

The answer from the walls entered her like a crescendo. At the same time she heard the sound of drums, magnified by distance, in the tunnels behind her. How could she make them see her? How would they know to follow her? The sound beat against her. She stumbled.

"G...o...o...o...o..."

The walls were waving. They seemed to be moving, pushing against her, driving her away from them and back into the tunnel. Ari had no choice. All she could do was run as if she were being pushed from behind. Without conscious volition, her heart thumping, her legs stomping, she tore through the blackness, aware only of the angry drum sounds that surrounded her in every direction as she ran.

Suddenly, she saw them. A huge band of dark grey mist was gaining rapidly on her! Spinning around, she never broke stride, but with all her might raced back the way she had come. Yes, there was the opening to the outside. She was running top speed toward it with hundreds of shadow renegades behind her. With her heart and legs pounding she raced forward. For an instant she felt fear. Would she emerge on the ledge and sail right off to her death?

Perhaps, but if she did the shadows would be right behind her, and they couldn't survive in the open!

She raced on, legs pumping faster now that she realized what she was doing and accepted it as her fate. Whatever happened next was surely meant to be. Perhaps she could at least try to be a savior, sacrificing herself for the good of others? Jonce was human as well as Las. He had survived daylight! In fact he loved light! So if the renegades could be captured in extrine, wasn't it likely that Jonce would be freed from their clutches? Perhaps if she could give all the Las renegades a chance for rebirth the Alph would see to it that Jonce survived!

Wasn't that worth dying for?

CHAPTER 42

Slowly Melas dared to relax, stretch out and descend. Miraculously, no shadow had been left behind to guard the unconscious boy. Every renegade had gone to the battle. Hovering over Jonce, Melas saw that the boy was deeply unconscious, curled in a fetal ball on the extrine. The new injury must be serious. Blood was still flowing from his nose and mouth. He needed more help than Melas could give him, and soon. How could he, in his new shadow form, get Jonce out of the tunnel where the renegades had left him? If Atrid was truly in the boy, could he get her to help?

Calling up his strongest Las voice, Melas mind-spoke to her. "Atrid, if you are truly in there, you must know that the boy is dying, and if he does, you will die with him."

"Who are you?" she thought back at him. "Obviously Shadow!"

"I am Melas, a friend of Talin," he replied. "Yes, like you I am Shadow. I am also your only hope!"

"I've never heard Talin speak of you."

Melas snapped his thoughts at her. "There are many things you have never heard Talin speak of," he reminded her. "If you don't get out of Jonce so I can carry him, he'll die and so will you. Then you won't hear Talin or anyone else ever again."

Atrid was silent. When she spoke again, her thoughts sounded petulant and selfish. "But I need a body! I will not go hang on a wall again. I am Queen! I am Star Woman! How dare you shadows treat me in this fashion?"

"As I see it you have only one choice," Melas told her. "You can join me until we get Jonce to safety, or both of you will die. I couldn't carry you both in my arms, even in my true form. Your dark energy is too strong. You must come out of him in order for either of you to live."

"How do I know you won't simply abandon me if I try to come out? Where would I go? I don't want to be a shadow again. No, I can't do it."

"I need your strength in order to carry him, Atrid. If there were any other way I would abandon you, but I have made a sacred vow to save him and I must at least try. If you will meld with me and lend me some of your power I will let you join me."

"Why should I believe you? You're just trying to trick me out of him."

"Atrid, I'm trying to save you both. This is your only option if you don't want to die!"

This time there was a long silence. Then Melas felt something pushing at the edges of his shadow form. Without a word he opened himself. For a moment he recoiled as he felt the surge of Atrid's powerful anger and determination, but knowing this was the only way to save Jonce, he accepted her darkness and let her in.

Immediately Atrid began to protest.

"There's too much light in here! It's too warm. I feel as though I'm shriveling! What have you done to me? Who are you?"

"I am Melas, one of the Las you turned to shadow with your

Change."

"I want you to understand that I do not take orders from shadows!"

Melas felt exasperated. Why had he taken her on? "I need you to be quiet so we can carry the boy to safety," he drummed.

"I don't take orders from you!"

"Then all three of us will die."

As if a wind had suddenly calmed, there was utter stillness.

"I need some of your power, Atrid," he thought to her. "We need strength and speed if we are to reach the surface before the renegades." For a moment he felt her wanting to fuss. Then, as if she had made a decision, her energy increased within him, and he knew she had agreed to help.

Immediately he enwrapped Jonce, just as he had previously done with Talin, and began to flow, carrying the unconscious boy through tunnel after tunnel at a velocity he had never experienced before. With the Queen's energy added to his own they might make it in time!

Finally they reached the place where he had previously left Talin and the youngsters. Now there was no turning back. The renegades were close behind. Soon the shadow band would burst into this space, charged for battle. In front of Melas lay an opening out to the compound. He knew that daylight awaited them the moment they stepped forth. Could he possibly establish contact with those outside before he turned to extrine?

In his arms Jonce began to stir, struggling to escape the net of Shadow that held him. Without hesitation Melas pressed a pressure point in the boy's neck, and he was still.

"We must go outside," he thought-whispered to Atrid. "If Talin is there with his troops you and the boy may both be saved." He didn't remind Atrid that she was still Shadow. Could she separate from him and survive the light of day?

Determinedly Melas went toward the tunnel opening. Now he could hear yells coming from the compound below. Talin must be there. He would know what to do if he found Jonce, but could he, Melas, drop both Jonce and Atrid before his own shadow self became extrine? He must try. The boy's safety came first. He had promised both the Alph and Ari.

"If you know any prayers now would be a good time," he whispered to Atrid.

In desperation he silently sent his own prayer thought to the Alph. "If you are listening, please help me do what must be done."

With that, Melas flowed forward and down. Letting the boy's body drop on a ledge overlooking the compound, the last thing he heard as the extrine took them was Atrid's voice calling from within him, "Talin, help! Save me!"

Then there was only darkness for them both.

CHAPTER 43

Melas had expected to find himself caught like a statue in the solidity of rock. Instead, to his astonishment, he found that he and Atrid were part of a wide, deep flow of shadows melting into black, viscous extrine that was slowly creeping through enormous tunnels and caverns.

"We are neither dead nor alive," Melas thought. "Am I still Shadow?"

He wasn't sure. All he knew was that he was still able to think, though he couldn't make a sound. He also knew that although Jonce had escaped, Atrid had not. He could feel her roiling around, trying to beat her way out. Melas tried to open his mind to her but there was no response.

Did he still have thoughts? Yes, and they were carrying images! Soon he found himself picturing a flowing river of former shadows. Many were shades of grey, while some were almost black; others were quite light, with a few almost white. What's more, the river was swelling constantly with the addition of multitudes of new shadows. Had the extrine taken the renegades? Had something called them all out into the light of day? Did this stream include all of his people? He wondered if those in the burrows had also been called.

"We are in the river between life and death," Melas thought. "How is this different from the last three hundred years? Is it what Earth humans called Purgatory, or the Bardo? Are there lessons to be learned here or do we just flow mindlessly, endlessly, without purpose?"

As he pondered their fate, he began to hear sound. Not the familiar drumming voices, but something like the whine of a power saw cutting wood, as when one of the Garden trees had died and was being turned into firewood. At first he felt puzzled. Finally he realized that the sound was that of frantic mind-voices screaming. They were the voices of his people, newly trapped in the same river as he. The only difference was that they were terrified, and he felt strangely calm.

Where was his calmness coming from? Not from the Queen he bore inside his shadow self. He was sure of that. He had willingly sacrificed both himself and Atrid in order to save Jonce: perhaps that was it. Slowly he became aware of other calm voices emerging from the river around him. To his astonishment he realized that they were singing!

"Melas!" they sang, as if they were rejoicing. "Leader. Welcome! We knew someday you would come for us, Sa...a...a...vior!"

The songs sounded strangely familiar.

"Do I know you?" he sang back.

"Y...e...es," the answer came back in the form of many chords, all vibrating with calm. "Y...ou...ou...rr Oth...er...r...rs..."

The joyous words were sung by some of the pale grey, almost white, shades in the river. These shadow beings were guiding the flood of viscous darkness.

"There are so many of us," Melas sang to them. He began to

feel full of surprise. "All different shades!"

"Yes...s...sss....All h...er...e."

Suddenly an actual mind-speaking voice popped in. Not a drum, not a song, but a familiar strong voice, coming not from the river but from nowhere and everywhere.

"The pale guides are your Others," said the Alph voice.

Melas wondered if he was in one of their dreams.

"Yes," the Alph voice commented, "the battle has ended. All of your people, including the Renegades, are in this flood, called by your Others to follow Ari into the light."

Melas's own calm seemed to split wide open. Was Ari in this river of souls? Was all he had done for nothing?

"No, she is safe with Jonce and Talin," the voice assured him. "It was not their time for transition."

"And for us?"

"That is up to you, Melas."

"To me?" He was shocked.

"Sa...aa...v...i..or," the soft voices in the river sang again. There were many now, as if the palest shadows were gathering near to give him support.

Melas felt agony. These were his people, his Las, the beautiful, the renegade, the radiant and the lost, all trapped in a moving river that seemed to have no destination.

"We're all trapped!" he thought.

"Trapped?" Atrid's thought voice sounded, weak and bewildered. "What happened? Who did this?"

"You did, Atrid," Melas thought to her.

"Nonsense," Atrid shot back. "I had nothing to do with this."

"You started it when you changed Zetti into Zed."

"Yes...ss...Th...he...e Ch...a...n...ge..." the pale voices sang.

"Nonsense. There was not a single human on Zetti. I made sure of that!"

"Not human, but Las, like the original Star Woman." The Alph voice broke in again.

"I am Star Woman and I am not Las." Atrid's thought had begun to sound desperate.

A titter rippled among the Shadow Others. It sounded like laughter. "No...oo...oo..." they sang. "No...tt...tt La...a...sss...n...o...tt As...tra...e...a!"

"But I have the hair! I have the star!"

The Alph voice sounded amused. "Those were cosmetic," it said. "You misunderstood. Your soul was too young."

"I am Star Woman!" Atrid's thought insisted.

"Ill...lu...u...sion...n."

"I was a good Queen." Atrid's desperation intensified. "I made the whole Galaxy my realm and kept it peaceful!"

"S...S...Slaugh...S...s...Slaugh...ter!"

"What do they mean?"

The Alph replied: "They are telling you that you achieved all that by slaughtering the Las."

"Las?" Atrid's thoughts were tired. "What is Las?"

"If you had listened to Talin and read the Folios you would know," Melas told her, his dream thoughts still controlled. "Astraea was Las."

"Nonsense," Atrid's thoughts weakly protested.

"You were always blinded by your own ideas," Melas thought back. "You missed the truly important things. We Las were here for generations. We had created a paradise."

"But the Las were giants! We could never have missed them!"

"When your probe came, most of us hid in the deepest tunnels. By the time the Change was completed, we had become shadows of ourselves. Those who stayed behind out in the open, mostly Las women and children, were caught by the Change in light and transformed into extrine. They have been in the cliffs for 300 years! Either way, we Las were all changed by your actions, Atrid, and we have been unable to either live or die all this very long time."

"I didn't know. No one told me."

"No," Melas said sadly. "You didn't know. You could not see beyond your own greed for power."

"Nonsense! All I wanted was the right kind of life for my people."

"Without considering the cost in lives and beings." Melas's thought was flat and sad. "Your changes were meant to make all your subjects obedient, in service to your own design."

"You mean the Survivors?" Atrid's thought was dismissive. "They didn't matter. They were simply the dregs."

"Your own bitter dregs."

There was silence within Melas as the river continued to flow. Finally, an Alph voice spoke to him again.

"Melas!" The voice woke him from his reverie. "We have

chosen you to gather all the shadows before you break free. Call them. It's their only chance."

"Sa...vi...or," the chorus sang.

Melas wished he could shake his Las head. He was only a shade, caught in an endless river of shades, yet he must call his people! Music began to pour forth around him. Soon the river widened and grew as more and more shadows poured into its slow inching flow.

"Sa...vi...or..." The chorus sang again.

"There is no way out," Melas thought.

"Yes, there is," the Alph voice assured him. "With Atrid's help."

"My help?" Atrid's thought was weak, almost exhausted.

"Yes. You must undo what you have done and free those you trapped in extrine."

"It's impossible. I'm too tired."

"Melas will give you his strength. You two are the only ones who can reverse the spell."

"I need my mages."

"Melas will be the mage. He is stronger and wiser than a hundred of yours."

As the Alph voice spoke, Melas began to see new images. A new tunnel was opening, as if the shining obsidian of extrine were splitting into shards sharper than knives, cutting a way through. At the same time there was a rumble.

"Are you doing this?" he asked Atrid.

"I don't know!" She sounded bewildered. "What's happening?

I can't see. All I want is to be out and back in my ship!"

"You must lead the flow, Melas," the Alph told him. "The pale shadows will help. The lava river must be guided to the Mesa of Song. We will bring Ari and Talin and Atrid's troops. They will sing you all to the Land Beyond the Stars!"

"I don't want to die." Atrid sounded weak. As she spoke, the tunnel ahead began to close, the lava hardening.

"You would choose a half life here in extrine instead?" The Alph voice was astonished. "Why would you choose that when you can pay your penance and be reborn?"

"Penance?"

"You can start by giving the shadow Las their chance at rebirth," the voice replied.

"Nonsense," came Atrid's weak and breathy thought.

"It's their only chance, as well as yours. The alternative is to stay in the extrine, perhaps forever!"

"But my people need me. My realm needs me. What will happen to the Galaxies if there is no one to rule and guide them?"

"Or destroy them! You even abandoned your Others, those you had melded. Atrid, look at yourself honestly. Here is your chance to redeem yourself. You and Melas, working together, can free this river of shadows and free yourselves to travel to the Land Beyond the Stars."

"A dr...e...e...a...m c...o...me t...r...u...e..."

"But I don't believe in dreams!"

"F...o...r us...ss...ss!"

Melas spoke. "Atrid, you must reverse the spell that was cast when you turned Zetti into Zed. We are running out of time. The tunnel is closing. Soon we will all be as hard and sharp as obsidian, unable to exist in anything but images and dreams. Is that what you want?"

"Get me out of you! I command you!"

"Yo...u ga...v...e a...w...ay y...o...u...rr co...m...m...an...dd!"

"Never!"

"A...t th...e w...e...b...bb."

"I gave..." The memory image struck Atrid's mind like a blow. She heard an echo of herself saying, "All I will give is my command!" and began to wail.

"Help me, Melas. Oh, someone help me!"

"We must help each other." Melas's thought was calm and strong. "But it must be immediate. Atrid, reverse the spell!"

"I can't remem..." Suddenly there was silence. Melas could feel Atrid's tension deep within his own mind. Into his dream came Atrid's memories. Mages stood in a throne room with the Queen at the center of their circle. Her hands were lifted. She said words, and the mages repeated them. The words began to fly around the space like wild birds and then were gone, like a bolt heading straight out across the Galaxy.

"Melas, stop them!" Atrid's mind screamed. "Change the Change!" He could hear her sobs.

In the dream Melas leapt after the flying words, sweeping them aside with a giant hand, disrupting their journey, sending them back to the throne room and into the mouths that had said them, where they died unspoken. Then all he could hear was Atrid softly crying within him.

The tunnel opened again, and their journey toward the high cliff began, the lava of shadows slowly flowing through the extrine toward the light.

CHAPTER 44

"Talin!"

For one moment Talin thought of ignoring the cry. Atrid was the last person he wanted to see or hear at the moment. All he wanted to do was curl into a ball like a wounded animal, clutching the pain. His efforts had been for nothing! He'd lost Jonce. The men were refusing to fight now that they knew what it was they battled. Thank Goddess Ari was safe with Melas in the Garden. That was the only good thing about this whole mess.

"Talin!"

It was the unforgettable sound of Atrid's voice, a terrified scream now, entering his brain like a bullet. At the same moment there was another cry from across the compound. Traveling like a swift wind, reaching Talin almost instantly, the news came. Guards had found Jonce lying unconscious on a ledge near the foot of one of the cliffs!

Half hoping, almost unbelieving, Talin got to his feet, straining to see across to where the men pointed. As he did, movement high up on the cliffside caught his eye. A woman came hurtling out of an opening in the cliff as if shoved from behind. Was it Atrid? It must be. She was calling her men once again, ululating her rallying call. It couldn't be Ari. She was safe back in the Garden with Melas.

Though he no longer heard Atrid's voice in his mind, Talin began to run, following the rush of men toward the cliff where she stood. Catching up with the men, panting for breath, he poured all his strength into the race and was soon leading the pack, leaving all but the speediest behind, never pausing to wonder why he was so eager to reach a Queen he had come to despise.

"Talin!" the woman on the cliff called, her voice desperate. Seeing the youth who lay bleeding and inert on the ledge, Talin paused to look up to where the woman stood as if she were ready to leap. Once again she called. This time he was near enough to hear her clearly.

"Father!" she shouted. "Help me!"

In terror, he realized that the woman on the cliff, soon to be surrounded by the shadow renegades, was not Atrid! It was Ari!

Nearly collapsing in horror, Talin saw behind her, in the tunnel from which she had emerged, dark shadows arriving!

"Help!" she cried. "Talin, help me!"

Terrified that he might be too late, he reached a spot just below her, barely aware of the guards rushing past him to reach Jonce.

"Jump!" Talin yelled, holding out his arms to Ari.

His heart in his mouth, he watched her leap just as the renegade shadows began to pour like a dark waterfall from the depths of the tunnel.

As she hurtled down from the height, he caught her, and both of them tumbled to the surface. Looking up from where he lay, Talin saw the shadow hoard instantly vanish as if they had never been.

Had the shadows retreated once again into the tunnel? No, he realized, they had followed Ari out into the light of day and vanished into the cliffs, taken by the extrine! The Alph's plan had worked, but it was Ari who had led them forth and won the battle, not any of the troops or himself or Jonce. It was Ari who lay in his arms shaking and sobbing as she watched shadows continue to pour forth onto the ledge high above and immediately vanish.

"It worked!" Talin told Ari. "The Alph's plan worked and you did it."

Ari's cry was filled with torment. "Yes, I did it, and brought them all to their doom!" She was crying hard now. "Oh, Talin, tell me. Was Jonce with them? Is he gone, too?"

"No." Talin spoke gently now, holding her loosely. "He's right over there on the ledge, but he's unconscious. The mages are trying to bring him round."

Helping his daughter up, he began to lead her to her young man.

Bending over Jonce, Talin saw that he was still unconscious. Ari fell to her knees beside him and put her ear to his chest, listening for his heartbeat. Immediately she turned to the guards who clustered around him.

"He's alive, but in trouble," she said. "Someone must go at once and get him a green patch. They work well for him."

Two guards immediately turned and ran back toward the Queen's ship.

"How did she know about green patches?" Talin wondered. "Did I teach her that?"

"No," she replied, obviously hearing his thought. "I've learned many things you didn't teach me."

"Yes," Talin thought quietly to himself. "She has become a woman capable of defeating a whole army of renegade shadows!"

As the others worked on Jonce, Talin found himself holding back, trusting Ari to use her healing skills. He had the same faith in her that he had had in Mag. She was his daughter and he loved her, but she was also a person in her own right, a woman who was bent on saving the life of the man she loved.

Jonce opened his eyes, took a deep breath and tried to sit up. He held his head with one hand as if afraid it might fall off.

"Where's Melas?" he asked.

Talin tried to reassure him. "Back at the Garden, I presume," he said. "He was going to wait there for Ari."

"I don't think..." Jonce's voice trailed off. "I think he saved me!"

Ari and Talin looked at each other in both astonishment and fear.

"What?" Ari exclaimed.

"Her, too."

"Her?"

"The Queen! Oh, Ari, the renegades captured us both. They made her a shadow like themselves. They beat me up and left me and while I was unconscious I think she melded with me! Then Melas came and took her out of me and into himself! Oh, my head, it's all so strange! I can't seem to wake up."

"If what you say is true, Jonce, then where is Melas now?"

"He brought me out. He laid me down. And then...Oh,

no...then..." Jonce began to cough and sob, rocking himself.

"And then?" Talin asked. "What happened then, Jonce? Try to tell us."

"He...he...oh, Talin...oh my Goddess...it took him! It took him!"

"It?"

"The extrine! It took him. Along with the shadow renegades. They all just vanished!"

Ari and Talin stared at him in horror. Both spoke at once. "Are you sure? Perhaps it was a dream?"

All Jonce could do was sob. Ari squatted down and held him against her, rubbing his back, her face against his cheek.

"You're safe now," she kept saying over and over again.

Jonce leaned into her. "The Queen, too! She was inside Melas's Shadow. They gave their lives for me. For ME!"

"The renegades were taken," Ari said, looking up at her father. "It would have been me, too, if you hadn't saved me."

"You saved yourself when you leaped," he reminded her.

Suddenly a familiar voice spoke in both their minds.

"We tried to keep her safe, but she was determined and wouldn't return to the Garden. There was nothing we could do. Nor could we save Melas. We did what we could, but we are dreamers, not Shapers. I don't know what we would have done if the walls hadn't helped Ari or if she hadn't had the courage to run."

"Or leap!" Talin exclaimed.

"You saved me!" she protested.

"What else could any of us do?" Talin helped Ari to her feet and knelt beside Jonce. "What could you do, Jonce? You were badly injured but Melas saw to it that you survived. You must use your energy to heal now. Don't let his gift to you be in vain."

At that moment one of the guards appeared with a green patch that was immediately applied to Jonce's head. Jonce reached out to Ari and she returned to his side. Talin stood again.

As he did, the Alph voice spoke again in their minds. "You must go to the mesa top where the dead were sung to the Land Beyond the Stars. Those who have been taken will need you to sing them forth. Melas and the Queen will release them and they must be sung out of the extrine. It is their only hope after three centuries in Atrid's purgatory. With your help they can die and either transcend or be reborn. Hurry! There's no time to lose. Jonce must come, too. Melas will want to know that he survived. Guards can carry him on a litter. It will take all of you and many other voices to sing all the shadows forth. Call your troops, all of them must sing as well."

Talin turned to call, but before he could, Ari leaped to her feet and went to the edge of a low ledge. She began to ululate. It was a Queen's call to her men. They all responded at once, rushing toward Ari. When the mass of them was gathered just below her, she gestured toward the highest cliff off to her right and strode forward, gesturing for the men to follow. As she climbed, she began to chant. Talin came behind the group, having waited for Jonce, who was being carried on a litter by the two medic-guards who had brought him the green patch.

Ari reached the mesa top first, followed by the troops. At her gesture they opened a pathway for Talin and Jonce, whose litter was placed at her feet. Few of the troops and mages had ever known such a place or song, but as Ari's chant rose into the twilight air, more and more voices joined in, until music rang like a great bell in the darkening sky.

As if in answer to the song, the mesa top opened right in their midst!

While they stood on solid ground, the extrine they encircled became as porous as a dream and a stream of Shadows began to flow forth, lifting out into the night air. To those chanting, many shapes in the stream became visible. Some were different shades of black and grey, while others were paler, even white. In a slow, steady stream they emerged and soared into the sky.

"Re...dee...mers!" The word, filled with joy, flew back from the flood into the minds of those singing.

Ari began to weep. The word was a gift from those who had been trapped in the cliffs, those she had known as a child, those who had helped her in battle. With every fiber of her being she sang, but she did not float with them as she had with the survivors. Leaning down, she took Jonce's hand in hers, to hold him fast as well. As if told by those who had been trapped and were now free, she knew they must stay behind. And Talin? Melas and Atrid were part of the flood. She watched them go. Would Talin follow?

"Oh, please, Pa," she thought as she continued to chant. "I need you for a while yet. Please don't leave me."

She felt Talin's touch on her shoulder and heard his voice singing in harmony with hers.

"Not yet," he thought back to her.

They all sang until their throats were raw, until dawn began to creep over the edges of the mesa and the last Shadow had flown. The singing stopped, and Jonce, who had managed a bit of singing too, slept in healing sleep as his litter bearers carried him back to the compound, following Ari and Talin. Exhausted guards and mages trailed along behind, staggering with fatigue. It was a new Queen they served now. Without being told, as Ari sang, they knew. The old Queen had been released. The job had been done, and well.

"Did you see Melas as he flew?" Talin asked Ari quietly.

"Yes. He looked like a great white bird filled with feathers of blue and gold fire, and within the fire was Atrid. They were beautiful. I shall never forget."

"Nor I. They were glorious."

Together they reached the compound, where Atrid's ship waited, looking like an enormous bird itself as it rested against the black extrine. As the morning light touched it, its color began to lighten. Soon it was white, pristine, as if it were waiting for what was to come.

"Waiting for its new King and Queen," Talin said. "Yes, it's time for us to go."

"Us?"

"Yes. Us. This is your time, Ari. I think you know that. You must go to Mem and be crowned, and Jonce with you. The Galaxy needs you both. You've done what you could here and you've done it well. It's time to go."

As if those who had flown were speaking once again in her mind, Ari heard the echo of their voices: "Re...dee...mers."

"Yes," she agreed. "Every one of us did our part, but there's still more to do. Zed is still Zed. Melas didn't have enough time to make that Change."

Suddenly, she heard Jonce's voice. He was awake!

"Together we can gather the mages and do that," he assured her. "The Garden is still here. Can't we imagine it spreading out over the whole planet?"

"We can try," Ari said, her voice trembling, "but first we must go to Mem."

"Yes," Talin told them both. "That was where the Change began and where it must very carefully end."

Motioning to the exhausted soldiers to follow, Ari took Talin's hand in one of hers. She leaned down to give the other to Jonce, and together all three came up the wide ramp into Shikari, and the journey to Mem, where the future awaited their arrival.

ABOUT THE AUTHOR

Jane Prétat is a retired Jungian Analyst and Marriage and Family Therapist who lives in New England. Long an aficionado of dreams and fantasy fiction, she is honored to have received the Iris Award from Rowe Conference Center And Woman Soul, for the production of this new book.

Made in the USA
Columbia, SC
23 May 2017